Beneath the Sands of Monahans

Beneath the Sands of Monahans

CHARLES ALCORN

La Reunion

DALLAS, TEXAS

La Reunion Publishing, an imprint of Deep Vellum
3000 Commerce St., Dallas, Texas 75226

Deep Vellum is a 501c3 nonprofit literary arts organization founded in 2013 with the mission to bring the world into conversation through literature.

Support for this publication has been provided in part by grants from the National Endowment for the Arts, the Texas Commission on the Arts, the City of Dallas Office of Arts and Culture, the George and Fay Young Foundation, and the Communities Foundation of Texas.

ISBNS: 978-1-64605-219-6 (hardcover) | 978-1-64605-245-5 (ebook)

LIBRARY OF CONGRESS CATALOGING-IN-PUBLICATION DATA

Names: Alcorn, Charles, 1961- author.
Title: Beneath the Sands of Monahans / Charles Alcorn.
Description: Dallas : La Reunion, [2022]
Identifiers: LCCN 2022058841 | ISBN 9781646052196 (hardcover) | ISBN 9781646052455 (ebook)
Subjects: LCGFT: Novels.
Classification: LCC PS3601.L3429 B46 2022 | DDC 813/.6--dc23/eng/20221209
LC record available at https://lccn.loc.gov/2022058841

Cover design by Dubzeey Wu and Justin Childress
Interior layout and typesetting by Haley Chung

PRINTED IN THE UNITED STATES OF AMERICA

To Charles and William
¡Mis hijos!
All-Time Texas Wingmen

May the Road Rise Up to Meet You
May the Wind Always Be at Your Back

It's not the pot of gold;
It's the rainbow!

Kinky Friedman

CONTENTS

Beneath the Sands of Monahans

CHARLES ALCORN

Prologue

A HOLY GHOST'S LAMENT

BIG SPRING, TEXAS
JULY 24, 2015

Archie Weesatche is alive, well, fit.

Not yet mingling with his kin beneath the sands of Monahans.

In full, long-boned stretch he flexes his well-marbled frame in the creamy pink light of dawn. Luxuriates on his fancy new mattress of high-tech foam. Floats in that nether space between wake and sleep.

A motion picture memory of crystalline lucidity projects on the back of his orphan's eyes. A reoccurring dream; a meticulously archived sliver of time where the adult Archie peeks in on his long-lost parents.

Lucky Room 7 at the Starlight Motel surrounded by undulating oceans of oil and sand.

A scene to which Archie returns again and again. Obsessed, some would say.

He can hear, almost touch, his beloved mom and dad.

Archie sees himself clearly; the buck-toothed boy. Eyes closed and smiling. Peacefully awake and aware; focused on the sound of Big Arch and Bunny rustling the bedsheets above him.

Sharp inhales. Breathless sighs.

Archie feels for the little guy, tucked carefully between the folds of a tidy roll-away. Wearing his favorite silk pajamas, a long-ago gift from honeymoon Hong Kong.

Archie reaches . . . strains for a touch; his sweet, beautiful parents . . . a fingertip away.

As the smell of Chanel and Old Spice drifts over the West Texas waif, a holy ghost's lament floats on the gusts of a softly rumbling swamp cooler.

A survivor's prayer . . . forever and ever . . . Amen.

KEEP ON TRUCKIN'

Archie Weesatche was running late.

After selling his oilfield hotshot company, Keep On Truckin', Archie gave himself three weeks to get all the paperwork cleaned up, but there he was, sitting in his banker's office in Big Spring, waiting to sign one more document when an Outlook alert popped up on his phone:

> KOT Exit Meeting
> 10–11 a.m.
> Mesa Building/Room 113
> UTPB – Odessa, Texas

As he sped down Big Spring's main drag, then out to I-20 West, Archie felt better. A large manila envelope with seven truck titles and eight bonus checks sat in the passenger seat—a little buffer for his drivers before their near-certain unemployment.

Admiring the otherworldly array of bone-white wind turbines spinning away atop the hogback ridges that rimmed his adopted hometown, it dawned on Archie that this was it—the last hurrah of his adult life's work. He never imagined when he started Keep On Truckin' out of his mom's garage that delivering oilfield equipment would keep him productive, happy, and solvent for fifteen years—most of it, anyway.

Archie sold Keep On Truckin' to a publicly-traded logistics firm out of
Omaha that offered $2 million in January 2015. During the negotiations,
another OPEC-instigated oil bust picked up steam. It was looking like a bad
one—as in, no end in sight. He closed the deal, six months later, at half the
original ask—$1 million.

The front page of the morning *Big Spring Herald* reported that Saudi
Arabia was dead serious about opening up their oil taps. The new head of the
House of Saud, Crown Prince Mohammed bin Salman, was playing hardball.
As the world's long-time swing producer, the Saudis were doing everything
they could to claw back market share from the U.S. shale producers. The price
of West Texas Intermediate crude was dropping daily, from a ridiculous high of
$104.92 a barrel when Archie received the Nebraskan's initial offer, to $38.24
a barrel on the Monday before July Fourth.

Drillers weren't drilling. Service company budgets were slashed. Keep On
Truckin's total deliveries were down by two-thirds year-over-year. Archie had
experienced similar downturns during the Great Recession of '08 and '09, but
felt fortunate—and guilty—about not having ride this one out.

The upshot: after retiring KOT's considerable debt, paying off the trucks,
and cutting bonus checks, Archie cleared $600,000.

Not bad; but about $400,000 less than he'd hoped to assemble for his
long-awaited gambling odyssey. Suddenly, the Tour of Texas Archie'd planned
for his one-year non-compete felt lazy. He needed to generate cash flow; not
float around the blue highways of Texas looking for sucker bets.

After a forty-five-minute drive, Archie rolled through the entrance of the
sprawling UT-Permian Basin campus in the no-man's land between Midland
and Odessa. He certainly admired the gumption of the UT administrators for
building a public research university in the middle of one of the roughest eco-
systems on the planet.

He'd decided to hold the final meeting at the regional hub of higher education because it was convenient for his far-flung drivers, but also because
Archie was curious about the university's new football team. Nobody knew
how good—or bad—the UTPB Falcons might be. Just the edge a football hustler needed when it came time to lure some lucrative hometown betting action.

As his faithful F-250 came to a stop in front of the Mesa Building, named after Panhandle billionaire T. Boone Picken's oil company, the fall of 2015 was looking bleaker than the parched chaparral surrounding the UT System's least glamorous campus. He grabbed his hand-tooled Mary Alice Palmer portfolio, a dandy present from a long-ago girlfriend, and rushed into the building, still worried if he was doing the right thing.

A lot of KOT's short-timers went for the easy money during the boom days of 2013 and 2014. Every oilfield outfit in the territory hired man, woman, or child—no questions asked. But the eight souls waiting for him had driven ten plus years for KOT. Four of 'em had worked for Archie the entire fifteen years.

When he pushed through the classroom door, Archie immediately noticed Ida Schustereit, KOT's long-time dispatcher, was on the job—as always. The hot glazed doughnuts and spicy sausage klobaseks she'd laid out were picked clean. The tray holding a wet array of fresh-cut fruit sat tooth-picked and undisturbed.

"Howdy, howdy," he said, setting his portfolio underneath the podium microphone. He adjusted the mic, then instantly felt silly. He turned off the speaker, pulled up a molded plastic chair in front of the lectern, turned it backward, and had a seat.

Six large, unshaven men in too-small T-shirts and oil-stained Dickies and two large women in too-small T-shirts and oil-stained designer jeans milled about in the fluorescent-lit room, a geology professor friend's unused classroom.

Archie asked everybody to take a seat.

"Don't really need a microphone," he said, laughing, as his employees went dead quiet. "How's everybody?"

Archie quickly checked his datebook to see how long it'd been (three weeks) since he'd told everybody to hang tight, that he was selling.

"Come on Arch, cut the crap," said Ida, a rail-thin chain-smoker and possessor of the tightest hairdo in Ector County, courtesy of a weekly wash and perm at the Kut 'N Kurl.

"Alright, alright," he said, waving off Ida with a big smile. "Damn, I miss you guys."

"Well, at least you ain't dead broke," said Bubba Howard, a native of Turkey, Texas, and one of the larger, stronger human beings in captivity. "Had me a helluva weekend out on Lake C-City. Noodled me a catfish as big as Ida, but that's about it. Let's get to work."

"Glad to hear it, Bubba," said Archie, giving the man mountain a wave. "It's really good to see everybody."

"Oh hush," said Ida. "What's up?"

"What's this Good News/Bad New stuff, boss?" asked Lonzo Hinojosa, KOT's Human GPS. A man with absolute encyclopedic recall of every lease road, ranch road, Farm-to-Market, state highway and Interstate in a 250-mile radius. And plenty of unmarked dirt roads, too.

"Here's what I got," said Archie, leaning over to retrieve the manila envelope from the portfolio. "Real simple. Keep On Truckin' is officially sold. That's the bad news."

"What's the good news?"

"You get to keep your trucks," he said, patting the envelope. "I got clean titles for all of'em, right here."

"Is that it?" asked Ida, looking extra-disturbed that UTPB was a tobacco-free campus. "You coulda mailed the damn titles."

"That's true Ida, but then I wouldn't get to see your pretty smile," said Archie, reaching into the envelope. "And I did get y'all a little bonus."

"How big a little bonus?" asked Lonzo, setting his spit cup down on the polished linoleum, tobacco-free campus be damned.

"Seriously?" said Bubba, swatting his friend with a welder's cap. "Let the man talk."

"Alright dammit," said Lonzo. "My wife left me again."

Archie exchanged a knowing glance with Ida.

"Yeah Lonz, I heard your girlfriend's got a meth problem," said KOT's only dedicated document deliverer, a blonde barrel racer from Stanton, whose name, at the moment, Archie couldn't recall to save his life.

Archie'd hired her straight out of Coahoma High to deliver contracts and court papers in a souped-up Camaro. She was a little worse for wear after ten years on the job, but every company man in West Texas knew, and loved, the girl.

Lonzo spit, "Girl, you better take care of your own damn meth problem."

"Órale *cabrón*," cried the barrel racer, launching out of her seat. "Don't be writin' checks your nerdy ass cain't cash."

"Alright, alright," said Archie, interceding before fists flew. "I figured ten thousand might help."

"Ten thousand! Seriously! Are you kidding?"

Archie smiled, crossed a Red Wing atop his knee. "I got truck titles and cashier's checks for every last one of you."

"Is it drug money?" Ida asked, with a straight face—the only kind she had.

"No Ida," said Archie, smiling. "Not unless the cartel's workin' outta Omaha. Although I did read where Warren Buffet's lookin' at some ground-floor pot opportunities."

"Probably not a bad idea, Arch," confirmed the catfish strangler.

"You're probably right, Bubba, but I've got other plans."

"What's her name?" said Ida, frowning prodigiously.

"No ma'am. Nothin' but clean livin'," said Archie. "I plan to watch as much high school and college football as possible this fall, then figure out next steps come spring."

"You need some ink, Arch," said the barrel racer. "We'll tat you up real good."

The barrel racer's girlfriend, an exceptionally stout young lady, with sleeves of tattoos running up both arms into a tight, Velvet Taco tank top, waved at Archie. "We're openin' up a new shop."

"Well, that's a bold entrepreneurial move. Especially during a down-turn," he said. "Can you put one where my mom can't see it?"

The girls tittered.

"I'll put something on you, your momma can't see," said the barrel racer. "It's Melanie, by the way."

"Dammit, of course. Thank you, Melanie." said Archie, by way of apol-ogy. "Y'all ready to whip a little cash out?"

"Hells yeah!" sang the chorus.

Archie was pleased indeed as he pulled checks and titles and read out names. It took a full thirty minutes to empty the envelope and say good-byes—shaking a man's hand and heartfelt hugs. Lots of, "Let's keep in touch."

When he called Melanie's name, she kissed her girlfriend and came up running. "I can't believe you did this," she said, leaning over to deliver a high hard one.

"Melanie Schoellmann, get your tongue out of that man's mouth," said Ida, swatting at barrel racer's backside. "Good Lord!"

"He ain't married."

"Not even close," said Archie, blushing. "But if that's what you're selling . . ."

"She's mine," announced the greatly tattooed girlfriend, hands on hips.

"Yes ma'am," said Archie, waiving his rights. "Good luck with your shop."

"We're gonna offer lots of services," said the girlfriend. "You should tell your friends."

"Y'all are crazy," said Ida, waving off.

After everybody cleared out, Archie helped Ida clean off the tables and trash the cups and plates. When all was shipshape, Archie asked her to sit a minute.

"So, you gonna babysit Lonzo and Bubba till they find a job?" he asked, helping his most indispensable employee into her chair.

"What, those knuckleheads? They both got good women. Lord knows how," she said, fidgeting with her hands. "You're the one I'm worried about. You ain't too good with free time."

"This is true. And you would surely know," he said, handing Ida her envelope. "But no worries, I promise you. I promise everybody, I'll stay busy."

"Twenty-thousand dollars!" she cried, the check fluttering in her liver-spotted hands.

"You can't afford that. Where's all this money coming from?"

"Million dollars goes a long way," he said, beaming as the toughest boot in the Permian Basin teared up. "You're the best hand in the whole outfit, Ida. You ran the damn place. Plus, you don't drive a truck . . . you deserve a little extra."

"Well, you know I still got the first dollar you ever paid me," she said, accepting Archie's clean handkerchief. "Did you save any for yourself?"

"You bet. Enough to buy me a brand-new Cougar Red Cadillac," said Archie. "I'm tradin' in F-250 number twelve, tomorrow morning."

"Well, look at you, Mr. Fancy Pants. I'm glad," she said, dabbing underneath her reading glasses. "You always loved them Houston Cougars."

Left unsaid, but well known to Ida, were Archie's family finances. His adopted parents, Sheriff Fuchs and Sister Ernestine, were probably the richest people in Glasscock County—every penny of their collective tens of millions, the result of the Sheriff's shrewd land purchases (with mineral rights) over the decades and Sister Ernestine's uncanny knack of enticing local oilmen to drill wildcats on heretofore worthless ranch land. With the invention of horizontal drilling and waterflood fracking, long-abandoned goat and cattle pastures were now producing prodigious amounts of oil.

"I'm glad for you too, Ida. Thank you for everything," he said, feeling a little misty. "Keep On Truckin' was a good ride, wasn't it?"

"Made me pull my hair out," she said, handing back the handkerchief. "Lord, we've had some characters."

"Nothin' but," said Archie, hoping they wouldn't go too far down memory lane.

But true to form, Ida Schustereit remained one of the few truly unsentimental people in these parts. She clawed a pack of Salems out of her purse, popped her polyester slacks out of the chair, and turned off the lights. "It's been real, Mr. Weesatche. Lemme know when you start something new."

As they pushed through the building's glass doors and out into the blast furnace that was Odessa, Texas in July, Archie leaned in for a hug. "You'll be the first one I call. Take care, Ida. Love you."

Ida squinted up at her old boss as she cupped her hands to light a menthol. "Love you too, Archie. God help us."

OKINAWA TAKES A POWDER

It was go time.

Bounding out the backdoor of his one-bedroom bungalow, recently made cheerful with a fresh coat of butter yellow paint and white trim, Archie waved at Okinawa Watkins, his old teammate at the University of Houston. The longtime Sports Editor of the *Big Spring Herald* rolled to a stop at the newspaper's side door in his too-small Honda Civic then—slowly—walked across the street to greet his long-time friend.

The baby boy of eight children in a hard-working, God-loving family of West Texas share-croppers, Okinawa Watkins was, as they say, hell for stout. Standing six-foot tall and barrel-wide, with thick slabs of muscle, Watkins was an all-state defensive tackle at Colorado City High and three-time 2A Texas state champ in the shot put and discus. A holy terror in his heyday, Oak landed a full ride at UH and was named second-team All-Southwest Conference nose tackle his senior year—even earned a free-agent tryout with the Houston Oilers, though he didn't make the team.

Fortunately, Okinawa also took his studies seriously. Graduated from UH with a journalism degree that led to a position with his hometown weekly, the *Colorado City Record*, then worked his way up the West Texas sports writer's ladder with positions at the *Amarillo Globe-News*, *Lubbock Avalanche-Journal*, *Odessa American* and the *Abilene Reporter-News*. He was named Sports Editor of the *Big Spring Herald* at the turn of 2000—the same year Archie high-tailed it out of South Texas and came back to Big Spring for good.

Talk about timing.

After five years of wandering, Archie and Okinawa were back in the Permian Basin and practically inseparable. And comical as counterparts.

Archie Weesatche was tall, skinny, and all white boy. At six-foot-five, the former UH slot receiver was long in the torso that spread across broad shoulders with sinewy arms and spider-thin hands. Archie was a star at an even smaller high school than Okinawa's—a four-year starting quarterback/linebacker for Garden City, perennially one of the finest Six-Man football teams in the state. Archie was also a splendid power forward on the basketball team as well as a gifted quarter-miler, discus thrower, long and high jumper for the Bearkats.

Archie still maintained his playing weight of 190, although a few of those pounds had admittedly migrated south. Okinawa, on the other hand, was probably closer to three bills, but still, cat-quick. Oak also maintained one the most devastating home run swings in all of West Texas softball.

In fact, Archie's best friend was a man of many talents beyond the newsroom and field of play. In Keep On Truckin's early days, he augmented his meager sports writer's salary by serving as the company's most persuasive repo man. When a KOT driver hit the skids, reality set in quick when they peeked out the window of their double-wide to see Okinawa Watkins striding up to the door with his favorite aluminum bat.

Needless to say, Oak had a 100 percent return rate.

After ten years of company-saving recovery efforts, the dean of Permian Basin sports writers retired from liberating wayward F-150's. Okinawa was now instrumental in actualizing Archie's Tour of Texas—a season-long high school/college football gambling extravaganza.

Problem was, Archie had a substantially smaller bankroll than previously anticipated. In the Permian Basin, everybody's livelihood was tied to the price of oil. And the price of West Texas Intermediate was in freefall.

Nevertheless, Okinawa had the names, and approximate net worth, of every high-roller in the territory. After three decades covering every local district from Six-Man to 6A, Oak could easily cite every West Texas game worth watching, on any week, from El Paso to Ft. Worth; Pampa to Eagle Pass.

"Okee-na-wah!," yelled Archie, across the wide, crumbling side street that separated his humble home from the brick-and-blue headquarters of the *Big Spring Herald*.

"Whattup, Mr. Weesatche?"

"How's that head?" said Archie, stepping into the soul shake/bro hug they'd perfected over the decades. "Heard you got your membership revoked down at the Settles last night. Our friend Deena was texting up a storm."

"Nothing but yap, man," said Okinawa, waving off. "I tol' that girl gin makes me sin."

"Gin and Juice on a school night!" said Archie, "Nothing a Goody's can't fix."

"My man," said Okinawa, looking over his aviator shades, revealing a flaming case of Tabasco eye. He tucked in the shirttail of his red and black Howard College polo and followed Archie across the street to his truck.

"Naw Arch, I tell you who was flexin' last night—that sweet sista from Midland. We hook up, then she goes home and starts sendin' me pictures. Check this out, dawg."

Archie did not require photographic evidence, but sure enough, there was the fabulous Ms. Pam Rogers, filling Oak's phone screen with provocative poses. Finally, a cobalt-blue pedicure filled the frame—ten painted toes pointing at the astounding digital numbers—267.7 lbs.

"Dude, that's crazy!"

"I'm tellin' ya," he said, whistling through his teeth. "The big girls love me, dawg."

He showed Archie more photos.

"Dude, please," he said, trying not to stare. "Damn Oak, that girl's gorgeous!"

"Arch, we was breakin' furniture, man," he bragged. "Dogs barkin' all over the damn 'hood. Straight up freak show."

"No wonder you're movin' slow," said Archie, grabbing the ever-present box of orange-flavored aspirin from his truck console.

"Hey, you got some water?"

Archie reached into the driver's side cubbyhole and produced a sixteen-ounce Ozarka.

"Voilà!"

"Good for what ails ya," said Archie, laughing, as his friend killed the bottled water in three pulls.

"Dr. Feelgood! Damn, I needed that!" he said, handing Archie the empty bottle, then instantly grabbed it back. "Hell, I'm gonna throw this at our new managing editor. Woman's got us hustling."

"Woman? Really?"

"Latina. UT grad. And fluent in Spanish, dawg. The press room dudes love her," said Oak. "She ain't half-bad looking either, but damn . . . ."

"What? Crackin' the whip?"

"Girl's way too smart for Big Spring," he said, shaking his head. "I think she grew up in the Valley. Edinburg. Pharr. Somewhere down there."

"Hell, she's happy to be in Big Spring. She's gotta job," said Archie, climbing in the truck and turning the engine.

Okinawa's meaty arm came in the window for a final handshake.

"Alright brother, wish me luck. I'm coming clean with Mom. Tellin' her all about the Texas Tour. And hey, she wants to know why they don't deliver the *Herald* to Garden City anymore."

"Print's screwed, Arch," said Okinawa, shoving his hands into his khakis. "It's all digital, dawg. Internet of Everything. Whatever the hell that means."

"Come on by tonight," said Arch. "Gimme the scoop on all those rich boosters you been scoutin'."

"Thanks for the powder," Okinawa said, turning for the *Herald's* side door. "I got three birds on the wire, Arch. They're for sure. But we better rake before this bust hits."

"Birds on a wire," said Archie, rolling away with a wave. "Line 'em up, Oak!"

A MAN WITH A PLAN

BIG SPRING, TEXAS

JULY 25, 2015

The Hotel Settles was fabulous—once again.

Fifteen stories of Art Deco grandeur rising inexplicably from the dusty caprock, the venerable Hotel Settles was, for many years, the tallest building between Ft. Worth and El Paso. The elegant Jazz Age oasis, opened shortly after the market crash of 1929, was a miracle of restoration. Bought in 2006 for $75,000 and restored to the tune of $30 million by a Big Spring boy done *real* good in the tax consultancy game.

Archie didn't know the taxman, G. "Brint" Ryan, a legitimate billionaire who hightailed it to North Texas State as soon as he graduated from Big Spring High, and stayed in Dallas to seek—and make—his fortune. But Archie fondly recalled the grand hotel's festive re-dedication. On a breezy, cold night, just after Christmas, the entire town crowded together to watch the lighting of the new $100,000 rooftop neon. It was quite a show as each floor blazed to life culminating in a brilliant burst of red, officially announcing the hopeful rebirth of the "Crossroads of the West."

An exemplar of West Texas hospitality, including—though not currently—the most accommodating brothel in the Permian Basin, the resurrection of the Hotel Settles was the best news to come out of once-prosperous Big Spring in a long, long time. Every time Archie walked into the opulent lobby, or attended an event in the meticulously restored second-floor ballrooms, he was thrilled and amazed. The transformation was just that stunning. If the city fathers could get the rest of its citizens to follow suit, Big Spring had a puncher's chance of becoming the next Marfa—truly, one of the most unlikely tourist destinations on the planet.

Archie strode across the hotel's polished lobby in a pressed khaki button-down and starched Levi's belted with an alligator strap he'd splurged on at the Houston Rodeo. He nodded good morning to an elderly gaggle of tourists, then turned into the Settles Grill, a thirty-seat restaurant built in the footprint of the hotel's old coffee shop.

Archie's mother was waiting—early as usual—the picture of non-ecclesiastic serenity.

Sister Ernestine was also in uniform, adopted the day she arrived in Texas from her native France. A white and maroon habit, hemmed well below the knee with white stockings that disappeared inside sensible white nursing shoes. A simple crucifix hung from a long silver chain. The former Evangeline Ducornet wore a wimple in the early years as a faux-nun but gave it up as she became more comfortable with her unconventional new identity.

"Hi Mom," Archie said, leaning in to kiss her cheek. "How's the tea?"

"Green; kind of," she answered, beaming up at her gentle man. "Oh good, Archie! You're finally rid of those awful dark circles."

"Slept till seven this morning," he bragged, helping himself to the decanter of coffee. "I was dreaming like crazy. I was a hawk, ridin' the thermals."

Sister Ernestine paused and smiled.

Archie knew, more than anything, that his mother prized an energetic life of the mind—essential to survival in their thinly populated piece of Texas.

"You don't look hawkish," she said, passing Archie a tiny pitcher of cream and packet of raw sugar for his coffee. "You look well-rested."

"Extremely," he said, pouring in the sugar. "That new mattress is a miracle."

Archie ordered biscuits and gravy, grits, and bacon. Sister Ernestine settled for oatmeal.

For a former college baller, Archie stayed in decent shape. He always talked about changing his diet, but knew he wouldn't, until an annual physical revealed a cholesterol problem, or worse. Basically, Archie was too vain to let his weight get out of hand.

He was also lucky to have a full head of hair and Sister Ernestine assured him he was so handsome, so often, that he believed it. Of course, the mirror said otherwise. So, Archie spent a lifetime staying trim and relatively clean-cut. Clothes pressed and boots shined. His momma and daddy were beautiful people. He'd seen pictures. He was rougher around the edges. In no way as elegant in bone or feature, which of course, suited West Texas just fine.

As their cheerful waitress, a young Latina recently graduated from tiny Sands High School, laid down their plates, Archie took a deep breath.

"Okay, Mom, I'm debt-free and ready for action."

"Oh, do tell!" said Sister, sprinkling sugar on her oats and blueberries.

"Couldn't have done it without you," Archie said, reaching for his glass of semi-fresh orange juice. "Especially those first, what, six years at the house."

"I loved having you at home. And the children adored you," said Sister Ernestine, putting away her reading glasses. "And by the way, we've hired a new Superintendent and Principle—a husband-and-wife team. They're wonderfully qualified."

After thirty-eight years, the parents and kids were reeling in the wake of their academic angel's long-anticipated retirement from her life's work at Garden City ISD. Sister Ernestine was over eighty years old—as far as anybody knew.

She had risen from school nurse, to nurse/teacher/Assistant Principal; to full-time Principal. After Archie graduated in 1990, Sister Ernestine was named Principal/Superintendent, a dual role she maintained till 2014. All of her promotions were earned in concert with degrees conferred: an Associates from Howard College, a distance-learning BA from Sul Ross, an MS in Secondary Education from UT-Permian Basin, and a Doctorate in Education from Texas Tech. Plus, she was the default counselor/college advisor, although never compensated for her extra-curricular efforts.

"Good thing you're right across the street," said Archie, thinking how the Ducornet homestead had expanded over the years from a two-bedroom ranch style to a compound encompassing the entire block. "I guarantee you'll get plenty of knocks on the door."

"They'll be fine," she said. "If they can put up with the bad internet."

"And bad DISH," said Archie.

"Thank goodness they're readers," said Sister, nibbling at her oatmeal. "Thank goodness *you're* a reader."

"I'm working on the latest Richard Ford novel, which are actually stories," said Archie, wiping at a slick of heavily peppered cream gravy. "Set in post-Sandy New Jersey."

"What's post-Sandy New Jersey?"

"Hurricane Sandy, 2012; wiped out the Jersey Shore."

"Yes, yes! I remember. You like?"

"I do. The guy's just . . . very thoughtful," he continued. "After McMurtry and John Irving, Ford's my favorite. And Cormac McCarthy."

Sister Ernestine read French novelists, almost exclusively—Balzac, Proust, Zola, Jules Verne. Marguerite Duras was her favorite. And she loved Roland Barthes—the playful French existentialist. Archie marveled at his intellectual mother, happy as a Mediterranean clam in a place the exact opposite of her birthplace on the French Riviera. He told her for the hundredth time that she was the best thing that ever happened to the children of Garden City; including himself, Matt and Tallulah, his fellow orphan siblings. "Even if you do dress a little funny."

"Oh, you know, thank god for uniforms," said Sister Ernestine, with a chuckle. "Growing up, I wore nothing but hand-me-downs. I couldn't afford to be French."

"You always look great."

Archie checked to see if she was smiling. The former Mademoiselle Ducornet hardly ever mentioned her childhood in Nice on the *Côte d' Azur*, but she didn't sound bitter. Bemused and defiant seemed to define her European memories.

"I look as I should," she answered. "Unadorned."

"Unadorned," he repeated. Archie couldn't love his mother more when she said stuff like that. He finished his biscuits and gravy, wanted to ask for more coffee, but knew it was ridiculous. He'd already had two re-fills and a big mug at the house.

"Well, I need to run something past you, Mom," Archie said, a little more haltingly than intended. "Do you have time? Nothing going on back at the house?"

"Officially retired," said Sister Ernestine, looking over her teacup. "You too. Can you believe it? How did that happen?"

"Not a clue," said Archie, steeling his nerves. "Although Okinawa and I have big plans."

"You and Okinawa," she said, waving to a foursome of older ranchers, each of whom pointed an index finger—out of respect—under the brim of their straw cowboy hats.

Archie cleared his throat.

"I'm taking a sabbatical. Highly educational, and with any luck, highly lucrative."

Sister Ernestine, pushed her chair back a bit. Folded her hands. "I'm listening."

"As you know, I've driven the highways and byways of Texas all my life. Mostly in trucks," he continued. "My only indulgence is a new Cadillac CT6."

"Good for you, Archie," she said. "I'm so proud of what you did for your drivers and Ida. I know they appreciated that."

He said all the drivers were grateful, but worried that it wouldn't be enough.

"Hopefully, I can hire 'em all back in a year," he continued. "Anyway, my plan is to wager on select high school and college football games carefully identified by Okinawa. The odds should be excellent."

"So, it's a gambling tour," she said, sipping her tea.

"Yes ma'am. Football season will take me through December at which point I plan to break for the holidays, spend a full month at the compound with you, and hopefully pay for some new Smart Boards for Garden City High with my winnings."

"That sounds lovely Archie."

"Now, if all goes to plan," he continued. "I'll widen my radius in the winter, play a little golf, maybe go to the Final Four, Texas Relays, stuff like that. Which will complete my non-compete, and then I'll sit down with you and Chuck and figure out what to do next. And maybe—maybe—think about starting a family."

"A family!" cried Sister Ernestine, clasping her hands. "Oh, Archie!"

Archie leaned back in his heavy wooden chair; threaded his fingers behind his head. Easy as pie, he thought. Easy as starting your own business or being a sportscaster.

"I know, a family sounds nice, but I am forty-five, and that basically puts me at sixty-five when my children graduate from high school," he continued, watching his mother's face, trying to read through her politeness. "And that's if I find the right lady, like tonight."

"I can think of a half-dozen girls who would marry you tomorrow," she said, beaming over her hot tea. "You'll be such a good father."

"I don't know, mom. I've got some pretty serious issues."

"Phooey. We all have issues," Sister Ernestine said, suddenly serious. "We all have fundamental problems that want to kill us. All of us. But we carry on."

"Yes ma'am, we do," he said, handing the waitress a credit card, happy that his mother was letting him pay for breakfast. "I didn't do well being engaged. I wasn't serious about being a good husband or a good sportscaster. Ridiculously immature."

"You're not immature now," Sister Ernestine said. "You're a grown man and a successful businessman who deserves to get married and raise a family."

"Well, then I'm foolin'," Archie said, shaking his head. "Why would I drive around Texas for a year if I was ready to settle down?"

Archie's mother averted her gaze. Took a deep breath.

"You're right," she said. "You don't want to start a family. You want to make up for missed opportunities, don't you?"

"Maybe," he said, wincing.

"Archie, you deserve my faith," Sister Ernestine said. "But a year away from your routine, gambling with rich men. What's that sound like?"

"Trouble."

"I'm not saying you don't deserve a break. I'm saying professors take sabbaticals to recharge their intellectual batteries and focus on a labor of love. Gambling on football isn't a sabbatical."

"You sound like a Pentecostal."

She laughed, put her hands in her lap. "So, what's your *real* plan?"

Archie looked at his boots. Hadn't he just explained?

"I didn't know your mother, or your father, but you've got some explosive blood running through your veins," said Sister Ernestine. "When you were living the high life with all those rich people in Victoria, I hoped you could handle it. But I could always tell you were anxious."

"Way over my head: personally, professionally, everything," he said. "I never believed any of it. Pretending to be in love with Patti; pretending to be a sportscaster; pretending to be rich. I was play-acting the whole time."

"So, we're not going to repeat that, are we?"

"No ma'am."

"You've done so well," she continued. "You can get married and raise a family if that's what you want to do."

"It's normal. But I'm not normal. I'm a loner."

"Nonsense. You're one of the most gregarious people I know," she insisted. "It's a gift."

Suddenly, Sister Ernestine rose from the table, walked behind Archie, and started massaging his shoulders.

"What's wrong, mom?" he asked, reaching back for her hand.

"I'm the loner, and thank God!" she said. "People . . . people need discipline. I wish we were both like Chuck, steady and true, but we're not. We're impetuous and smart, but we can't be left to our own devices."

"Come on, mom," Archie said, looking back, a little embarrassed by the impromptu kneading. "I've watched you do nothing but right, all your life."

"I want you to relax. Enjoy yourself," she said. She went back to her chair, a look of calm spreading over her face.

"Well, I *have* been planning this tour like a delivery schedule," he said. "I need to chill."

"And if you want to raise a family you need to practice."

"Practice what?"

"Parenting! That's it! Take Matt and Tallulah with you," she said, a gleam in her eye. "You can teach them how to grow up like I should have taught you."

"You did teach me," he said. "I just lost touch. I thought I was a grown man."

"Well, your mother and father never grew up," Sister Ernestine said. "I don't mean to be disrespectful. They were lovely, vibrant people, but you know, that didn't end well."

Archie didn't like to think about his parents, except in idealized terms. But Sister Ernestine was right. Big Arch and Bunny would be here if they'd been a little more—a lot more—mature.

"Mentoring your brother and sister," she said, clearly wanting to change the subject. "So exciting!"

"What kind of a parent would take a pair of impressionable teenagers on a gambling trip across West Texas?" asked Archie. "Matt's not going for it. He just graduated. And I love her, but Tallulah does not want to watch football games with Uncle Archie."

"I raised you to be an intelligent, thoughtful gentleman," said Sister Ernestine. "You will certainly take good care of your brother and sister."

"Alright, mom. I hear you," he said, a little exhausted. "Let me think about it."

"No, you let *me* think about," said Sister Ernestine. "Come out to the compound tomorrow and we'll figure out next steps and timetables."

Suddenly, Archie wished he was back on a lonely farm-to-market with fifty miles to go. He already missed those stretches of road; stretches of time; the beautiful simplicity of getting a load of oilfield iron from Point A to Point B.

"Okay mom; very good," he said, circling the table to help her out of her chair. "Be sure to give Matt and Tallulah a head's up before we get too far down the road."

"I will not," she said, welcoming her precious boy's kiss on the cheek. "I love them dearly, but those children require explicit direction."

Me too, thought Archie, smiling, as he ushered his sweet momma into the lobby.

A COUGAR RED CADILLAC ROLLS
TO THE GARDEN

The Cougar Red Cadillac was an absolute beast.

As he rolled across the cattle guard of Sister Ernestine's Garden City compound, Archie was not at all sure he could pull off driving such a "city-fied" ride. But the thought of it made him smile.

Referred to by Sister Ernestine as Chateau Nice (and by the locals as the "Nice House"), the main residence was a massive, rambling five-thou-sand-square-foot brick ranch-style with five bedrooms and five full baths. After four decades of additions and improvements, it sprawled across a full city block. A true oasis in the middle of the Big Empty.

The Nice House replaced the original bungalow (now the guest house) as Sister Ernestine's primary residence in 1983 and had been expanded and improved, many times, since. Each burst of work the result of successful oil and gas explora-tion on acreage in Borden, Scurry, and Glasscock Counties where she and the Sheriff jointly owned land—and more importantly—the minerals under the land.

His mother's five-acre homestead, ringed by a low wall of orange brick, was a complete departure from the modest frame houses and ubiquitous double-wides that dominated small-town West Texas. It was, hands-down, Archie's favorite place in the world—his sanctuary—an emphatic French/Texas denial of heat, cold, dust, and dreariness.

The entire property was beautifully landscaped with flower beds that changed with the seasons, azaleas that burst forth gloriously in the spring, and a spectacular canopy of spreading poplars, cottonwoods, and post oaks that blanketed the property with blissful shade. The backyard had a covered patio and orange brick sidewalks connecting a guest house, a greenhouse, an elegant swimming pool aproned in brick, and a three-car garage outfitted with a spacious game room/apartment above. The lawns and gardens had been completely re-created in the late nineties: the pool, guest house, and garage apartment all renovated in 2012 when royalty checks ballooned with $130 oil.

From the first year he was appointed (1970), Chuck Fuchs had wisely invested his small salary and small inheritance from the Borden clan (of condensed milk fame). He slowly accumulated parcels of land from distressed farmers and the sons and daughters of ranchers no longer willing to live in such unforgiving isolation. His and Sister Ernestine's lack of marriage vows did not dissuade them from being savvy business partners. All of the land they collectively acquired was in the Permian Basin. Most of it now ill-suited for raising cattle or growing cotton, but all, after the invention of horizontal drilling and fracking, proved excellent locations for the extraction of shale oil and natural gas.

As Archie exited the most expensive ride he'd ever owned, a gleaming black muscle car, running lights aglow, rumbled into the compound. Out of the Charger's passenger door popped Tallulah Hoffs. Long, tall, tan, and off-the-charts athletic, Archie's nineteen-year-old sister was an orphan rescue from a cult at the infamous YFZ Ranch outside Eldorado.

"Uncle Archie!" shrieked the six-foot, one-inch bundle of volleyballing energy. The recently graduated Garden City Bearkitten slammed the door with an airtight whoosh and ran to wrap her much older brother in a big hug. "Pimpin' ride, March!"

"Thanks," he said, always a bit perplexed why Tallulah added an M to his name. "And yes, you can take it to the Dairy Queen."

"No way! Way too scary," she said, running her hand over the fender. "Even Roger says it's pretty. And he thinks he's got the prettiest car ever."

"Hey, Mr. Weesatche."

The driver's window glide revealed a strapping teenager wearing wraparound shades and huge biceps.

"Hey Biggun," said Archie, reaching to shake a man's hand. "How'd you end up at State? I'm sorry I couldn't get down to Austin."

"Hell, I choked, Mr. Weesatche. Came out of the blocks like a damn turtle. Plus, I was in Lane 1," admitted young Tedesco, removing his sunglasses. "I'da caught' em if we were running two hundred and *ten* meters."

"But you're good for gold this year," predicted his proud girlfriend. "All the ones who beat you graduated, didn't they?"

"Except for that Mexican kid from Runge. He's a junior."

"Ooh, that boy was skin-ny!" said, Tallulah, squeezing on her boy-friend's arm. "I can't believe you've still got another year. I wish I was a senior again."

"Hell, I'd rather be up at Tarleton with you," said Roger. "Hey, I gotta run. Dad's gonna snatch my ass if we're not fishing by nine."

"Y'all got a tournament, or just fishing for fun?" asked Archie, who knew Roger's parents from the oilfield.

The Tedescos had a hundred acres outside Sterling City. Pioneer Natural Resources had just made them instant millionaires on land that could barely support fifty sheep. Mr. Tedesco bought a bass fishing rig, and put in a nice new kitchen for Mrs. Tedesco, but that was as far as the big spending went.

Folks in the "Big Empty"—the highly *un*populated parts of West Texas—didn't spend money like they did in the rest of Texas. "New money" out in these parts could only buy so many big screen TVs and Lazy Boys. And the newly wealthy might take a trip to Vegas, but they weren't inter-ested in flights to Paris or Tokyo. Most of the money stayed in the bank; improving herds, fences, barns and pastures.

Archie loved that about his people. They were happy as long as they had enough money to keep clothed, fed, and hunting. He'd delivered oil field equipment to at least a dozen new millionaires in the past three years, and everyone—to a man—would rather talk about his new bird dog or four-wheeler. Money might change the young people, but not that many young people owned land. Mainly, it was third, fourth, and fifth-generation farm-ers and ranchers relieved to be able to hold on to the homestead.

"Dad ordered a new fish finder from Cabela's," said Roger, revving his four-barrel. "Swears he's gonna catch one of them giant lunkers."

"I heard they're pulling some monsters out of Lake Fork," said Archie, who didn't fish, but was always amazed at the size of the bass caught in Texas' man-made lakes.

"I wish we were goin' to Fork," said Roger. "But Dad loves him some Acuña."

"I know what y'all love," said Tallulah, "You better stay away from those little sluts!"

"Come on now. I'm a good Christian boy," said Roger, giving Archie a wink. "Besides, who wants to get on your bad side?"

"You wanna find out?" she said, hands on hips. "And boy you will."

"No ma'am," said Roger, tugging her down for a goodbye kiss. "I got my girl."

"There you go," said Archie, pat-patting Tallulah's shoulder, as Roger racked the gearbox. "Plus, the border's closed to us *yanquis*."

"Cain't hardly cross anymore," said Roger. "Everything's closed down."

"Good!" said Tallulah, "How many fucks do you think those cartel guys give?"

"Tallulah?" said Archie, not shocked by his little sister's cursing, but always surprised.

"Sorry Arch," Tallulah said, batting her new woven lashes. "Mom says girls my age are the voice of new feminism."

"Come on man, don't be goin' feminist on me," Roger said, easing off the clutch. "Just kidding. I'm kidding. See you Sunday."

"If you're lucky," said Tallulah.

"I'm always lucky."

"Lucky to be with me."

Roger laughed and gave her the Hawaiian high sign.

Archie couldn't help but chuckle at the irrepressible Tallulah. They waved as Roger's gleaming ride rolled across the cattle guard headed back to Sterling City.

"Glad to see you two gettin' along," Archie said, ushering his sister to the front door. "Hey, I may need some backup with Mom."

"The Caddy? I love it," she said. "We need to roll that little red love machine down the road, March. ATX!"

"No, no. She's cool with the new car," said Archie, opening the heavy, hand-carved mesquite front door. "She's *not* cool with my Texas Gambling Tour."

"You play poker?' said Tallulah, adjusting to the sudden darkness of the foyer.

"Football," said Archie, enjoying the air-conditioned cool. "Okinawa's got prospects from here to El Paso. It'll keep me out of trouble till my non-compete runs out."

"What's a non-compete?"

"Can't work for any other hotshot company for a full year."

"Rip-off," said Tallulah.

"I signed the contract. Nothing I can do about it," said Archie, admiring his mother's dried flower arrangement atop a round antique entrance table. He looked out the floor-to-ceiling window at Hipolito, Sister's ancient *jardinero* pruning the rose bushes in front of the deep porch.

"You should go to Cabo Wabo," said Tallulah. "And take me!"

"No plans for Mexico, right now. But the OU-Texas game is in October. State Fair too," said Archie, walking into the den.

"We gotta go!" said Tallulah, literally triple jumping on the cool Saltillo tile. She grabbed the TV remote off the glass coffee table. "So lame to be a State Fair virgin."

"I'll take you, gladly," he said, picking up a copy of *Texas Monthly* with J.J. Watt on the cover sitting at the top of a pile of Sister Ernestine's subscriptions including the latest *New Yorker*, *Time* and *Architectural Digest*. "But you'll have a college flame by then."

"Is Mom gonna make me go?"

"What? I thought you were all set at Tarleton," Archie said, plopping down in his favorite overstuffed arm chair.

"Volleyball sucks," she said, flinging her lanky body on the spacious sofa. "I just wanna go . . . see some things! Travel. Not be stuck in Stephenville. So munch box!"

"Munch box?"

Tallulah giggled, "Sorry March, can't go there."

Archie was confused. He'd been thrilled when Coach Yeoman urged him to walk-on at the University of Houston. It'd been the best possible news; being wanted by a big-time program. But as he watched Tallulah's fingers fly over her phone, he understood—new generation. And Stephenville, Texas was a nice little college town, but no Houston.

"You're such a good athlete, Tallulah; I mean you're a sick striker," Archie said, wondering if "sick" was the right word. "You're going to light up the Lone Star Conference, I guarantee."

"Lone Star is lameness," she sighed, launching another text to heaven knows who. "I want a D-I ride, like you and Oak."

"Like Okinawa, singular," Archie said, suddenly thirsty. "I didn't get a scholarship till my senior year."

"Maybe I could walk on at UH."

"Maybe," he said, walking over to the wet bar with its walls of framed photographs. He pulled a longneck out of the mini-fridge, then replaced it with a Dr. Pepper.

Sister Ernestine sauntered in from the kitchen, sipping on a soup spoon. The aroma of sautéed onions wafted in through the swinging door.

"Hey mom," said Archie, leaning in to kiss her cheek. "How are you?"

"Hello loves," she said, offering Archie the spoon. "We're having French onion soup and a lamb roast with new potatoes and squash casserole."

"For lunch? A mid-summer's feast," said Archie, leaning down to sip the broth. "Wow, that's good!"

Sister Ernestine ran a hand behind her head and loosened a ribbon. She let her hair out with a couple of soft shakes. She never wore her wimple any more. Archie was glad.

"Matt's coming in from Alpine," she said, pat-patting Archie, then leaning into the couch to kiss Tallulah's head. "It's so nice to have you all at home."

"Mom, would you please, please teach me how to cook," said Tallulah, sending yet another text before making eye contact. "I'm never gonna cook like you."

"You'll cook when you're ready," she said, taking Tallulah's hands. "Right now, enjoy the food. Understand what you like to eat. Then we cook!"

Sister Ernestine had an uncanny knack for staying positive in the face of the fiercest pessimism. It was the quality Archie most admired about his Mother Superior.

Suddenly, Matt McQuaid, Sheriff Fuch's second orphan rescue, burst through the kitchen door; all shaggy hair, brilliant teeth, baggy shorts, and deep tan. He was practically vibrating from all the Red Bulls required for the four-hour drive from Alpine where, only weeks before, he'd graduated from Sul Ross State University with a degree in English Literature.

Matt—the middle child—was twenty-three years old, a shade over six-foot, red-haired like his Mexican-German mother and broad through the shoulders like his Irish father. Matt's parents, both professors at Angelo State, were killed during an ill-timed visit to the father's hometown of Belfast. Matt's newlywed parents were hoisting champagne cocktails at the Hotel Europa when a bomb ripped through the lobby bar.

A 1999 headline, on the front page of the Sunday *San Angelo Standard-Times,* announced the bewildering news:

Angelo State Professors Blown Up in Belfast
12 dead, 34 injured; Irish Republican Army claims responsibility

Sister Ernestine took Matt under her ample roof in 2001, only days after 9/11. Matt's maternal grandparents, who operated a small sheep ranch in nearby Wall, Texas decided—after two years of trying—they couldn't raise the boy properly in such a crazy, confounded world.

Not unexpectedly, Sheriff Fuchs caught wind of the boy's plight. He knew after Archie left for college, that Sister Ernestine longed for another child in the house. She was positively elated when Sheriff Fuchs arrived, for the second time, with an unexpected orphan in tow—ten-year-old Matt McQuaid—another soul saved. And saved spectacularly.

Matt was a three-sport star at Garden City High just like his big brother Archie, long before, and sister Tallulah, shortly after. So good, in fact, that Matt landed a full ride at Sul Ross as a two-guard on the Lobo basketball squad. By the time he was a senior, Matt was a three-year starter and two-time All-Conference.

Archie was very proud of the young man. Matt was cool, smart, level-headed, and wicked funny. He even knew how to study. Archie wished that he'd been half as put together as his brother when he was twenty-three.

"The return of the conquering hero!" cried Sister Ernestine, hugging Matt's neck. "How was your drive?"

"Boring," said Matt. "Man, that's ugly country. I mean it's okay between Alpine and Fort Stockton, but I forget how homely it is between Stockton and the Garden."

"Homely!" said Sister Ernestine. "What excellent usage! Our little Texas outpost is exuberantly homely!"

"Nothing but oil wells, dry creeks, and mesquite," said Archie, shaking a man's hand. "Congratulations again on the *Magna Cum Laude*. Sure was a nice graduation."

"Thanks for coming out," Matt replied. "Everybody loved y'all, although I quit trying to explain how we aren't really a family family."

"We most certainly are a family family," corrected Sister Ernestine.

"I know. Sorry, mom."

"Yo, bro," said Tallulah, bouncing off the couch to high-five her brother. "We're Sly and the Family Stone!"

La Familia, thought Archie, as his mother, brother and sister all single-filed into the kitchen, a melting pot of European mutts: French, German, Scottish, Irish, Mormon.

As he'd grown older, Archie recognized—haltingly—the complexity of growing up in such a mashed-up Texas culture.

How he'd been raised by loving Mexican housekeepers—Lily Hinojosa, Tina Fuentes, Connie Barrera and Florencia Villareal—and coached by scores of well-trained, super-enthusiastic coaches: White, Black and Latino. How he'd played ball with, and against, all manner of talented White, Black and Latino athletes. How his best friend, Okinawa Watkins, hailed from one of the only sixth-generation Black families in all of West Texas. All descendants of slaves who'd migrated north from Galveston after Lincoln's Emancipation Proclamation was finally announced on June 19, 1865.

And yet, as Tallulah laid the silverware, Matt set the plates, Sister

Ernestine eased a roast out of the oven and Sheriff Fuchs rolled his Borden County pickup into the compound, they were, truly, the best kind of family. Close as close can be. Come together for the first time since Easter to break bread and catch up.

As Archie filled water glasses around his mom's rectangle of black Irish oak, he pondered the origins of the Fuchs/Ducornet/Weesatche/McQuaid/Hoffs clan. Not so different from the pioneer families who settled early Texas. Single-minded seekers, provided land by Stephen F. Austin, the Republic of Texas, and finally, the United States, following laws that claimed that the property grabbed by the Sooners and sodbusters was legal and rightfully theirs. To own and protect by any means necessary.

Of course, the Native Americans, who'd been annihilated or unceremoniously removed from lands on which they'd peacefully co-existed for centuries, had an entirely different view of these so-called Texas pioneers. The Comanches and Apaches didn't think much of the white man. Or his laws. Or living on the Rez. Nor did the thousands of Mexican families in *Coahuila y Tejas* who lost lives, land and considerable wealth to wave after wave of hell-bent American colonizers.

But Archie also knew this about Texas. After decades on the road, and in the oilfield, myths were being exposed. Truths were being told. The state's White-washed history was being re-written.

Slow, but sure.

JOSEFINA WEARS A ONE-PIECE

DEL RIO, TEXAS
AUGUST 2, 2015

The Weesatche Tour of Texas was on.

And the stakes were rising.

Significantly.

Archie scanned the horizon beyond the Nice House compound as he and Matt crossed the cattle guard. They were beyond the Garden City limits in less than sixty seconds. Puffy morning clouds floated in a summer sky that promised a white-hot afternoon. The plentiful spring rains—miraculous after five years of hard drought—continued to provide mid-summer color: purple and red, yellow and orange popping in fields of green against the contrast of red dirt glowing with dew.

The brothers were headed out for some fun under the Pecos River High Bridge. First days of August meant no games. But two-a-days were in full swing across the territory—a Texas rite of passage if there ever was. There'd be plenty of ass-bustin' drudgery on display in the towns along the highways from Garden City to Langtry.

Archie's old friend from Victoria, attorney Billy Tuck, who represented clients in South Texas and Northern Mexico (or as Billy like to say, the Republic of the Rio Grande) had called earlier in the week.

Tuck said he was sorry to hear about Keep On Truckin' having sold out. "But I might have something in the works for you."

"Oh boy," sighed Archie.

Tuck explained that his client, an old paramour of Archie's, Josefina Montemayor of the fabulously wealthy family in Ciudad Victoria, wanted to create an "annuity" that would throw off enough cash to comfortably remove her from all family entanglements.

"She needs six hundred fifty thousand dollars to liberate six point five million that's sittin' in the Happy State Bank," said Tuck. "She needs it by December thirty-first."

"And this has what to do with me?"

"Since you sold Keep On Truckin', Josy thought you might have some cash handy for just such an investment," said Tuck. "But I'm guessing . . . maybe not."

"Good guess, Billy," said Archie. "And why December thirty-first? What's the rush?"

"Taxes," explained Tuck. "If Josy secures the money this year, it's a write-off. A day late, she's payin' big taxes."

"So, she needs me to raise six hundred fifty thousand dollars," said Archie. "In four months?

"Correct," confirmed Attorney Tuck. "I know you're light, but Josy thinks you're loaded. Let's go with it."

"I'm light because I gave my driver's the severance they deserve," explained Archie. "So, they'll come back to work for me when my dumb-ass non-compete expires."

There was a slight pause.

"Of course, there's the small issue of the virginity you stole from Don Montemayor's only daughter," said Tuck. "Apparently, while you were engaged to Patti Callahan."

Archie winced at the memory. "Come on, Tuck! I barely survived Old Man Callahan. Now Josy's gonna have me honor killed?"

"Calm down, Lothario," said Tuck. "Josy's gonna save your ass."

"I'm doubting that," said Archie, frowning at Matt, who'd gone wide-eyed at the mention of an honor killing.

"She's going to happily repay you the six hundred fifty K, plus a hundred K if you seal the deal at the Montemayor hacienda next week."

"Seriously?" asked Archie.

"Scout's honor."

Tuck patiently explained how Josy's partner of seven years, an alfalfa magnate from Wink whose family pioneered pivot crop irrigation along the Texas/New Mexico border, had suddenly died. Fortunately, said alfalfa magnate willed the bulk of her estate to Josy, but the partner also promised a 10 percent cut to her Happy State banker, whom for years had assiduously cleaned, deposited, and safeguarded the $6.5 million.

"You can get the six-fifty, right?" asked Tuck. "Aren't your mom and dad loaded?"

"I don't borrow money from my parents," said Archie, "So; yes, no and yes."

"Translation, please."

"Yes, I can do it," he replied. "No, I don't have six hundred fifty thousand dollars. Yes, I can get it."

"How?"

"Football."

"And you're willing to convince Josy?"

"That's your job."

"Fair enough," said Tuck. "*If* you have the money deposited in the bank by midnight December thirty-first."

"Deal."

"Deal," confirmed the barrister. "And to show my appreciation, come join us on the houseboat this weekend. It's Jet Ski Drag Racing under the High Bridge."

"Cool," said Archie. "Glad to hear business is good enough to keep the houseboat."

"Oh yeah, business is good. I'll send you the deets," said Tuck. "But let's keep our arrangement on the down-low. See if Josy and her brother are going to play nice."

"Ricardo's involved?" said Archie. "Dude, that's a deal killer."

"Curious choice of words, Weesatche," said Tuck. And he wasn't laughing. "Play it as it lays, Arch. We need to dance with these *fresas* whether we want to, or not."

"What's a *fresa*?"

"Children of Mexican oligarchs," said Tuck. "The good news is Josy's still total A-List."

"No doubt," said Archie, remembering well the stunning eighteen-year-old version. "You say she had a woman partner?

"Died of a stroke at forty-seven," confirmed Tuck.

"Rut ro," said Archie. "Stroke on a farm in Wink. Doubt it was from too much alfalfa."

"Another good guess," said Tuck, before hanging up. "*Hasta viernes.*"

Archie'd met the talented Mr. Tuck at the turn of the millennium, during an epic bender in *Ciudad Acuña*.

Billy the Barrister was holding forth at a famous border cantina called Ma Crosby's, buying beers for everybody who walked up to the polished 1920s oak bar. He was celebrating a case dismissed for a rancher client who shot—not accidentally—a Val Verde County Sheriff's deputy for trespassing. Fortunately for Tuck's rancher, Texas juries still confirmed frontier justice on a regular basis.

Archie and Billy had hit it off immediately.

So much so that Billy talked him into sharing a taxi to The Hill—*Acuña's* Boy's Town—where they proceeded to crawl through a series of increasingly tiny bars. They ended up under the all-night influence of two local profession-als, a handle of Hornitos, two cases of Tecate, several sizable blunts and an equally sizable baggie of white powder that never seemed to empty—until it did—as the eastern sun crept up the western wall of a tiny cinder block crib, one of a dozen identical "bedrooms" purpose-built for *gabacho* debauchery in the walled-off *Zona de Tolerencia*. After seventy-two hours of extreme bonding, it took a week for Archie to get right. But Billy the Barrister had remained a close friend ever since.

Fortunately, the following week's hangover, and missed business, proved a turning point for Archie. For fourteen solid years, summer 2000 to the fall of 2014, Archie didn't cross into a single border town. Not one. And he didn't miss many days of work, either.

That said, Archie still had fond memories of their frolic on the *frontera* back before the cartels made all the border towns into actual "Combat Zones."

THE COUGAR RED CADILLAC WAS HALFWAY TO SONORA BY THE TIME HE snapped out of his memory bliss. Archie could drive and drive, look down at the odometer, and be ten, fifteen, twenty miles down the road. Finally, he got so used to driving alone in the Big Empty that he wasn't even aware of his ever-lengthening road dazes.

"Hey, you're back," said Matt, putting a finger of Copenhagen between his cheek and gum. The recent graduate promised everybody big enough to listen he was going to quit dipping—cold turkey—on his thirtieth birthday. That was seven years away.

Archie took a big swig from his stainless-steel Yeti, half-full of piping hot Community coffee—road fuel of choice. "Hey, you ever seen a jet ski race?"

"Can't say that I have," said Matt, brushing specs of wintergreen off his Wranglers.

"There's a place on the Pecos, under the High Bridge outside of Del Rio. The rancher who owns the riverfront hosts jet ski drag races every year about this time. It's mainly an excuse to drink beer and look at girls in bikinis."

"Cold beer and hot bikinis," said Matt. "No place but Texas."

"You learn that at Sul?" said Archie.

Matt wiped a long sleeve across his mouth looking pleasantly surprised by all this bro banter. "You'd be surprised what you learn in college."

Archie knew that was right.

Miles of highway passed; the morning gray burned off into brilliant blue sky. The luxury sedan's noise-canceling silence was impressive, like riding in a tomb with windows. He pointed the Cougar Red Cadillac due south on Texas 33 with nothing but flat pasture and dry-land cotton in his rearview mirror. The route was one he'd taken many, many times during his appointed oilfield rounds. An easy 127 miles to Del Rio—nothing for a stepper like Archie, who'd often put in sixteen-hour days of pick-up, delivery, and pick up again. Up to a thousand miles in a single day when the price was right.

Oil companies paid top dollar for the equipment they had to have. Whatever price Archie quoted, company men would pay, because he delivered. He liked his work; he liked his customers, and most of the people he worked with. The sorry drivers ran themselves off, or his dispatchers would. Ida Schustereit in Big Spring, and Patty Ohrt in Victoria, tolerated no back talk, no delays and zero excuses.

Driving into downtown Del Rio, Archie pointed out the badass high school stadium with the funky vertical press box. He promised they'd return for the Del Rio-Eagle Pass rivalry game, probably sometime in November.

As they motored out of town, he remembered that the High Bridge was a full forty miles out of town, out toward Lake Amistad. He pulled into a Stripes off Veteran's Boulevard and yanked two ice-cold quarts of Budweiser from an aluminum trough.

After Archie paid, the girl sacking the beer looked out the window. "I like that red."

"Cougar Red, University of Houston," said Archie, trying not to swell up too much. "She's a spaceship."

"No shit, *chulo*," she said, whistling. "You should take me for a ride."

Archie smiled, tried to guess her age: twenty-five? thirty?

"I should," he said, trying his best not to creep out the young cashier as she brown-bagged the quart bottles.

"*¡Muchas gracias!*" Archie took the beer, waved off the change from a twenty, and shouldered into the plate-glass door. "Keep the change, *chiquita*."

"*¡Ay papi!*" she said, tucking folded bills in her bra. "Come see me on the way home."

"*Adios, adios,*" said Archie, making a quick getaway.

Matt was delighted to be handed an ice-crusted quart.

"Back in bidness!" yelped the baller, immediately cracking the cap and taking a throaty swig of the King of Beers. "Hell yes!"

"Cheers, brother," said Archie, clinking Matt's bottle and enjoying the sweet taste of cold beer rolling down his throat. "*¡Saludos!*"

THE PECOS RIVER HIGH BRIDGE HULKED LIKE A DEPRESSION-ERA MARVEL. The iron and rivet span bridged an impressively deep gorge gouged out of black and tan cliffs. The dam-swollen river looked so out of place in the vast expanse of Staked Plains that Matt almost spit up his dip.

"Damn!" he said, unscrewing his eyes from his phone. "That's a bridge."

"Comes out of nowhere, doesn't it," said Archie, admiring the gorge before heading down into the parking lot. "One of my favorite places in the whole state."

They rolled into the shadow of the gorge and slowly skirted the edge of the acre-sized lot. Archie scanned, scanned . . . and found it . . . a TCU-purple F-250 King Ranch behemoth, with the man himself standing in the bed, lifting two dripping cans of camouflage Lone Star. Archie eased up, glided his window down.

"Got a cold one for a hotshot?"

"As I live and breathe!" yelled a short, fit man in aging frat boy gear— blaze orange swim trunks, white long-sleeve fishing shirt, and flip flops. "If it ain't Mr. Keep on Fuckin' Truckin'!"

Billy Tuck let out a rebel yell and tossed a Lone Star directly into Archie's sweaty palms. "And would you look at that holy-smokin' Cadillac!"

Archie cracked his beer and watched, delighted, as the spry attorney leapt straight from the bed of his pickup, spread-eagle, on to the hood of the Cougar Red Cadillac.

"Hey Weesatche, Beyonce wants her car back!"

"That, believe it or not," he said, pointing to the crazy man crawling up the hood. "Is one of the most astute attorneys in the state."

As if to explain, Billy Tuck laid a pair of blowfish lips on the windshield and began to wiggle his disturbingly large tongue across the glass.

"Gimme some sugar, Weesatche," said Billy, sliding off the sheet metal to address Matt. "Pay him no mind. I've kept this errand boy out of jail many, many . . . .."

"I got your errand boy!" Archie cried, leaping from his seat and running around the car. "Too damn long, Billy Tuck!"

The two friends broke grip, raised their Tall Boys, and guzzled. Archie crushed his can, launched it into the immaculate bed of Tuck's truck, then hopped back in the car.

"Welcome to the wild world of William Woodcock Tuck," said Archie. He threw the Caddy in gear and wheeled to a stop under the green shade of an impressive mesquite.

"The guy's name is Woodcock?"

"One of several Billy Tuck oddities."

"Cool beans, bro. I can hang with the crazy dudes," said Matt, unbuckling as fast as he could. "Bring that experiential learning, Dr. Weesatche."

"Oh, we *will* study, young man. Hard!" said Archie, digging through the console for his dugout. "I like the sound of Dr. Weesatche!"

Archie instantly located the one-hitter: dug, lit, huffed, and passed to his brother.

"Don't mind if I do," said Matt, cuffing the dugout.

"Better to be under the influence with Tuck," promised Archie, popping the trunk to access his Igloo full of beer, soft-side Yeti full of set-ups, and wicker basket full of heavenly spirits: Havana Club, Maker's, Tito's, Boodle's, Jameson and Patrón.

Matt puffed prodigiously, then opened his door into a feathery swath of branches.

"Hey Uncle Arch, better not park under here. This mesquite's sweating bad."

"That's some fine Texas botany, son," said Archie, ever curious as to why Matt and Tallulah insisted on calling him "Uncle."

Archie scanned the parking lot for other shady spots, but saw nothing but empty pickups, empty trailers, and heatwaves. He quickly backed into a bare spot, clear of ding-producing vehicles. The glare coming off the caliche was blinding, but a hot car was better than one coated with *huizache* sap.

As they unloaded beverages in the blister of 105-degree heat, a mirage was forming.

"Holy moly," said Archie. A world-class one-piece and heels was coming in hot.

"Who's that?" asked Matt, peering over the top of the car.

As she walked closer, Archie recognized the exaggerated hip swing, the flawless oval face. Archie read her smile, her knowing look, and couldn't quite believe it.

"Who shows up to a jet ski race in that?" asked Matt.

"*Hola, guapo,*" said the phantasm, dipping slightly a pair of killer sunglasses framing her classic *mestiza* features—brown eyes, thick black lashes, creamy skin, topped with spectacular cascades of raven black hair.

Archie—startled—looked once, twice, then slammed the trunk.

"Cat got your tongue?" said Tuck, relishing his friend's state of shock.

Josefina Montemayor—*La Princesa*—waited impatiently for her long-ago lover to speak.

"Hey Josy," said Archie, clapping the dust off his hands. "Damn!"

"Damn!" Josy mimicked, with a spot-on redneck accent.

"You look great!"

"You sound surprised," she said. "It's only been . . . what?"

"Fifteen years?" said Archie, thanking the Aztec Gods that *La Princesa* was being civil.

They locked eyes as Josy stepped up in a pair of plexiglass Versace heels and a pearl white bathing suit with a plunge as deep as the Pecos Gorge. Archie had to hand it to Miss Montemayor; the girl could work a caliche parking lot like nobody's business.

He hugged her, careful not to press too tight, stepped back, let *Senorita Montemayor* artfully air kiss his cheeks.

"Matt," he said, beckoning his young charge to join the circle. "I am honored to introduce Ms. Josefina Montemayor, of the Tamaulipas Montemayors."

Josy dipped her sunglasses again as the lanky baller made his way around the Cadillac's expanse of hood.

"Josy, this is Matt McQuaid, my younger brother, and recent *Magna Cum Laude* graduate of Sul Ross University with a degree in English Literature *and* an All-Conference guard on the Lobo basketball team."

"*Hola, jugador,*" said Josefina, molding her thick black hair over shoulder before extending a hand to the gawking graduate.

"You should kiss that," said Tuck, nodding at the five-finger acrylic masterpiece.

"*Encantada,*" said Matt, doing just that.

"Oh, he's gorgeous," Josy exclaimed. "I didn't know you had an *hermanito*!"

"And a sister too," said Matt, clearly dazzled by her *telenovela* beauty and the gauzy nothingness of Ms. Montemayor's cover-up. "Our mom likes misfits."

"Archie!" she exclaimed, palming her cheeks in mock amazement, squealing, pulling Matt in for a hug. "He's your mini-me!"

"My professional advice is to control yourself," said Billy Tuck, gently prying the two beautiful people apart and wrapping an arm around Josefina's tiny waist. "Can you believe I ran into her, just last night?"

"Not for a minute. Where?" Archie asked.

"Laredo. Poolside at La Posada," said Billy, admiring Josefina's radiant hair as she grabbed the luscious locks, twisted slightly, then let the full length dramatically fall.

"I had every intention of retiring for the night, and was, in fact, walking to my room, when *this* rises from the pool."

"Oh yes, Attorney Tuck, you were quite chivalrous," said Josefina, batting her eyes at Archie, then Matt, then Tuck. "And so quick with that towel."

The men, forming a semi-circle of admiration, were suddenly struck dumb by Josy's spontaneous swimsuit adjustments.

"So Josy! You're here? With Tuck?" said Archie, offering his best little boy smile.

"Yes," she replied. "With an offer you cannot refuse."

"Really," said Archie, side-eyeing Tuck. "And you guys just accidently ran into each other. In Laredo?"

"That's our story," said Tuck, with a laugh.

Josy cut her eyes at Archie, her former possession, with a confidence that comes with thirteen generations of Spanish pedigree.

"I was bored to tears, in boring Laredo," she said. "Nobody plays at the border anymore. All the gringos and their slutty girlfriends are gone. Poof."

"You can be my slutty girlfriend," said Billy Tuck, hugging her waist.

"*Ay chiquito*, please," Josy said, gently removing his hand. "You can't afford it."

Tuck remained undeterred, "Ah, but who can offer you sunbathing on the only houseboat on the Pecos? And illegal wagering on jet ski races? Who provides the finest people watching this side of Cut and Shoot?"

"Where's Cut and Shoot?" asked Matt, trying his best to keep up.

"Piney Woods. Close to Point Blank," said Tuck, gesturing at Josefina like some deranged game show host. "The Big Thicket boys would make a nice rump roast out of this one."

The pregnant pause, combined with Josy's cloudy frown, made Archie jump.

"Twenty years since we were last seen on the streets of *Acuña*," he said, bouncing on the balls of his Pumas, rivulets of sweat running down the back of his favorite pair of aquamarine Birdwell Beach Britches. "How can that be, Tuck?"

"*Ay*, fifteen years for me," said Josy, fanning herself with no fan. "*Increíble!*

"Jesus H. Christ, it's hot!" said Tuck, raising arms to the heavens. "I ask you, *Princesa*, can you possibly hang with this posse of playas? For an entire afternoon?"

"Why not?" said Josy, continuing to adjust what little of the suit that wasn't cut out.

"How 'bout you, young buck?" asked Tuck, winking at the graduate, admiring his stylish three-day whiskers. "You gonna hang with the old folks."

"Speak for yourself, *abogado*," said Josy, finally pleased with the drape of her Spandex. She sidled up to Matt.

"I know you have a girlfriend," she purred. "She's blonde-haired, blue-eyed with big *chichis*."

"Careful Matt," Archie said, laughing. "She'll put you under her spell . . ."

"*Porfavor!*" Josy hissed, with mock fury. She ran a single fingernail up Matt's bare chest, across his cheek. "I can be your *novia*."

Matt smiled so hard it looked like his face was going to crack.

IN THE COOL SHADOWS OF THE PECOS RIVER HIGH BRIDGE, FLOATED A MASS of humanity ranging from daredevil teenagers—providing jet ski, water ski, and wakeboard entertainment—to grizzled river rats driving gurgling speed boats and souped-up SeaDoos. Along the length of the race course, marked off by small white buoys in the middle of the river channel, beer-bellied men in cutoffs and ball caps, and large women in scandalously-small bikinis and deformed cowboy hats, bobbed joyously, held up by a variety of inner tubes and rafts. The river's lazy current made it easy for people to stay close to their flotillas, but plenty drifted downriver, lulled to sleep by beer, fun, and sun. The pungent smell of hydro wafted across the dappled waters mixing with the ever-present exhale of Marlboro Reds and menthol Kools.

They came from every corner of West Texas and cities as far as El Paso, San Antonio and Ft. Worth. All part of a Texas tribe who worshipped Willie Nelson, voted Republican and worked hard at their white and blue-collar jobs—oilfield, construction, welders, mechanics; plus, the small-town bankers, lawyers, and merchants who ran their little towns with third, fourth and fifth-generation pride. It was sixty-forty white to tan; everybody getting along just fine. Mainly, because everybody had a little money in their pockets courtesy of the Texas economic miracle.

All-in-all, life was pretty good out on the serene Pecos River.

Meanwhile, the stars aboard the Good Ship Tuck floated the entire afternoon on prime water, betting any local who was willing. All afternoon, the winners would float beneath the house boat, waiting patiently as Barrister Billy launched hundred-dollar paper airplanes down to the winning jet ski jockeys.

Josy loved being the center of attention—and she did not disappoint—alternating on the upper deck between quick bursts of sunbathing interspersed with club-quality dancing to the blasting sounds of Tuck's wireless boom box.

DJ Matt impressed all within earshot with his skillful mix of country and hip hop, with liberal cuts of *norteño* and *Tejano* hits, and lots and lots of Kid Rock and Eminem—always a hit with the shots and reefer crowd.

Around 7 p.m., as the sun set behind the canyon walls and the breeze turned Josy's skin to goose flesh, the well-lubricated foursome had a decision to make. Stay in Del Rio with a crossover to *Acuña*, or hit the road for sixty quick minutes and get a suite at the Kickapoo Nation's Lucky Eagle casino.

According to Matt's Google Maps app, it was 93.7 miles from parking lot to parking lot.

"I don't want to go to *pinche Acuña*!" whined Josefina, as she tip-toed her way over male bodies sprawled across the upper deck.

"What, are you some kind of Texas Hold'em queen?" Tuck asked.

The host was finally getting a little sideways about all the attention his client was lavishing on young Matt. Not that Tuck resented the young man, who was unfailingly polite, and handled the adult's non-stop drinking with impressive aplomb.

"What's your best guess, Billy?" she said, pausing to scowl at Tuck, then sitting directly on Matt's lap.

Matt's eyes opened wide. "Howdy."

Josy raised up and plunged down on Matt's midsection. She laughed and cackled and playfully beat on the boy's torso, B-baller thin and muscular.

Archie raised his head from a lounge chair; took a quick look at Josy's gyrations.

As the saying goes: people change, but not much.

"Jesus, Joseph, and Mary!" said Tuck, waving off Josy with a petulant hand. "Weesatche, let's get that Cougar Red Caddy on the road! These two can roll around in the back . . ."

"*¡Ya! ¡Ya!*" Josy yelled, her eyes never leaving Matt. "I'm paying you to be jealous?"

"You haven't paid me *un peso, Princesa*!" said Tuck, eyes crossed. "But I hear your credit's good."

"Your retainer is paid in full, *abogado*," said Josy.

Archie smelled an exit. "*¡Vamonos amigos! ¡Vamos al casino!*"

AS THE GROUP WHEELED OUT ON TO THE EAGLE PASS HIGHWAY, ARCHIE WAS pleased indeed to be piloting this merry crew into the magical light of a summer's evening. He exchanged smiles in the rearview and thought back to when he'd met the fabulous Miss Josefina.

It had been the oddest of celebrations, sponsored by Laredo's Society of Martha Washington Colonial Pageant and Ball. An odd mash-up of American celebration and Mexican fancy dress featuring debutantes parading in highly-ornate costumes.

Archie was escorting Patti Callahan, his fiancé, the only daughter of Victoria, Texas royalty. Archie, Patti and the rest of the Callahan clan—plus assorted hangers-on—piled into an enormous stretch limousine and cruised through two hundred miles of brush country to the Mexican border. Archie was in high cotton—a jock/sportscaster squiring the only daughter of the richest man in the Coastal Bend. Drinking bourbon, talkin' smart, toasting Patti Callahan to the moon.

But little did the only Callahan child know, there was another Victoria girl—from *Ciudad Victoria*—come to town.

Josefina Montemayor, an eighteen-year-old senior at San Antonio's prestigious St. Mary's Hall, dominated the evening from start to finish. Demanding to be gawked, demanding to be danced, demanding to be wooed. Archie Weesatche was deliriously caught in her headlights—much to the delight of all involved. Except for a certain pouty Patti, who quickly drank the little bitch out of mind.

La Princesa's crowning glory was a $25,000 ball gown made of jade green velvet, sequins, and micro-mirrors; supported by spines of structural aluminum. Truly wearable art, the gown spread the floor like a colorful pondscape as she whirled and twirled to the crowd's delight.

Both Patti and Josy were main attractions: "Las Marthas" with family histories in the pageant dating back to 1910. All of the debs looked fabulous, floating throughout the ballroom floor like dancing mascarpones, ready to be snatched up and devoured by the eligible males of the wealthy elite.

Archie couldn't keep his eyes off Josefina while the belles of the ball performed their scrapes and bows, their hours-long introductions, toasts, and dances. It was an intoxicating bunch of business for a boy from Garden

City, who had managed his escorting duties at Fiesta in San Antonio and Buccaneer Days in Corpus Christi just fine, but was always nervous.

Now, finally, at this multi-cultural collision of a fancy-dress ball, Archie was relaxed.

He wasn't fretting about his tuxedo, or forgetting a hostess's name, or two-stepping instead of waltzing, or drinking too much. For the first time, he wasn't worried about being an orphan from small-town West Texas who had no business rubbing elbows with the playboys and glamour girls from both sides of the border.

He was intoxicated by Josy's pure laughter and the joy with which she worked the room. By the end of the night, the Callahan and the Montemayor parties were mixing and mingling like long lost friends. Old Man Callahan and Don Montemayor, resplendent in black tie and tails, eyed their progeny with pride—the debut of their respective daughters constituting one of the proudest days of their long lives.

When the festivities finally wrapped up, around 3 a.m., everyone waited for limos to make the short drive back from the event center to *La Posada*. Ricardo Jr., Josy's brother, and heir to the Montemayor fortune, ran up breathlessly.

"You've got to come," said Ricky. "Escobar is flying his footballers in from Medellín! My father hired *Club America* to represent the hacienda. It's going to be incredible!"

Archie and Patti looked at each other. What was the short-winded rich boy babbling about? Whatever it was, they were good to go.

All Patti Callahan remembered of the ensuing twenty-four hours in the lap of Mexican luxury was nothing. Nothing but a devastating hangover.

Archie suffered an equally debilitating episode—a full-frontal assault by Josy Montemayor. In a spotless barn full of million-dollar thoroughbreds, no less. The fleshy spell Josy cast only lasted six months, but Archie never recovered.

TRIPPIN' TO THE LUCKY EAGLE

The circus travels.

For the next ninety-three minutes, motoring ninety-three miles from the High Bridge to the Lucky Eagle in unsurpassed Cadillac comfort, Matt and Josy lounged in the backseat while Archie listened to Tuck recite random passages from Hunter S. Thompson.

"How's this for a little Gonzo wisdom: *'I hate to advocate drugs, alcohol, violence, or insanity to anyone, but they've always worked for me.'*"

"Can I getta amen!" said young Matt, as he settled in a comfy corner of the back seat.

The driver and navigator smiled. Tuck continued to scroll.

" *'Life should not be a journey to the grave with the intention of arriving safely in a pretty and well-preserved body, but rather to skid in broadside in a cloud of smoke, thoroughly used up, totally worn out, and loudly proclaiming "Wow! What a Ride!"'*"

"Ooh, I like that," said Josy, pausing to light a Davidoff. "Who is this man?"

"*Señor* Gonzo!" said Tuck, turning just in time to receive a face-full of exhale. "I wish he was around to take on Trump. They'd duel at ten paces!"

"Hey, Arch, let's read some Hunter S.!" said Matt, cracking a back window, while Josy stretched full length in the expansive back seat. "*Fear and Loathing.* That's a classic."

"I forget you're an English major," said Tuck, reaching back to squeeze Josy's thigh and promptly being hand-slapped. Hard.

"Jesus! Fear and Loathing in the Kickapoo Nation!" bellowed Tuck, thrusting his flask into Matt's chest. "Drink, Lobo!

"*¿Si o no?*" asked Matt, turning up the bottle like a true frat daddy. "*¡Si!*"

"You think I didn't know you're a Lobo?" said Tuck, pulling in the young baller's rebound for another deep drink.

"Tuck's the man who knows a little bit about everything," allowed Archie. "Just enough to be dangerous."

"*Poco peligroso,*" said Tuck, draining the flask. "*¡Y muy, muy intelligente!*" Tuck arched a small squirt of mezcal into the back seat.

"*Ay,* Billy!" cried Josy, swatting the rotgut off her amazing cover-up. "Archie, don't let him drink anymore!"

"*Tranquilo, tranquilo,*" assured Archie, with a smiling glance. "*¡No mas mezcal, abogado!*"

"*¡No! ¡No! ¡Mucho mas mezcal!*" yelled Tuck, followed by a terrifying yowl.

"Jesus, Tuck, stay with me, brother," said Archie, sliding his foot over the accelerator. "I think it's about time to stretch the belts on this V8."

"I cannot advise exceeding the speed limit," said Tuck, wiping his mouth on his sleeve. "But I will ask you to . . . make this bitch scream!"

And with that, the speedometer crept over a hundred, settled in at a smooth 110. In mere minutes the dim twinkle of Eagle Pass appeared mirage-like in the desert distance.

Despite his deft driving, by the time Archie navigated through Eagle Pass proper, and out the backside to the Lucky Eagle, his troops were in dire need of a bathroom. Archie pulled up to the casino entrance with seconds to spare and ordered Tuck to take Matt and Josy straight to the nearest water closet.

"Tell them to comp your rooms, *guapo,*" said Josy, woozily pulling her outfit together and sliding out the backseat with the help of the chivalrous shooting guard.

"What? Like you own the place?" said Archie.

"We *do* own the place," she said, dropping her head inside the backseat to give Archie a convincing leer. "They'll know who I am."

Archie didn't doubt that as he watched the trio stumble through the thick evening heat into the lobby.

After securing two rooms on his brand-new credit card from the Big Spring Bank & Trust, Archie cleaned up in an eerily empty men's room. He found the Mezquite Bar and Grill with his sidekicks looking out of sorts.

"Lone Star," Archie said, to the bartender. "You guys want a tequila?"

Josy and Matt looked at each other and then to Tuck. "Got some new marching orders."

"*¿Que pasa?*" Archie asked, laying down five dollars for his longneck.

"My brother's here," said Josy. "He wants to have dinner with us."

"When? Tonight?"

"At eight," said Josy, pushing away from the bar. "In an hour."

A chill ran across Archie's arms. How long had it been since he'd seen Ricardo Montemayor, Jr.? A lifetime. Not since the night he and Josy parted ways—post-abortion—outside the Menger Hotel in San Antonio.

Archie always knew it had been far too clean, practically antiseptic in its absence of drama or consequence. Now, all these years later, karma was knocking on his door.

Archie pulled out a barstool and joined his suddenly silent partners pretending to watch the Rangers thrash the Astros on a crisp flat screen floating above the bar.

Josy stood, sucked the last of her Topo Chico, asked Archie for the car keys. "I need to get my suitcase."

"I'll get it for you," said Matt, suddenly eager to have something to do now that the party was apparently over.

"You're so sweet," said Josy, squeezing his hand while they waited for Archie to fish his keys. "I'll meet you in the lobby."

"No problem," said Matt, looking at Archie, but only getting a paternal pat on the back.

Tuck finished off his *Dos Equis* and stood up.

"I need a disco nap or several fingers of *foco*. Think your brother could help me out?"

"Sure, go ask him," sneered Josy. "He's probably doing some right now. Fifth floor, Room 510."

"I'll get right on that," Tuck replied, unsuccessfully avoiding his client's death glare.

"We're on the ground floor," Archie said, handing Tuck a room key. "Sorry I couldn't get one with a view of the gorgeous Rio Grande."

Tuck snapped a salute and beat a hasty retreat.

"I knew this was going to happen," Josy said, as Tuck walked out of earshot. "Ricky's probably had us followed since we left La Posada."

"Anything specific I need to know?" Archie asked.

"He's such a macho prick," said Josy. "He's not . . . I'll protect my own fucking honor."

Archie sighed. "I'm sorry, Josy." They both turned, admiring Matt's youthful stride as he wheeled Josy's bag across the lobby. "Tell me what to do."

"Let me take a shower," she said.

She stomped off toward Matt, grabbed him by the arm, and rolled her oversized Louis Vuitton out of sight. Archie didn't have a clue how this was going to work out, except badly. He walked straight to Tuck's room and prayed for psychoactive deliverance.

"Tuck, what the hell?" Archie asked, trying to pry his sticky Lucky Eagle room key from the door's key reader. "Please tell me you've got a joint rolled for your padna'."

"No such luck, my self-medicating *amigo*," said Tuck, rolling over, red creases running the length of his face. "We need to talk."

"I'm sure. Hold that thought until my return with a bottle of Maker's and a six-pack."

"Do your thing," Tuck said, rubbing crust out of his eyes. "But tarry not, my friend. I'm in possession of life-saving intel."

"Come on, Tuck. Seriously?"

"I shit you not," said Tuck, looking as serious as he could muster.

"And one tidbit to chew on, on your whiskey run. I'm on retainer with the Montemayor family. So, what I'm about to reveal stays in this room or I face certain dismemberment *and* disbarment."

"What? Ricky's on the warpath?"

"Kinda," he said, shoulders slumped. "Don Montemayor's COPD is getting bad and now Ricky *thinks* he's in charge."

"So, I need to grab Matt and drive us the hell out of Maverick County?"

"Whiskey first," assured attorney. "It's nothing Archie Weesatche can't handle."

"I appreciate the vote of confidence, but I'm way out of playing shape."

"Come on, Weesatche!" insisted the barrister, throwing his legs off the bed with herculean effort. "Lest you forget, the last time we graced the bordellos of *Acuña, you* were the one who talked us out of harm's way with a nine-millimeter pressed to the base of your skull. Remember that?"

"Try not to," said Archie, turning on his heel. "I try to stay out of that kind of trouble."

As he opened the door, he called back to his attorney. "Tuck, you got to give me the straight scoop."

"It's nothing you don't know," said Tuck, massaging his face in his hands. "Mexicans have long memories."

HOW TO AVOID AN HONOR KILLING

The one-star dinner was ill-timed, unwelcome and a complete disaster.

Tuck, unapologetically disheveled, declared his ceviche was caught in the Rio Grande and ordered another double Jack and Coke. Matt, sporting a wrinkled Marfa Public Radio T-shirt and ancient Duck Heads looked ready for a Phi Delt kegger. Archie had showered but left his packed bag in Garden City. The best he could manage was a hurriedly-purchased Lucky Eagle polo and golf shorts.

Then there was Josy, glowing like a nuclear reactor in a gold halter top, white stretch pants, and yet another pair of Versace heels.

Josy's brother, Ricardo, made the foursome of river rats look terribly underdressed. He looked at once dying from boredom and deeply menacing behind gold-plated shades, black slacks, alligator boots, and a plum silk shirt, unbuttoned to the sternum all pulled together with a wheat-colored summer-weight blazer.

After a tense round of appetizers and several cocktails, Josy rose from her chair and announced, "This is ridiculous, Ricardo."

"This is business, *hermana mia*. Please leave."

"He speaks for no one, Archie," she said, pushing away from her brother's chair.

Josy walked backward, swishing her finger at Ricardo. She was suddenly surrounded by Matt and Tuck, choirboys with their heads bowed. Archie rose to join.

"You should stay."

So close, thought Archie, as his tablemates disappeared into the casino.

As Ricardo ordered coffee, Archie remembered his part in the Montemayor melodrama. He'd been bedeviled by Josefina Montemayor from the first stolen kiss, and more, in the pristine hayloft of the family's exquisite horse stable. After that fateful twenty-four hours, frolicking on the fabulous *hacienda* with the vivacious *Princesa*, Archie sought Josy out ceaselessly in San Antonio.

And paid for the privilege. In full.

During the ensuing months, Archie escaped his Victoria commitments—familial and professional—more and more. His producer at KAVU was tolerant, but worried, as were all the Callahans. Except for Patti, who gave a damn about what fresh hell her fiancé was cooking up. The heretofore clueless Miss Callahan knew Archie was chasing some whore. The private detectives who made it their business to know what the future son-in-law was up to, kept Old Man Callahan well informed.

Archie knew he was acting the fool. Completely whipped, he paid attention exclusively to his pleasure. Victoria was nice. It was growing on him, but nothing in the Coastal Bend could compete with the brand of enticement that preened and pranced in the Alamo City. Archie Weesatche—at best—a minor celebrity in the nation's smallest TV market, forgot his place; temporarily lost touch with reality.

"Seems like yesterday . . . George Washington's Birthday. In what? 1994?" said Archie, pouring a tube of raw sugar into his double expresso.

"Actually, February 1995," Ricardo corrected. "Josy was making one of her endless debuts: Las Marthas, Fiesta, Buccaneer Days. She even went to Waco. Some Pecan, Cotton . . . some asinine commodity festival."

"She's aging. . ." said Archie, clearing his throat. "Josy is maturing, beautifully."

"The finest maturity money can buy," said Ricardo. "I assure you."

"And I'm sorry to hear of your father's declining health," Archie continued, as formally as he could muster in shorts and tennis shoes. "I'll never forget that soccer match, or your *hacienda*."

"Was it my father's hospitality?" said Ricky, drilling into Archie with dancing hazel eyes. "Or Escobar?"

It was your sister, thought Archie, definitely keeping *that* to himself.

"Your father is a world-class host," said Archie meeting Ricky's gaze and holding steady. "But yeah, that whole *narco futbol* deal was way cool. In fact, I just saw a documentary called *The Two Escobars*. Amazing story."

"Really? That thug?" said Ricky, extracting a gold-filtered Nat Sherman from a polished silver case. He tapped the top of the cigarette, stabbed it in his mouth. "I'm surprised any filmmaker had the guts."

"Made after Escobar's death, no doubt, but fascinating. I'll send you a copy."

"Don't bother. We get every cable channel on the planet."

"Of course," Archie replied, regretting mentioning gifts to one of the richest men in Tamaulipas. "They had interviews with men from Escobar's inner circle in the eighties and nineties. They talked about how he was the Robin Hood of Columbia."

"Oof! Robin Hood with a machine gun," said Ricardo.

Archie paused a beat. "With all due respect, is it difficult for a family of your stature to stay clear of the *narcos*?"

Ricardo looked up from his coffee.

"I can hear, by your tone, that you *are* being respectful," he assured. "But that's not something one asks the executor of the Montemayor Estate."

"No, no . . . *perdoname*."

"Archie, please, I like you," Ricky said. "To answer your question—I'm being too sensitive—I'm still getting used to being the spokesperson for the family."

"Understood, Ricardo. None of my business."

"But I insist on explaining. Champagne?"

"Please."

Ricky waved his hand, "Champagne! And not that swill. Dom Pérignon! P2!"

The Kickapoo bartender disappeared into a room behind the bar and reappeared instantly with the famous smoked-glass curves of the French vintage.

"No, you see, Archie, it's precisely because we *are* a family of stature, as you say, that the Montemayor's can choose to participate in the admittedly lucrative *narco* trade, or remain *rancheros puros*, as we have for over two centuries. This land; right here. We owned it. This was ours. Before that villain Villa ruined it for everybody."

"What about the Kickapoos?"

The Don-in-training, rolled his eyes dismissively. "Can you believe this hellhole?"

"Josy says your family has a stake in the casino," said Archie.

"Did she?" asked Ricardo. "As always, the voice of discretion, my sister."

"My grasp of history isn't what it should be," said Archie, throwing back his expresso. "This was Montemayor land? I guess all of Texas *was* Mexico, back in the day."

"Yes, back in the day," he said, grimacing at the pop of the cork. "But enough about Old Mexico, tell me about your trucking business. I remember reading about a clever name, Keep On . . .?"

"Keep On Truckin'."

"Yes, that's it. With the hippy man logo!" said Ricardo, smiling like the former owner of *Tejas*, as the bartender slowly poured the champagne.

"I'm humbled that you know of my modest business," said Archie. "Oh, and by the way, I was granted permission, from R. Crumb himself, to use the hippy man logo. He refused royalties."

"Really? Well done," said Ricardo, delighting in his sip of Dom Pérignon's most recent creation, nodding to the bartender to fill Archie's flute.

"I've forgotten how agreeable you are, Archie," said Ricardo. "How well mannered."

"My mother and father think it's important."

"Yes well, we are a reflection of our families."

"Cheers then," said Archie, clinking glasses. "To your father's health. And to manners. May courtesy and respect carry the day. *¡Salud!*"

"*¡Salud!*" repeated Ricardo, dabbing his mouth with a napkin. He took a big drag off his Nat Sherman. "Archie, I want you to know that I intend to acquire Keep on Truckin' for the Montemayor family."

He let that settle for a beat, then carried on.

"The taxes are so high for acquisitions in *Estados Unidos*, no? I will set you up with accountants who are conversant in all the offshore strategies. Tropical bankers, who make taxes disappear—like Escobar's rivals, no?"

Archie raised his glass, paused. "It's good to see old acquaintances." They clinked again and drank, eyeing each other intently.

"It's good to see my new partner," said Ricardo. "To our continued success!"

Archie stalled.

He asked Ricardo for a cigarette which he quickly brought out and lit with a mother-of-pearl Dunhill lighter. Archie dragged on the cigarette, then spun out a beautiful smoke ring that floated just above Ricardo's head. "So, Ricardo, what you didn't read was that I sold my company," he said, ashing the cigarette.

"Really?" said Ricardo, eyebrows raised. "When?"

"We closed December 2014. KOT is now owned by a publicly traded company called Pro Logistics, based in Omaha. I signed a non-compete."

"How unfortunate."

Archie looked at a mysterious man—a tall, thin Kickapoo—who'd been staring at them the entire time. Montemayor security, he thought.

"So sorry about Keep On Truckin', Ricardo. Are we done?"

"Hardly," said Ricardo, waving his hand through another one of Archie's perfect smoke rings. "How is it that you survived dishonoring my family?"

Archie took another drag and made sure to exhale slightly left of Ricardo's head.

"We were young and dumb, that's for sure."

"You were neither," Ricardo spat. "Careless and reckless, no? Wouldn't you describe impregnating an eighteen-year-old high school senior of impeccable bloodlines and strict Catholic upbringing, as both careless and reckless?"

Archie lifted the champagne flute and drank deeply.

"Wake the fuck up," Ricardo said. "Cash call."

"Cash call?" said Archie, hiding wild eyes behind his flute. "So, this is extortion?"

"Archie, *Archito pendejo*. You think this is a game?" said Ricardo, lighting yet another cigarette. "That I'm bluffing?"

"Nope," said Archie, looking Ricardo in the eye.

"Let me refresh your champagne and your memory."

"Yes, please," said Archie, offering his glass.

"I picked up my sister from the Menger Hotel, with you by her side," he said, pouring. "Josy confessed that she had an abortion, performed by a doctor of your acquaintance. You are responsible."

"Ricardo, your fluency is impressive," Archie said, launching another beautiful, round smoke ring.

"What you should be impressed with is the gravity of your situation," said Ricardo. "Your former future father-in-law, Mr. Callahan, the father of your fiancée Patti, the woman you were engaged to while you were fucking my sister. ¿*Te acuerdas?*"

"No, but please continue," Archie said, nodding.

"This Mr. Callahan came to my father after his broken-hearted daughter came to him begging to defend *her* honor, seeking blood for your betrayal with Josy."

"Why am I not dead?" asked Archie, genuinely surprised by this new information. "And believe me, Old Man Callahan would have had me shot, no problem."

"Me too," said Ricardo, cocking his finger and shooting an imaginary bullet. "Truly. Boom! Done!"

"I can see that," said Archie, beginning to feel a bit unnerved.

"My father saved your life. *My* father, *mi padre*," said Ricky, thumping his chest. "Your bill is due, *Señor Huizache*. ¿*Entiendes?*"

"Look it. Here's what *I* know," said Archie, feeling his cheeks burn. "Old Man Callahan takes me out by the pool—after Thanksgiving dinner— tells me to never see Patti again. Tells me to go back to west Texas. And don't be fooling around in San Antonio anymore, is what he said. All of which I did; to the letter. Old Man Callahan never mentioned Josy or your father. It was plain and simple."

"Not plain, or simple!" cried the Executor. "Everything to do with stealing the virginity of, disparaging the honor of, ruining the good name of, my father's only daughter!"

"Disparaging . . . what's that in Spanish?"

Ricardo, the know-it-all, spelled it out for him.

"*De-shon-rar*," mimed Archie, tripping over the first r. "*Gracias*, Ricardo."

"Thank you," mimed Ricardo. "This is what you say to the man who's going to have you killed."

"Seriously!" Archie said, leaning back into his chair. "You're telling me this?"

"Here's my offer, and it's nonnegotiable," said Ricardo, standing. He shot the cuffs of his dress shirt; shrugged his sport coat into place. "*Nos debes*. Six hundred and fifty thousand dollars, delivered, in cash. December thirty-first. What is your answer, sir?"

"First, my answer is, yes. I appreciate the opportunity to make this right," said Archie, feeling the blood drain from his brain. "I sold Keep on Truckin'. I have four thousand in the bank. That ship has long sailed."

Ricardo drained his Dom Pérignon. Smiled at the country boy.

"Sounds like poor people problems to me."

A TALE OF TWO VICTORIAS

As he lay in his Lucky Eagle bed, with Billy Tuck in the adjacent double snoring off his blackjack losses, Archie pondered current realities and old hypotheticals.

He had not married Patti Callahan.

He had not married Josefina Montemayor.

What if?

Had he formed either perfect union, young Mr. Weesatche could have lorded over wedges of the world considerably larger than the Faulknerian postage stamp of Yoknapatawpha County.

This being Texas. This being Mexico. And all that entails.

Archie knew the stories. Old Man Callahan and his Irish pioneer descendants, landed on the Texas coast at Indianola and got to work. In a century and two score, they stitched together an enormous stake. Radiating from central command in Victoria County, their holdings stretched south to the bays of Copano and Aransas, west across the post oak scrublands of Bee and Goliad Counties, east and north over the rolling hills of DeWitt County, then back south to Carancahua Bay in Jackson County.

Not the King Ranch; but a damn respectable assemblage.

By the end of the twentieth century, the entire 137,268 acres—thirty-one leagues/*sietos*—were accounted for in pristine pastures fenced by rod-straight posts and guitar-tight wire. The barns, buildings, horse runs, and working pens were all painted iridescent white. Huge swaths of grazing lands were chained, burned, and carpeted with the strongest of A&M-engineered grasses providing plentiful nutrition for cattle bred specifically to thrive in the scorch of South Texas heat.

And the royalties!

As sedimentary and stratigraphic luck would have it the Callahan lands sat atop a bona fide petroleum bonanza. Lakes of shallow oil drilled vertically in the twentieth century and huge humps of shale drilled horizontally in the twenty-first century.

Decades of prodigious Callahan production from oil and gas wells provided the financial lubrication that made the ranching of cattle, the breeding of horses, the raising of feed and cash crops on carefully platted properties an enterprise of pleasure.

And the houses!

A stately mansion—the Big House—towered like a tintype mirage on the coastal prairie. A ranch-style compound commanded a full block of Old Victoria. Lakeside retreats. Bayside bungalows. Condos on the beach. Apartments in Houston and San Antonio. All manned by cooks and gardeners and housekeepers and secretaries and nannies and manservants and dog handlers and boat captains and jet pilots and helicopter pilots and drivers and foremen and cowboys. And more cowboys.

Oh yes, Archie could have ridden the Black Irish back of Patti Callahan into a large piece of heaven.

But he had not.

What in the wide world of matrimony was he thinking?

Thinking with his wedding tackle was the genteel Old Victoria response.

Young, dumb, and run-off was the real answer.

As for Mexico . . .

Hacienda Montemayor was an empire 222 years in the making. The long-ago Spanish father received his land grant from King Carlos II of Spain and established *El Rancho Palma*, near present-day Brownsville, Texas. Over the generations, mainly through marriage, but also naked land grabs when a revolution or other political instability proved fortuitous, the Montemayor holdings spread north to Del Rio, south to the *Sierra Madre Oriental* in Tamaulipas, then west to the edge of Monterrey in the state of Nuevo Leon. Thousands of hectares eventually consolidated at the turn of the twentieth century in an estate of such natural beauty, impeccable design, and progressive planning that it earned a national historical designation *and* continued as one of Mexico's most productive farming and cattle operations.

Archie never even considered being worthy of such a remarkable Mexican dynasty.

Archie Ducornet Weesatche knew one thing.

He was more saved than most. A foundling most fortunate.

Neither Patti nor Old Man Callahan could convince him otherwise. Not even the mercurial Miss Josefina, with her plentiful wiles, could wrest Archie out of his self-imposed deadlock. Archie Weesatche was destined to float in a world of his parents' making. The happy ward of Sister Ernestine and Sheriff Fuchs, his celestial keepers.

He did not articulate this hardened vow.

He did not care to explain.

He simply lived it.

And for his ornery insubordination, Archie Weesatche was lashed by tongue, tooth and nail. His skin practically melted from the hot breath of women scorned and captains of industry disobeyed.

"You be careful, son."

"*Cuidado, muchacho. Cuidado.*"

Archie got that a lot.

ON MY G5, G5

BIG SPRING, TEXAS – CIUDAD VICTORIA, TAMAULIPAS
AUGUST 10, 2015

Three days after agreeing to Ricardo's ultimatum in Eagle Pass, Archie watched as the Montemayor's muscular G5—call letters MTM420 stenciled below the Mexican tri-colors: green, white, and red—landed on the runway of the former Webb Air Force Base.

One of dozens of deactivated Air Force Pilot Training Wings in the United States' bloated military holdings, Webb AFB sent nine thousand plus pilots into the wild blue yonder during World War II, the Korean Conflict, and the Viet Nam War. Big Spring never recovered after the base closed in 1977. The city's population plummeted from a robust forty thousand to fifteen thousand in only thirty years.

The Permian Basin shale boom helped stanch the losses and the phoenix-like rebirth of The Settles Hotel had locals optimistic, but as Archie sipped his morning coffee, the words "military-industrial complex" made him shake his head. Who knew why the once-thriving Webb AFB was now relegated to a half-assed industrial park?

As the G5 taxied on the tarmac Archie admired the sleek lines of ultimate swag. He silenced the Cougar Red Cadillac, put the keys in the console, and sent himself a text with the keyless entry code. As he walked across the polished concrete floor of the one remaining commercial hangar at the base, Archie sang one of Matt's recent downloads:

"I'm a leavin', never coming back again, gonna ride in my G5, G5."

The jet stopped hard with engines noisily winding down. Instantly, the fuselage breeched, stairs hydraulically unfolding to reveal Josefina Montemayor, floor to door, filling the frame with pure female opalescence. Josy was smiling with such all-consuming confidence that Archie couldn't help himself.

"*Princesa!*"

"Have you ever been greeted by such a sexy flight attendant?" she asked, beaming as Archie bent his lanky frame into the cabin and planted two light kisses on his hostess's cheeks. Josy hugged him tight, held him for a few extra beats. "How are you, *guapo*? I hate how we left that stupid casino."

"I'm fine, Josy," he said, curious after the long embrace. "How are you?"

"I had such a good time on the Pecos. Matt's such a doll. He's so you, I swear!"

"A much younger me. And yes, flattery will get you everywhere," said Archie, stepping deeper down the aisle of the ten-passenger jet outfitted tip-to-stern in butterscotch leather and exotic wood trim. "Hey girl, this is . . . this is *nice.*"

He released his leather suitcase to a uniformed pilot who had silently materialized from the cockpit. The Mexican aviator took the bag with a tip of his cap.

"The Montemayor empire is flourishing."

"Appearances are deceiving," said Josy, removing her latest pair of fabulous sunglasses. "Wanna help me escape?"

"As best I can."

After topping off the fuel and smoothly lifting off for the state of Tamaulipas, Archie attempted to ingratiate himself. It had been fifteen years since their torrid San Antonio affair. The whirlwind day on the Pecos had provided zero opportunities to reconnect.

In her jet-set element, Archie could tell that Josy had grown up. She looked, dressed, spoke—even smelled—like a *hacendada*. Truly, a lady to the manor born.

"Josy, help a brother out," he said, gesturing at the palatial set-up. "Why escape?"

"Ricardo," she said, frowning. "He's such a macho. You'd think he built the *hacienda* himself. Really, Archie, it's disgusting. He thinks he's *el rey*! The King!"

Archie leaned back in his plush bucket seat; tried to relate.

"Old Man Callahan and your Dad, they got it right. Take care of the land; take care of the people; genuine *patrons*. But the heirs—Patti, Ricardo—they *expect* to live like royals."

"This sense of entitlement, no?" she said, flashing bejeweled fingers. "My name is Montemayor! I am the King of Mexico!"

Archie laughed. Josy *should* be running the Montemayor empire. She'd be terrific.

Sadly, that scenario, even as late as 2015, was DOA. The deeply traditional Mexican patriarchy wouldn't have it. Josy could more easily lead a publicly-traded company, even a cartel, than an old-school Mexican *hacienda*.

"*Ay, que lastima*," said Josy, reaching across the fold-out table to squeeze his hand. "What a waste."

"Why waste?"

"You and me," said Josy, unbuckling her seat belt. "Us!"

"Us." Archie smiled. Thankfully, Josy was smiling back. "I didn't have a clue about us."

"No?" she said, feigning surprise. "You seemed interested."

"Please, yes. I was obsessed with you. Not us. You were just following my lead. I knew better; didn't think straight for a minute."

"You sound like a guilty Catholic," she said, brushing some unseen lint from her blouse, leaning back in her luxurious seat. "I have a confession."

"Not necessary. You were eighteen."

"That's true. I was young, and you did take advantage, but not of me. No, no. I wanted what I wanted."

"And you had control," he said, raking fingers through his longish sandy hair. "But how so? What confession?"

Josy clasped hands and stretched coquettishly in a conservative white pant suit. "You treated me like a grown woman."

"You *were* a grown woman."

"With the mind of a devious child," she said, kicking off her pumps, pulling her legs up under her bottom. "I'd been practicing my *femme fatale* at St. Mary's Hall. When I met you at Las Marthas, I was *ready, chiquito. Lista!*"

"You were spectacular." Archie agreed. "I'd never seen such a thing."

"I could tell you wanted me. You tried to be respectful of Patti, at least until that crazy *futbol* match."

"Until we got pregnant."

"I was never pregnant."

Archie was shocked. "What? I took you to the clinic."

"I bribed the receptionist *and* the nurse. Right after they said to come back, you know, into the surgical suite, I gave them both two hundred dollars. I was going to bribe the doctor, too."

"Really?"

"Really. As soon as the door closed, I gave them the money. They knew just where to stash me."

"I waited for two hours," said an astonished Archie.

"I know, I was going crazy," Josy continued, laughing. "They stuck me in a janitor's closet. There was no light and all these stinky mops. But I waited. I kept looking at my glow-in-the-dark Rolex, the one *papi* gave me for making good grades—see, *muy intelligente*—and then, remember, I acted all hurt. I really wanted to be with you. That beautiful suite at The Menger! But I couldn't blow my cover."

"Educated by the *telenovela*," said Archie, laughing. "You were very convincing."

"Too convincing. I never saw you again," she said, looking out the window. "Not even *one* of your fabulous letters. I was devastated."

She swatted his leg for good measure.

"So, no *bambino*, huh?" said Archie, relieved to be really talking to Josefina, finally. "I didn't know about Old Man Callahan and your father cooking up some deal. Ricky told me last weekend. All this honor stuff."

"Of course, he did!" she said, looking out the window, the picture of petulance.

"What?"

"I was so stupid," she said, twisting a handful of hair. "I blabbed to Ricky that I hated you for not marrying me."

"Is that true? asked Archie. "You were so young."

"It was true at the time—a teenager's fantasy. I'm over it now, *guapo*."

Josy sighed and peered out the tiny oval window. "You know, Ricardo's trying to push me out of the estate. That's why I need you to win. So we can pay that fat banker and run away."

Archie massaged his temples, looked out the window at the craggy terrain of the Texas Hill Country. "Family dynamics," he sighed. "Always a challenge."

"Always," she agreed, then leapt from her seat. "What a bad flight attendant! Coffee, tea, or me?"

"You. And one of your famous blood orange and tequilas."

As Josy leaned into the aisle, Archie tried to avert his covetous eyes, but was caught.

"I miss you, *Archito*." She smiled sweetly, then hip-swayed back to the galley.

"Good to see you too, *dulce*," he said, to her bobbing backside. "I'll win that money for you, Josy. I will."

AN HOUR LATER, THE G5 LIGHTLY TOUCHED DOWN ON THE FRESH ASPHALT OF a runway hidden on a distant quadrant of *Hacienda Montemayor*. Archie automatically checked his phone for texts and emails. Matt had left a message that he was driving Tallulah to Stephenville to talk to the volleyball coach.

"That sounds good," he said. "I think."

"What?" said Josy, less effusive now that she was back on family turf.

"Your boyfriend's taking our sister to talk to her new college volleyball coach."

"Matt? He's such a good boy," she said, staring out the cabin window. "I'm embarrassed, Archie."

"Not for a minute. Matt's never met anyone remotely like you," Archie assured her. "He was thrilled."

"I was in such a mood! Ricardo put me up to the whole thing, with the help of your friend Tuck," she said. "You should be careful with him, *hermoso*."

"Tuck's harmless," he said, actually thinking otherwise.

"Probably, but you know. . . *cuidado*."

Archie wanted to tell Josy that Tuck had told him that he worked for the Montemayor family. But didn't. Archie'd worked long and hard to break the habit of sharing too much information. He'd visited a lot of trouble on himself confiding in people who didn't need to know, or worse yet, didn't *want* to know what was on his mind.

"So, we gonna have time to continue our catch-up?" said Archie, as the co-pilot brushed by. "Or is this all business?"

"All business, I'm afraid," she said, eyeing the co-pilot. "I was looking for our guests. Papa invited fifty of his closest friends from Victoria to your dinner party."

"Right," he scoffed. "I'm assuming that's Ciudad Victoria, not Victoria, Texas."

"CV, although I'd love to see what Patti looks like."

"Not as pretty as you," Archie said, watching the pilots stow their bags in the back of a waiting Escalade. "She went through a rough patch, but she's doing great now. I haven't seen her in years, except on Facebook."

"I hate Facebook; I can't do it," said Josy, fishing a hair doody out of her handbag. "As if anybody is interested in what my poodle ate for lunch! I don't even own a dog."

"I like keeping up with people," he said. "But I'm not much of a contributor. Maybe when I start the Texas Football Tour."

"That sounds fun," Josy said, giving him the gag sign. "I'll never forget when you made me go to that game in San Antonio."

"Alamo Heights," crowed Archie. "What? No love for the Fighting Mules!"

"Alamo Whites, is more like it. I was so bored," said Josy, busy fashioning her hair into a perfectly thick ponytail. "The *princesa* was ready to party. But I loved that you loved it; you know, your culture."

"I'm pretty sure we got the partying done, too," said Archie.

"American football is gross, in case you missed the last World Cup."

"No ma'am," he replied. "In fact, I'll take you to a Marfa-Presidio game with the Christmas Mountains backlit behind you and young men in tight pants in front. I'll feed you a warm Frito pie with a cold Dr. Pepper—tell me who plays the beautiful game."

"Very enticing, *Señor Huizache*," said Josy, touching up her lip gloss. "Matt said you haven't dated in years. You're not gay, are you?"

"Not that I know of," he said. "You want to check for sure?"

Archie and Josy looked at each other like adults who felt like naughty teenagers.

As they moved to the door, Josefina stopped. She demurely kissed Archie's cheek, then moved to his mouth. "See you tonight, *guapo*."

THE ENSUING TWENTY-FOUR HOURS, IN THE LAP OF MONTEMAYOR LUXURY, gave Archie time to consider that, perhaps, he'd made a mistake in not pursuing *La Princesa*.

The main entrance to *Hacienda Montemayor* was grand indeed, guarded by massive iron gates and fortress-like walls. The drive to the "Casa Grande" wound a couple of miles through flower-studded fields, across a lovely creek that plunged into the depths of close-set trees. Just outside the main buildings the shady road ran past servant's quarters and the elegant stone and timber stables where Josy and Archie had so enthusiastically rolled in the hay, years past.

The *hacienda* proper featured a verandah, thirty-feet wide, with a beautiful stone floor and high raftered-ceiling furnished with easy chairs, couches, rugs and tables where various breeds of dogs laid about barely raising their heads when Josy and Archie walked by. Long wings of bedrooms and salons rose on either side of the patio creating an immense three-sided court filled with broad-leafed palms and banana plants. The fountain-cooled air was lush with the smell of roses and orange blossoms.

"Holy moly," gushed Archie, stepping inside huge carved doors into a flower-filled entry hall. "Can I stay, like, forever."

"*Mi casa es su casa*," answered Josy, stopping to strike a pose midway up a graceful curved staircase. "Come see me."

THE EVENING BEGAN WITH A TWO-HOUR COCKTAIL PARTY ATTENDED BY FIFTY of the most beautiful people Archie had ever seen, all family friends from nearby Ciudad Victoria and the *haciendas* of southern Tamaulipas. All of the attendees were beautifully turned out in chic business casual, sipping mojitos, margaritas and wine under spectacular arched stone and timber arcades that wrapped around the enormous courtyard bursting with luxuriant landscaping and bougainvilleas of every color.

A band of mariachis, in full black velvet regalia, serenaded the guests with old favorites and requests. Cocktails were followed by a seated dinner in a formal living room featuring an enormous polished mesquite table groaning with chargers and plates and glasses and every conceivable utensil forged of the finest Mexican silver.

The English spoken around the table by three generations of Mexican aristocracy was as fluent as the Spanish, sprinkled with the occasional burst of French when the house chef paraded the delicious beef fricassee, grilled Tampico redfish, and a rolling silver cart with heaps of tender *cabrito* surrounded by grilled red, yellow and green peppers.

The third hour featured a citrus *flan* and *tres leches* cake complimented with pots of local coffee grown on the folded slopes of the nearby Sierra Madre. Dessert was followed by the finest Portuguese port and French cognac.

As the after-dinner liqueurs were being poured, Don Montemayor sidled up to Archie, as he exhaled a plume of iridescent white smoke from a perfectly humidified Cuban Montecristo No. 2.

"I'm so glad you could join us, *Señor Huizache*," said the Don, clapping his visitor on the back. "After all these many years."

"I'm so happy to be here! Such spectacular hospitality," said Archie, lifting his goblet, hoping he wasn't being too forward.

Don Montemayor, leaned down and whispered, "Let's steal away. *Vamos al jardin*."

The conversation quieted when Archie rose from the table. Before the host ushered him out of the room, Don Montemayor turned to the crowded table.

"Thank you all for coming. You are the best of friends and splendid ambassadors," he said. "*Muchas gracias, y buen viaje a todos.*"

As Archie followed Don Montemayor, meandering through indoor hallways and then outside to a secluded garden nook, dimly lit by *torchas,* he recalled, wistfully, the twenty-five-year-old Archie's inability to see this world; this colonial splendor. He'd never imagined the opportunity—the opportunity to weave a new Archie Weesatche; to create an original American-Mexican tapestry.

Why hadn't he manned up; broken up with Patti? Why hadn't he tried his luck? Why didn't he at least think of himself as a serious suitor? Surely, he could have built a relationship with Josy beyond the partying and San Antonio trysts.

"Come sit, Archie," said the Don, offering a choice of padded wicker chairs. "I want to tell you a story about our old friend, Señor Callahan. *Que en paz descanse.*"

"Thank you, sir. This cigar is a masterpiece—my first *Montecristo Cubano,*" Archie said, taking his seat. "What brand is your favorite?"

"A little known, but excellent cigar from the Philippines—Fighting Cock."

"Really, the Philippines?" said Archie, accepting the host's offer to inspect his cigar. He smelled the deep red wrapper tobacco; examined the band closely. "Look at'em—in mid-fight. I've read some fascinating stories about cockfighting during the Viet Nam war. They built a ten-thousand-seat arena in Manila just for the derbies."

"Oh yes, the Spaniards love good cigars and brave cocks!" crowed Don Montemayor, taking back the cigar. "I bought ten boxes of these from a man named Colonel . . . Colonel something."

"Colonel Rumbo? In San Antonio?" Archie guessed.

"*¡Exactamente!* He had a little shop in the Menger hotel . . ."

"And a big shop on San Pedro," said Archie, amazed at the memory.

"The Humidor. I used to buy all kinds of stuff from the Colonel during the cigar boom. Best sales tool in the book, next to women and whiskey; and a *whole* lot cheaper."

"Yes, yes, that's amazing," he gushed. "*El mundo es tan peque*ño. It's a small world."

Infinitesimally small, thought the star-struck guest.

"So, Archie, please indulge me," said Don Montemayor.

"*Porfavor*," said Archie, puffing on his Cubano.

"Tell me of Señor Callahan. When did you come to know him? I knew him for many years," said Don Montemayor, waving for his man to come re-light his cigar.

"I met Old Man Callahan at a Christmas party the year I moved to Victoria," recalled Archie. "December 1994."

"I met our old *amigo* in 1968," said the Don, as he puffed from the held flame of a thin cedar shake. "At the Mexico Olympics. We were seated next to each other at a shooting competition. The Skeet Finals."

"I love the Olympics," said Archie, admiring his elegant elder. "My Dad went to the Mexico City Olympics as well. He was a track and volleyball man."

"Did he take you to other Olympics? Mexico was my only one."

"No, not with my parents, but I did go to the Barcelona Games in nine-ty-two," said Archie, not wanting to go into his parent's accidental death. "I had a friend—Morgan Wooten—who competed in the decathlon."

"*¡Barcelona!*" cried the Don. "One of my favorite cities in the world. *Barca y Cartagena.*"

"*Las Ramblas* and all the Gaudi. I was in heaven in Barcelona."

"*Archito*, your enthusiasm is infectious," said Don Montemayor. "You wear it well."

They paused, drawing on their lush tobacco and laughing, enjoying the pleasant breeze that rippled the pool.

"Well, on with my Callahan story; it concerns you as well," said the host. "So, I met Señor Callahan at the shooting match and we got along famously. He even invited me to his *rancho*. Said that I must come to his annual pigeon shoot."

"The famous pigeon shoots," said Archie. "He built a covered grand-stand and these elaborate bird pens and shooting stations."

"Yes, a grand occasion!" said Don Montemayor, raising his glass for more port. "I took the invitation very seriously; too seriously. Here, more sherry?"

Archie picked up his goblet, then sheepishly set it down when the waiter stared at him.

"As I learned more of Señor Callahan's famous pigeon shoots, I heard the serious money was wagered on the "hired guns," he said, pausing to sip. "So, *por supuesto*, I brought the champion *pistolero* from my club in Cuernavaca, and at the dinner, I drank too much and danced too much with the beautiful Texas women. Then I wagered much too much on my man. But who could not? There were so many beautiful women and their rich husbands determined to impress each other. I was a prideful man from Mexico with all these Texas ranchers. Archie, I was foolish beyond measure."

Archie was spellbound, but couldn't guess how he might be involved in such a fabulous scene, right around the time he was born.

"So, I'm going to tell you how much I wagered because . . . *porque* it's the best part of the story."

"This is when? 1968?" asked Archie. "I was born in 1971."

"The spring after the Olympics."

"Okay, so sixty-nine in Victoria," said Archie. "You flew up from CV to Victoria, Texas."

"Yes, on our family's first private plane! A little Piper Cherokee," he said. "*Archito*, I bet one hundred and fifty thousand dollars that night."

"Wow!" was all Archie could say, trying to estimate what that would be in 2015 dollars.

"About six hundred and fifty thousand, in today's dollars," said Ricardo, entering from the arcade, gesturing to his father's man to bring him a chair.

"Ricardo! Come join us," said the Don to his son, who had changed from an elegant linen evening suit to boots, designer jeans, and vermillion silk shirt rakishly opened to display a tangle of gold chains and silver crucifix.

"Did you tell Archie how you were cheated?" said Ricardo, sitting next to his father.

"I think *cheated* is a bit much."

"Perhaps," said Ricardo, signaling for a glass of port. "But not inaccurate."

"My son is a talented linguist," said Don Montemayor, placing a hand on Ricardo's knee. "He's fluent in Spanish, English, and French."

"Yes, I'm amazed by the fluency of your family and friends," said Archie, annoyed by Ricardo's intrusion, but not surprised. "The *americano feo* must improve his *espanol*."

That got a rise from the men, who laughed and repeated, "*americano feo*."

"Okay, who's ready to party!" announced Josefina, decked for the disco in a turquoise halter dress and stilettos that clicked on the flagstones as she sashayed towards the men. "*Papi, vamos a bailar!*" She kissed her father's cheek, hugged his neck.

"*Yo soy un viejo. Esto es para jovenes,*" said the Don, enjoying his daughter's affections. "Go show our guest a good time. Archie, I'll finish my story over breakfast."

"I look forward to it," said Archie, taking a last puff of the heavenly Cubano.

"If she doesn't keep him out all night," sneered Ricardo, put off by Josy's intrusion.

An awkward silence ensued that not even the chirping frogs and dancing lightning bugs could soften. Long night, thought Archie, as they watched Don Montemayor being helped from his chair. As he trundled back into the main house, the *pater familias* waved without looking back. "*Buenas noches, hijos.*"

NEGOCIOS

CIUDAD VICTORIA, TAMAULIPAS—BIG SPRING, TEXAS

AUGUST 11, 2015

"Archie, you need to get up."

"*¡Archito, levantate!*" whispered *La Princesa,* in the ear of her dead-to-the-world guest.

Archie could not open his eyes. "No ma'am; wait."

The consequences of a straight tequila night with Josy and her coterie of boy toys— fashionistas, jocks, journalists, painters, sculptors, poets— banged on his skull.

Nausea was next.

After the fabulous four-hour dinner party, he should've repaired directly to his room. Archie knew he was in trouble as soon as Team Josy's phalanx of gleaming black Escalades rolled up to the throbbing, neon-bedecked Club Chaparral.

Archie could still feel the thump of endless *cumbias* closing in on him. The reek of dance floor sweat puddling at the small of his back.

He knew better. He was forty-five for goodness' sake; not twenty-five! And yet . . .

"Wait. The sun's up?" he said, incredulous, rising from the sheets zombie-like, cracking an eye. "Didn't we just go to bed?"

"It's seven-thirty, *precioso,*" Josy answered, giggling. She thrust an arm under Archie's pillow, pulled him down, pressed her body tight to the curve of his broad back. "You're having breakfast at nine."

"Just shoot me," Archie said, nestling back into the pillows. "Or am I already dead?"

"Don't say that," Josy whispered furiously, nibbling on his ear. "Come with me."

Josy doubled-backed the comforter and stepped out of bed to retrieve Archie's shirt, which *she* proceeded to put on and button—a single button.

Archie dove beneath the covers of the enormous California King and came up with a fistful of boxers which he slipped on and followed Josy out of her sumptuously decorated bedroom into a long hallway. As they tip-toed down the hall, a maid appeared at the top of the stairs holding a wooden tray with juice, coffee and water. Josy motioned for the girl to follow and all three padded silently down a precisely vacuumed purple and gold Oriental runner to a bedroom at the end of the hall.

"Go take a shower," said Josy, directing the maid to pour a cup of coffee and leave. "And no cat naps! You never wake up, remember?"

"You've got a sharp memory for odd details," Archie said, nodding thanks to the maid, who'd turned on the shower after pouring his coffee. His head was still murky, but now that he was awake, Archie felt relief. He was going to survive.

"I'm not invited to the meeting, but I'll take you down," said Josy, looking criminally seductive in his button-down, the shirttails barely covering *La Princesa's* pulchritude.

"I appreciate the escort," Archie said, trying to sip the scalding coffee, watching Josy follow the maid out the door. "Wait, Josy . . . hey wait, does your brother know about the money? About the banker?"

"Take a shower, *guapo,*" she said, poking her head back inside. "Josy's got your back."

"Excellent news," said Archie, loving her confidence, but not trusting that all was well. "Come back and have some coffee. We need to talk."

Josy was gone.

ARCHIE WAITED IN THE ROOM, FULLY DRESSED IN KHAKIS AND A LIGHTLY starched *guayabera,* until 8:55. He couldn't text Josy because he'd left his phone in her room. When he cracked the door and looked down the hallway, the maid was waiting.

"*Conmigo, porfavor,*" she said, motioning for him. "*Porfavor, Señor Huizache.*"

The crisply uniformed housekeeper escorted him to the pool. Every step of the way, Archie was agog at the pleasures of the Montemayor's perfectly assembled home—plush and impeccable, but not fussy; perfectly rustic.

Ricardo, Jr. and Don Montemayor were seated at a round concrete table inlaid with orange and turquoise tile under a shady, vine-crowded pergola. In the morning light, he noticed the Olympic-size swimming pool's perimeter was layered with more multi-colored tiles and mosaics. The craftsmanship on display, even in the tiniest nook of the *hacienda*, was stunning. The furnishings, the landscaping, the fixtures; every detail was thoughtful, authentic, precise.

The Montemayor men nodded as Archie approached. They exchanged *saludos* and *buenos diases*.

"I'm so taken with your *hacienda*, Don Montemayor. Such an elegant home."

"You're too kind, *Señor Huizache*," said Don Montemayor. "It is an honor to host a man who appreciates *why* we, as you say, maintain such an extravagant house. We are standing on the shoulders of many generations; hard-working men and women who allow us to take our ease. My family tamed these lands and built these walls."

"Ricardo, I see where you inherit your facility with language," said Archie, giving his rival a wan smile. "My mother would love to sit at your table, Don Montemayor. She is a native of France, but speaks English with great felicity."

"*Dios quiera*, your mother and I will share a bottle of French Bordeaux someday."

"She would enjoy that very much," said Archie, basking in the warmth of the Don's natural paternalism. He sipped his *café con leche*, watching the oligarchs—father and son—lean back into their padded wrought iron chairs.

"This family . . ." said Archie, searching for the right words, raising a blue, hand-blown glass of fresh guava nectar. "*¡Yo saludo Don Montemayor y Ricardo!* What you have built; what you have maintained through the centuries, through the troubles, is truly amazing. Thank you for your kindness and hospitality."

"You are most welcome," said Ricardo, as his father nodded.

At that, a uniformed squad served the three men from plates heaped with *chilaquiles con pollo*, scrambled eggs with diced ham, crispy bacon and a choice of six salsas. Next, a colorful platter of farm-fresh citrus was passed including mango, papaya, guava, melon, pineapple and blackberries. Sweating on an outdoor sideboard were five beautifully etched carafes with freshly prepared juice: *toronja, naranja,* beets, carrots and mandarin surrounding a dessert platter filled with crisp *campechanas* and soft *cuernitos*

Archie ate quickly, hoping to vanquish the pulsing in his skull.

"Josefina says you visited many years ago," said Don Montemayor. "I am sorry that we have not made our *hacienda* your Mexican home."

"It's an honor to return to *Tamaulipas* after so many years," said Archie. "I understand your love for this country. I love Texas. I know your pride."

"So, you *have* visited, yes?" asked Ricardo. "With Josy?"

"Yes, fifteen years ago. I'll never forget it," said Archie. "Your son was gracious enough to invite us to the famous *futbol* match against the Columbian all-stars."

"*¿Si, es verdad?*" asked Don Montemayor. "*¿Cuando? Noventa . . . cinco, seis?*"

"*Si, Papi, despues Las Marthas en Laredo,*" said Josy, walking up to the table barefoot and noticeably unrestrained beneath a robe of shimmering jade green silk. "Ricardo was trying to impress Archie's fiancé, the daughter of your friend from *Tejas*. And I had such a crush on this one."

She draped her arms around Archie, allowing her wet hair to cascade across his face.

Ricardo sighed loudly; rolled his eyes to the heavens.

As Archie squirmed, Don Montemayor chuckled, indulging his favorite child.

If she were alive, this brazen display would not have been tolerated by Doña Montemayor. But Josy's mother was long gone, felled by a fatal breast cancer when the only daughter was but fourteen. Don Montemayor was advised to send her to boarding school in *los Estados Unidos* but only relented after Josy's infamous *quinceañera* in Ciudad Victoria. The precocious *princesa* graduated from the fine girl's school in San Antonio, St. Mary's Hall, just after her eighteenth birthday.

Finally, Ricardo exploded out of this chair. "What? Not enough attention last night? Why don't you go back to your shower and let us attend to business?"

"What business?" Josy replied, unwrapping herself from the blushing Archie. "Have you told our father about your plan to extort hundreds of thousands of dollars from our guest?"

"*¡Josefina!* You forget yourself," said her father in a tone pained, but patient.

She crossed arms across her chest, stared down her older brother.

"I see that you have a woman's business on your mind," said Don Montemayor. "Perhaps now is not the time."

"Archie, *con permiso*," Ricardo pleaded. "Josy clearly doesn't understand the nature of our partnership."

"Why are you lying, Ricardo?"

"*¡Josefina!*" said Don Montemayor. "*¡Basta!*"

"*Idiota celoso*," she hissed, then pulled her own chair.

Don Montemayor took the measure of his quarreling children, rose slowly from his chair. A manservant hustled to help him. He wiped his mouth with a tasseled linen napkin, folded it, and placed it on his half-eaten plate of *chilaquiles*.

"*Señor Huizache*, our guests were delighted with your spirited conversation last night," said Don Montemayor. "Many remarked of your charm."

Archie stood up, "Don Montemayor, the pleasure was all mine," shaking a man's hand. "I appreciate you surrounding me with such beautiful, interesting people."

Josy helped herself to her father's plate. "What did you expect? Peasants in hemp?"

Don Montemayor shot his daughter a withering look. "Goodbye, *Señor Huizache*. Please visit us again, soon. *Buen viaje*."

"*Gracias, Don Montemayor*," replied Archie. As the *jefe* took his leave, he glanced at Josy and Ricardo, both of whom avoided his scolding eyes.

They all watched the Don, elegantly attired in linen slacks and a pearl white *guayabera*, shuffle behind his walker, the length of the galleria and into the house.

"Okay guys," said Archie. "What's up?"

"*Nada*," replied Josy. "We're not taking *uno centavo* from you to protect my honor. *¿Esta claro, Ricardo?*"

"You have no honor," Ricardo said, glaring at his sister. "Archie and I struck a *business* deal. And would you please close your robe?"

Josy smiled at her brother, then slowly adjusted her silky green garment; eyes glued on Archie.

"Wow, wow, wow!" said Ricardo, whistling as he rose from his chair and backed away from the table. "You think he's impressed?"

"Run away, *Ricardo*," she said, flicking a wrist at her retreating brother. "*¡Andale!*"

Archie took a healthy spoonful of *caldo de res*, albeit a bit bug-eyed amidst Josy's astonishing display. Ricardo motioned, from across the pool, for Archie to join him.

Josy's arm-barred his exit. "Relax, *guapo*. Ricardo, go away!"

The brother followed his sister's orders, much to Archie's surprise.

"Finish your *campechanas*," she said, shooing a fly, while eyeing Ricardo's retreat.

Archie did as he was told, then laid his napkin over a clean plate. "Hey," he said, pointing to her robe. "Can you do that again?"

"You're such a little teenager, *Archito*," she said. "And you are not to do business with Ricardo! I forbid it."

"*Tranquila amor, tranquila*," said Archie, making a strenuous point *not* to look at the sizeable vent descending down Josy's robe. "Did you just save me a bunch of money?"

Josy cinched her belt, beckoned for Archie's hand. "You wish. *Vamos*."

"*¡Si! ¡Si, mi Princesa!*" said Archie, throwing back the last of his *jugo de naranja*.

"WHO'S TEXTING YOU NOW?" SAID JOSY, LOOKING FOR ALL THE WORLD like a sated puma, curled up in her regular seat on Air Montemayor, claws twisting her glossy black mane, dressed to kill in red skinny jeans and a body-hugging blouse.

"It's so flattering to be courted by Listserv," Archie said, leaning back into the glove-soft leather, beyond ready for the flight to Big Spring to be over.

Archie's post-coital attitude made Josy frown. "What's Listserv?"

"Every football player who's ever played for UH," he answered, softening his tone for the sake of pleasant travel. "We're all on a Listserv at UH Athletics."

"So, you're being a smart ass?"

"I *am* a smart ass," he said, reaching to pat-pat her powerful thigh. He was lucky not to pull back a bloody nub. "They've invited all the former players to meet Tom Herman at a Touchdown Club luncheon. He's the new football coach. American football, in case you were wondering."

Josy smiled sweetly, playing along. "That's sounds nice. Are you going?"

"Actually, I think I will," he said. "I haven't been to a UH function in forever. Exactly the kind of thing I should do now that I've got a little time on my hands."

Josy unfolded her legs, sat up straight, buckled her seatbelt. "I forget you were a famous football player before you were a famous sportscaster."

"Right," Archie said. "I'm relieved that's your enduring impression."

Josefina waved away his petulance. "You should take a nap."

As the jet taxied and the engines roared, Archie took the opportunity to be quiet. He turned off his phone, tried to fathom why in the world he was annoyed. He closed his eyes and thought about big Mexican cats—jaguars, pumas, panthers, ocelots.

He'd seen a sizable one recently, while surf fishing, courtesy of one his Eagle Ford shale clients whose hunting camp was outside of Brownsville, on the beach where the Rio Grande empties into the Gulf of Mexico—*Boca Chica*.

Man, did he long for the simple days of Keep On Truckin'! Dropping off drill bits and blowout preventers. Casting for redfish was a lot less stressful than predicting the next move of Hurricane Josefina.

The native cat he'd seen on the beach—maybe a jaguarundi, was spotted and smallish—ten kilos max. The *gata* across from him was sixty kilos plus and not shy. He sneaked a peek of her scanning her phone. There was no telling the range of admirers flirting with *La Princesa*.

He wondered if big Mexican cats, in their endless search for prey, ever found themselves in Texas. For the past two decades this one had roamed the *frontera*; Juarez to Ojinaga to Nuevo Laredo to Matamoros—a singular beast; surely the only black panther in Tamaulipas. And hungry.

Yes, Josefina had been busy in the decades since she and Archie were ripped asunder. She'd made her name in a purely Mexican realm—with people, in a time of which Archie was unaware. In fact, the things that Archie *didn't* know about Ms. Montemayor could fill the fuselage.

As soon as the jet lifted into Mexican airspace, Josy was ready to talk.

"Okay, *guapo*, do you want to be my lover or my business partner?"

"Both?" he said, tentatively.

"Good answer, but I don't believe you," she said, sitting up in her seat. "Ask me if I saved you six hundred and fifty thousand dollars."

"*¿Si o no?*"

"No, I saved you from my idiot brother trying to mix business with pleasure."

"Yeah, I'm still not clear what your brother wants," Archie said, "He says he wants to buy Keep On Truckin'. But I explained—a couple of times—that ship has sailed."

Josy pondered for a bit.

"He thinks he can dominate you," she said, tossing her phone into her purse.

"Wonder what he made of all that breakfast commotion?" Archie said, praying that the heavy turbulence would pass quickly. "That was quite a show."

"I'm going to kill him."

"We're both full of good answers," he said, feeling suddenly nauseous as the buffeting continued. "I need a stake horse."

"A what?"

"You," he said, trying to focus on anything but air sickness. "I need you . . . excuse me." He closed his eyes and prayed for nausea deliverance.

"*Pobrecito*," she said, unbuckling. "Do you want some water? You need to hydrate."

"Yes, please."

He looked out the oval window at the black clouds boiling below the jet. By the time Josy returned from the galley, the sailing was considerably smoother.

She handed him a cold bottle of *Topo Chico*. "Archie, do you realize that I have a degree in Spanish from St. Mary's *and* an MBA from Rice?"

"Really? From Rice!" Archie gushed. "I knew you stayed in San Antonio for your undergraduate. I was strenuously told *not* to, but I kept up with you."

"You were stalking me?" she asked, resuming her feline pose. "How romantic."

"I knew better than to try to see you. Old Man Callahan's men were watching me like a hawk," Archie said, stopping to guzzle, not realizing how thirsty he was. "Plus, you started showing up in the *Express-News* with that handsome plastic surgeon."

"Who, him?" she said, clearly reveling in Archie's recollection. "He wanted to marry me so bad."

"You guys made a handsome couple," said Archie, taking another long draft, feeling the bubbly water work like an oil change. "Was he Spanish? From Mexico?"

"No, Spain! And only second generation. All he could talk about was how his mother was related to the King—Juan Carlos this; Juan Carlos that. My parents begged me to marry him. But I could see my future—boring!"

"Sounds like money to me."

"He was. Handsome, successful—he already had a nice practice. But I couldn't do it. You were a bad influence on me."

"We had a good time. Not sustainable, but fun," said Archie, recalling fondly the night crawls through San Antonio and Austin, the road trips to the border with his irrepressible eighteen-year-old.

"We were fun AF," she purred.

"So, Miss Multiple Degrees. That's awesome."

"Are you really impressed?" said Josy, batting her lashes. "I always thought we broke up because you wouldn't get serious with anyone but a rich *gringa*, like Patti."

"Come on," he said, incredulously. "We were too young. Although, lookin' back . . . .."

"I expected you to propose. I did," she said, looking out the window. "That's how naive I was. My mother married my father when she was twenty. And the girls I went to school with—they all knew who they were going to marry by the time they got to high school. Married as soon as they graduated. Crazy, no?"

"It worked for your mom; not you," said Archie, finishing his *Topo* and settling in now that the jet was at a cruising altitude well above the weather. "No telling when Matt and Tallulah's generation are going to get married. Hopefully in their late twenties, early thirties."

"I love the name Tallulah; I want to meet her."

"Tallulah's a trip; you'll love her," said Archie, remembering that his sister was with his brother in Stephenville. "Of course, not as much as you love Matt."

She rolled her eyes.

"*Porfavor*," he said, reaching out to pat-pat her knee when she hid her face in her hands. Archie recognized the theatrics. Josy wielded sex like a scimitar.

"But back to me being a racist," he said, laughing. "I was crazy about you, Josy. Because you *were* Mexican. Smart, fun, fiesty—the South Texas trifecta."

"Whatever," she said. "You chased me into the arms of a woman from Wink."

"I doubt that, but yes, tell me about your alfalfa magnate," he said, glad to change the subject. Not so much when he saw Josy's heart-stricken reaction.

"She was wonderful," said Josy, dabbing at her eyes. "*Es lo que es.*"

"*¿Que?*"

"It is what it is."

Archie was sure he'd hear more about Josy's long-time lover—just not right now.

"So, you're up for the Presidio-Marfa game?" he asked. "First game of the year. Biggest rivalry in the Big Empty."

"The Big Empty?"

"That's what the locals call far West Texas, Big Bend."

"You're taking me to the Big Empty?"

"I'm taking you to the Rock Hudson Suite at the Hotel Paisano in Marfa. Plying you with fine tequila and enchilada dinners," said Archie. "Have a little faith, *dulce*."

"Come sit by me."

He got out of his seat, eyed the situation. He offered his hand, helped her up, took a seat, and coaxed her back into his lap. Archie spent the final thirty minutes, streaking across the former Mexico, feeling the weight of a full-grown *gata* bearing down on him.

"*La pantera negro*," he whispered.

"*La pantera ne-gra*," she corrected.

"*Gracias maestra*."

"*De nada, guapo*."

Josy lifted her head off his chest as the wheels touched down on *tierra Tejana*, ran her hand through her lanky wide receiver's sandy hair; heaved a deep sigh. "*Huizache, Huizache*," she said softly. ¿Como *te sientes?*"

"Little bleary," he said, not quite sure of what he was being asked.

Archie looked past Josy, as the outlines of the Big Spring raced into focus, the G-forces pressing them closer, tighter. Archie felt the big cat dig into his bark; her feline hooks,

lifting and sinking,

lifting and sinking,

lifting and sinking.

TOM TERRIFIC

A three-mile run around the Garden City track in the books, Archie paused to gulp the pristine West Texas air under the wide porch of the Nice House.

It was a fresh Monday morning, with birds chirping their thanks for the night-time cool, the sun just peeking above the orderly orange bricks of Sister Ernestine's compound wall. In the distance, brown and cream bands of sedimentary rock piled into hogback ridges, the sun-struck beauty of the buttes and mesas thumbing their noses at the plains below pockmarked with clots of salt cedar, creosote and mesquite.

He sipped high test coffee; stared at his cellphone newsfeed.

Across the street, rooster tails of water arced over the vibrant green of the high school practice field where three football coaches waited under the goal posts, inserting wads of tobacco, then passing the pouch, as their wiry warriors—the 2015 Garden City Bearkats— in shorts and helmets, filed out of the field house.

"Thanks be to Allah," Archie muttered. "*Allahu Akbar.*"

He shook his head, thinking how strange it was to call upon the Muslim deity.

His plea was prompted by a ghastly morning report. Somewhere in the Arabian Desert, ISIS jihadis were creating a Syrian-Iraqi caliphate. And committing atrocities—videotaped beheadings, public hangings and serial rape—all in the name of religion.

He closed his eyes; prayed for the soldiers, the men and women from places like Big Spring and Garden City. He wanted them home; yearned for their safe return.

The Serenity Prayer and the Lord's Prayer, every morning. Every so often, a plea for forgiveness. The occasional request for strength, courage and patience. And many, many calls for comfort and safety for friends, family and total strangers.

That was about all the religion Archie could muster. But he did have faith. After a lifetime of driving the most beautiful, most god-forsaken space in the world, Archie Weesatche understood clearly:

God is Mother Earth.

And she was going to swallow us whole.

He never questioned who was in charge; was never at odds. Never fought what could not be vanquished. Only paid humble respects. Of course, Archie never said any such thing out loud. Out in West Texas, there wasn't much call for New Age spirituality.

As he opened the hermetic seal of the Cougar Red Cadillac, Archie felt a little guilt, but mostly relief. He was so happy to be doing what he did best—driving Texas; driving *his* blood's country after forty-eight hours of Montemayor melodrama.

It was becoming clear to Archie that a period of indentured servitude was at hand. The Montemayor crew were masters with benefits to be sure—flesh, money and lifestyle to spare—but also entanglements that would snare him like the dew-bejeweled web he admired hanging from the rough-barked hackberry that shaded his car. It was a dazzling display of arachnid craftsmanship, the web spread wide by the lady of the limbs casting her silk in elegant, suspended curves.

"I'll get your money, Josy!" he yelled at his on-again flame, smoldering in his mind's eye. The image of Josy's thighs, Josy's eyes, Josy's kisses pulling him closer and deep. "Count on it, *mi novia*."

But this was no lark. No easy task. Winning a little money on football was tough.

Winning $650,000 was ridiculous.

Archie was no longer allowed to simply cruise into hand-picked hamlets with money to be made. No leisurely bets against men whose red necks burned, waiting to sling fistfuls of cash on their hometown heroes. It was all business now—carefully constructed wagers, against men of means, in far-flung counties.

Archie loved'em.

He didn't want their money. He wanted the THWACK of their luck-scorned fists pounding on the warped wood of rising bleachers as the visitor's tailback raced to the end zone with the ball held high.

But not today. The Point Spread Whisperer was on sabbatical this week.

It was going to be such a joy to decompress on a long, solo eight-hour road trip—488 miles through the heart of the heart of the Lone Star. Nothing but badlands—Big Spring to Eden; then a jog through sheep country—Eden to Junction; down along the spine of the Hill Country—Junction to Boerne; then the welcome monotony of flattening coastal plain—San Antonio to Houston.

Nothing but caffeine and road food: coffee and peach Blizzard at the Wall DQ; liver and onions at the Hungry Horse in Boerne and a Tres Hombres plate at Leo's in Montrose. It was rumored that Leo's shut down, but Archie refused to believe such a mortal sin.

It was Archie's first "alone time" in his curve-hugging, road-gobbling CT6, which was quickly turning into his all-time favorite iron horse—right up there with the tricked-out K-10 Blazer from his Victoria days, bought from Atzenhoffer Chevrolet the very same day he accepted his offer to anchor the sports desk at KAVU.

"You need a name, girlfriend," he said, pat-patting the dash.

He'd put Tallulah on it. The Nickname Queen.

As he cruised in Cadillac comfort, Archie watched the gridiron hopefuls in every small-town toil under the Texas sun, enduring two-a-days on their pristine patches of irrigated green. The boy's dreams of glory slowly being ground to dust by squat-bodied tyrants in polyester shorts and wide-brimmed hats. Coaches yelling unspeakable motivation at lithe young men who threw themselves on the glistening ground; steeling themselves for Friday night and the glorious rewards of the end zone.

He saluted the Bobcats in San Angelo, barked at the Bulldogs in Brady, waved *ole* at the Matadors in Seguin; paid his respects to the fiercest of Tigers in Katy.

It was nearing September, the cruelest month. Football promising the coolness of fall only to be bitterly sandblasted by gales of hot wind and hurricane gusts boiling up from the Gulf. Every day delivering drenching humidity that sent every able-bodied ballplayer into spasms of cramping calves and hamstrings; every player slathered in sweat pulled out of every pore by a cruel barometer called the Heat Index.

Archie ached for the players he passed, the dream of a cheerleader's kiss still real as the starters began to separate themselves from the boys on the bench; rugged individualism reigned supreme as the coaches taunted and prodded, unleashing the beasts, the raw testosterone, in tackling drills called "Bull in the Ring" and "Oklahoma."

IN AN EFFORT TO UNWIND IN STYLE, ARCHIE SPENT HIS FIRST NIGHT IN Houston in twelve years at the J.W. Marriot, an orange brick fortress across the street from America's original shopping mecca, The Galleria. He enjoyed a solid night's sleep and lined up the next morning with a pack of yawning millennials of every race, color and creed at a Starbuck's on Post Oak. Properly caffeinated, he quick-stepped across Westheimer and down into the famous Men's Department at Neiman-Marcus.

Guillermo, a dapper young sales consultant, guided him by the elbow into sartorial heaven, instantly outfitting him with a perfectly seasonal ready-to-wear ensemble: brown plaid Zena sport coat with threads of Cougar red, tan twill slacks (no pleats this season), a white spread-collar shirt with a subtle herringbone pattern complimented with a red silk Ferragamo tie featuring a spray of gushing blue oil wells. Archie balked as guileful Guillermo sat him down in the shoe department, but relented when presented with a pair of gorgeous brown leather lace-ups.

"Pradas," he purred.

"Sold," said Archie, shooting his cuffs in the three-way mirror; grateful for maintaining a playing weight of 190 now that he was so artfully displayed in slim fit forty-four long.

Now he understood why the concierge sent him directly to Guillermo, who, while inserting several straight pins, suggested that Archie go people watching for an hour while his in-house tailors altered the garments.

"Guillermo, this was fantastic. Totally pain-free."

"You have wonderful taste, Mr. Weesatche," Guillermo said, inserting a final pin on a trouser cuff. "It's a pleasure to work with a man who understands style."

Archie didn't know about all that, but he was sure pleased that Neiman-Marcus was around to dress country boys with a few extra dollars in their pocket.

"Leave the pants and jacket," said Guillermo, guiding him back to the dressing rooms. "Take the escalator all the way to the top floor. Café Mariposa's on the right."

"Perfect," said Archie. "See you at eleven fifteen."

He went up the escalator, delighting at the sight of a truly "grand" mother doddering to her dressing room with a personal shopper who rolled a rack stuffed with carefully curated outfits.

On his way down the escalator, enjoying a café latte, Archie nodded to a stunning mother-daughter team on their way up to women's couture. Wowsa! he thought.

The peacocks are on parade!

He strolled the concourses past Tiffany's and Armani and Gucci and Porsche and Lacoste and every other posh multi-national retailer on the planet. He popped into a steakhouse for a dram of Irish whiskey, divining that the demographics had changed dramatically since his days at UH, from majority Big Hair Blonde to majority Global Smoke. And the confidence projected by these female alphas was unmistakable. Queens of the Urban Playground.

Archie wasn't quite sure where a forty-something West Texas guy fit in the mix, but he couldn't wait to regale his mom with tales from the Sun

Belt. Houston was overgrown, outrageous; in the throes of permanent business overdrive. But it still felt like home.

The short walk to the hotel—in the midday heat—had Archie sweating through his undershirt, threatening to ruin his new clothes. He dove into the Marriot's air-conditioned lobby, not a second too soon.

The hotel's Liberty Ballroom was packed and electric. Filling up with hundreds of old school football fanatics more than ready for the gospel according to Tom Herman, the newly-crowned National Champion and Assistant Coach of the Year from Ohio State.

At the dais, sat the Houston Touchdown Club directors led by Don Trull, a '63 Baylor All-American, who Archie admired for his lean frame and gray brush-cut. Chris Gilbert, the UT tailback from the legendary '69 National Championship team, was yukking it up with Jim McIngvale, a scrub on the '63 UT National Championship team, who'd parlayed a walk-on's work ethic into a million-dollar furniture empire. Next to "Mattress Mac" was the star of the show, the hyperkinetic Coach Herman who'd brought his defensive coordinator Todd Orlando and offensive coordinator Major Applewhite, himself, a former football god during his QB days at UT.

Pretty damn cool, Archie thought, as he scanned the room and took a seat.

He introduced himself to his table mates: a new UH Regent from Midland, Spencer Armour; Moon Mullins, a late sixties Cougar quarterback from San Angelo was sitting with Coach Yeoman, the legendary UH coach and inventor of the Veer. The final pair was a couple of head coaches from local high schools--Matt Meekins of Houston Westfield and Nathan Larned of Kinkaid, the oldest private school in the city.

The coaches offered firm handshakes. They said they remembered Archie during the run-and shoot days. He seriously doubted that. But it was nice that they were being nice to the Coog slot receiver whose best season was twenty-four catches, 488 yards and one touchdown.

It was big-time Texas football, with everybody telling war stories as fast and as loud as they could. The rubber chicken went untouched before the man-of-the-hour stepped up to the microphone.

Coach Herman was a fire-breathing true believer, preaching "H-Town Takeover" a new social media war cry deployed to convince fair weather fans that UH football was not simply back—UH *Athletics* was going to be nationally relevant. It was a masterful display of young man bravado and MENSA-caliber intelligence in a twenty-minute pep talk that had the UH faithful ready to run through a brick wall for the man.

Even old Coach Yeoman had a smile on his face.

"Hell, I'd strap it on for that guy!" said Archie.

"If you're down this way again, come see a Kinkaid game," urged Coach Larned, as they exchanged handshakes around the table.

"Hell, I'll make a weekend of it, Friday Night Lights, UH on Saturday, Texans on Sunday. I think Herman might be on to something with this H-Town Takeover."

"And UH's got a nice new stadium—TD something," added Coach Meekins. "We're playing The Woodlands there Week Two."

"Cool," said Archie, admiring the crisp demeanor of these big city coaches. "It's great they built it on campus."

"TDECU," said Regent Armour, reaching across the table to shake Archie's hand. "It was designed by the same people who built BBVA for the Dynamo. Big step into getting us into the Big Twelve."

"'bout damn time," said Archie, matching the Regent's enthusiasm. "Took us a while to get into the Southwest Conference, as I recall."

"Football and politics," said Regent Armour. "Blood sport of Texas."

"Hell, let's send Herman up to the Legislature," said Coach Yeoman. "He'll get us in the Big Twelve. Or die trying."

LET THE GAMES BEGIN

"*Archito!* You brought your own team!"

Josy stepped out of the Hotel Paisano elevator to find her new-old *novio*, Sister Ernestine, Sheriff Fuchs, Matt McQuaid, and Tallulah Hoffs waiting in the lobby.

"*¡Hola, Princesa!*" said Archie, immediately covering her up in a big hug. "I got to meet your family, I figured it was your turn."

Sister Ernestine stepped up from the cluster, looking angelic in her fresh-pressed ecclesiastic garb. She took Josy's hands. "*Hola, Josefina, encantada,*" she said in French-accented Spanish.

Josy was struck demure in the presence of the spry, but elderly, member of an uncertain religious order. Archie stepped beside Sister Ernestine, put a hand at the small of her back.

"Josy, this is my mother, Sister Ernestine Ducornet."

The seeming contradiction; this short, beautiful, beaming woman, both mother and Sister, took Josy by the tongue. The two women looked at each other—they shared the same height—and smiled silently during a pregnant pause.

"Oh my god I love that color!" said Tallulah, wedging her hands between her mom's simply varnished nails and Josy's glistening cobalt manicure. "I'm Tallulah! Hi, hi, hi! Matt has a crush on you."

"No way, Tallulah!" cried Matt. "No way you're saying that!"

Everyone laughed nervously. The sound ricocheting off the hotel's terrazzo floor.

Thankfully the only people in the lobby were a pair of tourists captivated by the photographs and artifacts in the *"Giant"* movie display case. Before its late twentieth century transformation into the most unlikely of art colonies, Marfa came to fame as the staging area for the infamous Texas blockbuster. Hence, the Rock Hudson Suite.

"I'm Josefina Montemayor. It's an honor," she said, taking the non-nun in one hand and Tallulah in the other. "And Tallulah! Look at you. *Porfavor!* Give me a hug!"

"Really!" cried Tallulah, bending down a good nine inches to rest her head on Josy's shoulder, incidentally taking a whiff of Josy's soft black mane. "Oh my God, your hair smells like a magic garden!"

"*Jardin magique.* I love it," said Sister Ernestine, nudging the Sheriff, while the girls embraced and the boys raised their eyebrows.

Josy deftly swept her hair into an over-the-shoulder offering for her young admirer. "It's pure glycerin and crushed herbs. I make my own shampoo."

"Your own shampoo?" Archie said, loving Josy for putting his family so at ease.

"*Por supuesto,*" said Josy, giving Archie a sweet side-eye. "I'm very talented. And you must be Sheriff Fucks."

More tittering.

"*Fewks* is the way most folks pronounce it," said the Sheriff, tipping his hat, then taking her extended hand. "It's a pleasure to see you again Miss Montemayor. How was your trip from Victoria?"

"Very nice, thank you," said Josy, batting long lashes at the husky lawman. "I love what they're doing with Marfa. It's charming, no?"

"Thanks to Mr. Judd and his artist friends. Very cosmopolitan," added Archie, watching the Sheriff loom over the Mexican aristocrat, somehow, non-threateningly. The Sheriff had that way about him—serious, but not mean.

"*Hola, Mateo,*" said Josy, extending her hand, pulling Matt in for a hug.

"Thank you again for being such a *caballero* during our day on the river."

She turned to Sister Ernestine. "You must be so proud of raising such polite young men and this beautiful daughter. Such a wonderful family."

"We're blessed. They're all very spirited," said Sister Ernestine, clasping her hands to her heart. "Just the way we like it."

"Little too spirited in spots," allowed the Sheriff, with a laugh.

"*Mon deaux*! Never!" said Sister Ernestine, locking her arm inside the Sheriff's "They've saved us from a life of boredom and treachery."

"Aww, that's sweet!" said Tallulah, hugging her mom's shoulders, but looking at Josy. "They saved our lives. They're angels."

Tallulah pointed at herself, then Matt, and finally Archie. "The Three Musketeers! We wouldn't have had a chance without Sister E. and the Big Man."

"That sounds like a Mexican band," said Josy. "*¡Sister E. y los tres mosqueteros!*"

She made them all laugh and laugh.

"Josy, you look like a million bucks," Matt blurted, obviously taken with *La Princesa's* form-hugging black catsuit. "You're going to a 6-Man game in that?"

"Of course, she is," cried Tallulah. "Josy's cool, unlike some people I know."

Tallulah grabbed her hand and spun Josy around once, then twice. They skipped out a set of French doors, arm, and arm, to the patio.

"Hey *hombre*," said Archie, jabbing at Matt's washboard abs. "Go get us a table before the girls start dancing on top of 'em."

"Oh hurray!" said Sister Ernestine. "Let's dance!"

"Don't look at me," said the Sheriff. "Your sons are the fancy dancers."

"I'll dance a little two-step with you. Any time," said Archie, giving his mom a twirl.

The Hotel Paisano had an enclosed courtyard with a gurgling stone fountain in the middle, and again, they had the space to themselves. Once Tallulah and Josy finished skimming across the flagstones, everybody seated themselves at a round wrought iron table. Archie ordered a pitcher of sangria.

"Uncle Archie taught me how to dance," said Tallulah, blowing a wisp of strawberry blonde off her forehead. "He can waltz across Texas."

"Absolutely! If Ernest Tubb's playing," said Archie, leaning his chair back on two legs.

"You should have seen him at the club in Mexico!" said Josy, "Sister Ernestine, all the women were swooning for your handsome *Archito*. I had to swat their hands."

"Those Mexican girls do like a little gringo two-step," he bragged, winking at Tallulah.

"It's good you weren't there, Matt," said Josy, flipping her hair in his direction.

"Why's that?" he asked. "Sounds like my kind of town."

"No, no! Too much Texas *suave*," said Josy. "The Sheriff would've had to arrest every woman in the club."

"Archie! Where have you been hiding this dear girl?" said a beaming Sister Ernestine.

The waitress arrived with a tray of glasses and a giant pitcher of deep purple *sangria* swimming with sliced orange and peeled grapefruit, followed by a barback with baskets of yellow corn chips and bowls of *salsitas*.

As Matt poured everyone their daily serving of Vitamin C, Archie webbed his fingers behind his head, took in the clean desert air, and thought maybe this little hook-up was going to work out just fine. After the *sangria* was depleted, Archie checked his watch and signaled for the check. He clapped a couple of times, as was his excitable habit.

"Alright troops, who's ready for some Friday Night Lights?"

"How far is the stadium, Sheriff Fuchs?" Josy asked, careful to pronounce his name like a Bavarian instead of her favorite four-letter word.

"Stadium's just past the square a few blocks," he said, standing up from the table and stretching out his long frame. "Nothing's too far in these parts, 'cept the next town."

"Y'all hear they're playing in Presidio," said the waitress, placing the bill in front of Archie. "My son's on varsity. Somebody trapped a bunch of feral hogs and let'em out on the field last night. And man, did those pigs do some damage."

"Really? That's a first," Archie asked, signing the ticket and digging in his jeans for a cash tip. "Did they catch the hogs?"

"*No se*, but they moved the game to Presidio," said the waitress. "Coach Davila was so mad. You should have seen him stomping around. All summer, he had that field perfect. Those pigs damn near destroyed it."

"Wow, that's crazy," said Matt. "I never saw any feral hogs around Sul. Didn't think they were out this far West."

"What? What's happening?" Josy said, making duck lips in her compact mirror. "Is the game cancelled?"

"No ma'am," Archie said, placing a twenty on top of the bill. "Game's in Presidio. Now you'll get to see one of the prettiest views in Texas high school football."

"I'll do you one better," said the Sheriff tipping his hat in Josy's direction. "How 'bout a VIP escort?"

"Can I ride with you?" asked Josy, taking Sister Ernestine's hand.

"You bet," said the Sheriff smoothing his thick grey hair, replacing his sweat-stained Stetson. "If you don't mind straddling a stick shift. And that damned computer. No, you girls better sit in the back. I'll be your chauffeur."

"How nice," said Sister Ernestine, squeezing Josy's hand.

"And I'll take these hoodlums," said Archie, jerking his thumb at Tallulah and Matt.

Matt pulled a phone out of his hard-starched Wrangler's. "Google Maps says we'll be there in . . .."

"We'll be there in thirty-five to forty minutes, tops," said the Sheriff, mapping the highway in his mind's eye.

"Let's make a mile," said Archie, plunging his hands into the catchment surrounding the fountain. Everybody laughed when he splashed his face with cool water.

"*Vamonos*. Can't get a bet down if we miss kickoff," he said, drying face and hands with his ever-present clean handkerchief.

"And do you still carry a sharp knife like the Sheriff taught you?" asked Josy, as they pushed through the lobby doors.

"Of course," said Archie, proudly pulling out his Swiss Army knife. "See there, Tules. I'm still in possession of your very thoughtful Christmas gift."

"Wazedik bro!" said Tallulah, triple jumping out the front door and into the bright afternoon sunshine.

They piled out onto the sidewalk and stopped in front of the Sheriff's Borden County pickup and the Cougar Red Cadillac side-by-side against the high curb.

"Blue Devil Stadium is exactly fifty-nine point seven miles away," announced Matt, reading his screen. "It's five forty-seven p.m. Kickoff's at seven. We gonna make it?"

"Due south and all downhill," claimed the Sheriff. "We'll be there before the National Anthem."

"South on Texas Sixty-Seven," added Archie. "If I'm not mistaken."

"On this, sir, you are *not* mistaken," said Matt. "Highway Sixty-Seven South. And not a single stop till we hit the border."

"*¡Vamos a Presidio!*" said Archie, opening both passenger doors with a flourish. "Come sit up front with me, Tallulah. Take in some of this breathtaking Big Bend scenery."

"I'm good," she said, diving headfirst into the caramel leather backseat. She wiggled the soles of her turquoise cowboy boots in his face. "Thanks for asking."

"I'll try not to lose you," said the Sheriff, smiling at Archie while Josy and Sister Ernestine buckled in the backseat. "Watch those S curves around Shafter."

The Sheriff and Archie backed out and turned on to Highland Avenue which transformed into Highway 67—an absolute straight shot through the Trans-Pecos wilderness. Once they were a mile out of town, the Sheriff turned on the flashers embedded in the grill and back bumper. Archie followed close as they made the road shoulders stream with dusty rivulets.

When they hit the outskirts proper, the scenery turned—all craggy mountains and cattle grazing in the khaki-colored pastures. With plenty of daylight, and conditions dry and clear, the Sheriff settled in at one hundred miles per hour.

"Now Miss Montemayor, you couldn't be safer if you were walking a *sendera* on your *rancho*," said the Sheriff, winking back at Sister Ernestine, who was peeking at the speedometer. "Sit back and enjoy the Far Empty at its finest."

"*Muchas gracias*," said Josy, smiling at her seat mate. She looped her arm through Sister Ernestine's. "I love your family. So much fun!"

AS PREDICTED, THE TWO-CAR CONVOY COVERED THE MILES BETWEEN Marfa and Presidio in record time—thirty-seven minutes and thirty seconds from city limit to city limit, according to Matt's stopwatch app.

As the posse swung down into Presidio proper, they hung a left at the Mexican Consulate then cruised down Erma Avenue past the Tres Palmas Motel. Archie fought the flashbacks, but couldn't help but dive back into memories of unruly Labor Days around the motel pool.

The party was officially, *La Fiesta de la Paloma Blanca*—aka the Presidio Labor Day Hunt—consummated annually during the North Zone Opening Day by a Mongol horde of otherwise highly-civilized Texas gentlemen. Over the years it became an increasingly fractious three-day Bacchanal featuring the frat boy elite from UT, TCU, SMU, Texas Tech, and the occasional UH outlier.

Archie chuckled, then blanched, at the thought of the five dove hunts he'd attended (he called it quits at the tender age of thirty-one). He thanked God and Allah and Buddha and every other benevolent higher power who'd seen fit *not* to exterminate every single thick-skulled celebrant for excessive entitlement, excessive Ugly Americanism and the toxic mixing of tortured brain cells with:

Odessa strippers, Ojinaga strippers, Lot Lizards, Ft. Stockton fun girls, locals, tourists, Halliburton crews, H.B. Zachry crews, roughnecks, roustabouts, Mormons on bikes, Banditos on Harleys, *carne asada*, *barbacoa*, *cabrito*, *menudo*, *tequila*, more *tequila*, *mezcal*, *sotol*, skinny dipping, more skinny dipping, Presidio police, Presidio County Sheriff's deputies, Texas Parks & Wildlife game wardens, Customs & Immigration officers, DPS troopers, Texas Rangers, Border Patrol, *federales*, more *federales*, Browning over and unders, plugless Winchesters, handguns, potato guns, deer rifles, M-16s, cattle prods, electric shock sticks, electric shock boxes, rental cars, tow trucks for wrecked rental cars, more tow trucks, guitar picking, off-key serenading, coyote howls, boom boxing with Public Enemy, the Geto Boys, *Intocable*, the Doobie Brothers, Asleep at the Wheel, Commander Cody, Willie, Waylon and the Boys, and lots and lots of Ernest Tubb.

And not a single cartel encounter.

Archie recalled vague memories of wrestling a thirty-pound catfish onto the banks of the Rio Grande, the smoking of dirt weed, the taking of dirt naps, the wearing of trucker hats, cowboy hats and candelabras, the ingestion of trucker speed, Dot Races, rental car rescues, room trashing, dehydration, food fights, chicken fights, pool cues upside obnoxious white boy's heads, shouting matches with Mama San, fistfights with steroid abusing college football players, cockfights, arm-wrestling, Indian wrestling, Baby Oil wrestling, table dancing, tap dancing, vomiting, binging, purging, weeping, more barfing, shallow-water drowning rescues, *Paloma Blancas* on the Barbie, sweating buckets, sweating bullets, Gatorade, Goody's and BC Powder till you come back strong.

And mostly, the most soul-crushing hangovers ever visited upon unshaven, unwashed horned beasts left to rot on the tarmac of the Midland/Odessa Airport while the Southwest flight attendants called for backup, the Southwest ground crew called for gallons of Pine Sol, and the Southwest pilots informed the tower that Flight 666 was being delayed while certain bleeding, passed-out passengers were forcibly de-planed, attorneys were retained, and ambulances were dispatched with bags of saline and every vial of penicillin available in Ector County.

Archie Weesatche peered into the rearview mirror, grateful for his mid-forties, safely removed from the motherlovin' *La Fiesta de la Paloma Blanca.*

SIX-MAN BORDER BRAWL

"Earth to Uncle Archie."

Tallulah stuck her pony-tailed head in between the front seats. "Come in March?"

"What? No! Wait!" Archie snapped from his reverie; braking hard as the stadium entrance neared. "Here we go! Hard right! Here we go!"

He swung the Cougar Red Cadillac off the last piece of paved road before the bridge to Mexico. A cluster of Presidio ISD buildings appeared at the end of the road that paralleled dense green tangles of river cane concealing the banks of the Rio Grande.

"Blue Devil Stadium," he said, cruising into the gravel parking lot, half-full of old cars and a few shiny pickups. "Troops, I got Marfa plus thirteen. And a secret weapon."

"What? You and Okinawa?" said Matt. "Y'all gonna suit up for the Shorthorns?"

"Please," said Archie, in search of shade and finding none. "Superman's name is Viviano Molina, a dual-threat quarterback who ran for fourteen hundred yards and passed for fifteen hundred at El Paso Austin last year—transferred to Marfa, like, two weeks ago."

"Yeah Matt," said Tallulah, punching his shoulder. "Don't be such a cyberpunk."

Archie and Matt exchanged smiles.

"Girl, if you were any goofier . . ." said Matt, turning violently, only to gently tug on his sister's ponytail. "You'd be dangerous."

"Oh my God," Tallulah cried, in mock distress. "So aggressive!"

The Sheriff circled the lot, as was his law enforcement habit, then pulled in beside the Cougar Red Cadillac. The posse of six made their way to the stadium entrance where five dollars got everyone a front-row seat and a Xeroxed game program. Three dollars at the food truck bought a split-sack Frito Pie with extra jalapenos and a cold cup of Dr. Pepper. The girls' bottled water was expensive—a buck apiece.

Archie herded his troops around a blue rubberized track to the visitors' bleachers with Josy and Tallulah eliciting a few wolf whistles from the fence-line crowd.

Archie thought he heard—knew he heard—an "*¡Hola Josefita!*", but blew it off.

The visitors' side was mostly empty save for a cluster of Marfa parents on the fifty-yard line. The Sheriff, Matt, and Archie settled in on the top row so the Sheriff could rest his back and enjoy clear sightlines. The ladies set up on the row below.

"*¡Futbol americano!*" said Archie, soaking up the game-time festivities—twirlers tossing, the tiny bands warming up horns and drums, the clearly Anglo public address announcer consistently mispronouncing names as he introduced the all-Latino lineups.

"There's my mark," said Archie, standing up in the aisle. "The big one in the Presidio letter jacket putting a half-pound of dip in his lip."

"That's a big dude, Arch," scoffed Matt. "I thought you were betting rich ranchers."

Archie smiled at Matt, then turned to the Sheriff. "I bet you know Rudy."

"Oh yeah," said the Sheriff, patting the Glock nine-millimeter holstered on his hip. "Muscle for the Ojinaga Plaza. Heard he got promoted."

"He did," confirmed Josy, looking up from her seat between Sister Ernestine and Tallulah. "In July. Plaza Boss of OJ."

"So, you know Rudy?" asked Archie.

"For many years," she said. "I should introduce you to his *pistolera*. She says she knows you. Right there, on the fence next to Rudy."

The Sheriff and Archie exchanged glances.

"Is that Wacey?" asked the Sheriff, thumbing the focus on his field glasses. "I thought she was workin' in Juarez."

"She was," said Josy, casually. "Her boss was assassinated and Rudy offered her a job."

"She works security for a cartel?" asked Archie, squinting to get a better look. "That's pretty stout."

"Wacey's from Forsan," answered the Sheriff, handing Archie his binoculars. "Good bit younger than you. Her daddy was one of the best rodeo clowns in the business. Back in the eighties, nineties."

"Forsan?" asked Archie, trying to read Josy's expression. "That's a long way from El Paso. How'd she end up in Juarez?"

"Best natural shot I ever seen," said the Sheriff.

"And you know her, too?" he asked Josy, handing back the Sheriff's binoculars.

"We used to date," said Josy. "I dated both of them, actually. Rudy and Wacey."

Archie suffered a sinking feeling. He was out of the loop—way out. All he knew about Rudy Leos was that he was a Presidio football star done good, kind of like Archie. Okinawa hadn't let on about any cartel connection, much less being the Plaza Boss of Ojinaga. He also knew nothing about this gun-totin' daughter of a bullfighter from Forsan—which was a damn shame. Wacey the *Pistolera* sounded pretty damn interesting for a Howard County native.

Archie scanned the field, watched the players finish their warm-ups and trot to the sidelines. The team captains walked to the fifty-yard line. He checked the program and smiled. "I'm 'bout to put some Viviano on his Plaza Boss ass!"

"You better hurry," said Josy, pointing at the clock.

"Yep, time to get a handshake," he said, pulling two envelopes from his Carhartt; one sealed with $5,000 inside, the other unsealed with $5,000. He handed the sealed envelope to the Sheriff. "Hold that for me. Time to see if ol' Rudy's for real."

The Sheriff shook his head, smiling, then slid the envelope inside his black Borden County windbreaker. With the bands finally silent, the referees introduced themselves to the players.

"Y'all stay here," said Archie. "I got this."

And with that, Archie was down the bleachers, two at a time, and headed to the track as the National Anthem played through tinny bullhorn speakers nailed to telephone poles bristling with old sodium vapor lights.

Okinawa, the man who'd assiduously cultivated Rudy Leos for two years, gave Archie a wide-eyed grimace as he walked up. "Didn't think you were gonna make it, hoss!"

"Sorry about that," Archie said, bro-hugging his former teammate. "Got my whole family in tow, then got the home field wrong. Game was scheduled for Marfa."

"Crazy 'bout them hogs, ain't it?" allowed Okinawa, giving Archie a look, then proceeded with the introductions.

"Archie, this is Rudy Leos, All-State linebacker at Presidio High, Class of Ninety-Three; second all-time leading tackler for the Tarleton State Texans. One of the proudest Blue Devil boosters you'll ever meet."

Archie was much more interested in catching the *pistolera's* eye, but she was all business, scanning the track and stands behind a pair of killer wrap-around shades.

"Hey Rudy, *mucho gusto*," said Archie, replicating the soul shake, bro-hug routine preferred by machos the world over. "Oak tells me you got a dual-threat nephew playin' quarterback."

"*Primo*," Rudy corrected, removing his aviator shades to get a better look at Archie. "Glad you made it. You get lost?"

"Nah, just a little detour in Marfa," Archie said, pulling an envelope from his inside jacket pocket. "So, I got Marfa plus thirteen." He slapped the envelope against his thigh for good measure. "For five grand."

"I thought the bet was ten," Okinawa protested. "I told Rudy ten grand."

"Well, I been thinking ten's pretty rich for a Six-Man season opener," Archie said, looking Rudy in the eye.

"So, you changin' things up?" said Rudy, in a tone most dead serious.

"Could be," said Archie, lowering his gaze. He pulled his phone out and punched a recent call. He held up one finger when Rudy gave Okinawa a, "what the hell?" look.

"Hey Sheriff, would you mind coming down for a sec. I got someone I want to introduce you to."

"What's up, Arch?" asked Okinawa, looking none too pleased.

Archie waved at the Sheriff, then put the phone in his back pocket. "Right after Rudy tells me how that field in Marfa got all torn up."

"What is this shit, Oak?" asked Rudy, ignoring Archie. "You said this guy's for real."

"I'm real alright," Archie said. "Just wondering about this *hog* story."

"What hog story," said Rudy, laughing. "We got hogs all over this country. Pull'em out of the river bottom all the time. We bettin' ten grand, or what?"

"I guess hogs coulda come up from Alamito Creek," Archie said, looking at Okinawa.

"Why you talkin' shit? Like you know this country," said Rudy, crossing arms across his barrel chest. "We bettin', or what? It's kickoff."

"No, it ain't," said Archie. "Go tell your zebra friend to hold up a minute."

Rudy looked at Wacey, who shrugged, then motioned for a young tough standing at the fence to come over. A light-skinned teenager in a ball cap, T-shirt, and roach-killer boots trotted up. Rudy said something to him in terse Spanish. Sheriff Fuchs joined the circle as the young man jogged out on the field, straight to the referee holding the ball.

"How's it hangin' Oak?" said the Sheriff, shaking the sports editor's hand. "How you doin' Rudy? Heard you're movin' up in the world."

The referee blew his whistle and signaled an official's time out. He sent the captains to the bench, then joined the other referees at the thirty-yard line.

"Yeah, man. Business is good," said Rudy, shaking the Sheriff's hand. "Come on over to OJ someday. Buy you an enchilada dinner."

"Might just do that," said the Sheriff, checking out Rudy's posse of fence-sitters. "Looks like your payroll's growing."

"Trying to keep the young ones off the street," said Rudy. "No jobs in OJ."

"Hey Sheriff," said Wacey, reaching to shake his hand.

To Archie, she looked more punk rock assassin than a cowgirl in her T-shirt and skinny jeans, distressed leather jacket, and Doc Martens. Not as long as Tallulah, but lean. And strong. *Muy fuerte.*

"Evenin' Wacey," said the Sheriff, reaching inside his jacket.

Wacey quickly reached behind her jacket.

"Whoa now, just getting' some cash," said the Sheriff, slowly extracting the envelope. "Y'all set for your bet?"

"Marfa plus thirteen for five thousand . . . *and,*" Archie said, nodding to Sheriff Fuchs." And five thousand more says Marfa has two hundred yards total offense in the first half."

"Wait, what? Total offense," Okinawa said, "Why not ten grand, plus thirteen, like we said?"

"You said this guy's straight up! Oak," cried Rudy. "What's all this side-bet shit?"

"Nobody holding a gun to your head," said the Sheriff, slapping the envelope.

"No sir. No, they ain't." Rudy laughed and gave the sheriff some side-eye. "But you, *compadre,* can fuck a buncha side bets."

By this time, every player, every student, every administrator, every band member, every cheerleader, and every fan were staring at the big men below the scoreboard.

"Take *my* bet for ten grand," said Archie. "Or take your ass back to OJ."

That snapped Wacey's head. And everybody else's.

"What you know about OJ, *gringo*?" Rudy hissed, turning to Okinawa. "What's up with your friend, Oak?"

Archie stepped up, toe-to-toe; stared down the bristling Plaza Boss.

"Man, y'all worse than a buncha roosters," Okinawa said, pushing Rudy one way while the Sheriff yanked Archie the other. "Make a bet. Or don't."

"*Oye, pendejo*," Rudy said, straining to get at Archie, but being held tight by Okinawa. "I'm gonna shut that smart fuckin' mouth of yours."

"Round and round, *baboso*," Archie said, clenching his knuckles white, as the Sheriff stepped between. "Round and round!"

"*Cabron*! I'm gonna kill this guy!" yelled Rudy, shaking off Okinawa, but not the Sheriff.

"You're not doin' a goddamn thing 'cept watch a football game," said the Sheriff, watching Rudy's hands closely. "I got eyes on you."

"I got eyes on you, too," Rudy said, careful not to rush a law enforcement officer, but unable to resist giving the Sheriff the "I'm watching you" hand sign as he stepped back.

The Sheriff stared down the line of Rudy's lieutenants as they peeled off the fence and followed their leader into the home stands.

"Small-town bullshit," seethed Archie. "I guarantee you, Rudy ruined that field."

"Probably, but Rudy's connected," added the Sheriff. "Cartel connected."

As Archie'd grown older, he'd made peace with having to go to war with a certain breed of idiot. Small towns, in particular, were sorry with them. In times like these, Archie'd learned that turning the other cheek was a little like dying. A man who backed down from a bully wasn't worth a bucket of warm spit.

But, thought Archie, walking back to the stands. Plaza Bosses fight to kill; not for honor.

FIRST RATTLE OUT OF THE BOX, MARFA RECOVERED A PERFECT ON-SIDE KICK.

"Hell yeah, Shorthorns!" said Archie, yelling at the top of his lungs. "Hell yeah!"

Matt, Tallulah, Josy, and Sister Ernestine, all turned simultaneously to see if Archie was having a seizure. Unfazed, Archie stood on the top bleacher and raised his fist to the home stands. "Twenty-three's gonna break your fucking heart!"

"What the hell, son?" said the Sheriff, slapping the aluminum bleacher. "Take a seat."

"C'mon Chuck, nobody can hear me."

"Sure they can," he scolded. "Sit down."

Again, Archie looked down to find Josy and his family staring at him, dumbfounded. And again, he stood, undeterred. Adrenaline flowing. "Let's go, Viviano! Let's show'em how to run and shoot!"

"Sit down, son," said the Sheriff, tugging on his jacket. "Calm the hell down."

"Alright, I hear you," said Archie, exhaling a deep breath, easing an arm around his step-sister's shoulder. "Whatcha thinking, Tallulah Bankhead?"

Tallulah's face broke into pure relief. "Whoa Arch, I never . . . I've never seen you get all krunk and shit."

"Me too neither," said Matt, grinning at his older brother. "Me too neither."

"Archie," said Sister Ernestine, reaching out for his hand. "Are you okay?"

"I'm fine mom. Just a little riled up."

Archie peeked over at Josy, whose sly smile meant something. What, he didn't know.

After the fumble recovery, Marfa broke huddle and sprinted to the line. Viviano Molina looked like a shiny blue puma as he scanned the Presidio defense.

On his first play as a Marfa Shorthorn, Molina took a shotgun snap, rolled left to the wide side, faked an option pitch to his tailback, then cut back through the grasping, over-pursuing Blue Devil defense and sprinted seventy yards, untouched, into the end zone.

"*¡El mejor jugador!*" yelled Archie, as the quarterback's teammates power-lifted him high in the air. "*¡Viviano! ¡Viviano!*"

"Is that the transfer?" asked Matt, high-fiving Archie.

"Straight from El Paso to the Presidio end zone."

"He's good," said Tallulah, tugging on Josy's luxurious shawl. "And cute."

"He does look cute," said Josy.

And in short order, the Marfa footballers and their electric transfer backed up Archie's pre-season intel. Viviano Molina racked up 216 yards on the ground and 47 through the air to take a commanding 35–8 lead after the first *quarter*.

And that's when things got local.

Real local.

As in Rudy Leos had the Marfa quarterback shot.

Literally.

Fortunately, number 22 wasn't shot with an assault rifle. Not even a .22. No, after his *fifth* touchdown, the shifty Viviano was shot with a laser-sighted pellet gun. Repeatedly.

In both calves.

At first, the quarterback acted as if he'd been bitten by a horsefly or a mean mosquito. But then he noticed blood seeping through his knee-high socks and limped over to the bench. The student trainer took one look and immediately ran to the coach.

"Rut-ro," said Archie, craning to get a better look. "That's not good."

When the Marfa coach waved over the EMS, the Sheriff and Archie immediately made their way down to the Marfa sideline.

"Oww! What the hell?" yelled the quarterback as an EMS tech squeezed a pellet out of his calf.

The EMS guy didn't say anything. Just kept his head down and dug for more pellets.

But the Sheriff and Archie knew the score.

"That's ridiculous," said Archie, as the Sheriff took the two envelopes out of his jacket.

"What's ridiculous is betting against cartel muscle."

Archie shook his head as the tech finished bandaging both Molina's legs with gauze and athletic tape. "Holy crap."

"You need to . . ." said the Sheriff, handing Archie the envelopes. "Give the sumbitch his money back before somebody really gets hurt."

The Sheriff grabbed the envelopes out of Archie's hand. "Hell, I'll do it."

Before Archie could stop him, the Sheriff was off. He spoke to Viviano Molina, shook the coach's hand, before walking briskly around the track, into the stands and straight up to Rudy.

Archie watched the Sheriff hand Rudy both envelopes, then say something to Wacey. When the Sheriff started back, Archie watched Rudy's posse and prayed they didn't do anything stupid. It was a tense few seconds, broken by sudden cheers for a Presidio breakaway touchdown.

"Let's get the hell out of this stadium," said the Sheriff, passing Archie on the sideline. He stepped up the stairs to the first row, whistled, and gave the "head'em up" sign.

"Let's go!" he yelled.

He didn't have to say it twice.

As Sister Ernestine, Matt, Tallulah, and Josy hustled down the stairs, Archie stood with the Sheriff. "What'd he say when you gave him the money."

"*Vaya con Dios.*"

"And why'd you give Rudy Leos *my* five thousand dollars?"

"Peace offering."

Archie chewed on that for a second. "Guess so. You're the peace officer."

"Let's go," said the Sheriff, as the rest of the family breathlessly stepped up. "Now."

Archie watched a visibly shaken Viviano Molina hang a towel over his head and stand, alone, as his teammates got ready for the kickoff.

"Matt, Tallulah, Mom, y'all go on back with Chuck," said Archie, stealing a look at the Marfa quarterback as he limped to the locker room. "Josy, you mind riding with me?"

"*Claro que no,*" she said. "I don't mind."

"Thanks for coming all this way," he said, bending to kiss his mother's cheek. "Don't y'all wanna come stay at the Paisano? I bet there's plenty of rooms."

"We'll get on back to the Garden," said the Sheriff, looking across the field in Rudy's direction. "And no OJ. Y'all drive straight to Marfa."

"Yeah! Can I ride with Josy?" asked Tallulah, clapping twice, then executing a perfect round off on the track.

"Tallulah, just come with us," said Matt. "Before we *all* get shot."

"Shot?" yelled Tallulah. "Who got shot?"

"Tallulah Hoffs! This instant!" said Sister Ernestine, urging her chicks behind the Sheriff, who kept his head on a swivel all the way to the parking lot.

MOON OVER OJINAGA

OJINAGA, CHIHUAHUA, MEXICO
AUGUST 22, 2015

It was time for a howl.

After signing off for the weekend and following the Sheriff out of town, Archie hung an impetuous right at the Tres Palmas and started up an impossibly rough, rain-gullied county road. Up ahead, two colossal tanks, containing the city's water supply, reigned in the Trans-Pecos twilight overlooking the breadth of well-lit Presidio and great swaths of darkened Ojinaga.

"Archie, your car!" cried Josy, as he bounced the Cougar Red Cadillac up the steep ravine, loose rocks popped against the undercarriage.

"It's all-wheel drive," said Archie, white-knuckling the wheel. In the fading light, a black-brown piece of fast-moving gristle—a roadrunner—led them up the arroyo through creosote bushes, towering century plants, and spikes of sotol.

"Where are you taking me?"

"To the top of the world," he said, praying that he didn't crack a muffler, or worse. Archie remembered well ramming many a rental car up this very road with carloads of derelict dove hunters. It was ridiculous to subject a new car to such abuse, but it was also a rite of passage—all Weesatche vehicles passed this kind of test at some point. He grimaced when the bumper dug into loose rock, the victim of an unseen washout. Undeterred, he punched the accelerator, crested the hill, and skidded to a stop at the edge of a dangerously steep ridge. The view across the *Rio Bravo* was breathtaking.

"*¡Mira! Mira!*" he said, motioning Josy to join him outside the car. He hopped up on the hood of the hyper-ticking car and waited for his date.

After a quick makeup inspection, *La Princesa* joined him on the hood. Down below— visible from a couple of miles away—small packs of Marfa Shorthorns and Presidio Blue Devils made their way to the locker room at halftime.

"How's this for a Six-Man Skybox?"

"Beautiful," said Josy, leaning back to enjoy the expansive view. "*¡Bravo, guerito!*"

Archie excused himself, and for a blissful minute, was a cow on a flat rock, swaying to the marching band beats wafting across the valley. He lingered in the gloaming, serene amongst Big Bend's flora and fauna, listening to the yips and chirps and coos of an unseen desert multitude settling their roosts.

As he strolled back, the game announcer, clearly audible in the pristine desert air, broadcast the halftime score: Marfa 35–Presidio 35.

"Nice comeback, Blue Devils," he cried, shaking his fist at Rudy Leos and his pellet gun posse. "Buncha damn cheaters."

As he neared the car, Josy was gone. Upon closer inspection, it seemed his skybox suitemate was moving fast and stripping off. Archie tip-toed up to the windshield to get a better look. And there she was, in nothing but underwire and a thong. She gave him a come-hither look, then vaulted—ass over teakettle—into the back seat.

"Hells yes!" he cried, with a boy's joy, pounding on the hood.

Archie drummed every window on his way to the remotely opened trunk, immediately uncovering a jumper cable bag, containing, in all its Zig Zag glory, the fabled "emergency joint."

"Touchdown Jesus!"

Archie quickly lit, hit, and hustled to the back seat, then dove full-length, into the vise grip of Josy's thighs. He slowly elbow-crawled up and over her mountain of bosom just in time to give the giggling heiress a deep-lunged shotgun.

The smoky kiss unleashed a round of petting and clutching and squeezing. And soon enough, belt buckles cracked, jeans flew and pashmina ripped. Every square inch of backseat was enveloped in flesh and moonlight and eucalyptus-scented hair; gasps and inhales and cat shrieks, and finally, so much muscular thumping that the coyotes howled and owls screeched as an American *güero* and his Mexican *princesa* pawed at each other like the desperate teenagers they were not.

JOSEFINA, IN FULL BEDRAGGLED GLORY, REACHED FOR THE HALF-SMOKED joint. She took an epic pull and spoke in a cloud of exhale. "*Ahora*, my acrobatic lover."

"*Si, la pantera, ahora!*" he said, admiring her buxom density, her exquisite curves. Shameless objectification, but please, there it was. "Pulchritude."

"Pulchritude," she repeated, cradling Archie's head in her lap. "Such a show-off."

"But accurate."

Josy toked some more, clearly pleased. Then demurely wrapped herself in blue pashmina; stroked Archie's longish hair. "How much money did you lose tonight?"

"Not a penny, why?"

"Because I want that money, *guapo*," she said. "For us."

"And so it shall be," he said, smoothing the silky cloth, not wanting to control his hands.

"*En serio?*"

"*Por supuesto, Princesa.* The Gods of Texas Football will abide."

"I thought you were a good gambler."

"Terrible card player. Excellent sportsbook," he said, sliding a hand beneath Josy's pashmina.

He wanted more.

She did not stop him.

And just like that, they were at it again.

And didn't stop till the dark was complete, the joint smoked, and the narcotic drowse of lovemaking had worked its magic on their sprawled backseat bodies.

All the while, Archie was monitoring the football proceedings down below. He was more than pleased as the headlights of three school busses and a string of parent pick-ups pierced the darkness of Shafter Pass. The road-runner tough quarterback from Marfa, Viviano Molina, and his bleeding calves, had turned the Blue Devils into butter.

Final score Marfa 94 Presidio 80.

"About the money," said Archie, pressing the ignition and running the A/C full blast. "If I don't make it betting—and I will—I have access to other resources."

"I know you do."

"Yeah, I know you know I do," said Archie, directing a vent to cool his passenger's glowing skin.

"Look, this game; this bet. That's *not* how I roll. I bet with gentlemen."

"I need that money, Archie," she said, mopping her hair into a sweaty ponytail.

"*Me entiende*, girl. It's gonna happen," said Archie, smiling as she struggled back into her outfit. "I *will* get this done."

"I believe you," she said, basking in the moonlight.

"What else do I need to know," he said, leaning to kiss her neck. "Whose six point five million dollars are we talking about?"

"A bad man."

"How bad?" he said, lifting himself away from her salty skin.

"As hard as these mountains, *hermoso*," she said, pulling at him. "The first boss of OJ."

"For the Juarez Cartel?"

"Sinaloa. The original," she said. "He smuggled *mota* back in the seventies. Then they consolidated all the plazas and made a deal with the Columbians to smuggle cocaine through *Chihuahua y Coahuila*. Which made Pablo—the man I'm talking about—very rich. Too rich."

"Pablo Escobar?"

"No, no. This Pablo was Mexican," she assured. "This Pablo was from *Chihuahua*. He buried a lot of money all up and down this part of the river."

"I think I read about this guy, Pablo . . ."

"Please, Archie," she said. "Never mention his name."

"Got it," he said, in all seriousness. "Did Rudy inherit the plaza after the Chihuahua Pablo passed?"

"No, no. Long after," she said, sighing. "Lots of turf wars and blood. There's been three or four Plaza Bosses since Pablo—all dead. Rudy's just the latest."

It was exactly the kind of news Archie *didn't* want to hear. He'd seen it with his own eyes in the past fifteen years. Any serious disturbance with the cartel was basically a death wish.

"That's why Pablo loved Windi, my friend from Wink. He needed someone soft and smart," she said. "She talked to him. She loved him."

"He looked pretty rough?"

"You knew him?" said Josy, clearly shocked.

"No," laughed Archie. "I saw his picture on the cover of a book. Great shot. Total *narco*—straight out of central casting."

"I never met Pablo," she said. "He was long dead before I met Windi. I don't know if he really meant to leave her the money, but she said he did. Either way, it's ours now. If you win, *Archito*. Only if you win."

"Scary stuff," he said, retrieving his shirt and jeans from the floorboard. "Re-stealing cartel money."

"All taken care of, *guapo*," said Josy, kissing his neck. "I just need your six hundred fifty K to bring it back home."

"And I'm your best option," said Archie, wiggling into his Levi's. "I mean I'll do it. But all I really want to do is drive around Texas, with you and Tallulah and Matt, bet on some football and eat Frito Pies."

She looked up at him, silent. And stayed silent as she carefully tucked her blouse.

"I trust you, Archie. I don't have anybody else. Maybe my father, if he wasn't so sick." said Josy. "Why did the Sheriff give Rudy that envelope?"

"You were watching that close?" he said, with a hint of exasperation. He decided to lie. "I've got five and Chuck gave Rudy the other five. Said it was a peace offering."

"Peace offering." Josy didn't look convinced. "I know Sheriff Chuck's got your back, but you trust that other guy?"

"Who? Okinawa? Sure, I trust him," demanded Archie. "You trust Rudy Leos?"

"No," Josy said, rolling her eyes. "I only know him through Ricardo. And Wacey."

"Why didn't you come down and say hello?" said Archie, pulling on his Red Wings. "You could've stopped all that macho crap."

"Rudy doesn't listen to women," she said, wrapping herself tightly in pashmina. "He's the worst kind of macho. Small-town macho."

Josy opened the visor mirror, brushed a speck of mascara off her cheek. "*Mira*, Rudy's the price of doing business. He's a bad guy who's going to get me out of trouble with worse guys. You've heard of the Zetas?"

"Yes, I've heard of the Zetas!" Archie felt his blood pressure jacking. "As in the psychopath ex-Mexican Marine Zetas?"

"That's who's threatening my brother, my family. And my brother's such a clueless idiot . . . I had to do something," said Josy, batting her lashes. "Rudy can keep the Zetas off me for a price. We're still negotiating."

"Who's negotiating?"

"Me and Rudy."

Talk about a buzzkill.

"*¡Ay, Archito! Porfavor,*" Josy said, picking the roach out of the car ashtray. "I'll tell you the whole story on the way back."

"You think an amateur *gringo* like me is going to get your family out of trouble with the fucking Zetas?"

"*I'm* getting my family out of trouble with the fucking Zetas," she said, slamming the mirror shut. "That's why I've been in Ojinaga since Wednesday."

"Wednesday? Where'd you stay?"

"With Rudy."

"Holy . . . No wonder he was all up my ass!" said Archie, scooching a tad further down the bench seat. "You're sleeping with both of us?"

"I'm fucking Rudy Leos because I have to, dumb ass!" she said, opening the door and stepping out. She quickly returned, pointing a finger at Archie. "I'm fucking you because I want to!"

Right, he thought. He wasn't touching that one.

Archie got out of the car, met Josy at the trunk and hugged her. He looked over her head, over the top of the car, past the Tres Palmas, to the stadium lights, glowing in the distance like six skinny ghosts.

He leaned into Josy's thick hips. Pushed her hard against the Cadillac's smooth sheet metal. He tried to unpack all she'd said and then didn't much care.

"Thank you," she said, kissing him like she meant it. "You're the only one I trust."

"I'm in, Josy," he said, easing off her hips. "I'm in."

"You're too nice, *Archito*," she said, nuzzling his neck. "People take advantage of nice boys like you."

"Not so much," he laughed, taking his *novia's* hand, kissing her long, strong fingers. "Not if my girl's got a gun to their head."

ARCHIE GETS THE MIDDLE FINGER

On the drive back to Marfa, through the pitch-black of the Big Empty, La Princesa clarified and amplified—manicure flashing; lip gloss glowing—her plan to retrieve, repatriate and put to work, $6.5 million in unburied treasure. In fact, so lucid and compelling was the Rice MBA's business plan that by the time Archie slowed to cruise Marfa's bohemian main drag with its galleries, bookstores, restaurants, and bars, he was truly curious. A little skeptical, but pretty much won over.

"Rule number one, Mr. Weesatche," said Josy, with a perfectly executed hair toss. "The less you know, the safer we stay. ¿*Comprende?*

"*Si, comprendo.*"

"You're gonna be super safe," she said, as her on-again lover parked the Cougar Red Cadillac in front of the Hotel Paisano. "I've got someone to protect you. She's the best."

"*She's* the best?"

"Yes, she is. You met her; Wacey," she said, wiping lipstick off her teeth in the mirror. "Rule number two: Keep your hands off her."

"Correct," Archie laughed. "No hands on the female assassin."

"Smart boy," she said, rushing for the lobby. "*Ya sabes.*"

"I thought she was working for Rudy."

"Wacey's mine," she said, as the lobby door closed.

Who isn't? he thought, following Josy's rhythmic sway up the stairs to the third floor.

Archie knew the time was right for some black-market magic. Whatever the job required. Whatever the boss told you to do, you did it. If that meant raising $650,000, you didn't ask questions.

As he watched Josy unlock the door to the Rock Hudson Suite with an actual metal key, Archie Weesatche, the former aw-shucks owner of a modestly successful hotshot delivery service, suddenly realized he was in the laundry business. "And I don't mean dry cleaning."

"*¿Que?*" Josy asked from the toilet. "What are you saying?"

"*Nada, nada, Princesa,*" he said, flicking on the TV in the suite's parlor hoping to catch the late-night high school scores.

Josy returned from the bathroom in the same jade green robe she'd worn to smashing effect at *Hacienda Montemayor*.

"Wow," said Archie, as she plopped on the couch. "Howdy."

"Here's the only thing you need to know, *guapo*," she said, scooting closer. "You wire my fat bastard banker six hundred fifty K by December 31 and I'll wire you seven hundred fifty K on January 1."

"Just like that?"

"Just like that."

Archie smiled at *La Princesa* as she parted the jade green sea and said no more.

THE NEXT MORNING, AFTER CHECKING ALL THE WEEK ZERO TEXAS HIGH school football scores, Archie closed Josefina's state-of-the-art laptop. He crawled back under the covers while his friend with benefits rubbed the sleep out of her eyes.

"You know what this feels like?"

"What *what* feels like?" said Josy, petulantly pulling the sheet over her head. "It feels like you're up too early."

"It feels like old times," he said, pulling up the sheet and peeking under. He crossed his arms across his bare chest, stared at the ceiling, took a deep breath, thought about shutting up . . . but didn't.

"It feels like I don't know what the hell I'm doing. Just like sportscasting—just winging it. Piss poor preparation. Piss poor delivery, piss poor everything. I was a joke. Never thought about learning how to deliver my lines like I wasn't reading the fucking TelePrompTer. Broadcasting 101. Such a joke."

Josefina folded the sheet back to reveal eyes only. "So, we're a joke. That's what you're saying? That we're a joke?"

"No . . . I don't know," he said, exhaling. "I hear you, but here's the thing. I deliver oil field equipment. That's what I'm good at."

"Jesus, Archie, really? You're such a baby . . . always running away . . . 'I can't do it mommy, make it better!'"

"And you?" he replied. "You're using your feminine wiles for the good of mankind?"

He felt her unsmiling eyes bearing down. He breathed deeply, tried to recall what game Okinawa had lined up next—maybe Forsan-Coahoma. Maybe Big Spring-Sweetwater.

"I'm calling Chuck," he mumbled, stripping the covers off his legs.

"No! You can't tell him," she said, gathering the sheets under her chin. "He's a Sheriff, Archie. No way. You can't tell him!"

"Woman . . . I swear."

"Please go smoke," she said, sending him away with a flick of her wrist. "You're so emotional."

Archie got up to do just that. "Six point five million! Stolen! From a cartel!" he yelled from the bathroom. "Can you say, 'death wish'?"

He lit and took an enormous drag off the fat roach he found on the edge of the sink, stared at a framed glamour shot of Rock Hudson, wishing *he* was a movie star instead of a dumbass sitting on the toilet *looking* at a movie star.

"Fuck my life! You passive-aggressive *pendejo*," Josy yelled, from under the sheets.

He sprang from the toilet.

"No ma'am," he said, squeaky-voiced and buck naked, exhaling a boiling cloud over her body. "You cannot make me fuck your life."

Josy sat straight up, looked him in the eye, and declared, "What if I want babies?"

Archie stopped short, took another drag.

"You don't want babies. That's what rich plastic surgeons are for," he said, offering her the last of the roach, which she pretended not to want. "You *think* you want babies. We can't even take care of ourselves. Seriously, I know first-graders who are more mature."

"I hate you," she said, blowing smoke in his face.

"Don't hate me 'cause I can't launder money," he said. "Hate me because I'm too sexy for my boxers."

She evil-eyed him as Archie danced around the bed and sang riff, after god-awful riff, of the "I'm Too Sexy" song. "I'm too sexy for the Border Patrol. I'm too sexy for my *chorizo*. I'm too sexy for my . . ."

"Quit swinging that thing."

"See," he said. "You like the lanky, don't you?"

"*Tanto* . . . no more *mota* for you," she laughed, throwing the roach on the tile floor.

He left the *cucaracha* to die, dove on the bed, ascended the Tetons, buried his head, and just stayed there.

But not for long.

Josy shouldered him off and planted a vicious stiff-arm when he went in for a kiss.

"Denied at the rim!"

"*Si, guapo*," she said, demurely clutching handfuls of bed linen. "*No respeto; no chichis.*"

He gracefully pirouetted from above her, to beside her, lingered on the edge of the bed, pondering the joy he felt parrying with this fine woman.

He looked over his shoulder, met her smiling eyes.

"*Hola Princesa.*"

"*Hola guapo.*"

—

THEIR FULL DAY OF BIG BEND ROAD TRIPPING STARTED WITH A PEPPY JAUNT to Terlingua, introducing Josy to Texas's most famous ghost town, featuring shots of *sotol* and Lone Star chasers with the decidedly irregulars at the town watering hole, *La Posada Milagra*.

Next, they cruised the Cougar Red Cadillac up to Panther Junction, where they dutifully rest stopped at the Big Bend National Park Visitor's Center. After a siesta under the shaded delight of giant poplars, they repaired to tiny Marathon where they fortified themselves at the Gage Hotel with saddle-blanket-sized chicken fried steaks, mashed potatoes with cream gravy and fried okra.

They extended their Big Empty circuit with a drive-by of Alpine's famous baseball venue, Kokernot Field, and Matt's alma mater, Sul Ross State University. Their final stop was the Marfa Lights station, but by the time they got there, they were too tired to witness even a hint of extraterrestrial activity. In fact, they were so weary, climbing the staircase of the Hotel Paisano, that the now famously reacquainted couple proceeded to snooze way past the 10 a.m. checkout.

Fortunately, Archie'd made the Marfa-Midland trip in less than five hours, many times.

He vowed, hurriedly loading the last of Josy's four bags, not to talk about football, or money laundering, or anything even vaguely cartel-related. He also didn't ask why she was flying commercial to Laredo. And he sure as hell didn't ask what (or who) she was doing in deep South Texas.

As they headed out of town, Josy ignored Archie's finger pointing out the Chinati Foundation army barracks where Donald Judd's modernist aluminum boxes were on display. She couldn't wait to hear more about the small-town millionaires he'd identified and how much he was going to bet on each game. Archie kept reminding her that regardless of how well he and Okinawa knew these big-time boosters and their small-town teams, there were no guarantees.

"Please!" she seethed. "If I was some tall, skinny *gringa*, you would have already married me. That's your real problem. "Deep down, you're a *Yanqui* snob."

Archie remembered these turn-on-a-dime moods in San Antonio only he hadn't been nearly as patient back then. Thinking back to their fights—full-on shouting matches; in public!—made him shake his head.

"Seriously," he objected. "You're playing the racist card?"

"Because it's true," she said, crossing her legs and folding her arms. "Tell me why you won't help me. It's going to save my life. My family. You're backing out. Aren't you?"

"No," he said, keeping his eyes on the road. "My hesitation has nothing to do with race, color, creed, sex . . . nothing. It has everything to do with how fucking stupid it is to re-steal six point five million dollars from a cartel. I'm paranoid. Shoot me."

"How come you're not paranoid about sleeping with me?"

"Cause I love sleeping with you," he said, shooting her a glance.

"Don't talk to me like your fucking girlfriend!" she screamed. "I am not your girlfriend. I'm your business partner. And from now on, you are *not* sleeping with me."

"Come on . . . I was a perfect gentleman."

"But you had to fuck me when we got back to the hotel, didn't you?"

"Seemed like a decent idea," he said, hoping for a break. "Was it really a problem?"

"Maybe."

"Maybe what? Come on Josy . . . I'm forty-five years old," he said, giving her a truly puzzled look. "You know damn well . . . ."

"You should be careful," she said, staring straight ahead.

Archie took Josy at her word.

Things were very quiet the last four hours of the drive. When the Midland-Odessa International Air and Spaceport sign flashed by, Josy wheeled in her seat.

"How do you spell respect?" she demanded. "In Spanish."

It was a curious thing to ask, but Archie could tell she was serious.

He punched the accelerator and began to pass a long line of eighteen-wheelers.

"How do you spell it?" she insisted.

"Jesus Josy, can you wait a second?" he said, topping out at 110, then decelerating to eighty as he moved back into the right lane. "Now, how do you spell, what?

"Respect!" said Josefina, jabbing at the radio presets until Chris Stapleton's beautiful country drawl went silent. "The word respect, in Spanish."

"I don't know," he cried, looking at the letters in his mind's eye. "R-E-S-P-E-C-T-O."

Josy laughed. A painful laugh. She reached over and delicately moved a strand of Archie's hair.

Archie kept his eyes glued on the broken white line.

"You don't respect anything about my family, do you?" she asked, "Not me, not my father. I'm not good enough for you. Please just say that."

Archie breathed deep, exhaled slowly, blinked a lash out of his eye. Finally, he spoke.

"I do respect you, Josy. You and the Montemayor family. I do."

"No, you don't," she said, slamming her hands on the dashboard. "It's *respeto*, Archie. *¡R-E-S-P-E-T-O!* Not *respecto*, like some fucking redneck!"

Archie raised his eyes to the Mexican heavens, turned pale with shame.

It was true. He'd done it all his disrespectful gringo life. He'd always said, always texted *respecto*, never once considering if his lazy Spanglish was incorrect. Clearly, he didn't care. It was beyond embarrassing.

"Didn't you notice? You signed off with that stupid, *Con Mucho Respecto*. I'd text you back with the correct spelling and you kept right on using *respecto*. When I first met you at *Las Marthas*, I thought you were funny, the charming *caballero*. Fifteen years later you're still doing it. Why is that?"

"*I'm loser, baby*," he sang. "*So why don't you kill me.*"

"*Chingao*," she said. "You don't have a serious bone in your body."

They pulled up to the Departures gate with twenty minutes to spare. Archie hopped out, hustled her bags to the check-in counter, slid the porter a ten, and waited, while Josy got her boarding pass.

"I'll give you my answer day after tomorrow," he said, as she scrolled her texts.

"Great, so you're out," she said, not looking up. "*¿Si o no?*"

"No," he said. "I need forty-eight hours."

"Like the last time?"

"The last time was fifteen years ago," he said, not even attempting a hug, or to hold her hand. Nothing. "You owe me some time to think about a very serious situation; a life-changing situation."

Josy carefully placed her phone in her purse, then jabbed her finger in his chest. "You owe *me*, Archie *Huizache*!"

"You're gonna miss that flight," said the porter. "Ten minutes."

"Go, go," he said, leaning in to kiss her cheek.

La Princesa was having none of it.

She pushed Archie's face away with both hands, turned her stilettos right into the revolving door. Bursts of unintelligible Spanglish popping off the plate glass as she spun away, raking at her hair.

"I'll call you," he said.

Josy's answer: two bedazzled middle fingers. Up high.

"*¡Mamon!*" she cried. "*¡Mamon!*"

IN OVER YOUR HEAD

GARDEN CITY, TEXAS

AUGUST 24, 2015

"So, did you like, do it all weekend?"

Tallulah smiled slyly at Matt, sitting next to his sister at Sister Ernestine's kitchen table set for five. The matriarch looked quizzically at her daughter while Sheriff Fuchs and Archie helped themselves to serving dishes filled with squash casserole, mashed potatoes, green beans, and a platter heaped with pan-fried liver and onions. The salad, halved pears with sour cream, shredded cheddar and crushed pecans, was not getting much attention.

"Yes, Tallulah, to answer your titillating query, Miss Montemayor and I did many things, including 'it'," he said, watching Tallulah fail to stifle her laugh. "If by 'it' you mean fighting like banshees and enjoying lots of epic Big Bend scenery."

"So, you were having incredible make-up sex?" Tallulah asked with a straight face. "Me and Roger do that all the time. It's like we fight so we can make up."

"Lots of it, Tules," he continued, passing the green beans to his irrepressible sister. "All kinds of make-up activity."

A shriek of pure teenage bliss cut through the droning of the overworked air conditioner as the West Texas sun blazed in the evening sky.

"Young lady," said Sister Ernestine. "The only sex you need to be thinking about is protected, or preferably, abstinence."

"What's abstinence?" said Tallulah, cutting her eyes at Matt.

"Matt, please remind your sister that playing dumb doesn't work in this house," said Sister Ernestine, watching everybody dig in, beaming at the rarity of having her entire family seated for supper. "I know that Miss Green explained "safe sex" in the fifth grade."

"Mom! I didn't get here till sixth grade," insisted Tallulah. "And no biggie on condoms. I keep some in my purse. When I have a purse, which is like, never. But Roger always has some. He knows."

"TMI, Tules!" said Matt, trying unsuccessfully not to talk with his mouth full.

"We've raised you to be intelligent adults," said Sister Ernestine, looking at the Sheriff. "Be smart about sex; all of you. That's all we ask."

"Don't look at me," said the Sheriff, as the entire table, did indeed, look at him. "My parents never said a word about sex. Not even the word. Not once."

"The Puritans are still alive and well in America," chuckled Sister Ernestine. "It's always baffled me."

Archie took a slight pause from one of his all-time favorite meals to reflect. He'd never been smart about sex. Ever. Although he *was* the master of the withdrawal method. But that probably didn't count.

"Mom, thank you so much for this wonderful meal."

Everybody looked up and offered thanks and praise to Sister Ernestine, who drank it in, the picture of contentment. The silverware clinked and the small talk waned as every bit of comfort food was systematically inhaled.

"So, tell us about Josy's business plan," said the Sheriff, carving through the delicate sear of his pounded-thin liver.

"I think Josy's lovely, by the way," chimed Sister Ernestine. "And that figure, oo-la-la."

"Matt's got a crush on her," said Tallulah, punching his shoulder. "On her tiddies."

"Partially true. But super wierd," said Matt, eyes down on his entré.

"So, let's hear it, Arch," said the Sheriff. "Lots of keen minds around this table."

"No sir. No business talk at the table," he said, wiping his mouth. "How 'bout on the porch, with a cigar?"

"Sounds good to me," said Matt, wiping his plate clean with a crust of wheat toast. "Got any more of those Fighting Cocks?"

"Yes sir, got a beautiful box of Texas Reds," assured Archie. "Aged to perfection."

"Don't even think about getting up," said Sister Ernestine. "Dewberry cobbler and French press for dessert."

"I'll help, mom," said Tallulah, grabbing her own and Matt's plates. Archie was still eating, of course, he being the slowest eater in Glasscock County.

On her way around the table, Tallulah piled the Sheriff's plate on top.

"Thank you, ma'am," he said, winking at his favorite female orphan. "You're a good hand, Tallulah Bankhead."

Sister Ernestine pulled a steaming Pyrex dish out of the oven filling the room with the smell of warm, ripe berries. Evening light poured through the overpainted panes as Archie savored his last bite. "Say, Chuck, are you up for re-election this year?"

"Twenty sixteen," said the Sheriff. "Might hang it up after this one. "Twenty twenty will be fifty years."

"Fifty years! That's about a career," Archie said. "Especially if you have to arrest me for money laundering."

"Say what?" said Matt, reaching for a toothpick.

"I figured it was something sketchy," said the Sheriff, leaning back in one of the old ladder-back chairs Sister Ernestine had recently re-caned. "What's she got in mind? Running it through Keep On Truckin'?"

"Nah, she needs cash for cash," said Archie, leery of the lawman's uncanny intuition. He took his plate to Tallulah who was rinsing dishes at the sink. "Thank you, Tules."

"You're welcome, *Archito*," said Tallulah. "I love it when Josy calls you that."

"Me too," he said, as Sister Ernestine handed him a plate of cobbler. "It's a pretty good plan, actually. Josy says it's airtight."

"Airtight, huh?" said the Sheriff, accepting his dewberry dessert and a sweet kiss from his girlfriend. "Am I gonna have to put you in cuffs right here and now?"

"No sir," said Archie, noticing that the Sheriff wasn't smiling. "All hypothetical."

After dewberry cobbler and coffee, their conversation continued under the porch trellis, overgrown with vines and climbing flowers. The breeze freshened after the sun finally set for good around nine thirty. Archie talked about Josy's scheme, assuring the Sheriff it was a good opportunity for him to earn a decent payday while he was non-competing.

"You don't want to get within a mile of those cartels. In any way, shape, or form. Those boys play for keeps," said the Sheriff, stubbing the butt of his Texas Red in an overflowing ashtray. Matt and Tallulah had only smoked a third of their Double Coronas. "Don't get mixed up in something you can't handle."

"I hear you," said Archie, taking one last drag on his Fighting Cock before the draw got too hot. "Josy says she's got it handled. I just need to win a lot of football games."

"Sounds like Josy's got you handled on all sides," said the Sheriff.

"She's a stepper," said Matt, sipping on a cold Shiner Bock. "I can vouch for that."

"Young man, I expect you to be blind-sided," said the Sheriff, patting Matt on the shoulder. "Archie, you've got no excuse."

"Well, she's mighty persuasive," said Archie, feeling the heat rise in his cheeks.

"You keep saying that," said the Sheriff, hitching up his pants. "You sure she ain't takin' advantage?"

Archie gave the Sheriff a look. He knew all he had to do was tell Josy no and get on down the road. But looking at the Sheriff, then down at his boots, then to the ashtray; he also knew he wasn't going to do that.

And couldn't say why.

"I'll keep my eyes open," said Archie, stubbing out his cigar, unable to look at the Sheriff or Matt. "Come on guys, a little chivalry never hurt anybody."

"Your daddy used to talk like that," said the Sheriff, shaking his head.

Archie let that piece of information settle.

"Well, there you go," Archie continued. "All genetics. Got no say in the matter."

The Sheriff picked up his hat, squared the cream straw Stetson on his salt and pepper head. "I've said my piece, son. But remember what happened to your dad. Your mom and your dad."

Archie was shocked. Chuck Fuchs never, ever called out Big Arch and Bunny.

Archie stood up and stepped up, not quite toe-to-toe, but real close. They were both big, tall men, but the Sheriff seemed a lot more substantial. Archie shuffled his boots. "I heard you. Why you bringing mom and dad into it?"

"I hear you too, son. You sound just like your dad."

"What the hell, Chuck?" Archie stammered. "I'll do whatever the hell I need to."

"I'm sure you will, but this ain't no game, Archie," said the Sheriff, standing tall. "You're in over your head."

"Hey, come on now," said Matt, bravely stepping in between the two. "Let's . . . let's calm down."

The Sheriff stepped away from Archie and yanked open the sliding glass door with a bang. "Be sure to tell your mom thanks for that good meal."

"We did," said Archie and Matt, in unison.

"Then tell her again, goddammit," he said, stepping inside and slamming the door.

"Yes, sir."

FAST EDDIE AND THE MUSTANGS

"Hey Oak, how 'bout we start makin' some money."

On the field below the two former high school standouts, swarms of black-clad Big Spring Steers and solid-red Sweetwater Mustangs warmed up in the spacious Mustang Bowl, a Civilian Conservation Corps masterpiece, built in 1939 by Nolan County's Depression-era laborers smack in the middle of the Staked Plains—not a drop of water in sight, sweet or otherwise.

In the pre-game swelter—over one hundred degrees—Archie set up his stadium seat high above the fifty-yard line. Per the usual, Okinawa was at his disrespectful best. "What kinda high-stakes gambler sits in an old lady seat?"

A firm middle finger was the only proper response for the man who always had the best seat in the house. In an air-conditioned press box, no less.

The Farmer's Almanac said it was closing in on the Autumnal Equinox, but the oven-like conditions reminded Archie of just one thing: cramps— out-of-nowhere, bolt-of-lightening seizures that grabbed an unsuspecting football player and sent him to the turf in fist-pounding agony.

There were lots of things Archie missed about football, but cramps, gobbling big orange salt pills, and watching a coach stretch your hamstrings to the shredding point, were not among them.

Okinawa was mystified by the Texas Tour's dramatic change of stakes. He was still in for ten percent, but didn't cotton to working for Josy, even if she was Mexican royalty.

"That good stuff ain't free, dawg," said Okinawa, who knew a few things about the realities of modern romance. "That baby needs all kinds of new shoes."

"Yeah, and I'll buy'em unless you've got some more plaza boss surprises," said Archie, scanning the stadium for his mark, a rancher-oilman named Fast Eddie Lau, who owned most of the cattle, and all of the oil and gas, in Scurry County.

"Naw dawg. No more of that mess," agreed Okinawa. "Fast Eddie ain't no gangsta."

That was a fact.

Fast Eddie Lau wasn't going to do anything but shake a man's hand and bet $10,000 on his beloved Sweetwater Mustangs. A team he firmly believed was going to beat the boys from Big Spring by at least a touchdown. In fact, Fast Eddie was so confident, that he'd given Archie a touchdown and two points, +8.

"So how many games you figure we gotta win to raise all that money?" asked the skeptical sportswriter, waving at a gaggle of young Big Spring ladies in the latest Texas Mom uniform of Daisy Dukes and cowboy boots. "I'm with the Sheriff. You in *way* over your head. Six fifty's monster money, dawg."

"You line'em up," said Archie, breathing in the superheated September air. "I'll take care of the money."

"Alright, hoss," he replied, with a chuckle. "I like it when you get all bowed up."

Archie quickly spotted Mr. Lau's distinctive LBJ-style Stetson, coming through the end zone. "Josy's got a plan. And she's got her man."

NOT FOR A MINUTE.

Turned out, Fast Eddie could've spotted Archie *three* touchdowns.

In a total blow out, the Big Spring Steers lost their season opener to the pass-happy Sweetwater Mustangs, 35–7, and just like that, Archie was down $10K.

BENEATH THE SANDS OF MONAHANS

They met under the scoreboard after the game as parents hugged their sweat-soaked sons and little kids ran wild on the field.

"Pleasure doing bidness with ya," said Fast Eddie, accepting a Keep On Truckin' envelope full of hundred-dollar bills. "Y'all come on over to Buck's; buy you a steak."

"I appreciate it, Mr. Lau," said Archie. "You figure it's gonna get under ninety tonight?"

"Hell no," he said, done counting after a few bills. He shook Archie's hand and hitched his khaki britches up high on his skinny waist. "Must be something to this global warming stuff. I's born in twenty-five and never seen it this hot. Even during the drought."

"'bout to turn the Mustang Bowl back into a Dust Bowl, ain't it?" said Archie, sleeving the sweat under the bill of his black and gold Big Spring ball cap.

"Looks like we might have us a team this year," said the old rancher. "I'da given ya a few more points if I knew our quarterback could sling it like Sammy Baugh."

"Throw'd it like a frozen rope," added Okinawa, back from the press box, a tad embarrassed that Archie was on the wrong end of one of his "sure things" for the second week in a row. "That boy's going D-1 for sure."

"Sure hope he signs with Tech," allowed Fast Eddie.

Okinawa and Archie said their goodbyes and promised Mr. Lau they'd be back in October for his annual dove hunt and goat roast. Before they left, Archie couldn't help but ask about the pretty lady sitting with Fast Eddie and the wife.

"She's my Relationship Manager," he said, grinning. "Works in what they call Advancement over at Tech. I donated an Endowed Chair to the Ag Department, and she came with it."

"Do tell," said Archie. "That's a pretty nice perk."

"Man, I could use me a Relationship Manager," agreed Okinawa.

"All it'll cost you is a cool million."

Okinawa whistled through his teeth. "That's some strong relations, Fast Eddie."

They all stopped to admire the comely Relationship Manager's silhouette, quite discernible, even from a distance, as she visited with the lovely Mrs. Lau and her Sweetwater Country Club pals.

On cue, obviously feeling all manner of manly gamma rays, the women turned to wave.

"Yeah, hidy there," said Mr. Lau, in a stage whisper. "Can't touch that girl with a ten-foot pole, but I shor' can look."

"Beats hell out of the girls working The Settles," said Archie.

"Buncha damn meth heads is what I heard," added Okinawa. "Nobody pays for a skinny hooker."

"Whaddaya mean, *heard*?" asked Archie. "I bet you're the first one on the twelfth floor come payday."

"Payday? At the *Herald*?" he said, incredulous. "You think they're payin' sportswriters a living wage?"

Everybody sighed at the mention of the twelfth floor of the Settles, Big Spring's House of the Rising Sun.

"Yeah, that Ryan boy cleaned up the old Settles nice," said Mr. Lau. "I tell ya, I left a pretty penny on the twelfth floor. In my younger days, of course."

"The Settles is something," Archie exclaimed, proud of his adopted hometown's unlikely skyscraper. "Got a great bar and real nice restaurant. Bring Mrs. Lau and I'll take y'all to dinner."

"Aw, you've been plenty generous, Archie," said Mr. Lau, jerking his thumb in the Relationship Manager's direction. "Hell, I'll bring her."

"You gonna buy me dinner, Mr. Lau?"

"You bet, Okinawa," said Fast Eddie, winking at Archie, and stepping up to clap the former defensive tackle's broad back. "You just put me together with ten thousand dollars. Least I can do is buy you a nice rib-eye."

PISTOL-PACKIN' MAMA

BIG SPRING, TEXAS
SEPTEMBER 7, 2015

"Who in the Wide World of Sports is that?"

After a Monday morning workout and run around Scenic Mountain, Archie opened the seldom-used front door to find a woman walking up his sidewalk. He was always glad he didn't have children, seeing as his street, North Gregg, doubled as the busiest highway in town.

Pedestrian foot traffic was highly unusual in Big Spring, but this woman was clearly on a mission. As she quick-walked up to the house, Archie could tell she was no Texas Leaguer—shoulder-length asymmetrical hairstyle, silver aviator shades, hip-hugging jeans, and a tight Juicy t-shirt.

She walked hard. Boots pounding the cracked concrete. And not a hint of smile.

"Mornin'," he said, extending a hand into which the woman put an envelope.

"From Josy."

Archie looked at the sealed envelope, then up at the woman, who stood, cross-armed, waiting.

"And your name, ma'am?"

"Wacey."

"Hey Wacey, I'm Archie Weesatche," he said, looking for her car and/or her accomplice. "I think we met a coupla weeks ago in Presidio."

Crickets from the tough girl.

"This for me? To open?"

"Handed it to you."

"Alrighty. Hey, let's grab some shade," Archie said, offering to step beneath his shallow, furniture-free porch. He tried to be careful with the envelope, then went ahead and ripped it open.

The letter was typed on *Hacienda Montemayor* stationery:

> *August 31, 2015*
>
> *Mr. Weesatche,*
>
> *This letter intends to clarify the ongoing business arrangement between Archie D. Weesatche and Josefina Montemayor.*
>
> *Please wire transfer $650,000 to the agreed upon account at the Happy State Bank & Trust no later than 12 a.m. (midnight) December 31, 2015. Upon receipt of the funds Josefina Montemayor will return $650,000 plus $100,000 for services rendered to the bank account of your choosing.*
>
> *Buena Suerte,*
>
> *Josefina Del Rocío Montemayor*
>
> *Ciudad Victoria, Tamaulipas, Mexico*

He peered at the woman, who'd removed her sunglasses, but still had a hip cocked and arms crossed. Was she DEA? Was this the bodyguard Josy promised? Was she working for Rudy Leos? Was she working for Chuck?

"Hey, let's take it from the top," he said, a little self-conscious in his ancient UH Football T-shirt and droopy red basketball shorts. "I'm Archie Weesatche."

He held his hand out until she reluctantly shook it. The woman looked very disappointed when Archie tried to hand back the letter.

"I don't want it."

"I can see that."

"See what?" she said, swatting at the envelope. "Josy hired me to keep you alive."

"Excellent news," said Archie, eyeing her straight up. "I'm in mortal danger?"

"Yep," allowed the deeply-tanned, slightly wind-tooled woman. "Pretty dumb to be messin' with Rudy Leos."

Archie guessed Wacey was thirty-five years-old; forty tops.

"You from West Texas?"

"Here's all you need to know about me," she said, putting her shades back on. "That six and a half million is just as much mine as it is Josy's."

"Is that right?" said Archie, trying his best to be serious.

"Damn right, that's right," she snapped. "Christ, you're annoying."

He laughed, nervously. Clasped his hands, raised up on his toes, wanting desperately to communicate with this perfectly agitated stranger.

Finally, he asked if she wanted a cold beer.

"At nine o'clock?"

"Yep," said Archie, holding her gaze steady. "Price of explaining why it's your money."

"Chuck said you were different," she said, softening just a tad.

Not as different as the likes of you, he thought, taking a halting step toward the door.

"You like Bud or Lone Star?" said Archie, spotting a faded tattoo in the space between her skinny jeans and ankle boots.

"I like that Cadillac parked behind the house."

"Me too," said Archie. "You casin' my house?"

"You wish."

Now we're talking, he thought. Archie pushed open the door and motioned Wacey inside. "So yes, you hail from West Texas. And no, you *don't* want to discuss my Mexican love interest?"

"Lost me," she said, walking inside as Archie held the door. "Where'd you learn to talk like that?"

"My Mom."

"Your Mom a teacher, or something?"

"No, but she does have a Ph.D. from Texas Tech," Archie said, flipping on the living room lights, then closing the door. "My mom's a nun."

"A what?" said Wacey. "Jesus, you're weird."

"Yeah, it's a long story. You got any appointments today?"

"Baby sittin' you," she said. "And getting my money."

"Well, ma'am . . ."

"Wacey."

"Yes ma'am, Wacey," he said, folding up a blanket from the couch and placing it just so on the ottoman. "Please, make yourself at home. Can I get you some coffee; some water with that beer?"

Wacey took stock of her seating options, looked at the ottoman, the wing chair, then decided on the couch. "Water'd be great. And a steak."

"You bet," he said, ducking into the kitchen.

"I'm just kiddin' about the steak," she shouted after him.

"I'm not," said Archie, returning with two beers, handing her a cold Lone Star.

Archie clinked the top of her bottle, beaming at his unexpected guest. "Here's to pretty girls with pistols in their pockets?"

Wacey clinked, drank, then reached behind her back for the aforementioned gun. "Never leave home without it."

She racked a shell into the chamber and sighted down the barrel out the window.

Archie was visibly impressed. "Now, who sent you, Sheriff? Or Josy?"

"Both."

"Damn," he said, enjoying a big swig of ice-cold Budweiser. "Must be my lucky day."

"Don't get your hopes up," she replied, taking her own big swig.

"Don't mind if I do," said the committed bachelor.

AFTER A QUICK DRIVE TO TJ'S STEAKHOUSE, TWO T-BONES, TWO BAKED potatoes, two slices of Key Lime pie, and several Coronas later, Wacey the Assassin was revealed to be the wild-child runaway of a recently passed rodeo star and a long-dead C&W-singing momma.

Wacey Foyt had dropped out her junior year at Forsan High, crawled into the hip pocket of a way-older piece of oilfield trash, moved to Odessa, moved to El Paso, where she promptly got mixed up with the cartel crowd; got busted when she was nineteen, and ever since, remained a highly-prized asset for the DEA and DPS under the care and protection of the original orphan wrangler himself, Sheriff Chuck Fuchs.

Feeling the need to reciprocate some family history, Archie confessed his eternal debt to, and unconditional love for, Sheriff Fuchs and Sister Ernestine.

"They took you in when you were five?" said Wacey, fingering a dollop of Cool Whip off Archie's pie. "You're a lucky man."

"All day," he agreed. "And most of forty-five years."

"Forty-five!" she exclaimed, "What kinda fountain of youth you been jumpin' in?"

"Clean livin'."

Wacey clucked her tongue. "Deal with the devil is what I'm thinking."

They also concluded that her appointment as Archie's bodyguard, was very likely, the first step in Sheriff Fuch's long-awaited plan to release Wacey from undercover duty and transition her back into the general population.

"I've been doin' this stuff for thirteen years."

Archie couldn't imagine what kind of stuff she meant, but he did do the math: nineteen plus thirteen. Wacey Foyt was thirty-two! And by the end of lunch, he also understood, clearly, how desperate the tough girl was to get out from under the Sheriff's thumb.

"Listen, I'm not gonna be any trouble," said Archie, waving to Rosa, his regular waitress, to bring them another round. "I might be your ticket out of the shadows."

"Out of the shadows," said Wacey, suppressing a frown. "That sounds kinda cool. Except there's nothing cool about living in a dump-ass duplex in Lamesa, Texas."

"That where he's got you?" said Archie.

Wacey took a drink and a vape pen out of her purse. She pointed it at Archie.

"You go ahead; jump through Josy's hoops," said Wacey, exhaling a cloud of something that smelled like tropical fruit. "It's my money, too. I helped Josy get it across and in the bank. And now you're helping her."

"Where's the lady alfalfa farmer fit in? She your girlfriend?"

"How'd you know about Windi?"

"Josy."

"That bitch, first she steals Windi, who I introduced her to. Now she's bangin' you senseless."

Archie tried not to laugh at the uncanny accuracy of that statement.

"Maybe, but who'd the alfalfa queen steal the money from?"

"Her name is Windi," Wacey replied.

"Who'd Windi steal it from?"

"A plaza boss who hid it in Mexico."

"In the canyon, down from Ojinaga. Santa Elena?"

"Really? You know this shit?" said Wacey, accepting a sweating bottle of Corona from Rosa. Turning to Archie, she added, "She's so cute. You better tip her good."

"Rosa's got the nicest smile in two counties," assured Archie. "And yeah, I do know this stuff. What I don't know is about you and Josy and Windi the alfalfa heir from Wink. Sounds like a lover's quarrel to me."

Wacey lifted an eyebrow. "You think I quarrel or shoot?"

"I bet you do whatever the hell you want," he said. "I bet on high school football."

"I heard that," she said, sliding the check tray over. "Wow, you are a big tipper."

"Hard to make a livin' 'round here, ain't it," he said, handing the tray to Rosa.

"Especially with three kids under five," Rosa agreed, folding the cash into her bra. "Thanks, Archie."

"You're welcome." He wanted to introduce Wacey but thought better of it. Might blow her cover. He raised his arms above his head and stretched for all he was worth. "So, you gonna keep me out of trouble. Even when I don' know it."

"Exactly," she said. "Smartest thing you've said all day."

"I just read books and watch movies," said Archie, relieved that this tough-ass woman had his back. "I'm not living it, like Miss *Sicaria*."

"Yeah, but I'm so over it," she said, taking a healthy swig off her fifth cold beer. "Which is where *you* come in, cowboy."

"Did the Sheriff mention anything about me being in over my head?"

"First thing out of his mouth."

"Nice," said Archie, finishing off his last beer. "How 'bout we call Sheriff Mastermind and get everything on the table."

"Why? You're acting exactly like he said you would."

"No doubt," said Archie, dialing the sheriff's cell. When the call began to ring, he put it on speaker. "Listen, in all seriousness. I owe Sheriff Fuchs my life—literally."

"Ha-lo!"

"Hey Chuck, this is Archie. Guess who I'm plying with beer and steak down at TJ's?"

"I bet she's drinkin' you under the table."

"I bet you're right," said Archie, smiling at Wacey, who nervously put her aviators back on. "Hey, come on down. Wacey wants you to explain the plan. And shed a little more light on whose money we're talking about."

"You tell Wacey, and you listen close, too," answered the Sheriff. "That's my money."

"Really?" said Archie, recognizing the Sheriff's tone from a mile away. "I know a girl from Mexico who would strenuously beg to differ. Come have a beer."

"I would, but I got sheep loose at John Ferguson's," said the Sheriff. "Let's meet back at your house. Five thirty. And get a cup of coffee!"

Archie raised his eyebrows at Wacey, who looked grim-faced.

"Got it. Five thirty at the house," said Archie. "Good luck with the sheep."

"I'll need it. Little bastards are all over his cotton field," he said. "Had us a haboob come across south county this morning. Knocked Ferguson's pens flat."

"Sounds like you been listening to that cute weather lady outta Lubbock," said Archie. "Calls her dust storms, *haboobs*."

"Yes, she does," said the Sheriff. "And so do I."

ARCHIE PULLED INTO HIS DRIVEWAY AND PUNCHED THE GARAGE DOOR OPENER.
"Welcome to *Casa Huizache*," he said, just now realizing how proud he was of his half-acre. "Or welcome back, I should say."

"I can't believe you live here," said Wacey, as he pulled into the half-light of the sheet-metal shed. "I passed by this house a million times, growin' up."

"Yeah, right here on the main drag," said Archie. "I like Big Spring."

The garage was tight, front-to-back, but the width was roomy enough for the Cadillac, a four-wheeler, a dirt bike, and piles of home improvement junk. Archie came around and opened Wacey's door. While she was checking her face in the visor mirror, he pulled the string for a single halogen bulb, then opened her door.

"Wow, somebody's got some new toys."

"Car's new," he said, kicking the tire on his dirt bike. "Everything else looks new 'cause I never use'em."

"This is nice," she said, looking around at the spotless concrete floor with ladders, a push mower, a Weedeater, and all manner of yard implements hanging on the walls. "Never once thought about who lived here."

"Since 2000," said Archie. "Hard to believe it's been fifteen years."

Wacey took his hand as she stepped down off the garage slab into a patchwork of pea gravel and clover that doubled as a backyard.

"Yep, this is it," he said, motioning to the two shotgun houses raised on piers, the crawl spaces under each bordered by freshly painted lattice. The afternoon glare and heat were giving way to a fresh, low-humidity breeze. Archie admired Wacey's strong stride as she walked over to the flower beds bordering the back of the house.

"These are pretty," she said, settling on her haunches to admire the swaying xenias.

"Home Depot promised they'd hold up in the heat," he said, joining her in the shade. "Long as you keep'em watered."

"So, you cook, too?" she said, absently fingering the bright orange petals.

"Nope. Pretty much heat and eat."

"I was about to say," she mused, raising up and stumbling a bit. "Whoopsie. Don't see too many clean garages and flower beds around here. You sure you're not gay?"

"Yeah . . . but I am an orphan," said Archie, pleased that this undercover operative accepted his hand up. "I guess people get to wonderin' if you're a bachelor too long."

"You don't seem too worried about it," said Wacey, as Archie fished the keys out of his jean's pocket. "Maybe we should make some coffee. I'm feelin' a little drunkish."

"Comin' right up," he said, opening the back door into the mud/laundry room. "Make yourself at home."

"You want me to take my shoes off?"

"Naw, you're good," he said, holding the door. "It's all laminate anyway. I ripped up some pretty disgusting shag when I moved in."

"Sounds like my place," she said, pulling a chair from the kitchen table set for two. "And no dirty dishes in the sink! Dude, I've been looking for a roommate like you all my life."

"No dishwasher, either," he said, pleased that his place looked presentable. "Not that I dirty up too many dishes. I eat a lot at mom's house. She lives in Garden City."

"That's nice," said Wacey, absently picking up a water glass off the table, while Archie started the coffee. "I don't think I ate dinner with my mom and dad a single time at the dinner table. They were always working nights. Clubs, rodeos—took me everywhere they went, till Mom died. Then we moved to daddy's place in Forsan. And he died."

"I'm sorry about your mom. And your dad," he said, pouring water into his ancient Mr. Coffee. "You're kind of an orphan, too."

Wacey drained her water and put the glass down. "Momma was sweet. I was the one who was tough on everybody."

"She was a singer?"

Archie liked the way the sunlight hit Wacey's hair when she pushed a strand away.

"Back-up singer, mostly," she said, smiling wistfully as Archie poured her more water from a cold gallon jug. "She met my dad out at The Stampede."

"The Stampede!" he said, pouring himself a glass. "I love that place. Haven't been out there in way too long."

"They were semi-celebrities; at least that night. Mom was touring with the Flatlanders and Daddy won the bull riding *and* the bronc riding at the Big Spring Rodeo. Joe Ely dedicated a song to him and daddy jumped up on the stage and asked mom to dance."

"Hey now, that's West Texas legit. I'da loved to seen the Flatlanders in their prime," Archie said, sitting across from her. He raised his water glass. "Here's to sweet-singing mommas and bull-doggin' daddies."

"Cheers," she said, clinking the hand-blown *vasos* he'd brought back as a souvenir from Ciudad Victoria. Actually, a gift from Josy.

Archie wanted to say all kinds of things to his new friend. About how he'd seen Joe Ely down in Austin; how he'd won some money on her daddy at the Ft. Worth Rodeo and why they should go two-stepping at The Stampede, tonight.

Instead, he let the silence settle; snuck a peek at this unusual woman; marveled at the dust bunnies floating in the sunbeams behind her, then got up to pour them a couple of mugs of coffee. By the time he asked how she took hers (little milk; no sugar) and fixed his own (lots of milk; little sugar), Sheriff Fuchs was rolling up in the backyard.

Archie walked everybody to the living room with their coffee. He sat the Sheriff in the wing chair, then sat next to Wacey on the couch, but not too close. He muted Lester Holt and the *NBC Nightly News* and re-set everybody's coffee on his junior college coasters: one from Frank Phillips in Borger, one from Odessa College, and one from Western Texas in Snyder.

"How you like that new bull TV?" asked the Sheriff, seemingly pleased to be sipping coffee with Archie and a new lady friend, even if he'd orchestrated the whole thing.

"Using about five percent of its capacity, I'm sure," he said, laying the remote down on his old pine coffee table. "You'll have to pry me out of here during football season."

"Gimme that," said Wacey, reaching for the remote. "I'll show you how to drive."

"Hallelujah!" said Archie, leaning back on the same Scotch-Guarded couch he'd had since his sportscaster days in Victoria.

"You two seem to be gee-hawin'," said the Sheriff. "He treatin' you proper, Wacey?"

"He's okay," she said, suppressing a smile while surfing the cable channels. "What's this about *your* money?"

"One hundred percent *my* money; as in the State of Texas's money" said the Sheriff, taking a sip of his coffee. "And whatever we say in this room, stays in this room, right Archie?"

"Yes sir."

"Good. I don't mean to be hard on you, son. But like I said the other night, the people we're dealing with, and the amount of money we're talkin' about, attracts a lot of attention. The worst kind. Wacey can vouch for that."

The Sheriff and Wacey exchanged knowing looks.

"Plenty of people get dead stealing six and a half million dollars," said the Sheriff, scooting up in his chair. "I don't know how the hell you gals got it across and into that bank, but I intend to make good use of every dime of it."

"Josy didn't do a damn thing," said Wacey, in her snarkiest tone. "Windi brought it across, cleaned it, and banked it. Josy's just trying to steal it back."

Archie's eyes rolled to the heavens. "And," he said. "What's this got to do with me?"

"You're great cover," said the Sheriff.

"You think?" said Wacey. "You think Josy's not gonna figure this out?"

"You're Josy's idea," said the Sheriff. "She wants you to protect her stake horse."

Archie cursed himself. "Long as nobody gets hurt if I *don't* win."

"It'd be better if you *do* win. Some," said the Sheriff. "You know, keep the Princess happy. But nobody's expecting you to win six hundred fifty thousand dollars."

"She does," said Wacey. "I promise you."

"Oh yeah," Archie agreed.

"Well, Josy ought to know better," said the Sheriff. "She must think nobody knows she's tryin' to re-steal six point five million dollars."

"Worst kept secret in West Texas," said Wacey.

"My show now," assured the Sheriff. "And I got lots of eyes on me. On both sides of the border—alphabet soup: DPS, DEA, ICE, Border Patrol, Homeland Security. Every single person involved is looking to get paid, get promoted, get even, or get dead."

"He's not kidding," said Wacey. "The people I run with; kill you for fifty bucks. No problem. Life is cheap—blah, blah, blah. But it's true. They know they're going to die, like tomorrow."

"Hey, hey," said Archie, waving his hand. "I didn't sign up for dyin' tomorrow!"

"Me neither," said Wacey. "That's why I do exactly what he says. I mean *exactly*. And I'm still going to die."

"No, you're not," said the Sheriff. "You're gettin' out for good."

Archie felt the heat rising in his cheeks. "So, can I like, opt-out, like right this second?"

The Sheriff chuckled and Wacey scooted a little closer to her new assignment.

"Oh honey," she said, putting her hand on Archie's knee. "I know. It's scary."

¡OYE PAYASO!

Archie slept on the couch.

Outside, in the early-morning dark, a lonesome dove cooed behind the pulled blinds.

Josy had been texting him, nonstop, for two hours.

Her final text, simply: *WTF??????*

Now his cell phone was vibrating angrily. He grabbed the offending gadget off the pine table, watched it buzz in his hands.

He swore at the phone, glared at the glowing screen. Let the call go to voice mail. He sensed that his guest was awake, and was loath to let her hear Josy's voice, but couldn't help listening to the message.

"Call me, *Archito*. You promised. Call me, *precioso*. I miss you. Call me."

As a battalion of frac trucks rumbled down North Gregg, Archie swore to god, he *was* going to get Josy her money. He was. But he was *not* going to be denied a better understanding of the mysterious miracle sleeping in the next room.

He sat up straight, closed his eyes, and prayed. Same as he ever did.

He opened his eyes; tried to sit still. But all this newness, so different from the routine of delivering oilfield equipment, was unnerving. Josy, and now Wacey, made him flinch. He was a dog-paddling in the deep.

But at least he had some partners.

Some women he could trust.

The gun-for-hire had talked around the future all night. But by the time he tucked her in he knew Wacey Foyt was thinking—maybe, just maybe—her years of living dangerously were coming to a close.

As dawn painted the edges of his shaded windows, he slipped out from under the quilts to make a pot of coffee, then crawled back under. Kept thinking. It was a lot to process and pretty damn exciting.

Josy Montemayor was a force of nature. He admired the woman. Greatly. He also lusted after her. Wanted to possess every inch.

But he did not love Josy.

Which was a damn shame. But the damn truth.

As a single ray of light pierced the room, at 7:03 a.m. he decided.

He'd throw the pigskin dice. Do right by Josy. Get on with the rest of his life.

If he was lucky, he'd make a life with this brave, tough, smart girl in the next room. He didn't know why or how, but he knew. Knew he owed Wacey something different. Something bigger—a chance to see what they could create. He wanted something more at the center of his universe than a Technicolor SurroundSound Dream featuring his star-crossed mom and dad.

It was time.

"We can do it, Wacey."

"Do what?" she immediately replied, as if she'd been listening, through the sheetrock, to his internal monologue.

"You watch," he said, hopping off the couch, pushing the hollow bedroom door open.

"Watch what?" she said, stretching tan, taut arms above her bed-head.

"Watch us."

Archie pulled out a foam mat from under his queen-size frame and positioned it, just so, on a well-worn section of Oriental rug that covered the entire room; yet another Continental treasure from his mother.

He cranked out fifty sit-ups, thirty-five leg lifts, fifteen push-ups. Then hurdler's, groin, hamstring, and lat stretches. Then thirty lunges, twenty reach-for-the skies, and a final twenty-five side-to-side pushups;

moving left on toes and tips—up/down; moving right on toes and tips—up/down.

After the rigorous routine, Archie crawled over and sat below his guest. Wearing nothing but boxers, he looked up, skin glowing.

"Never happens," he said, panting.

"What?"

"Morning exercises after drinking."

"We didn't have that many, did we?" she said, throwing back the duvet and sitting cross-legged on the rumpled sheets. "I feel pretty dang good."

After a breakfast of bananas and orange juice, Wacey asked Archie to drive her home.

"I'm glad you slept good," he said, pouring dark roast coffee into two Yetis.

"It's nice to be normal," she said, accepting the caffeine, gladly. "Every guy I know, their places are disgusting—trash, dirty clothes, dirty dishes. My place sucks, but it's clean. And empty. Seven years and not a single guy through the door."

"What about girlfriends?"

"A few, but they're bad news, too," she said, reaching in her jeans for a Scrunchy. She quickly tied her wettish hair in a funky side ponytail. "It's fucking depressing."

"I'm lucky to have the family I do," he said, locking the back door behind Wacey, who'd jumped off the concrete steps and was bouncing around the backyard. "Hell, I'm an old man and my parents are still lookin' after me."

Wacey bolted for the clover and broke out some crazy, hip-swinging moves, completely oblivious to Archie's musings.

"So how come we didn't do it last night?" she asked, coming at him with a rolling hip thrust. Archie squinted into the morning sun, shaded his eyes.

"You wanna go burn some calories?" he said, fishing the keys out of his jeans and punching the garage door opener. "We can dial that up, real fast."

"Just checkin'," she said, slapping Archie's butt as she skipped by and into the garage.

ARCHIE ROLLED THE COUGAR RED CADILLAC TO A STOP IN FRONT OF WACEY'S as-ugly-as-advertised four-plex, the bottom unit of a two-story built into a hill of red dirt. Her apartment was surrounded by a dozen more units slowly being reclaimed by creeping sand and mesquite. He knew the Sheriff had his reasons for stashing Wacey in this place, but she was definitely paying some dues.

"Seven years!" he said, circling the broken asphalt cul-de-sac, trying not run over a rusty tricycle. "That's a tough stretch."

"Tell me about it," she said, "I'd ask you to come in. I really would, but I don't want you to park your car 'round here; not even in the daylight."

"Hell, I was lookin' forward to being the first man to darken your door," he said, shaking his head at a windshield-busted Saturn parked next to a bank of waist-high dandelions. "I sure want to see you some more, you know, off-duty."

"You ought to let me stay in that spare house," she said, chewing on a finger nail. "Nobody's in there, right?"

"Not since I sold Keep on Truckin'," Archie said. "Although, I 'magine the Sheriff will have something to say about that."

"God, that would be awesome."

"What about your neighbors? Aren't they gonna miss you?"

"Who? The tweeker and his pitiful girlfriend," she said, trying to scoot closer, but thwarted by the console. "She's nice, but he's a dickhead. Actually, he *is* nice, when he's not using."

Archie stared out the windshield, past the dirt hills, out to the hogbacks in the distance.

"What's the matter?" she asked, slipping her little finger underneath his little finger. "Thanks for taking me to lunch and letting me spend the night."

"Absolutely, I'm glad for the company," he said, curling his pinky around hers. "Nah, you know, Keep on Truckin's been my life. I'm kinda flailing since I got bought out."

"What do you mean, flailing?"

"Figuring out what to do," he said, surprised when she webbed all her fingers through his. "I got a good plan. Been plannin' it for years. Just got a little high-centered's all."

"Is that what you call what Josy's doing to you?"

"What would you call it?"

"Pussy whipped."

Archie laughed. He loved this hard-nosed woman. She reminded him more and more of Sister Ernestine, even if she cussed a lot more. "I hear ya, but I got to do right by Josy. I owe her."

"Fuck that," said Wacey. "I didn't tell you last night, but I've known Josy a long time; since my El Paso days. I hung out with her one year down in OJ—not with her, but around her—when she was shacking up with Rudy. That's when us girls got the money across. Our insurance policy is what Windi called it."

"How long did Josy date Rudy Leos?" he asked, truly surprised that a girl of Ms. Montemayor's social stature would deign to hang out in a dusty outpost like Ojinaga.

"Cartel guys don't date, Archie," she said, letting go of his hand. "They use."

"How long's Chuck known about all this?"

"Forever. Sheriff Chuck knows everything about everybody," she said, sounding as if she'd rather not talk about her past life.

"I thought you ran with an oilfield crowd."

"Nope. Dope runners and thugs," she said. "Me, Josy and Windi—*¡Somos locas!* The bad boys loved us."

Archie knew he'd be learning a lot more about Wacey for a long time. She'd been busy.

"Windi's family's been around Marfa and Ojinaga for a long time. Her folks had a place on the river," she continued. "That's why she knew where the money was buried."

"Is she the one who got it in the bank?"

"No, Josy was the mastermind," Wacey admitted, with a sigh. "Josy's smart. She's the one who hooked us up with the banker who cleaned it all."

"So, it *is* your money," Archie concluded. "Helluva a lot more than the State of Texas."

"I don't know. Chuck doesn't want you mixed up in any of this," said Wacey, raking off the Scrunchy and re-positioning her ponytail. "He told me not to talk about it."

Archie leaned his head back on the headrest. "That's cool. The less I know the better," he said, setting both hands on the steering wheel. "Chuck's a funny dude. Like an Arch Angel or something."

"Thank God," she said. "He's the only reason I'm alive, by a long stretch. Thank God."

"Me too."

She tried to lean her head on his shoulder but the console kept her too far away. Wacey looked at Archie then sat up straight with her hands in her lap.

"So, what's next, secret agent girl?"

"Whatever the Sheriff tells me." She took a deep breath and closed her eyes. "I'm so tired of this shit. I want a real life. You know?"

They both jumped—completely startled—when a black Chrysler 300 crested the hill, bass thumping furiously. They watched carefully as the four-door sedan with blacked-out windows slow-rolled around the cul-de-sac.

"Fucking, fuck," said Wacey, hunkering down in the seat. "Don't look at'em."

Archie stared straight ahead as the Chrysler rolled to a stop, inches from his door. The passenger window glided down to reveal one low-riding skinhead and a driver staring holes through the Cougar Red Cadillac's lightly-tinted windows.

"Friends of yours?"

"No," Wacey said, turning so she was partially hidden by Archie. "They're looking for Jesse—the meth head."

Archie looked at the pair, then back at Wacey. "So, we sit?"

Although the Cadillac was sound-proofed to the max the reggaeton blasting from the trunk, made the entire car shake violently.

"These fucking guys," she said, pulling her gun from her purse on the floor.

"Come on now, I can deal with 'em," he assured his new partner, gliding his window. Archie tried to talk but was completely drowned out. He made a hand sign that cracked up the passenger.

Suddenly, the music muted.

"Mornin'."

The pair made no effort to acknowledge Archie's salutation. Just blank, tough-guy stares. Fortunately, Archie had vast oilfield experience dealing with this brand of attitude. He hung his arm on the window; took off his shades.

"Help you with somethin'?"

The younger of the two, in the passenger seat, with a red ink dagger bisecting his eyebrow and cheek, sneered at Archie, then turned to the driver, whose wife-beater revealed tattoos crawling up his neck and down both sleeves. "Yeah homes, you wanna help me with somethin'?"

Archie shrugged, "*¿Qué onda?*"

"*Oyé payaso*," said the driver, much to his passenger's delight. "*Pinche gringo.*"

"Fuck you, Chuy!" yelled Wacey, lunging across the console.

Archie, never taking his eyes off the two, talked her down. "*Tranquilo, tranquilo.*"

"*Tranquilo, tranquilo*," mocked the passenger, flashing a golden grill.

"I'll show you *tranquilo*, you fuckin' . . .."

Wacey crashed out of the passenger seat, flattening herself across the hood of the Cadillac. Archie watched—in utter disbelief—as his bodyguard fired three quick shots through the Chrysler's open passenger window. The passenger headrest exploded, raining chunks of foam rubber and leather onto the interior.

The driver instantly floored it, spraying the Cougar Red Cadillac with gravel as it fishtailed across the cul-de-sac.

"Comin' up on me! Motherfucker!" she yelled, two hands on her pistol, tracking the car with locked-arm precision. "You better fuckin' haul your ass!"

She continued to scan, arms locked, as the four-door disappeared down a hill and immediately reappeared in the distance tearing down the highway access road.

"I'll blow your motherfuckin' head off."

Archie burst out of the car.

"Damn, girl!" he yelled, banging the rooftop with both fists. "Damn nation!"

"Comin' up on me!" she yelled, completely oblivious to Archie—raging, furiously stomping the asphalt until the heel of her ankle boot flew into the weeds.

Archie watched in awe and instinctively hid behind the trunk as Wacey lost it.

"It's cool, Wacey. It's cool . . . Everything's cool."

She shoved the gun behind her back, turned to Archie, who was peeking over the roof. "Fucking assholes!" she screamed.

"Holy Moly, girl," he said, stepping out from behind the car.

She continued to stomp, then finally stopped, and slumped on the hood. "Those little fuckers. They know better."

Archie couldn't stop grinning as he joined her. "Did you mean to shoot that close?"

"I can handle my nine," she said, taking it out of her jeans and slapping the ceramic barrel. "You wanna try?"

"Hell no!" he said, waving off. "I hate 'em."

"Good," she said. "All they do is make you dead."

"Maybe not you," he said, touching the still-warm barrel. "That scared the crap out of me. Hell, I'm still shakin'."

"I know, sorry," she said, ejecting the pistol's magazine into her palm. "Kinda snapped, didn't I?"

"You think?" he said, raising a high five. "Hell yes, you can live in that house!"

Wacey left him hanging. Took off her shades and squared him up.

"I'm not kidding, Archie. You don't . . .."

"No, no, I get it," he said, taking hold of both hands. "I mean it. Whatever you need."

She didn't say a thing. Just wrapped her arms around a man for the first time in forever.

Archie stood still.

Wacey Foyt could hug on him as long as she wanted.

MPFB

"Talk about a pistol-packin' mama!"

The entire family was gathered around Sister Ernestine's dinner table listening intently to Archie's exuberant recounting of Wacey's morning security measures.

"Shot him in the head!" said Tallulah, hanging on her brother's every word. "All Ninja and shit!"

"Not *in* the head," corrected Matt, rolling his eyes. "*At* his head."

"Girl can shoot," agreed the Sheriff, helping himself to a serving dish brimming with broccoli and cauliflower. "She's as fine a gun handler as I've seen; male or female."

"I'm the safest human being in West Texas," Archie allowed, forking a ketchup-topped slice of meatloaf. "Hey mom, so you think it's okay if Wacey lives in the KOT house? You know, while it's empty."

"All taken care of," said Sister Ernestine, pleased her entire family was enjoying a home-cooked meal.

"Really?" Archie said, thrilled that he didn't have to lobby. "Do y'all own those houses? I didn't know what to tell her about rent."

"I bought'em from the Widow McAlester, but your mom owns'em now," said the Sheriff, giving Sister Ernestine a bit of a grimace. "That and a good bit of West Texas ranchland that *was* worthless."

"*Was* worthless? What do you mean?" asked Matt, snatching Tallulah's phone. "No technology at the table, Tules."

Tallulah stuck out her tongue but didn't make a fuss.

"Thank you, Matthew," said Sister Ernestine, patting her daughter's hand.

"It's a good story," continued the Sheriff. "I bought five hundred acres of tired old pasture on the Howard/Dawson line, 'round Ackerly. Bought it cheap from an old ranching family's kid. Back in '88. Twenty-five years later, Pioneer drills a wildcat. Now they've got five horizontal wells pumpin' and more on the way."

"Wow, you got the mineral rights?" asked Archie, in the general direction of his mom. "Not that it's any of my business."

"Of course, it's your business. And yes, we did retain the mineral rights," said Sister Ernestine, fixing her lover with a surprisingly stern look. "Thanks to our friend, Mr. Greene, they found lots of oil that's paid for lots of improvements around here."

"Good for Mr. Greene," said the Sheriff, frowning as he passed a basket of buttered rolls. "He can stack some more millions on top of his billion."

The Sheriff's girlfriend gave him a curt smile. "Let's hope you kids don't have to pay too steep a price for all that fracking."

It was a fair point. Fracking had revitalized the Permian Basin but at what cost to the aquifers? Not to mention the pollutants released into the air from flaring gas twenty-four seven.

"Archie, I'm personally supervising Wacey's move," added Sister Ernestine. "That young woman deserves better."

"She deserves to be alive," said the Sheriff, pushing back in his chair. "A lot easier to keep her safe in Lamesa than the busiest street in Big Spring."

"Chuck Fuchs, I can't believe you made her stay in that awful place for seven years."

When he objected, Sister Ernestine shushed him. "Disgusting. Absolutely disgusting."

Archie had to know. "Wacey let you in her house?"

"She most certainly did," said Sister Ernestine. "Her neighbors are ghastly."

The Sheriff stood up, carefully placed his napkin on top of his clean plate. "Do what's best, Sister. You always do."

On that, no one could disagree.

"So," Archie said, eyeing his fellow orphans. "Since I'm supposed to be mentoring you two, it's time for a field trip to Dallas. Time to meet Big Tex up close and personal."

"Mom! Can you believe I'm finally goin' to the State Fair?" said Tallulah, leaping up from her chair and hugging Sister Ernestine's neck.

"Yo, genius donkey," yelled Matt, tapping on his phone after cleaning his plate. "The State Fair doesn't start for two . . . no, three weeks."

Tallulah shot Matt the bird behind her mom's back.

"So, where's Wacey tonight?"

The Sheriff gave Archie a look.

"Over at the Settles," he said, under his breath. "I've been keeping a room pretty regular since they fixed it up."

"Have you now?" said Sister Ernestine, rising from the table. "Sensible of you not to drive back to Gail every night."

"They give me a free room in exchange for a night deputy," he said, in a more chipper tone. "They get some pretty rowdy folks in off the Interstate."

"Well, then *you* can tell Wacey I'll be at the house at eight a.m.," said Sister Ernestine, pulling two empty serving dishes from the table. "Can you drive me, Archie?"

"Yes ma'am."

"I'll have her there at eight," said the Sheriff, angling in behind his gal. He put his hands around her waist and kissed her on the cheek. "Thanks again for the supper. Sure is nice to have the kids home."

"I should say." She turned to give her long-time boyfriend a peck and a hug. "Take care of her, Chuck. That girl's not as tough as you think."

"I'd like to take care of her," said Archie, quietly.

AFTER DINNER, ARCHIE WAS ANXIOUS.

He wanted to text Wacey *and* Josy, just to check-in but stopped himself.

Instead, he sat with Tallulah on the sofa in the living room and chilled. The Tennessee Titans were crushing the Houston Texans on Thursday Night Football.

"Don't ever bet on NFL football," he admonished his sister, who was laughing at Roger, via text, who was winding down from stacking hundred-pound bales of alfalfa.

"I got a hundred pounds of love you can throw around," said Tallulah, talking to Roger's text. "Wait, what? Roger thinks my ass weighs a hundred pounds."

Archie had no comment.

After signing off with Roger, Tallulah jumped up from the couch and effortlessly lifted in the air for an imaginary spike. "BAM, mothertruckster!"

"Tules, why are you not playing volleyball?" said Archie, impressed by the spontaneous display of athleticism.

"Come on, March," she said, slouching back onto the couch. "I'm side out. I'm ready to hit the road."

Archie picked up Tallulah's phone. "What's P911 mean?"

"Dude!" she cried, snatching the phone out of his hands. "Never snoop a girl's text."

"My bad," said Archie, blushing at his transgression. "I'm just so social media clueless."

"Be like Sister," said Tallulah, fingers flying over the tiny keyboard. "She gives two fucks about all of it—texting, social media."

Archie would never get used to Tallulah's cursing, but she made a good point.

"BTW, P911 means 'Parent Alert'."

Archie chuckled; promised himself not to try too hard to keep up with teenage lingo.

"Thank God I'm nobody's parent."

"You're kinda my parent," said Tallulah, eyes back on her phone.

"How 'bout good influence; maybe teacher," said Archie, aimlessly surfing the sports channels: Australian Rules football; Premier League soccer, professional billiards.

"Do you know what MPFB means?" asked Tallulah.

"No," admitted Archie, frowning at his endless cluelessness.

"No biggie," she said, carefully placing her phone on the glass-top coffee table, screen down. "Do you really want me to play volleyball?"

"Mainly, I want you to go to college."

"Can't you teach me?" she whined. "Be like me and Matt's personal professor. That would be so cool."

"That would be cool," said Archie, fascinated by a Filipino pool prodigy, who was magically shooting his way around a nine-ball table.

"I bet *he* didn't go to college," said Tallulah, pointing at the big screen. "Dude's got skills, doesn't he?"

"Mad skills!" she said. "Did he just hit that ball *over* that other ball?"

"He did," said Archie. "And my guess is Dennis Orcollo never set foot in a college classroom. But I guarantee you he'll make his children go."

"Who's Dennis Orcollo?"

"That guy," said Archie, pointing at the pool shark sinking the last ball with a razor-slice into the side pocket. "Maybe you can be as good at volleyball as he is at pool."

"I hate volleyball. I really do," said Tallulah, punching the couch cushions. "Please don't make me play."

Archie pondered a few seconds.

"You should go to UH," he said. "Bright Lights. Big City. You'd love it."

"I'd be too scared," said Tallulah, getting teary-eyed. "FML!"

Archie scooted a little closer, so he could pat-pat her leg. "Don't stress. I felt the same way. I didn't have a clue what I wanted to do, except play ball."

"So what?" she said, wiping tears, but smiling. "What am I gonna do?"

"Walk on. Play volleyball. Give yourself some time to figure it out," he said, pat-patting. "Find out what you're passionate about, besides blasting a volleyball. You're damn good at that."

"You're sweet," she said, reaching for her phone. "Roger wants me to stay here so I can be his MPFB."

"Am I going to be embarrassed if you tell me what that means?"

"You don't get embarrassed," she said, punching his shoulder. "Except when you try to talk Mexican."

"My Spanish is embarrassing," said Archie. "It's shameful to live in Texas and not speak fluent Spanish."

"So you can be sexy with Josy in two languages."

"Maybe," he said, not able to look Tallulah in the eye.

"Arch the March!"

"So, you gonna tell me what MPBP means?" he asked, getting up from the couch to retrieve a way overdue beer.

"MP*F*B," she sighed. "It starts with My Personal and ends with Buddy."

"My Personal . . . Yep. Got it," said Archie, disappearing behind the kitchen door.

AFTER WALKING THE SHERIFF OUT TO HIS TRUCK AND SHOOTING A FEW HOOPS with Matt and Tallulah in the driveway, Archie wandered back to the master suite. Sister Ernestine, reading glasses on, was diagramming furniture placement for Wacey's bedroom, living room, dining room, and kitchen.

He took in the comfort and style of his mother's bedroom décor—an overstuffed reading chair and lamp, a chaise lounge in seafoam green velvet and a huge, gaily painted chest of drawers; her beautiful writing desk crammed with framed photos and topped with shelves of books, all in perfect harmony with the king-size bed heaped with pillows with its pleated silk headboard and matching dust ruffle. The house's cumulative splendor—all completely redecorated over the past five years—got him to thinking that his mom's royalty checks must be sizable.

He took a seat on a funky zebra-striped bench at the foot of her bed, stared between his boots at the intricate patterns of a gorgeous Oriental rug.

"How's Mr. Sonny Greene doing these days?"

Mr. Greene and several of his oilfield friends were early investors in Keep on Trucking.

Sister Ernestine finished her drawing and turned her chair to Archie.

"Sonny's good; or as good as can be expected for eighty-eight. He still smokes and drinks like there's no tomorrow."

"He should donate his body to science," said Archie, remembering fondly the day he introduced Mr. Greene to his mother at the Wall Street Bar and Grill in Midland, shortly after he'd returned from Victoria.

Archie and Sister Ernestine had come to town for an afternoon reading by Larry McMurtry at Midland College. McMurtry was Archie's long-time literary hero. He'd gotten hooked after reading *Hud* and *The Last Picture Show* in high school, then kept on reading the Houston trilogy at UH, and all of the *Lonesome Dove* books upon his return to Big Spring. Archie thought McMurtry was the best he'd ever read at understanding the way Texas people walked and talked. Especially his women—a magic act he held in the highest esteem.

"You know, Sonny's been taking care of my investments for some years now," said Sister Ernestine. "Chuck's never put his mind to making money."

"So, you've got a billionaire looking after your money and fifty-year lawman watchin' your back," said Archie, sitting on the edge of the pil-low-top mattress. "For a penniless French immigrant, I'd say you've got this American thing figured out pretty good."

"I was given every opportunity," said Sister Ernestine, capping her pen. "I just hate all this immigrant bashing."

"Politics has gotten to be such a freak show," said Archie, grimacing. "You're still the only person in Glasscock County I can tell that I voted for Obama . . . twice."

"Isn't he splendid," said Sister Ernestine. "It's fascinating to watch people watch President Obama. Especially people in West Texas."

"I still can't believe it," said Archie, smoothing the sides of his freshly barbered hair. "Never thought I'd see a Black President. Maybe in Tallulah's baby's day."

"Is Tallulah pregnant?"

"No, no. Sorry," said Archie. "Tallulah is *not* pregnant."

As far as he knew.

"Oh Archie, look!" she said, pulling a legal-size envelope out of a stack on her desk. "Sonny's found this fabulous wealth manager. At Raymond James."

"Wealth Managers? In Big Spring?" he asked, surprised. "I do my banking at Big Spring Bank & Trust."

"Bob Martin's his name. He's a Kappa Sig from UT. Sonny and all his oil pals just rave about him."

She glanced at the date on the big white envelope, then handed it to Archie. "You should think about letting him manage your money, now that you're so successful. I don't want you to waste a dime betting on football games."

"No worries, mom. I'm just stimulating the local economy," said Archie pulling a dozen sheets of paper marked "Confidential" on each page.

"Seventeen million!"

"Can you believe it?" she said, pressing her hands to her heart. "Sonny has the final say, but this Martin boy's been managing both our accounts and quite a few of Sonny's friends. He started buying distressed assets during the recession. I think he's a genius."

"That's great, mom," said, Archie, poring over the printouts. "Good Lord, look at all these blue chips. And bonds. And options. This guy knows what he's doing."

"It's all a bit unreal. I've never had money before. Real money," she said, watching her oldest son's rapt attention on the reams of financial information. "My father's family was very wealthy, a long time ago. They were fishmongers in Nice. For over a hundred years. My father had no interest in fish or selling his paintings. Can you imagine? He never worked a day in his life. I loved him, but he was from another time."

"So, that's what brought you to balmy West Texas," said Archie, carefully replacing the printouts in the legal envelope. "Tell me again; how'd you end up in San Angelo?"

"Oh, you know, I picked up that *National Geographic* and thought Big Bend was the most beautiful place on Earth," she said, eyes bright with nostalgia. "Mama was gone. And Papa didn't care. I wanted to escape. I hated the ocean. I hated the beautiful people. I was surrounded by wealth and beauty with no way to enjoy it. I loved France, but I had to get away."

"So off you went—the indomitable Ducornets!" said Archie, never tiring of his savior's colorful odyssey. "GTT! Gone To Texas."

"With the clothes on our backs," she said, with a heavy sigh. "I guess it killed Papa."

"Is that why you changed your name?"

"Oh, I don't know . . . I was sooo impetuous," she said. "I was like Tallulah. I spoke a completely different language. My mother could hardly stand it."

"We've got wild stories, mom. Mine's not half as wild as yours, but I swear that's why I'm a believer," said Archie, taking her hands. "Who else would bring me to you?"

"Chuck Fuchs."

"Exactly," said her son, gently squeezing her hands. "How in the world did he know?"

"Know?"

"Know to bring me to you."

"Oh, Chuck's been in love with me since I got here," said Sister Ernestine. "You were his dowry."

"Josy got really mad when I told her," said Archie. "She couldn't believe that nobody in my family took me in."

"Well, Josy's right," said Sister Ernestine. "Your Aunt Ida *did* come to get you, but I talked her out of it—broken English and all. She could tell I adored you and I was taking good care of you. I'll never forget, I was feeding you scrambled eggs in your high chair, in our little kitchenette behind the Sanatorium. Aunt Ida was watching us very carefully, and the next thing I knew, she was at the door with her suitcase. She kissed us on the cheek and left. Straight back to East Texas—Palestine, I think. I never heard another word. I hope that doesn't make you sad."

"Why? I'm the luckiest man in the world."

Sister Ernestine gave him a grateful smile.

Archie almost started to tell his mom about his recurring Big Arch and Bunny Dream— the Technicolor DreamScape—but didn't.

"Well, it's excellent news about your finances," said Archie, bending to kiss her forehead. She smelled like Chanel and meatloaf. "I love it, even if Chuck doesn't sound too thrilled."

"He's just jealous of Sonny," she sighed. "Always has been."

"Hard to compete with a billionaire in the money department."

"Oh Archie, it's like funny money. I can't spend it, except on this house. And yours. And Wacey's," she said, luxuriating in a long hug. "It'll all go to you kids."

"Nothing to the Sheriff," said Archie. "He's been awfully good to us."

"I should say, but he wouldn't think of it," she said. "He's mad that I let Sonny talk me into letting that oil company drill on that land we own."

"I doubt it," said Archie. "He's just sorry he didn't think of it first."

Sister Ernestine looked pained. Gave Archie a knowing smile. "We should go to Midland and have lunch with Sonny."

"I'd love to," he said. "All those guys, the lunch bunch at the Wall Street Grill, they were the key to Keep On Truckin. Sonny introduced me to just about every oilman in the Permian Basin."

"I wish you hadn't sold your company," Sister said, lingering with his hand. "I'm proud of you, but . . . I don't want you to drift into bad habits."

"I will, if I'm not careful," he said. "But listen, mom, I'll start a new one as soon as this non-compete is up. And off we go."

"Oh, perfect," she cried. "I'd love it if you'd train Matt to take over the next one."

"Not sure Matt wants to get into the hotshot business. He'd be a great coach. I think that's on his radar—coaching basketball."

"Oh really?" she said. "Where? In Garden City, I hope."

"His coach at Sul Ross offered him a grad assistant job," said Archie. "But I think he's little burned out on Alpine."

"I'm on the couch," said Matt. Suddenly, he appeared at the door separating his mother's bedroom from a commodious sitting room.

"Come in darling," she said to her favorite middle child. "Are you going to coach the Bearkats? The children would be thrilled!"

"Well . . . I hadn't really been thinking about working in the Garden."

"What do you want to do, Matt?" asked Sister Ernestine. "The world's your oyster."

"I'm thinking about trying to get on with the *Herald*," he said, stepping around Archie so she didn't have to crane her neck. "I've known Mr. Watkins for a long time. You think he'd take me on?"

"Absolutely; if he can," said Archie, delighted at the thought of Matt as a sportswriter. "Times are tough on newspapers these days. But Oak says they need digital people; social media and stuff. Can you do that?"

"I mean, I'm on Instagram and Twitter and Snapchat."

"What about Facebook?"

"That's for old people," he said, grinning at Archie. "I mean it's okay. You know, for keeping up with family and stuff."

"Listen, little brother," said Archie. "I guarantee the *Herald* can use an English major who's digital media savvy."

"And I can help," agreed Sister Ernestine. "While you're getting started. So exciting!"

Matt kissed her on the cheek.

Archie was glad he was from such a kissy family.

All at once, the sound of a basketball came caroming off the walls of the long hallway connecting the living area with the bedrooms. Tallulah popped her head inside, still dribbling.

"Tallulah, stop that racket!"

Tallulah picked up her dribble, clearly not cool with being scolded.

"You're such a doofus," said Matt. He knocked the ball out of his sister's hands and darted away, dribbling down the hall with Tallulah screaming in hot pursuit.

"Isn't it wonderful," said Sister Ernestine, as she and Archie enjoyed the sound of orphan laughter.

GONE TO TEXAS

The Mediterranean breeze, blowing soft and salty behind Nice's most popular tourist restaurant, was redolent with the aromas of exquisite French seafood. Papa Ernest and daughter Evangeline waited in the alley behind *La Gauloise* for their daily leftovers—a long-time accommodation in exchange for fresh bread delivered by the two Ducornets, morning, noon, and night.

"Papa, let's go to Texas."

"Yes," he said. "Let's go."

The eighty-four-year-old painter, whose luxurious white beard and leonine head resembled that of the American poet Walt Whitman, looked lovingly at his daughter in the fading spring light as she slowly turned the pages of a *National Geographic*. The magazine was thick with stunning photographs of a strange and beautiful landscape—a new national park in Texas—Big Bend.

"Oh, Papa," she exclaimed, kissing his head. "Wouldn't you love to paint this!"

The mistress of *La Gauloise* appeared with two heaping plates in exchange for three dozen fresh baguettes. "*Bon appetite, Ducornets!*"

"*Bon voyage,*" replied the cheeky teen. "*Au revoir!*"

Two months later, the resourceful twenty-eight-year-old French nurse trainee and her frail, but game, father boarded a Moroccan freighter and set sail for America.

After three weeks of daily battering on the brutal Atlantic Ocean, Evangeline slid her peacefully passed father into the cerulean seas off St. Kitts. After another week, drifting with no fuel in the balmy Gulf of Mexico, the ship was boarded by the U.S. Coast Guard. In time, Evangeline and the stowaways were transferred to Galveston, then unceremoniously herded onto a train for Chicago, with a sudden stop on a seemingly endless plain.

Evangeline found herself at a crossroads.

San Angelo, Texas to be precise.

"Nurses! Nurses!" came a cry from the dusty station platform. A formidable woman in all white, hands on hips, stood bellowing at the passenger cars. "Any nurses on board?"

Evangeline, the only detainee with any English, waved her hand and grabbed her valise reinforced with twine.

"Are you a nurse?" asked the administrator, eyes squinting in the blowing sand, as a stout young woman approached, positively beaming. "What's your name?"

"Sister Ernestine."

"You're a nun?"

"Yes. And a nurse."

"Come with me."

And just like that, the self-made, self-educated, self-proclaimed Sister Ernestine arrived in the New World; with no ecclesiastic sanction whatsoever—washed up on the shores of San Angelo; a place that could not have looked less like her home on the *Cote 'd Azur*.

But no matter.

Evangeline was now Ernestine. The south of France was now West Texas.

Soon enough, the stern administrator and her bevy of newly-trained nurses marveled at their young French protége's endless energy, her soothing accent, her supernatural ability to calm the anxious, especially the swarms of tubercular children under her care.

No one could believe a woman from the French Riviera was living in Tom Green County. As such, the in-name-only nun's transformation from undocumented immigrant to certified American citizen went completely unquestioned. Undoubtedly, it also, helped that Sister's skin was as white and smooth as alabaster.

In fact, the only question Sister Ernestine ever entertained were from grateful doctors, staff, and patients: "Are you from heaven?"

"No, no. I am from east of Monaco. West of Cannes," she replied, smiling. "From the city you call, Nice!"

And so it went, for a solid decade, Sister Ernestine growing, maturing, utterly transforming from European stowaway to super-competent Texas nurse, reveling in her independence. Totally at peace in her carpet grass oasis, her institutional island, with names that changed from Anti-Tuberculosis Colony No. 1, to McKnight State Tuberculosis Hospital, and finally, San Angelo State School.

All the while, a young Sheriff from Borden County, keeper of the peace in Gail, Texas, remained vigilant; eye on the prize—the radiant, elusive Sister Ernestine Ducornet.

Problem was, nobody knew how to date a nun. It just wasn't done.

Nevertheless, and despite being married to his job, Chuck Fuchs fell in love with the ample, wire-haired nun-nurse from Nice.

And don't think the good sister didn't notice.

The Sheriff was all lawman. Tall, wind-tooled, and stern. A man of distinct German ancestry, but in no way a threat, unlike her parent's Nazi tormentors. Chuck Fuchs was a kind man, as well. Arriving regularly with tubercular urchins in tow.

And so, for ten long years, the Sheriff waited.

Kept his council.

Made no move.

FRANCIS MCCOMBER HANGS IN MCCAMEY

MCCAMEY, TEXAS
SEPTEMBER 10, 2015

The Big Empty was not forthcoming.

While Sister Ernestine and the Sheriff helped Wacey move into her new digs, Archie took Matt and Tallulah on a three-day search for an edge—injury reports, player/girlfriend gossip, coaching irregularities—anything that might tip the scales in his favor now that he was $10K in the hole and slightly panicked. He trusted Okinawa's picks, but after the Sweetwater loss, Archie was looking for an edge. Real-time, actionable intel.

Off they drove in the Cougar Red Cadillac—Garden City to Big Lake, Big Lake to Balmorhea, Balmorhea to Pecos, Pecos to Monahans, Monahans to Crane, Crane to McCamey. After canvassing school yards, barbershops and game rooms, Dairy Queens and C-stores, beer joints and motels, shooting the bull with lots of likely informants, not a single morsel was gathered. In three whole days!

Except how to successfully avoid arrest in the Permian Basin barrens of Reagan County.

"Mr. Weesatche," said the DPS trooper, scanning Archie's driver's license. "Do you realize you were driving ninety-nine miles per hour?"

"Yes sir. I'm sorry about that."

"Is there an emergency?"

"No, sir."

"Where are you headed this morning?"

"Yes sir, taking these two to the swimming hole in Balmorhea," he said to the trooper, handing over his registration and insurance. "First time she's ever been."

"Mornin' sir," said Matt, adding a tiny wave.

"Hi, officer!" yelled Tallulah, sticking her pony-tailed head between the front seats.

The young trooper, looking razor-sharp in pressed uniform and mirror shades, packing all manner of armaments on his thick patent leather belt, seemed bemused by the cutest teenager in Texas. He nodded at Matt, nodded at Tallulah, then stepped away to check Archie's information.

As the lawman strode back to his black and white supercharged Camaro, Archie prayed it wasn't a canine unit. He assured his passengers that he appreciated their respective salutations but warned against any further conversation.

"Come on, March," cried Tallulah. "Po-Po needs some love!"

Matt wheeled in his seat. "Zip it, Hopalong. He's serious!"

Fortunately, Tallulah rolled in her tongue just as the trooper reappeared in the window.

"Mr. Weesatche," he intoned, scribbling on a steel-case ticket pad. "I need you to keep your speed at the posted limit."

"Yes sir," he said, maintaining a chipper tone.

"Due to the clear visibility and dry road conditions," said the officer, handing Archie a citation. "I'm only going to issue you a ticket for excessive speed.

"Yes sir," answered Archie, grimacing as he reached for the slip of paper.

"You need to set a good example for these young folks."

"Yes sir. Thank you, officer," said Archie, looking the lawman in the eye.

The trooper leaned forward to peer in the backseat. "Enjoy your swim, ma'am."

"I will! Thank you!" gushed Tallulah, sitting up straight. "Is it so cold? I hear the water is so cold!"

"Yes ma'am, the water temperature is a constant seventy-two degrees," replied the trooper. "It's the largest pool in Texas at one point three acres and cycles through over fifteen million gallons of spring-fed water a day. No chlorination required."

"That's so cool!" said Tallulah, all aflutter. "Do you want to come swimming with us?"

"Yes ma'am, I would," he said, offering the slightest of smiles. "Duty calls. Y'all be safe."

As Archie glided the window closed, Tallulah fell between the seats in full swoon. "OMG, he's *so* gorgeous! Can I please have his baby? Oh my God!"

Archie and Matt cracked up, pat-patting their prostrate sister.

"Goals, Tules," said Matt, laughing. "Goals."

"How much'd he get me for?" asked Archie, handing the ticket to Matt.

It had been a few years since he'd received one. A miracle considering how many miles he racked up every year. Archie's brother flipped the ticket over and read the fine print.

"Ninety-nine in a seventy-five," said Matt. "Let's see, twenty-four over the speed limit. You owe Reagan County Two hundred and ninety-eight dollars."

"Two hundred ninety-eight dollars!" cried Archie. "Damn nation!"

"You're lucky, bro," crowed Matt. "One more mile an hour over would have cost you three hundred and thirty dollars."

"Seriously?"

"*En serio, vato,*" said Matt, handing Archie the ticket, pointing to the schedule of fines.

"That's some mad cheddar, March," said Tallulah, easing into her back-seat lair. "Better slow your roll."

"Yeah, yeah," whined Archie, accelerating back onto the empty two-lane. "Y'all better find me a quarterback with some baby mama drama."

AS THE SUN'S LAST RAYS LASERED THROUGH THE MINI-BLINDS OF ROOM 127 at the La Bonita Inn in McCamey, Archie morphed into teacher mode.

Matt was sprawled out, face down, at one end of the queen-size while Tallulah sang, eyes-closed, along with her pop chanteuse of the moment, Iggy Azalea.

Archie made hand motions once, twice, then got up off his bed and stood above the catatonic teenagers, arms crossed.

"Hey! Earth to students! Hey!" said Archie, tapping Matt's shoulder and grabbing Tallulah's tennis shoe.

He explained that he'd read the first few pages of Sister Ernestine's handpicked selection *The Short Happy Life of Francis Macomber* out loud, to get in the mood, and then they'd trade off a page apiece.

That plan met with silence. Airbuds jammed deep inside ear canals.

"Come on now; you're gonna love it," said Archie, turning off the TV and propping two pillows behind his back in the recently remodeled room, renting for a weekday $67.50; down from a boomtown $125, six months ago.

"Do we have to?" whined Tallulah, willing, at this point, to take out a single Airbud. "We need a little *me* time."

"And what is your answer when Sister Ernestine asks how you liked Hemingway's masterpiece?"

Matt turned off his phone and attempted to look interested. "How 'bout it Tules?"

"Ask IGGY!" cried Tallulah.

With that, Archie took three double-spaced copies of the story from his leather portfolio, threw one copy to Tallulah, one copy to Matt, sat down in bed, and read.

The sound of Archie's slow drawl, reciting line upon line of Hemingway's elegant, muscular prose, had a mesmerizing effect. The forty-eight-page story about a rich American couple behaving badly on African safari, some-how took hold of the youngsters.

"Y'all want to read?" Archie said, "Out loud?"

"I wanna read! I wanna read!"

"Excellent, Tules," said Archie, leaning across the beds. "Right here. Top of page three."

When Tallulah began at a painfully slow pace, Matt looked up but didn't say a word. Just shook his head.

What Matt didn't remember was how far his sister had progressed. He forgot that Tallulah was "homeschooled" at the Yearning for Zion Ranch by her brainwashed, overburdened mother. He forgot that Sheriff Fuchs brought Tallulah to Sister Ernestine when she was thirteen, reading at, maybe, third-grade level.

"I like it better when you read," she said, after gamely slogging through a page.

"You did fine. That was good," assured Archie. "Matt, you read a page."

"Yeah, you read, Mr. College," she said. "Let see how smart you sound."

Plenty smart, as it turned out.

Matt read on about Mr. and Mrs. Macomber's glamorous Jazz Age lifestyle full of luxurious travel to exotic destinations—Francis, the wealthy scion of a Chicago financier; Margot, the spokesmodel for a famous brand of hand soap.

They all felt bad for Francis when he pleaded with his wife not to seduce the manly Mr. Wilson. "You promised," scolded Francis.

Margot's response was a beeline straight for the Englishman's double-wide cot.

Tallulah followed along for a page or two, then stared blankly.

Matt finished his page after Mrs. McComber slept with the gruff British hunting guide.

"What a piece of work!" Matt said, eager to continue. "Margot thinks her husband's not going to notice she's sleeping with Wilson?"

"'The rich are different from me and you,'" quoted Archie. "That's what F. Scott says."

"Cold-blooded is more like it."

"What do you think, Tules?" asked Archie, hoping to re-engage his pupil. "What's Margot up to?"

"I'm bored."

"What? Come on Mud Hut," said Matt, slapping the top of her jutting hip.

"Shut up, Matt," she said, flying upright, eyes watering. "Y'all read."

Archie and Matt looked at each other.

"Nah, listen, it's cool. We can pick it up tomorrow," said Archie, wishing he'd seen this coming. "We're not even halfway through."

"I really like it," said Matt. "I can't believe I haven't read it before."

"*I can't believe I haven't read it before,*" mocked Tallulah. "Hey, nerd."

"Really?" said Matt. "Says the genius who can't even read a full page."

"Matt . . . no sir," said Archie.

Tallulah launched her copy straight at Matt's head. She cursed her brother, then ran to the bathroom and slammed herself inside.

"Aw hell," whispered Archie.

"You too, Uncle Archie! I don't want to play fucking volleyball. You too! Just leave me alone."

Matt giggled into the crook of his arm like he was covering up a sneeze.

"Hey, you can't be saying that," whispered Archie, signaling to cut it out. "Hey, Tules, I'm sorry. We aren't picking on you. We . . ."

"Are too!" she screamed behind the door. "I hate . . . why are y'all pickin' on me?"

"Wait. No, ma'am," pleaded Archie.

"Come on, Tules!" said Matt.

"I wanna go home," she continued, literally stomping in the tiny bathroom. "Such assholes!"

This outburst terrified Archie. He'd probably triggered all kinds of bad memories from Tallulah's days in the YFZ cult.

The toilet seat slammed. Toilet paper furiously unrolled.

He pointed at the bathroom.

"Go!" he whispered to Matt. "Talk to her."

The English major frowned mightily, but rolled off the bed and talked to the door. "Come on, Tules. I was just giving you a hard time. Calm down, okay?"

"I'm sorry about the volleyball, too," added Archie. "Do whatever you want. I won't say another word about volleyball."

They could hear their sister crying behind the door, her breathing jagged.

"Come on, Tules," pleaded Matt.

The toilet finally flushed. The crying slacked until all they heard was the fan.

"Okay, okay," she said. "Just gimme a minute. Fuck my life!"

"Yeah, yeah, FML," said Matt, in a weary tone.

"Matt!" whispered Archie, worried that he'd set her off again.

"I'm sorry," he said, then started banging on the door. "Hey, lemme in. I drank like a gallon of Mountain Dew."

"Fine!" she screamed, bursting out the door.

Archie sprang off the bed and followed her outside into the floodlit parking lot.

"Tallulah, I'm . . . ."

"Chill, Arch," she said, bent at the waist as if she'd run a race. "I'm not going postal. Just chill."

"Got it. Chillin'," assured Archie, hot-footing it on the sidewalk. "Right here chillin' . . . not saying a word."

Archie's barefoot antics made Tallulah hiccup and laugh at the same time. "I'm just so . . . so . . . you know!" she said, swiping at the rings of black mascara under her eyes. "I just wanna . . . think!"

"I hear you," said Archie, putting one foot on top of the other. "That's exactly what we can do; for the rest of the year. I promise. Drive Texas, eat Dairy Queen, watch football, and chill. That's it. All the time in the world to figure it all out."

"I'm sorry," she said, standing there, long-armed, slump-shouldered, but smiling. "Can I get a hug?"

Archie took a step, then hesitated. "I'm sorry Tallulah."

"It's fine," she said, shrugging. "You don't have to hug me."

"No, no . . ." he said, gingerly walking to her and wrapping her up, but not too tight. "I'm sorry about the volleyball stuff, you . . ."

"You're fine. I deserve it," she said, laying her head on his shoulder. "I just need a hug."

Archie swayed with her, tightened his hug, admired her sinewy strength. Seconds later, Tallulah twirled away and bopped back inside.

THE NEXT MORNING, WHILE HIS STUDENTS SLEPT, ARCHIE WAS UP WITH THE sun, knocking out his morning exercises and twelve laps on the McCamey High School track. He called Sheriff Fuchs on his way back to the La Bonita.

"Your mom's got Wacey all squared away," said the Sheriff, who was driving in from Gail. "She also said Sterling City's playing in the Garden on Friday. Tallulah's gonna want to watch Roger, I'm sure."

"That'd be good. She's strugglin' a little bit," said Archie. "She's not goin' to Tarleton."

"Aw hell," said the Sheriff. "I don't even pretend to understand that nonsense."

"College'd be good for her, but you can't force it," said Archie, thinking back to the previous night's upset. "How old was Tallulah when you got her out of that cult?"

"Thirteen, I believe," said the Sheriff, cussing a coyote, who'd darted out in front of his truck. "She had . . . six, seven sisters and a momma at her wit's end. Lord, I'm glad I pried her loose from that place."

"What was it called? The XYZ Ranch?"

"The YFZ Ranch—Yearning for Zion," corrected the Sheriff. "Damndest bunch of zealots you ever saw. Not quite as crazy as the Waco bunch, but damn close."

"Oh, damn!" said Archie. "I forgot about Waco, who was that—David Koresh? Those Branch Davidians were loaded for bear. Shot the hell out of the ATF, didn't they?"

"Yes, they did. And some," said the Sheriff. "The YFZ fella—Tallulah's daddy—he's as crazy as Koresh; just not as well-armed. Thank goodness. He's more interested in knocking up little girls than getting in a gun battle with the State of Texas. After Waco, I guaran-damn-tee you, the State of Texas isn't gettin' outgunned again."

"I 'magine not," said Archie, not wanting to admit he was wandering the Trans-Pecos—the $650,000 a million miles away. "So, all good, Chuck. I'll have'em back in time for the game, if not sooner. Tell Wacey howdy."

"I'll do it," assured the Sheriff. "Drive safe."

YEARNING FOR TALLULAH

ELDORADO, TEXAS
MARCH 29, 2008

Sheriff Fuchs couldn't tell if the gangly girl in the passenger seat of his Borden County F-250 was listening to the radio, or not. Her thousand-yard stare indicated not. He turned down the volume on the police scanner and focused on an AM radio report:

> *"Texas authorities have taken physical possession of the YFZ Ranch bringing an end to the place known as a refuge for polygamous sexual assault in the name of religion. The Fundamentalist Church of Jesus Christ of Latter-Day Saints, a rogue offshoot of the Mormon Church, bought the "Yearning for Zion" Ranch for $20 million in 2003. Located in remote Schleicher County, the ranch consists of nearly 1,600 acres with living quarters, barns, classrooms, and a towering temple, that on a clear day, can be seen in the county seat of Eldorado. When officers visited the ranch on a welfare check, they found evidence of underage marriage and sexual abuse. Criminal charges were filed against a dozen men, including FLDS leader Warren Jeffs, for allegedly sexually assaulting two girls, ages 12 and 15, he took as spiritual wives."*

The Sheriff peeked over at his third orphan rescue.

"He never touched me," said the soon-to-be Tallulah. "Not him. Nobody."

Before the Sheriff could think, he was pat-patting the tall, thin girl, who was still wearing twin pigtails, a full-length homemade dress, and tennis shoes.

"Good," he said, grateful that she didn't flinch at *his* touch.

The Sheriff wanted to say more. To assure her that no one would harm her; that he would protect her. But Chuck Fuchs had made similar trips with his sons, Archie and Matt. And remembered well, that during these first lonely miles, on an unknown journey, it was best to keep his own counsel.

OAK BALES A COTTON FARMER

POST, TEXAS

SEPTEMBER 11, 2015

Archie, Matt, and Tallulah trudged out of Karen's Kountry Korner in Post.

The orphan trio had each ingested extra-large Chicken Fried Steaks for the third time in a week. As Archie stretched his long wingspan, his phone's distinctive bongo ring tone bounced off the heat waves.

"What's up, Oak!" he said, hitting the unlock and start engine buttons on the Cougar Red Cadillac. He watched Tallulah dive into the back seat, a move she'd perfected over the past days of fruitless West Texas wandering.

"Got a live one, dawg," crowed Okinawa. "Tors plus ten over Dimmit *in* Lamesa."

"Lamesa!" said Archie. "Dude, they've lost like forty straight."

"Arch, this one's good, I'm telling you," said Okinawa, lowering his voice till he got back to his cubicle at the *Herald* Sports Desk. "Met him last night at The Settles. Big cotton farmer in town for some Co-Op meeting. Anyway listen, the guy's from Dimmitt. Played ball for Tech; his son's the big dog for Dimmitt this year."

"Was he drinking?"

"Hell yeah! Seven and seven out of a damn hose," he continued. "Dude was talkin' all kinds of smack."

"Perfect!" said Archie, attempting to pull up MaxPrep's intel on Lamesa and Dimmitt on his cell phone.

When Matt came scuffling across the parking lot, Archie threw him the keys. About the only positive thing he'd managed on the trip was teaching his roommates a few Weesatche rules of the road.

"Listen, dawg. It's the coach—he's in a bind," said Okinawa. "Man ain't gonna live long enough to get fired if he don't win tonight. You know Darryl?"

"Yeah, I know Darryl," said Archie. "He was a damn good coach at Klondike."

"Exactly, but he ain't worth shootin' right now," said Okinawa. "Him and his girlfriend got a bad meth jones. Wacey probably knows her. Real freaky chick."

"So, this is a tragedy; not a damn football bet."

"Whatever Arch," said Okinawa, as if his feelings were hurt. "Look, you asked me to find good bets, and this a good bet. Come on, dawg! I could use the juice."

"Hell, I'll loan you some money."

There was a long pause. Archie could hear Okinawa's labored breathing.

"I don't need no damn handout," said Okinawa. "You always actin' like you wanna be a playa, but you ain't got no heart, Arch."

Now it was time for Archie to catch *his* snap.

"Lamesa plus ten," said Archie, opening the passenger door and grabbing his sunglasses to cut the midday glare. "That's what you're selling? For ten K?"

"All day."

Archie dropped down into the seat; catching Matt and Tallulah staring.

"Book it!" he said. "And tell that boll weevil I'm bringing cash."

"Now you talkin'!" said the *Herald* Sports Editor. "Kickoff's at seven. I'll be in the box by six."

"Alright, I'll see ya," he said, buckling his seat belt. "Might even bring these two cherries I got tagging along if they'll grow a pair."

"You should buy me a pair," yelled Tallulah, stretched out in the back. "I want some fun bags."

"Is that your crazy sister?" asked Okinawa.

"Oh yeah!" laughed Archie. "Say hi, Tallulah."

"Hey Okinawa!" she said. "How's tricks?"

"What? I'm on speaker?"

"Yes, you're on speaker. The Cougar Red Caddy is always dialed in," said Archie. "You're right about one thing. It's time for the Golden Tornados to twist up on ol' Dimmitt!"

"I'm tellin' you, Arch," assured Okinawa. "This one's for real."

"Better be," he said, punching end call.

"Uncle Arch, gettin' all krunk!" said Tallulah, lifting herself between the front seats.

"Well, we've been out here three days, diggin' up nothin'," said Archie. "This is real intel. Human condition intel."

"What's up with the coach?" asked Matt. "He huffin' meth?"

"That, and owes his dealer a bunch of money," said Archie, motioning for Matt to go.

"Him and his skank girlfriend," added Tallulah.

"Tallulah, you better stay the hell away from that stuff," said Archie.

"Yeah, Tules," said Matt, piling on. "Don't be such a meth head."

"Lameness," said Tallulah. "I'm totally pure, unlike some dudes I know."

"Whatchu know?" asked Archie, whiplashing in mock surprise.

"I know that you smoke ratchet dirt weed," she said, punching Archie's shoulder. "March, you need to upgrade."

"Don't be dissing the dirt—I'm just keeping it five percent, *vato*," said Archie, trying to pop the top of Tallulah's hand, but she was too quick.

"I bet Mr. Matt can get some dope dope," said Tallulah.

"Rocky Mountain hydro!" said Matt, with a sly grin. "But you better bring your bank."

"Uncle Arch is slingin' all kinds cheddar!" said Tallulah, digging her bare feet into the padded roof. "All Daddy Warbucks and shit."

"That's good bullshit, Tules," allowed Archie. "But I'm also eight hundred years old, and ostensibly, your mentor."

"What's ostensibly?" asked Tallulah.

"In theory," said Matt.

"As in, ostensibly," Archie continued. "I should be modeling responsible adult behavior instead of devising illegal gambling schemes and debating marijuana potency."

"Don't be trippin', Marchabout!" said Tallulah, throwing her hands up. "We're the West Texas Posse. Orphan's rule!"

Archie was impressed with Matt's steady hand as they sped west on Highway 82. When they turned south on Texas 87 and picked up cell coverage, Sheriff Fuch's voice beamed in over ten speakers.

"Where you at, son?"

"South of Post, headed for Tahoka."

"Glad I caught you," said the Sheriff. "Sister wants you to bring Matt and Tallulah back to the Garden. Tallulah, you promised Roger's folks they could tailgate."

"I-G-G-Y! I totally forgot," moaned Tallulah.

"Sweet!" said Matt. "Tailgating with the Tedescos!"

"Please, can I go with you to Lamesa?" pleaded Tallulah.

"No ma'am. We're headed straight to the Garden," said Archie, eliciting a fresh round of howls. "And then I'm headed to Lamesa. The Golden Tornados are about to take your boy to the promised land!"

"Lamesa!" said the Sheriff. "They haven't won a game since the Tet Offensive. How much?"

"Ten K," he said. "Oak lined up some guy named McIntyre out of Dimmitt."

"I know him," he said. "Big cotton farmer. Simple as salt. You'll win. Bye."

Matt made it back to the Nice House in record time, covering a hundred miles just in time to watch Roger Tedesco Sr. setting up his massive rolling BBQ pit under the ample shade of Sister Ernestine's live oaks. Archie and Matt got a kick out of Tallulah, instantly making nice with her future father-in-law, lifting a thin volleyballer calf as she leaned in to hug the barrel-round former sheepherder.

Inside, they found Sister Ernestine scurrying around the house wearing her famous "Bearkat Flow" a billowy caftan, custom-made in France, with kaleidoscopic swirls of red and black silk. Archie pecked her on the cheek then took a seat to call Sheriff Fuchs.

Archie was half-glad he wasn't going to be around to see Garden City whip up on Sterling City. Both teams were 2–0, but Roger Tedesco Jr. was the Eagles' only chance of staying close with the Bearkats, who had a trio of quick-hitting scat backs and a defense that hit much harder than their 150-pound average. Garden City probably wouldn't "forty-five 'em," but they'd win handily.

"What's cooking, Sheriff?" asked Archie, watching his mother's favorite tabby cat, Martin Buber, slide under the table and arch her back against his boots. "Roger Senior's got about fifty lamb kabobs on the grill if you're in the area."

"I'm in Gail," said the Sheriff, sounding frazzled. "Wacey's gonna be busy tonight."

"Aw, hell," said Archie. "I was hoping to take her to the Lamesa game."

"Got her up on Gail Mountain; spyin' on some new smugglers. Looks like Josy and Rudy might have some competition in OJ," said the Sheriff. "And hey, and I know that blowhard McIntyre. He ran for Castro Sheriff a few years back. Got his ass stomped."

"Okinawa says he's plenty rich," said Archie.

"Hundred years of irrigated cotton will do that for you."

"As long as he's payin' cash, I'm good," said Archie, stroking the tabby's grey and black striped fur. "Tell Wacey I miss my bodyguard."

"She'd rather be with you, I guarantee," said the Sheriff. "I think she's smitten."

"Me too."

GOLDEN TORS TO THE RESCUE

"Friday Night Lights, baby!"

The excitable Archie Weesatche yelled into the windshield of the Cougar Red Cadillac as he wheeled into the bustling parking lot of Lamesa's Tornado Stadium. There was still plenty of daylight savings time left as he locked the door and adjusted his pretty new UH ball cap. Archie sniffed a wee nip in the air and, perhaps, the promise of more football-like weather.

The stadium scoreboard read twenty-eight minutes to kickoff. Archie joined a multi-generational throng of Lamesans—youngsters, graduates, and good citizens—ambling to the gate. He stepped up to the ticket table where a grumpy lady with a face and hairdo from the fifties stared at him blankly.

"What's the UH stand for?"

"University of Houston," he said, cheerfully handing her a twenty.

"Never heard of it," said the cashier. "Don't you have nothin' smaller?"

"No ma'am," he answered, as she pulled bills from her metal box. "Guess you're not a fan. You look like a Cougar."

"That's a funny thing to say," she declared, frowning prodigiously. The woman adjusted her visor, licked her finger, then counted out fifteen singles.

The Anti-Cougar slapped the stack of one-dollar bills in one hand while Archie gave her the three-finger UH sign with the other.

"Thank you," he said, with an oversized grin. "Go Coogs!"

"Next!"

Upon closer inspection, Archie wished he'd traded with the other cashier—clearly a recent graduate—wearing a smallish Lamesa Chicken Fried Steak Festival T-shirt. Archie made a mental note to look up the festival date.

As he walked through the peppy hometown crowd, covered in shade by the towering erector set bleachers, Archie was proud to be participating in this much-revered small-town ritual. It was true, the Lamesa Golden Tors hadn't won many games of late, but that didn't stop the natives from swarming into their sixties-era stadium.

While waiting in the concession line, Archie pulled up a *Texas Monthly* article on his phone about Governor Perry (from nearby Paint Creek) signing a Texas Legislature Proclamation recognizing Lamesa as the official home of Chicken Fried Steak, invented and first served by a Lamesa short-order cook in 1915.

When he stepped to the counter, he was thinking corndog, then ordered his go-to: Frito Pie and a Dr. Pepper. "Unless y'all got a chicken fried steak hiding back there."

"No sir, but you should come back for the festival," said a spirit-teamer manning the chili pot.

"When is it?"

"In the spring sometime," she said, ladling Wolf Brand into a side-split bag of Fritos.

"Last week in April!" confirmed a nacho assembler with a towering blond beehive.

Archie scooped up his Friday night dinner and left the chili ladler five dollars.

"Thanks, Mister!" gushed the girl, folding the bill into her apron. "Go Tors!"

"Go Tors!"

Archie climbed the aluminum bleachers to the top and knocked on the press box window. Okinawa was pecking away at his computer. He always wrote his lead and first draft before the game, so when the score went final, all he had to do was fill in the stats, re-cap the game's stars and big plays, and email it to the *Herald* Sports Desk.

While he waited, Archie admired the Golden Tornado dance and pom squad warming up their gold and black sequins in the setting sun. Grooved with the line drummers tapping out little riffs while the horn section toot-tooted their mellifluence.

"What's up Archie Bell and the Drells!" said Okinawa, bounding down the aisle, giving his old friend a big hug.

"Where's Big Papi?"

"Who the hell is Big Papi?" said Okinawa, giving him the fish eye. "Man, you always talkin' code. Like your crazy-ass sister."

"Where is the cot-ton far-mer from Dim-mitt," said Archie.

"Oh, McIntyre. He up in Lubbock geehawing with his new Chinese partners," he said, nodding to the field. "Big Fifty-five's his boy."

"Where?"

Okinawa pointed to a white and purple behemoth swivel-stepping across the width of the playing field.

"Oh man! He's a big ol' Bobcat," said Archie, admiring the linebacker's lightness of foot. "Bet that sucker can fill a hole."

"Big Cat's averaging fifteen tackles a game," said Okinawa. "He had twenty-one last week against Panhandle."

"Twenty-one! And you think ten points is gonna get it done?" said Archie, pulling his trusty Zeiss binoculars from the back pocket of his jeans. "Against that beast?"

"Darryl's gettin' em fired up," Okinawa promised. "I was down in the locker room. He's breathin' fire, brother."

"He better be," said Archie, following young McIntyre as he trotted back to the visitor's bench.

"He'll have'em jumpin'," said Okinawa, cracking his bull neck with an awful pop. "I wasn't the only visitor in the locker room, if you know what I mean."

Damn, thought Archie. Nothing to get the competitive juices flowing like a bunch of drug thugs lurking in the locker room shadows.

"Hey, shoot me a text when our farmer gets here," said Archie, knowing that Oak needed to get back to the press box. "Sheriff Fuchs says McIntyre doesn't have enough sense to spit downwind."

"Your Dad says that 'bout everybody," said Okinawa, pulling the press box door open. "Ten K, comin' your way, Arch!"

Archie waved him off, found a prime spot above the fifty-yard line, and sat tall in his "old lady" seat. After a long Baptist prayer, a moment of silence for 9/11, and a lovely, off-key rendition of the Star-Spangled Banner by the Golden Tor band, Lamesa kicked off into a semi-cool breeze.

Though clearly unintentional, the squib kick was perfect; crazy-bouncing clean through Dimmitt's front line. A Bobcat return man finally chased down the ball, but had to cover it in the end zone. A gang of Golden Tornados piled on for a safety.

Lamesa 2–0. Excellent start thought Archie. Up twelve, with two lifetimes to go.

Unfortunately, the miscue woke up the visitors who immediately scored four unanswered touchdowns. Four! As in twenty-four points! As in another $10K down the drain.

The only silver lining in the entire first half was that Dimmitt's kicker was hurt, forcing the Bobcats to go for two after every touchdown. Somehow, Lamesa stopped Dimmitt's two-point conversions each time. Otherwise, it was a complete rout—Dimmitt's well-drilled, well-conditioned White Boy/Mexican-American mix against Lamesa's uninspired, outhustled all-Latino welterweights.

Dimmitt trotted into the locker room at the half, up 24–2.

Archie got up to stretch. It was a gorgeous night, not quite crisp, but increasingly temperate as the sun set. He banged on the press box window. Okinawa was on his cell, looking none too pleased.

"Ridiculous, man! I'm talkin' to his no-play-calling ass, right now," said Oak, stomping down the bleachers. "Had all the momentum after that safety; then nothing!"

"Hell, don't sweat it, Oak," said Archie.

But Archie *was* sweating it, he was not looking forward to talking to his mom about a bridge loan. A big bridge loan.

"I'll set his ass straight," grumbled Okinawa, heading for the Lamesa locker room.

While his bookie properly motivated the Golden Tornado coach, Archie sweet-talked the Chicken Fried Steak cashier into letting him out without having to buy another ticket. He moseyed out to the Cougar Red Cadillac. It was high time for a puff.

In fact, it was going to take all manner of self-medication to adhere to Archie's one ironclad rule—a man's got to finish the game. Four quarters; forty-eight minutes. In person.

And sure enough, when Archie returned to his stadium seat, the Lamesa Golden Tornados were born again. The Tors ran back the second-half kickoff ninety-one yards for a touchdown, then converted a sweet two-point option: 24–10.

Lamesa pick-sixed Dimmitt's first pass of the second half and converted another two-point play: 24–18.

Lamesa recovered the ensuing on-side kick, then executed a flawless Hook-and-Ladder.

Young McIntyre, personally stuffed the two-point conversion, but Lamesa had miraculously tied the game: 24–24.

And just like that—total bummer to utter euphoria—in the space of six minutes and fifty seconds.

Archie breathed easy; his ten-point spread restored. "Come on, Tors! Hold 'em!"

Midway through the third quarter, a track meet broke out. For the rest of the game. Dimmitt scored. Lamesa scored. Dimmitt scored. Lamesa scored. Six times! Every player, on both sides, was so dog-tired, so completely gassed, that nobody could tackle.

Except for Big Number 55.

With seven seconds remaining in the game, Lamesa went for a game-winning touchdown from the two-yard line.

Unfortunately, for the Golden Tornados, The Beast was waiting.

On an ill-advised sweep, two hundred-thirty pounds of pissed-off Bobcat rammed Lamesa's 160-pound tailback into the sideline, snuffing out the Golden Tornadoes last chance for gridiron redemption.

The horn sounded. Lamesa had lost its thirty-fourth game in a row.

Final score: Dimmitt 50 Lamesa 42.

But . . . hold the phone!

Who wins $10,000 on a ten-point spread?

"Archie F . . . ing Weesatche!"

In the press box, none of his fellow sportswriters could figure out what Okinawa Watkins was cheering about, until they did.

Oak was still jawing as Archie slapped ten crisp Benjamins into his sweaty palm.

"Can you believe it, man," shouted Okinawa. "Tornados played 'em tough!"

"Yeah, but did you see The Beast come to eat!" said Archie, pocketing his field glasses. "Lowered the Bobcat Ka-BOOM! when ol' Castillo cut it up in the hole."

"And I do I think I see Mr. McIntyre," said Okinawa, nodding at a huddle of giant adults, surrounding Number 55, who looked even meaner, and sweatier, with his pads off. "Let's go catch him, while he's happy."

"You think?"

"Hell yeah, let's go," said Okinawa, bounding down the stands. "My story's filed."

"Go for it, Oak," said Archie, hesitating. "Save the man a trip to Big Spring."

This was the part of the gambling game that Archie liked least: collecting. As he walked down the stadium steps behind his bookie's wide back, he was grateful to know, first-hand, that Okinawa harbored no such reservations.

By the time they hit the six-lane synthetic track and made their way across the AstroTurf, it was just Big Number 55, his even bigger Dad, and a Mom/Step-Mom/Girlfriend trio.

The girlfriend wore a T-shirt proclaiming: *Texas Girls – Just Like You, Only Hotter.*

"Helluva game, Fifty-five," said Okinawa wading in, offering young McIntyre an old-fashioned handshake. "Had you down for seventeen tackles, two sacks, and five tackles for loss. Helluva game!"

"Thanks," said the linebacker, seemingly surprised by the sportswriter's crisp re-cap.

"Hello, sir. I'm Archie Weesatche," extending his hand to the elder McIntyre, who at this point in his post-football life resembled a barrel of West Texas Intermediate crude stuffed into starched Wranglers and a 3XL fishing shirt.

Archie looked the cotton farmer in the eye before shifting his attention to his son.

"Helluva fill on that last play."

"Thank you, sir," said the man-child.

"I can't believe you let those pepper bellies come back on you," said Senior.

"I hope you're thinkin' 'bout playing for UH." said Archie, half-kidding.

"Yeah, I seen your hats," said Senior. "Y'all play down there?"

"Long time ago," said Okinawa.

"Ninety-one to ninety-five," said Archie, "Played for Old Man Yeoman. I was a walk-on. Hoss, over here was All-Conference nose tackle."

"I played for Tech. Southwest Conference," said Senior, folding his arms above a giant belly. "Back before all this Big Twelve bullshit."

"How come it's the Big Twelve if they only got ten teams?" asked Junior, trying his best to keep up with all the jock talk.

"Damn good question," said Archie. "They ought to let UH and Memphis in and start kickin' ass in football *and* basketball."

"OU and UT ain't *about* to let that happen," opined Senior. "They wouldn't let U of H in back when I was playing. Hell, they barely let Tech in the Southwest Conference."

"They ought to let 'em in," said Junior, loosening up noticeably. "That'd be badass."

"Y'all showering here? Or back home?" asked Senior, clearly not agreeing with his son's Big 12 expansion ideas.

"Here," said Junior, picking up his shoulder pads and helmet. "The showers suck."

"Go on, wash off the salt," said Senior. "You can jump in the hot tub when we get home."

"Really? Cool!" said Junior, turning for the locker room. "Nice to meet y'all."

"I'll look for you in Lubbock next season," said Archie. "Guns Up!"

"I wish," said Junior, smiling over his shoulder as he trotted away.

"Kingsbury got his eye on him?" asked Okinawa, closing the circle of three.

"Preferred walk-on, right now," spit Senior. "Tech don't look at nobody under 5A."

"I hear you," said Archie. "Recruitin's tough on the small-town boys."

"Say, gents," interrupted Okinawa. "I'd love to shoot the shit, but we need to exchange a little cash."

The cotton farmer scuffed his boot on the artificial turf.

"Had ya beat, if we coulda' scored a damn two-point conversion," said the farmer, producing a roll of bills thick enough to choke a stallion.

Archie was positively amazed when McIntyre peeled off hundred dollar bills right there in front of God and everybody. "Left a few points on the table."

"Ten, exactly," said Okinawa, in a hushed voice.

McIntyre, Sr. looked up at him, licked his finger, and kept on counting. Didn't say a word until he was finished. "That look like ten?" he asked, staring at Oak.

"Count's right," said the bookie, nodding at Archie to take the money. "I 'preciate ya, Mr. McIntyre. If you ever wanna bet Tech, I gots all kinds of action on the Raiders."

"Can't say that I will," said McIntyre, handing Archie the stack of bills. "I guess this what I get for bettin' on my home team."

"Your son's a helluva player," said Archie, stuffing his winnings into a back pocket then reaching to shake a man's hand. "Hope Tech figures that out. He's a baller."

"He's better than me, that's for sure," allowed the proud Dad. "He's got offers from places where he'd start right away. Abilene Christian and Angelo State."

"That's good ball," said Archie. "Lone Star Conference is stout."

"Yeah, we'll see," said Senior, taking his John Deere cap off to smooth a full head of salt and pepper bristles. "I don't reckon these boys love it like we did."

Parting words on which they could all agree, as the grown men walked their separate ways, stiff-arming gridiron ghosts and the fade of glory days.

GUNS UP!

Archie drove fast from Lamesa, hoping to find Wacey home from cartel surveillance.

No such luck.

So, he laid his fat stack of cotton farmer cash on the top of the coffee table, set up a Jawbone speaker to wirelessly croon some classic C&W, spread out his large-scale road atlas, and got to work.

Two hours, six beers and half a hog leg later—the Josefina Cash-Fix Football Tour was taking final form. Archie sat back in his favorite wing chair, Budweiser in hand, joint smoldering, Ernest Tubb pleading with his honky-tonk angel in stereophonic glory. He clapped his hands as Mr. Tubb's final refrain floated on a cloudbank of Sinaloa Special.

"Come on girl," he cried, pining for a certain *pistolera*. "How 'bout a storybook ending?"

Archie heard nothing but crickets: real and imagined.

He scanned the scattered intel—2015 issue of Dave Campbell's *Texas Football* (Play the Game! shouted the cover at UT and A&M); laptop open to the MaxPreps football website; a legal pad filled with scratch outs and stars; dates, times and venues for the final eleven weeks of the high school and college season: Dallas, Mason, El Paso, Amarillo, Round Rock, Abilene, Waco, Houston (for the UIL State Championships), all marked in Sharpie red on the road map of Texas.

The final destination, during the week between Christmas and New Year, was Las Vegas, where, with any luck, he would lounge with his fellow football fanatics in the biggest sportsbook on the planet (Westgate, Caesar's, Bellagio—who knew?) and watch his beloved Coogs compete in a coveted New Year's Day bowl.

It was all coming together and, of course, subject to massive change. Teams upset. Unknowns ripping through the playoffs. Matt or Tallulah—likely both—desperate to attend an Iggy Azalea concert instead of a boring football game. Sister Ernestine insisting on a weekend feast in Garden City. Sheriff Fuchs arresting Archie.

Archie knew it was a fall fraught with peril. A plan whose success was predicated on the physical and psychological well-being of the world's most unpredictable animals— teenage boys. In other words, way too many variables.

Not that any of that mattered to Archie. He was beyond fired up. "And thank you Golden Tornados!"

He said a little something for the Lamesa head coach as well. Hoped he and his girlfriend could find their way home. Knowing well that addiction cared not.

Archie was re-lighting the hog leg when he heard hard fist-knocks on the back door.

He shot up from the couch, opened the mudroom door, took Wacey's stern face in his hands, and pushed a Sinaloa Shotgun straight down her undercover throat.

"What up, soldier?"

Wacey held the smoke as long as she could then proceeded to cough, so hard and so loud, that the neighborhood dogs began to howl.

"What's up with you?" she said, stepping inside and immediately helping herself to the bottle of Pinot Grigio in the refrigerator. "That's a helluva greeting."

"Post-surveillance gift. You deserve it after a day on Gail Mountain," he said, clinking her wine glass with his bottle of Bud. "Come check out my masterpiece."

Wacey followed him into the living room, waving her hand through the cannabis fog.

"Oak hooked me up with some new sativa," he said, nodding to the smoldering joint. "It's called Northern Lights. From Boulder."

"Ya think," she said, giving him a look, but quickly helping herself.

Archie offered her a seat on the couch, sat back, and watched her take a big swig of wine and adjust her underwire.

The undercover agent had changed out of her camouflage work clothes, and was looking camera-ready in a pearl white Adidas tracksuit. He observed her tan face. She looked stronger, healthier since the Sheriff and Josy dropped her into his world. Thriving, now that she was out of that dump in Lamesa, eating regular meals and sleeping regular hours. Plus, Tallulah had introduced her to the amazing world of online shopping. They'd both done exceedingly well with their recent wardrobe, makeup and hair care purchases.

"*Mira!*" he said, pointing to the fat stacks.

"What's all this crap?" she asked, tracing the highlighted lines on the road map with a white acrylic nail.

"You got your finger on the Promised Land," he said, trying not to sound defensive. "How was your day? Sorry I didn't ask when you came in."

"Quit saying you're sorry," she said, not bothering to look at him.

"Damn, girl," he said, setting his beer down and scooching up next to her. "What's up?"

"I got a call from Rudy."

Archie waited a beat. A couple of beats. "And?"

"He's out. Some guy named *Lobo Loco's* taken over the Ojinaga plaza," she said, staring blankly, her voice a monotone. "He's scared as hell."

Buzz killed, Archie exhaled and fell back into the couch cushions. "Who's *Lobo Loco*?"

"Fuck if I know."

"Then what's up?" he asked. "Is he the guy you were looking for today? The new smuggler?"

"Again," she said, exasperated. "No clue."

"Did you ask Rudy?"

"No," she said, staring at him. "I work for your dad, remember? Sheriff Fuchs?"

And don't forget Josy, he thought.

Archie turned on the ten o'clock news, tried to stay calm, but felt his heart begin to race.

"Rudy was trying to tell me something," Wacey continued. "But couldn't."

"Like somebody was listening?"

She began waving her hands furiously.

"I don't know. It's all fucked," she said, leaping up from the couch, pacing around the room, then accidentally kicking the table leg with an unclosed toe. "Damn it to fuck!"

"Here, Jesus," said Archie, springing up to move the coffee table back to its normal position. "What's going on? Why so agitated?"

"Agitated?" she said, giving him a look. "I'm so fuckin' tired. I meet you; I think I'm getting out, but you're in it too. You and fucking Josy. How the hell did you ever hook up with her?"

"In Laredo," he said, stubbing out the joint. "Fifteen years ago."

"Bullshit," she yelled. 'You were sleepin' with her two weeks ago."

It had been nearly two months, but he said nothing.

"So, what next?" Archie asked. "Wait for *Lobo Loco* to come blow *our* heads off?"

Wacey stood there; hands on hips. "I DON'T FUCKING KNOW!"

Archie wanted to do something. But didn't know what Wacey wanted or needed. He walked back to the kitchen to get a beer, surprised that she followed.

"I'm scared," she said to his back.

He turned in the kitchen doorway. "I can tell."

He hugged her, tried to *show* her, something. "You're scared because you've been there."

"I'm surprised he isn't dead already," she whispered, then started to sniffle.

"Damn," said Archie, holding her tight, pat-patting her heaving shoulders, kissing her hair, the top of her head.

"Should we tell Chuck?" said Archie. "Maybe he can help Rudy out."

"No. That'd make it worse," she said, holding on tight. "It would."

Wacey held him, talked into his shoulder. "I'm just so fucking tired."

"I know," he said, as she finally loosened her hold. "Let's get some sleep."

"Can I stay with you?"

"Of course," he said, "That's what I meant."

"It's kind of spooky over there."

"I hear . . . I understand," he said, pointing to the fridge. "Split one with me?"

"Sure."

Archie wrestled a longneck out of its cardboard carton. "Want one of your own?

She wrapped her arms around his waist, laid her head on his back. "I want one of you."

He straightened up, turned to his bodyguard. "Careful what you wish for."

Wacey twisted the top off Archie's Bud, drank, then kissed him. Kissed him good.

THE NEXT MORNING, ARCHIE WOKE UP EARLY. NOT ON THE COUCH.

Soft dawn filtered through the sides of the bedroom blinds casting Wacey in a dreamy light. The *pistolera* was half-dressed—T-shirt bunched around her neck—splayed on top of the covers as if, maybe, she'd had a hard time getting to sleep.

Archie didn't remember a minute past hitting the pillows.

He crawled next to her and snaked an arm under her pillow. Kissed her head, but she didn't twitch. Then busy brain attacked. He wanted to talk to the Sheriff; wanted to talk to Josy, kinda. Mainly, he wanted to understand who this *Lobo Loco* cat was and what a new plaza boss in Ojinaga might mean for *his* health, forget about Rudy.

He slipped out from under the covers, turned on the shower, put on a pot of coffee. He was so happy not to exercise; loved lazy Saturday mornings. He stripped down and looked at his ESPN app while the water got hot.

Texas Tech v. UT-El Paso 6 p.m. Jones Stadium - Lubbock.

"Damn! That's perfect!"

He tiptoed past Wacey in the buck nude to retrieve a phone charger. He plugged-in and planned the excursion right there in the bathroom. Called the Overton Hotel in Lubbock, which, of course, had been sold out for weeks.

"Except for the Honeymoon Suite," said the perky desk clerk. "It's three fifty a night, but it's real nice."

"I'll take it. Can I check in early?"

"The room's ready right now if you want," she continued. "Groom got cold feet."

"Too much pressure, eh?" said Archie, hoping the hot water hadn't run out in the shower. "You got any tickets to the game?"

"Two," said the very helpful clerk. "But they're in the student section."

"Perfect!" said Archie. "And your name, Miss?"

"Crystal."

"Okay, Crystal. Book the Honeymoon Suite and I'll pay you cash for your tickets. Double the face," said Archie. "We'll see you around noon. Guns Up!"

"You don't owe me nothin'. I got'em for free," said Crystal, giggling. "Guns Up!"

TWENTY-FOUR HOURS IN RED RAIDER LAND PROVED TO BE THE PERFECT TONIC. The early evening kickoff allowed Wacey to snooze till ten o'clock. As soon as Archie explained the spontaneous Lubbock road trip, she'd jumped out of bed and ran to her house. She came back looking like a frat boy's dream in cactus-inlaid cowboy boots, Daisy Dukes and a black, sheer long-sleeve blouse over a red-lace bra.

When Archie pointed the Cougar Red Cadillac due north, there was still plenty of time for a barbecue pilgrimage to Evie Mae's in Wolfforth.

Wacey was not a big barbecue fan but seemed pleasantly surprised by the jalapeño cheese grits which she devoured while Archie took his time with a two-meat plate. He even went back for round two when he overheard a local bragging about Burnt Ends.

"Man, this is unbelievable," said Archie, forking a heaping helping of blackened brisket.

"That's supposed to taste good?" asked Wacey, who was considerably cheerier after a good night's sleep and a slice of coconut cream pie.

"Nothing better," he said, toasting Evie Mae with a can of Robert Earl Keen Honey Pils. "Hardly ever see Burnt Ends on the menu. Righteous buncha carcinogens!"

Wacey's look explained all Archie needed to know about mixing cancer and barbecue.

"So, you bettin' on Tech tonight?"

"Nope, no gamblin' today," said Archie, handing his girl a moist towelette. "Paying strict attention to my date. I 'preciate you letting me stop here. Lubbock's bound to have some good restaurants."

Wacey dabbed at herself carefully so as not to disturb her over-the-top makeup.

"Maybe Italian," she said. "I love spaghetti."

When they arrived at the Overton Hotel (on Mac Davis Lane!) the Honeymoon Suite *and* Wacey, were ready for bidness. She'd waited till they got in the room to break out a bat of Northern Lights. She sealed the deal by blocking Archie's view of ESPN Game Day in a neon-orange negligée.

"Holy Moly!" was the best Archie could do, before he took hold of her outstretched hand and retired to the bedroom featuring an enormous four-poster bed.

"Hell, maybe we'll watch the game from here," he said, lounging in a sea of pillows as Wacey closed the black-out curtains. "I guarantee we'll know when Tech scores."

Fortunately, Archie at forty-five was smarter than the twenty-five-year-old version, who would have fired up another bat and never left the room. Instead, he wisely watched the Tech game on TV *and* ordered up two tickets for Los Lonely Boys at the Cactus Theater (on Buddy Holly Avenue!), took his date out for a romantic Italian dinner, then walked her to the venue just in time for a rowdy second set by the guitar slingers from San Angelo.

All in all, a full-service Saturday.

"I hope you get used to this," he said, slowly promenading his *pistolera* back to the hotel in the dry cool of a West Texas night. "You saw my map. Eleven straight weeks of football heaven, comin' your way."

"I am read-y," she said, steadying herself on a pair of big-girl stilettos. "Ready Freddie!"

GUN PLAY IN PYOTE

PYOTE, TEXAS
DECEMBER 23, 2010

Karma came to call during the blizzard of 2010.

Visibility was less than zero as Sheriff Fuchs drove into the teeth of the pre-Christmas snowstorm. He rolled to a precisely designated stop on a desolate, windy, pitch-dark stretch of I-20 West. A mirror-polished Silverado with Chihuahua plates and tinted windows waited in his headlights.

He was parked in Pyote, Texas. It was freezing cold. It was three o'clock in the morning.

With one hand on his service revolver, Sheriff Fuchs walked up to the rumbling pickup and reluctantly rapped on the driver's side window with his Angelo State class ring.

The black glass descended revealing Rudy Leos, a soldier for the Ojinaga Plaza. The Sheriff's new undercover operative, Wacey Foyt, hands and feet bound, struggled in Rudy's lap. A bulky satellite phone balanced atop the young woman's jutting hip.

"She wants to talk to you," said Rudy. He handed the Sheriff the phone, then jammed the barrel of his Desert Eagle in Wacey's mouth. "I swear I'll blow her head off."

"Don't do anything," said the Sheriff, grimacing as he took the phone.

"Do you want Wacey to die?" asked Josefina Montemayor, on the other side of a satellite connection deep in the Sinaloa jungle.

"Josy?"

"Answer the question."

"No," said the Sheriff, looking away from Wacey's wild eyes. "Don't do it."

"Then listen to me."

WILD TIMES AT THE WHITE ELEPHANT

FT. WORTH, TEXAS
OCTOBER 10, 2015

Road trip!

The Cougar Red Cadillac, freshly hand-washed and filled with a gang of four—Archie, Wacey, Matt, and Tallulah—left Big Spring at a high rate of speed headed for a weekend of State Fair and OU-Texas madness.

Four hours into the drive, clipping along I-20 East, Barrister Billy Tuck beamed in.

"Tuck, the only rooms in Dallas I can find are on Harry Hinds," said Archie, observing that his passengers, front and back, were sound asleep. "No-Tell Motels are *not* going to cut it."

"*¡Huizache!* my man! Where are you?"

"'bout ten miles east of Cisco."

"Well, it just so happens," said the garrulous attorney, "I keep a two-room suite at the Stoneleigh Hotel."

"Damn Tuck, that's fancy!"

Recently relocated from Victoria to Ft. Worth, for reasons undisclosed, Tuck was eager to introduce Archie to his local bookie—a giant named DC!!! from the Red River bottom country near Pottsboro. DC!!! played defensive tackle for OU back in the late nineties, and as Tuck explained it, was a prime example of a certain North Texas oddity—a Texas-born OU diehard.

"Does he sign his checks with exclamation points?" asked Archie, thoroughly intrigued by yet another of Tuck's colorful friends.

"He's cash only," said Tuck. "I don't even know his last name, but I do know he's giving you ten points if you're man enough to bring twenty-five K. And in case you missed it, the Vegas line is UT plus seven."

"Tuck, In Case *You* Missed It," answered Archie. "You're on speaker."

"Hey, Mr. Tuck!" yelled Tallulah. "How's it hangin'?"

"Hey crazy teenager, who I don't know, but can't wait to meet," replied the ever-clever attorney.

"Tuck, as you well know, I'm officially playin' catch-up," he said, smiling at Tallulah in the rearview, who beamed right back. "I've got twenty-five K itching to be doubled."

"That's a bingo, *Huizache!*" replied Tuck, "Our mutual acquaintance. Or, how should I describe Ms. Montemayor?"

"Mexican Slut!" said Wacey.

"That's Wacey, by the way," said Archie, "She's not in love with our client."

"I can hear that," said Tuck. "Hey, Wacey. That's the best West Texas name, maybe ever."

"Archie said you were a charmer."

"Yes, ma'am," said Tuck. "Charming AF."

"Hey, Mr. Tuck, this is Matt. I'm really looking forward to dinner at Joe T.'s. My frat brothers swear by it."

"Smart buncha Phi Delts."

"SAEs," corrected Matt.

"Alright, Mr. Sigma Alpha Epsilon," continued Tuck. "Here's what you need to do. Order a large queso with taco meat, a shot of Patron, a cold Modelo, and a frozen margarita."

"Sounds good," said Matt, playing along.

"Shoot the Patron, chase the Modelo. Then dump the margarita in Tallulah's lap. How's that sound?

"Like frozen beaver!" shrieked Tallulah. "OMG! I'm on such a roll!"

"Wacey," said Archie. "Get that under control."

"That's your job," said Wacey, turning to smile at her new BFF in the backseat.

"Y'all are nothin' but a rollin' menace to society," allowed the lawyer. "Drive safe!"

"Always," said Archie, moving fast past an abandoned Willie Nelson Bio-Fuel station. "Tuck, we'll see you at Joe T. Garcia's in one hour. Seventy-five minutes tops. Grab us a table by those pretty fountains."

"Frozen beaver!" added Tallulah.

AFTER A LONG, LUXURIOUS OUTDOOR PATIO FEAST, WASHING DOWN FIVE JOE T.'s Enchilada Dinners with a dozen frozen margaritas, Attorney Tuck and the gang of four repaired to Ft. Worth's brick-paved Stockyards. They immediately encountered throngs of college football fans—equally obnoxious crazies from OU, Texas, Texas Tech, SMU and TCU—all dead set on out smack-talking each other.

As they pushed through the White Elephant's swinging doors, a band called The Cropdusters—crowded guitar-to-drum kit inside a tiny bandstand—could be heard over the dull roar. Solid introduction to OU-Texas, Archie thought, as they single-filed through the crowded saloon. Wacey, Matt, and Miss Tallulah were taking it all in with mouths wide open.

Soon after their arrival, Wacey and Tallulah took control of the shuffleboard table. They only won a one game, but were so convivial and cute that a gaggle of TCU co-eds promptly adopted them. Meanwhile, Matt re-discovered the considerable bar pool skills he'd honed at Sul Ross, holding the table for over an hour, much to the consternation of a string of frat boys who just knew they could kick his country ass.

Archie and Tuck took it all in from corner bar stools. The raucous swirl was reaching a fever pitch when the man-mountain himself, DC!!!, crashed through the doors.

"Holy crap, Tuck," said Archie, watching a sea of drunks part in the giant's wake.

Out of nowhere, a cute blonde in a SMU ball cap and several layers of bra and camisole, grabbed the tip jar off the bandstand and fast-balled it into DC!!!'s 4XL chest.

The bar went quiet as the giant kicked aside the jar, grabbed an unsuspecting Kappa Sig, powerlifted him overhead, and launched his walrus-ass at the many-layered blonde, who, of course, neatly sidestepped the incoming pile of preppy blubber.

Fortunately, the rotund pledge bounced off the top rail of the bandstand, landed on his feet, and screamed: "Please sir, may I have another!" eliciting thunderous approval and an absolute hail-storm of longnecks against the Cropduster's chicken-wire stage.

"Welcome to OU-Texas!" shouted Tuck, as he waved over the former defensive tackle.

"Glad to be back!" said Archie, giving Wacey, Matt, and Tallulah a double thumbs up.

After the obligatory introductions, bro hugs, and tequila shots, Tuck quickly brokered the bet between Archie and his raging bookie.

DC!!! nodded. Archie shook a man's hand. And the deal was done: UT +10 for $25K.

"I 'member them Coogs back in the day," said DC!!!, knocking back a double tequila. "Buncha speedballin' motherfuckers!"

"Yes, we were," said Archie, barely surviving the bookie's backslap. "Not quite up to OU standards, but we could damn sure run up the score."

"Yeah man, never take the Under on the Coogs," agreed the giant. "Buncha goddamn speed freaks!"

"Wacey! You hear that?" screamed Archie.

Wacey, fortunately, couldn't hear a thing, as she waved corn starch on the shuffleboard.

"She your girl?" inquired the giant, casting a covetous eye on the *pistolera*.

"Hope so," said Archie, mooning over his bodyguard. "*Fuerte muchacha!*"

"Whatever the fuck that means," said the giant, thoroughly unimpressed with Archie's Spanish. "Looks like she could suck the chrome off a trailer hitch."

"Yep," agreed Archie, resigned to the fact that even a straight right to the giant's jaw would do nothing. He took a last sip of Lone Star and plotted a hasty retreat.

As luck would have it, the gang of four survived the first night—always the most dangerous in Archie's experience—without incident. A minor miracle considering DC!!!'s amorous intentions for Wacey as well as Matt and Tallulah's insistence on late-night munchies at a Waffle House in White Settlement, every table filled with bad-acting drunks.

After they piled into their swanky Stoneleigh rooms, Archie was relieved indeed. He fluffed his pillow and dreamed of a giant payday, still baffled how Tuck paid for such a splendid suite.

Wacey knew.

"Spoiler alert," she said, struggling to pull off her adorable cactus-festooned cowboy boots. "Your Mexican love interest is sleeping with Tuck."

"Sounds about right," sighed Archie, Sheriff Fuch's admonishment ringing in his ears.

AS THE FOOTBALL GODS INSIST: THE RED RIVER SHOOTOUT ALWAYS KICKS OFF at 11 AM. Sharp.

The hangover was fierce, and the only coffee available was K-Cups, but once Archie emerged towel-wrapped from an ice-cold shower, he quickly went into action, shaking the corpse-like teenagers and his own matte-haired shuffleboard queen out of bed and into the shower with a minimum of fuss. In the interim, Archie perched himself in the sitting room, enjoying ESPN Game Day from Dallas where the morning Heat Index was already edging toward ninety degrees.

The show-stopper of the Game Day coverage was a UT fraternity skit featuring a kamikaze SAE pledge going complete wedge-buster on an unsuspecting Sooner smack talker— in a classroom, no less! Archie guessed it had to be staged, but man, did it look real!

"Matt, come here. Check this out!" he yelled, cueing up the blindside obliteration for a third time. "Coach Strong needs to sign this kid up!" screamed Kurt Herbstreit, the longtime ESPN college analyst. "I mean, that's a takedown!"

"Dude!" said Matt, watching the fratricide unfold. "That's broken ribs, minimum!"

In a show of miraculous assemblage, the group gathered in the hotel lobby by 9:35 a.m. Archie wasn't sure about this Uber thing. He always drove to the game but was leery indeed of parking the Cougar Red Cadillac in the sketchy lots surrounding Fair Park.

"Welcome to the House That Doak Built," said Archie, pointing to the famous stadium in the distance, as the gang of four cruised down Elm Street.

"And Tallulah love," said Archie, tapping her shoulder from the back seat. "Would you please ask our excellent driver about the availability of that spleef in the ashtray."

"Papa Smurf be comin' true'" said the nice young man with a lovely Caribbean lilt. With no wasted motion the driver lit, puffed, then reached back and stuck the blunt straight in Archie's mouth. "Pray tell, prophet, who is this, Doak the Walker?"

Archie dragged deeply on the herb, exhaling a cloud out the moon roof. "Oh my Jamaican god! Can you say, Uber customer for life!"

As the incomparable Cotton Bowl came into focus, a torrent of intel rolled in from Matt in the cloudy backseat.

Doak Walker was the 1948 Heisman Trophy-winning halfback for the SMU Mustangs. A local sensation from state champion Highland Park High School, Walker went on to star for the hometown Mustangs and the Detroit Lions in the NFL. Walker is famously known as the singular attraction that convinced local boosters to expand the Cotton Bowl and earn the moniker, the "House that Doak Built."

"I-G-G-Y! I'm comin' every year," yelled Tallulah, pointing out the window at one of the dozens of graffiti-scrawled bars. "Look! The Double Wide! We gotta go."

"In due time, Tules," said Archie, marveling at how much Deep Ellum had changed since his cruising days during the Grunge Era. Not as gritty as the nineties, and a lot more storefronts open for business. Even a bookstore—Deep Vellum.

"I've got to take Wacey to Adair's for a burger after the game," said Archie. "But we'll definitely head over to the Double Wide."

The chillest of Uber drivers dropped them off at the Parry/Exposition gate. Archie was amazed that no cash was exchanged; not even a tip.

"It's cool," reassured Matt, when Archie fished bills out of his pocket. "All covered."

It was Wacey's first Uber ride as well. "What? It's free? You millennials are crazy."

"All on the app," said Tules, pat-patting Wacey as they exited the car into a river of Crimson and Cream and Burnt Orange revelers, a fraction of whom might actually have attended the University of Oklahoma and the University of Texas.

"One more toke for the Jolly Rancher," said the driver, reaching out with the joint.

Archie instantly obliged and slipped the driver a folded twenty upon return.

"Appreciate you, prophet!" said the driver, waving the spleef out the moon roof as he rolled away.

And with that, the day was on.

"Alright troops, welcome to the State Fair *and* OU-Texas!" shouted Archie joining the Commerce Street throngs yelling, singing, screaming, Boomer Sooner! and Hook'em Horns! as UT's Pride of the Southwest band blew the Eyes of Texas as loud as their leather lungs would allow.

Fortunately, it was only ten o'clock, which gave them an hour to promenade the fairgrounds and take in some of the finest people-watching east of the Trinity. Archie purchased two hundred carnival coupons and handed out fifty to each of his herd.

After dutifully checking in on Facebook (Archie) and Twitter (Wacey) and Instagram (Matt) and SnapChat (Tallulah), the gang of four wandered through the Art Deco fair grounds and proceeded on a long walkabout marveling at the culinary insanity also known as State Fair food.

The range was stunning with row after row of booths serving heaping helpings of: Bacon Wrapped Deep Fried Garlic Pepperjack Sausage, Deep Fried Root Beer and Chicken Fried Lobster with Champagne Gravy, just to name a few.

After a full circuit of the carnival, Wacey opted for the tame, but delicious, Crawfish Lollipops; Matt tucked into an enormous basket of Chicken Fried Spam Fries; Tallulah went ballistic for the Deep-Fried Chicken Noodle Soup on a Stick, and Archie located the salt-sweet center of the universe with a half-pound Funnel Cake Queso Burger.

At this point, Archie knew they were going to miss kick-off—a cardinal Weesatche sin—but this trip being as much about the State Fair as football, he chilled and texted Tuck to re-confirm the bet.

ARCHIE: DC!!! still allowing UT +10?

TUCK: Confirmed: UT + 10. Let's meet under Big Tex after the game.

ARCHIE: Done. Thx! Hook'em Horns!

TUCK: DC!!! sends his regards. Horns Down! :) Boomer Sooner!

Archie had scored four decent seats on the Texas side, but access proved a challenge. After a full twenty minutes of inching up crowded ramps and steep stairs, they folded down their narrow seats just as UT scored the game's first touchdown.

Just like that, Archie was +17.

"Little different than Sul Ross-Austin College, ain't it," Archie said to Matt, who was actually watching the game while Wacey and Tallulah freshened their makeup and surfed their social networks.

Matt simply smiled through the roar of the UT cannon.

Two minutes later, an alert UT receiver jumped on an end-zone fumble to give the underdogs Longhorns a delirious 14–0 first-quarter lead.

"Man, oh man, oh man!" whispered Archie, trying not to get too excited.

"Plus twenty-four! Lookin' pretty sweet, Arch," said Matt, nudging him in the ribs.

"Lotta football left," said Archie, glaring.

"No jinx," swore Matt, with a big grin. "Charlie Strong might keep his job."

"Yeah maybe, if the Horns win."

The first half ended 14–3 with an inspired Texas defense holding the Sooners to a field goal. Archie was +21, but OU came into the game averaging 42 points. No time for overconfidence. Meanwhile, Wacey and Tallulah were nowhere to be seen after complaining of "creepers"—West Texas parlance for time-delayed hangovers.

To start the second half, Baker Mayfield and Company covered eighty-seven yards in just eight plays, edging the Sooners back within seven, 17–10.

Fortunately for Archie, the Longhorns answered spectacularly, when D'Onta Foreman, a former Fightin' Stingaree from Texas City, peeled off an eighty-one-yard scamper. "How 'bout them apples, Mr. Matt!"

"Hey, I just got a text from Tules," said Matt. "They're in the shade drinkin' Red Bull."

"Tell'em we'll meet'em under Big Tex. I'm not movin' till the clock hits zero."

"Got it," said Matt, fingers flying over the digital keyboard. "They'll be grateful."

"I tell you who I'm grateful for!" yelled Archie. "The Texas defense!"

Naturally, as soon as he said it, Mayfield and the Sooners drove straight down the field for the tying score, with plenty of time left in the fourth quarter. But when Texas needed a final stop, big Poona Ford collapsed the pocket for a huge seventeen-yard sack. OU never got the ball again.

Final score: Texas 24 Oklahoma 17.

Archie could scarcely believe it. He'd won the biggest bet of his life, straight up—no points required! He instantly texted Tuck, leery of payoff problems.

ARCHIE: How's your man set for cash?

TUCK: Cash being delivered to a bar called the Double Wide–3510 Commerce. Big Man's got the red ass, but bookies always pay.

ARCHIE: What time at Double Wide (great name btw)?

TUCK: 6 p.m.

ARCHIE: Perfect! Time enough to scarf a victory burger at Adair's

TUCK: I'd join you, but babysitting the giant.

ARCHIE: Understood. Thank you. 6 p.m. at Double Wide.

TUCK: We'll be there. Nice bet! Josy's impressed. :)

THAT WAS SELF-DEFENSE

DALLAS, TEXAS
OCTOBER 11, 2015

And there they were.

Wacey and Tallulah, mesmerizing a large semi-circle of UT fans with long-legged cartwheels and aggressive round-offs. Even the surly OU fans seemed impressed, trudging back to their cars, although none were in the mood to join the gymnastics.

"Damn girl," said Archie, sauntering up to his date after a sweaty thirty-minute migration from the Cotton Bowl's treacherous upper deck down to Big Tex, who was looking extra sharp in his new Dickie's duds and ten-thousand-gallon Resistol hat.

"I was a cheerleader at Forsan," said Wacey, hands on hips. "Before I dropped out."

To finish the impromptu display of tumbling skills, Tallulah got a running start on the smooth concrete apron surrounding Big Tex, then whirled from cartwheel to back handspring to backflip.

"Tallulah Bankhead!" yelled Matt, unleashing a super-loud two-finger whistle. "What the hell, girl!"

"I haven't done that in forever!" screamed Tules, the reluctant show-off, running to hide behind Archie and Matt, red-faced from the applause.

Wacey did one more round off then slapped Archie high-five as the crowd drifted away. "You won your bet, didn't you?"

"He sure did," said Matt, eyeing a squadron of Longhorn co-eds in the uniform of the day—white Daisy Dukes with burnt orange tops and cowboy boots.

"Beers on March!" yelled Tallulah.

"Hells yeah!" said Archie, leaning in to give Wacey a big kiss. "And Tules, you're in luck. We're meeting DC!!! at the Double Wide."

"Aren't you afraid he's gonna throw you like that frat boy?"

"Absolutely!" said Archie. "Throat punch him if he tries, would ya?"

"Absolutely!" yelled Tallulah. "I'll kick his fat ass."

Archie relished the thought of Tallulah's Day-Glo high-top buckling the ogre's green teeth with a perfectly placed heel kick.

As the gang of four slid through the pedestrian street zoo, following a broad-shouldered huddle of UT Cowboys walking Bevo back to his trailer, debauchery was on display at every turn. Boys turning up flasks; girls twerking; obliterated Sooners knee-walking back to their cars; Longhorn inebriates barfing into gutters; all manner of teenagers making out in broad daylight.

As the sun descended behind the ultra-modern Dallas skyline, they finally hit Commerce Street, traffic barely crawling. The post-game madness came to head in the form of a monster F-350, with a bed full of UT rowdies, cruising side-by-side with a charter bus full of OU rowdies, windows wide-open.

Politically incorrect does not begin to describe the foulness being hurled between the two frat wagons. In due time, a beer bottle came flying, conking a UT idiot trying, quite successfully, to urinate on the moving OU bus. As soon as their UT brother hit the deck, a fusillade of cans and bottles rained down from the Monster Truck. Which, of course, had the OU sodomites practically crawling out the open windows.

The rolling riot quickly gained the attention of a team of black-clad Dallas police, a unit specifically trained to snuff out all OU-Texas nonsense, especially the invariable winner/loser brawls.

The DPD SWAT teamers waded in between the now stopped bus and truck, smashing undergraduate heads by the double handful. One cop proceeded to spread eagle the UT urinator on the pavement, while his partner yanked the Monster Truck driver from behind the wheel and straight to the street. Fortunately, somebody jammed the monster truck in neutral allowing the colossal toy to harmlessly bump to a stop against a parking meter as the OU bus rolled merrily away. Scads of Sooners hung out the windows, loving every second of SWAT team brutality—a small consolation for the loss to the hated Longhorns.

Wacey tapped Archie on the shoulder. "Did that just happen?"

"Oh yeah," he said, spying the Double Wide, steering his charges toward an aluminum tornado hovering above the door. "Now I remember why I *don't* come to OU-Texas."

"I thought biker rallies were bad," said Wacey, looping her arm inside Archie's.

"Uncle Archie, can we come every year?" asked Tallulah "It's so I-G-G-Y!"

Archie, head on a swivel, expertly navigated the last two blocks and herded his troops to their Double Wide destination. Inside, it was wall-to-wall hipsters—dudes with Bluetooths and chicks with attitudes—everybody drinking Yoohoo Yeehaws, Hurri-Tangs, and enough keg beer to float an aircraft carrier. Everybody groovin' amongst the wall-to-wall kitsch, including: Elvis, many times over; a velvet Kenny Rogers, lots of Willie, Waylon and the Boys; stately pink flamingos, random driftwood, signed trucker hats, signed jockstraps, signed sports bras, Lone Star neon, Raquel Welch in her Stone Age bikini, a giant *Giant* poster, Roy Orbison album covers, stuffed javelinas, stuffed jackalopes and lots and lots of in-the-weeds waitresses yelling drink orders—all in all, a true OU-Texas melting pot of hormones, testosterone and chemical imbalance.

A country-punk band called the Bang Angels were setting up in a small open-air patio featuring a mural of Barry Manilow in prison stripes and toilet tanks filled with cactus. At the end of the twenty-foot bar, sat Tuck and DC!!! looking like a Crimson and Cream volcano spewing hate from every orifice.

As the kids peeled off for the patio, Archie and Wacey approached the pair with caution, stepping gingerly through slicks of spilled drinks. Tuck caught Archie's eye as they forded swirling eddies of handsome frat boys and scores of immaculate confections also known as UT and OU sorority girls. As they drew closer, Tuck lifted a bulging Angelo's BBQ bag.

"Fuck Texas!" roared DC!!!, violently thrusting the Horns Down sign. Archie assiduously avoided the strings of spittle roping out of his raging bull mouth.

"Hey, Billy Tuck," said Wacey, giving him a big hug. "What the fuck?"

"I love this woman, Weesatche!"

"Shut up, Tuck," said DC!!!, mashing down on the Angelo's bag. "Show 'em!"

Tuck timidly opened up the bag for Wacey to peek. Her grin changed to a frown when she came up with a fistful of . . . *pesos.*

Archie pulled a bill and read: "*El Banco de Mexico; Dos Mil Pesos.*"

DC!!! grabbed the sack and dumped every last note of legal tender on the bar.

"It's all there," said Tuck, trying to keep the bills from dropping behind the countertop. "Three hundred fifty thousand *pesos* at the very liberal exchange rate of fourteen to one."

"That work for you?" inquired the blood-boiling bookie.

"Yeah, *pesos* are fine," said Archie. "*No problema.*"

"Fuck Texas," spewed DC!!!, not listening to a word.

"Yeah Biggun, I hear you," said Archie, scooping and stuffing stray *pesos* back in the bag. "Lemme buy you a drink."

"What you drinkin', Big Man?" said Tuck, rolling up the Angelo's bag tight, handing it to Wacey.

"Jack and Coke."

"Let's have four of those bad boys, and call it a day," said Archie.

"I call you a lucky sombitch," said DC!!!, leering at Wacey. "She still with you?"

Archie caught a bartender's eye and the man actually stepped up to take his order.

"Jack and Cokes all around," said Archie, standing tall, calculating. He looked over his shoulder and spied Tallulah and Matt talking to a studious looking fella in a Rastafarian beanie next to a former toilet now sprouting a pipe organ cactus.

Soon enough, the bartender set down four drinks. Archie peeled a twenty and told him to keep the change.

"I would, but it's twenty-eight."

"Aw hell," grimaced Archie, peeling off another twenty. "Stuck in the nineties. Thank you."

"No, thank you," said the musclebound bartender sporting tip-to-stern tattoos under a black wife beater. His matching black hair net was a nice touch.

Archie handed Wacey her Jack and Coke, raised his own. "Hook'em, Horns!"

"Fuck Texas! And double fuck your n*****r head coach," yelled DC!!!, slamming his drink in one gulp and firing the glass—ice and all—straight through the patio door and into the wall, splintering shards above Matt, Tallulah, and a covey of hipsters.

When Archie looked back the badass bartender was striding up to DC!!! with a sawed-off, pistol-grip shotgun. "You! Out! Now! Now motherfucker!"

DC!!! instantly launched a haunch up on the bar, but got hung up. Hung up just long enough for the bartender to flip the shotgun and swing its thick rubber stock straight into DC!!!'s ear. A blow of such force and baseball precision that it knocked the ogre's eyeballs clean out of their sockets—a hideous mess of dangling ganglia wriggling on the bar in a puddle of beer and blood.

"Holy shit!" cried Wacey, ducking under the giant's flailing arms.

Archie grabbed Wacey and headed for the porch. As the crowd surged toward the bar to watch the screaming DC!!! lash out in blind fury, Archie directed his charges out through an alley and up the still crowded street until he identified an actual Yellow Cab, dome light shining.

He urged Tallulah, then Wacey, then Matt into the back seat. As soon as his passenger door slammed shut, they were off, with barked directions to the Stoneleigh Hotel.

"Holy crap!" said Archie, taking his first deep breath, just realizing that he was carrying the Angelo's bag like a football. "Is everybody okay?"

"I never . . ." started Wacey. "And I've seen a lot."

"What just happened?" asked Tallulah. "Total fugazi!"

"What the hell did he say to that bartender?" yelled Matt.

"Who knows!" said Archie, replaying in his mind's eye, the bartender's shotgun flip and perfect swing into DC!!!'s ear. "Man, that was nuts."

"You think?" said Wacey, wiping her face, up and down. "God, I'm glad to be outta there. Idiots! Nothin' but drunk idiots."

"His eyeballs were on the bar!" screamed Tallulah, pulling herself up on the seat by the driver's headrest. "That's so . . . that's so . . . totally out there!"

"No, no; he was goin' nuts," said Archie, trying to ascertain if they were going the right way now that the car was clear of Deep Ellum. "I swear they're gonna have to shoot him. Thank you, sir, for getting us out of there."

"I hate this weekend," said the cabbie, in a thick Nigerian accent. "Too much crazy. Too much drinking, man. People gone foolish!"

"Too, too crazy, man. Thank you, sir," said Matt.

"Thank you, sir," said Tallulah, finally sitting back and curling up against Wacey.

"It is my responsibility," assured the cabbie, checking his side and rear-view mirrors, expertly maneuvering through back streets. "You are safe."

Archie firmed his grip on the money bag.

"Let's get the hell out of here," said Wacey, holding Tallulah's hand. "Like now."

Archie turned in his seat. "We'll get some sleep and leave early."

"No, I mean, now. Tonight," insisted Wacey.

"I say we go right now," agreed Matt. "What about DC!!!'s friends?"

"Please Uncle Archie can we leave tonight?" pleaded Tallulah.

"Fine with me," he said. "Let's pack up and go. We'll drive straight to the Garden."

Ten minutes later, they were in a Stoneleigh elevator, talking non-stop about how fast they were going to pack and scat. As Archie struggled to extract the card key from his tightly packed wallet, Matt and Tallulah jostled behind him to get in the door first.

After several attempts, he finally got a green light and opened the door.

"*Hola guapo*," said Josy, blowing on her fingers, stabbing a skinny wand back in a bottle of nail polish. Rudy Leos was sitting next to her, on the wide couch, smoking a cigarette.

"Hey Josy," he answered, holding the door. "Hey, Rudy."

Tallulah rushed in, but stopped mid-stride, dumbfounded. "Josy!"

"Tallulah, *hermosa!*" she said, up from the couch with open arms. "It's so good to see you. And *Mateo! Hola! Hola!*" she said, unwrapping from Tallulah, just in time to give Matt a big hug.

The group hug gave Wacey an opening. She walked straight past Josy, straight into Rudy's lap.

"*Hola guapo!*"

Rudy tried to play cool but had to laugh when Wacey wrapped herself around his lap.

"Hey Josy," she said, swishing her hair in Rudy's face. "What's up?"

Everybody, including the wryly smiling Rudy, running a hand through his thick black hair, stopped for a beat.

Josy clucked, slowly approached Archie, then jammed her tongue down his throat.

"*Decias* . . . You were saying," she sneered, turning so Wacey could see her brush the front of Archie's jeans. "Your boyfriend misses me. No?"

"Hey *pendejo*," said Rudy, pointing at the Angelo's bag. "What's in the sack?"

"Barbecue," said Wacey.

"Smells like money," said Josy, easing the bag out of the crook of Archie's arm.

Archie clenched, but let her take it. Josy sat back down on the couch, unrolled the bag on the coffee table, and peered inside. "Oh, look. *Pesos. Muchos pesos.*"

"*Pesos?*" said Rudy, easing Wacey off his lap, then turning to the bar. A big chrome-plated pistol was jammed in the back of his jeans, glinting. He patted Wacey on the butt as he stepped up to the bar.

When Rudy uncorked a full bottle of Patron, Wacey clapped her hands. "So, what the fuck, guys? Did the new *jefe* run y'all out of OJ?"

"Matt, Tallulah," Archie called out to the teenagers, who'd ducked into the master bedroom. "Come tend bar, please."

Archie stepped up next to Rudy and gestured for the bottle. "Relax my friend; *con permiso*." He waved for Matt and Tallulah to join him.

Rudy raised his eyebrows, but handed Archie the bottle, sat back down next to Josy, who promptly dumped the contents of the Angelo's bag on the table.

"Tallulah, let's get some drink orders," said Archie, trying to catch Josy's eye. "It's the least we can do for our hostess."

Wacey took a seat in an overstuffed chair and started counting the scattered pesos, placing them in neat stacks. Josy sat back and watched.

"How are you, Wacey?" she said, flipping her hair. "Long time, no see."

"What can I get for you, Miss Josy?" asked Tallulah, stepping up with surprising poise. "Would you like a blood orange and tequila? I hear it's your favorite."

"Ooh, that sounds nice," said Josy, unable to ignore the teenager's cheery enthusiasm.

"And for you Miss Wacey; you want one, too?"

"I'll have a shot, with one cube of ice," said Wacey, looking up from the money to give Tallulah a knowing smile.

"*Tequila con hielo solo y tequila con jugo*," recited Matt, taking down a tumbler and a shot glass from the bottom shelf of glasses.

"Wait, Matt!" cried Tallulah. "Wait to see what Mr. Rudy and Uncle Archie want."

"*Perdón*," said Matt, cutting his eyes at Archie.

"May I get you something to drink, Mr. Rudy?"

"*Si, flaca*," said Rudy, eyes moving up and down Tallulah's considerable length. "*Tequila solo, sin hielo*."

Tallulah giggled, hiding her face behind her notepad.

"*¡Ay Tallulah, que linda!*" said Josy. "He wants a shot of tequila; no ice."

"Hey bartender," said Archie. "How 'bout shots all around and I'll have a Bud back. Be sure and pour one for yourself and our fine waitress."

"Got it," said Matt, wiping his hands on his cargo shorts and getting to work. "Six shots, one blood orange and tequila and a Budweiser. Anything else."

"That's my job!" said Tallulah, hands on hips.

When everyone murmured thanks, Tallulah silently joined Matt, whispering in his ear. "We don't have shot glasses."

"Use those," he said, gesturing at the top shelf.

"We're going to get drunkity drunk drunk," she said, bringing down six wine glasses.

Meanwhile, Wacey's *peso* stacks continued to fatten.

"When did you learn to count?" said Josy, giving Archie a knowing smile. "Did you get your GED?"

Wacey looked up, didn't stop counting, then did. She lifted two middle fingers for Josy's inspection. "Fuck off."

"They say, Forsan High is the St. Mary's Hall of West Texas," said Archie, looking out the window for a fire escape. "Helluva lot better school than Presidio, huh Rudy?"

Rudy stared at Archie, gave Wacey a wink, then pulled the huge Desert Eagle semi-automatic from behind his back and racked a shell. "You talk like a *pinche vieja*."

"Please shut up; both of you," said Josy, exhaling a cloud of cigarette smoke. "*Mateo*, may I have my drink, please?"

"Yes ma'am; coming right up," said Matt, anxiously setting Josy's drink in the middle of a round tray circled with wine glasses of tequila.

Tallulah looked at the tray, hesitated.

"Let me get that," said Matt, expertly balancing the tray in one hand above his shoulder. "You can serve."

"Where'd you learn that?" asked Tallulah, visibly impressed.

"Alicia's in Alpine," he said, setting the tray down on the coffee table as Wacey made room by stacking the stacks. "I tended bar during the lunch shift."

"That's where I know you from!" said Rudy, waving the Desert Eagle at Matt. "I eat at Alicia's all the time. I knew I knew you."

"*Rudy!*" yelled Josy. "The gun. Please!"

"Oh, sorry," said Rudy, sheepishly setting the firearm back in his lap.

"I'm a *narco*, I think," said Tallulah, setting Josy's tumbler down in front of her.

They all looked at Tallulah, puzzled.

"*Narco, no. Loquita, si,*" said Rudy, chuckling as Tallulah handed him a wine glass.

After all of the drinks were distributed, Archie proposed a toast.

"To the mighty Texas Longhorns!" said Archie lifting his wine glass. "And to DC!!! May he see all the more clearly."

"Ew, gross!" cried Tallulah, "His eyeballs were all squiggly and . . ."

"You didn't even see it," complained Matt.

"Did too!

"*¡Viva Mexico! ¡Salud!*" said Rudy, raising his glass.

He and Archie chugged their shots in one gulp.

Matt and Wacey took two tries to get their shots down. Tallulah balked as soon as the liquid hit her lips; Josy left hers on the table, choosing to sip the delicious blood orange.

Seconds after the heat of the shots began to spread through their bodies, they were all startled by the sound of the door's electronic lock.

Billy Tuck came blasting in, sweat-soaked, with greetings and salutations.

"Hello, hello! *¡Hola amigos!*" he shouted, drunkenly weaving toward Archie, who instinctively rose from his chair to shake a man's hand.

But before Billy and Archie could press the flesh, the roar of Rudy's Desert Eagle filled the room with ballistic cacophony. The entire room, watched speechless, as Tuck bent at the waist, clutching his gut. He fell to his knees, swayed, then face-planted squarely, a hole gaping in his back, blood blooming across the back of his white OU polo.

Before anyone could think, another shot—a much quieter bullet— introduced itself to Rudy Leos's thick skull, boring through bone, brain and a silk lampshade on its way out the window.

As Rudy slumped on the couch, everyone froze.

Except for Wacey, who slowly turned her nine-millimeter on Josy.

"That was self-defense."

Josy frowned at Wacey, glanced at Rudy, stubbed out her cigarette, gathered her purse and calmly left the room.

By the time the EMS arrived, Tuck was dead; completely blown through.

Rudy was also dead; his razor-cut scalp precisely penetrated.

Archie, Matt, and Tallulah sat shell-shocked.

LATER THAT NIGHT, WHEN SLEEP WOULD NOT COME, AND MORNING LIGHT bled through the blinds of the Stoneleigh suite, Archie thought about disembodied eyeballs and jellyfish.

He thought how the gelatinous threads of the giant's eyeballs resembled the tentacles of a Portuguese Man 'O War he'd tangled with during a drunken swim off Mustang Island.

His future fiancé, the skinny-dipping Miss Callahan, had known just what to do, as he emerged, writhing in pain, from the shallow salt waters. Patti sat him down in the sand, squatted over his length of bone, and peed right on the welts. "It's a Victoria thing," she laughed, as the hot liquid ran down his legs.

And it worked!

That same Port Aransas night, his searing stings miraculously soothed, Archie Weesatche popped the question over spectacularly fresh seafood at the Tarpon Inn.

Patti Callahan said yes, casually forking a bite of redfish and lump crabmeat.

Archie could tell the richest girl in South Texas was not impressed, with the diamond, or her landlubber husband-to-be.

As he tined a final bite of succulent soft-shell crab, Archie Weesatche knew one thing for certain—he *was* in over his head.

And cared less.

RETURN TO PUNCHER DOME

One dead giant.

Two bodies in a fancy hotel.

Three straight-up murders.

The Weesatche Tour of Texas had taken an ultra-violent turn.

As soon as they received his one call from a breathless Archie, Sister Ernestine and Sheriff Fuchs drove straight to Dallas.

After the authorities confirmed that Matt and Tallulah were innocent bystanders in a bizarre hotel shootout, Sister Ernestine quickly extracted the youngsters. The three were back in Glasscock County by sundown Monday.

Sheriff Fuchs, on the other hand, worked long and hard to extricate Archie and Wacey from their respective web of complications.

For starters, there were twenty-five thousand dollars in Mexican pesos stacked neatly on the coffee table. A lengthy interrogation also revealed Archie's long relationship with Tuck; his even longer relationship with Josy, his short but complicated relationship with Wacey, followed by a recounting of Rudy's now-infamous pellet gun attack in Presidio, and finally, his weekend OU-Texas wager with DC!!!, the now-deceased bookie who'd survived for two days on a ventilator at Parkland Hospital.

"Mr. Weesatche, you keep some interesting company," said the Dallas Police Department detective assigned to the case. "You can thank your lucky stars—and your dad—for getting you out of jail. We're not finished with you by a long shot."

Wacey was in an even stickier predicament, due to a modest rap sheet, mostly from her teens and early twenties, mitigated somewhat by the fine undercover work she'd performed for Sheriff Fuchs, the DEA and DPS over the past decade. Wacey's claim of self-defense was semi-reasonable, but the accuracy of her single shot and the fact that she and Rudy had once been close, called her deadly action into question. Wacey's close ties with the Juarez cartels also put her in grave danger.

All that said, after five full days of investigation, no charges were filed. Rudy Leos, for reasons unknown, shot Billy Tuck in cold blood. Wacey Foyt killed Rudy Leos in self-defense. Both motives were shaky, but both men were also in the ground. And Texas being Texas, another drug-related double murder investigation went cold.

By the following Friday, Sheriff Fuchs was able to talk the Dallas DA's First Assistant into a suitable arrangement for Archie's and Wacey's release back to Big Spring.

However, the *real* reason the gambler and his bodyguard were set free was due to the curious case of the disappearing District Attorney. As in, no charges could be filed because the District Attorney could not be found to sign the court orders.

"Chuck, if you can keep close tabs on these two until we finish the investigation, I'd sure appreciate it," explained the Assistant DA. "Ever heard of a high-ranking public official just up and disappearing? How is it possible that nobody's seen or heard from the District Attorney of Dallas County in two weeks!"

"I never," said the Sheriff, winking at Wacey and Archie, as the four ambled down the polished halls of the Frank Crowley, one of several massive court buildings in downtown Dallas. "This one's scared witless and Wacey knows the drill. They're not going anywhere, 'cept where I tell'em."

TWO WEEKS LATER, AFTER NUMEROUS ROUNDS OF NEGOTIATIONS WITH VARIOUS Dallas County law enforcement and prosecutors, the entire family reassembled for a spectacular lunch around Sister Ernestine's Irish oak table. She'd been cooking all morning. The kitchen was filled with savory smells from stove, oven, and sideboard.

"Can you believe it?" said Sister Ernestine, passing a dish of mashed potatoes to Sheriff Fuchs, "We're all here!"

"Wa-zedic," said Tallulah, giving Matt bug eyes, as she passed a platter of venison.

"I sure am glad to be back in the Garden," agreed Matt, exchanging with his sister glazed carrots for backstrap. "D/FW is way too urban for this boy."

"Amen for West Texas," said Archie, passing fresh-baked cornbread.

"And amen for the Sheriff and Sister Ernestine," said Wacey, helping herself to a crumbly square.

"I mean! Three cheers for the cavalry!" said Archie, raising a glass of *Beaujolais nouveau*. "Thank you both, to the moon."

The Sheriff nodded, raised his glass, and drank a big sip. He then helped himself to carrots, mashed potatoes and venison, relieved to have delivered his troops from certain incarceration. "Here's to family."

"And not one of us with the same name," said Matt.

"I'll drink to that," said the former Evangeline Ducornet, clever creator of alternate identities.

As the plates passed and the food was distributed, the family settled in once again.

"I hope Josy's okay," said Tallulah, choking down a short swallow of wine.

Archie knew that she was. He snuck a peek at a scowling Wacey and said nothing.

Josefina Montemayor, a person of interest as defined by the DPD, was safe in Mexico, being shuttled from apartments and haciendas from Ciudad Victoria and Monterrey to Ojinaga and Nuevo Laredo. Archie's lengthy text exchanges with Josy revealed that her father, Don Montemayor, was more afraid of retaliation by the cartels battling *Lobo Loco* for control of the Ojinaga Plaza than incarceration in Texas. He was determined to keep Josy safe and that meant keeping her on the move for the foreseeable future.

"I 'magine she's scared," said the Sheriff. "She's also pretty damn resourceful."

"That's called feminine wiles," said Sister Ernestine, pat-patting the Sheriff's liver-spotted hand.

"Ooh, I like wiles," purred Tallulah, "How's that spelled?"

"W-i-l-e-s, as in Wile E. Coyote!" said Matt.

"He was my favorite," added Wacey. "I wanted him to wring that Roadrunner's neck."

"You remember, Mom," said Archie, "I'd get up every Saturday and watch *Looney Tunes* all morning. I loved the rooster."

"Foghorn Leghorn!" recalled Matt.

"All created by Mel Blanc," added Sister Ernestine. "A Frenchman, of course."

"Ooh-la-la," cooed Tallulah, cracking up the table.

The laughter was a balm to Archie. Matt and Tallulah seemed at peace. Even Wacey was edging closer to normalcy. He wanted to re-start the Texas Tour as soon as possible but was waiting patiently for Sheriff Fuchs to give the all clear.

"Chuck, we good for a little regional travel?" he asked, forking a thick cut of venison and red-eye gravy. "Or are we still under house arrest?"

"Can't hold you, if you're not charged," he said. "What'd ya have in mind?"

"Local rivalry. Mason-Junction," said Archie, enjoying a sip of the choice vintage. "I'd love to take everybody over to the Puncher Dome. It's a classic."

"The Puncher Dome!" cried Tallulah. "Road trip!"

"Yes sir, I'm familiar with Mason," said the Sheriff with a sly grin. "That's where my granddaddy got knee-deep in the HooDoo Wars with Johnny Ringo and the Rangers."

"The HooDoo Wars! Oh, Chuck, for heaven's sake," sighed Sister Ernestine.

"Hand on the Good Book," the Sheriff exclaimed. "After the War Between the States, a bunch of Confederate soldiers hooked up with the outlaw Johnny Ringo and started rustling cattle around Mason. Granddaddy hired on with the Texas Rangers. They went after'em for nearly two years— all kindsa' shoot-outs and hangin's."

"Hope we're done with that kind of trouble," said Archie, looking at Wacey. "Right?"

"Don't look at me," said Wacey, sopping her cornbread. "I'm not the one with all the crazy friends."

"Wacey Foyt, I've met plenty of your crazy friends," reminded Chuck. "I introduced you to him, didn't I?"

Wacey laughed at that, snaked her little finger through Archie's.

"Can we please go to the Puncher Dome?" said Tallulah, cupping her face in her hands, mooning at the Sheriff.

"Yes, let's all go," said Sister Ernestine. "There's a man in Coleman who has the most delicious honey. I haven't been to see him in years."

"I knew a bull rider from Coleman at Sul," said Matt, having cleaned his plate in less than five minutes. "Bad, bad *hombre*. I think he was an All-American."

"My Daddy rode bulls," said Wacey, offering seconds of venison to Matt, who patted his flat belly and dug in.

"Your Daddy was the best bullfighter I ever saw," said the Sheriff, clearing his throat. "Saved a whole lot of fellas from being gored, stomped, or worse."

"I didn't know there was bullfighting in Texas," exclaimed Sister Ernestine.

"Let me take this one, Chuck," said Matt, wiping his mouth and placing his napkin on top of his plate. "Mom, he means the rodeo clowns who keep the cowboys safe after they're thrown off; not like the European bull-fights with pikes and swords."

"Oh, the clowns! I love the clowns!" exclaimed Sister Ernestine. "The men in the baggy clothes who let the bulls chase them."

"That was my Daddy," said Wacey, "But Lord he took a beatin'. Momma finally wouldn't go. Quit rodeos; quit singing; quit everything, 'cept drinkin'."

"Y'all wanna tequila shot?" asked Tallulah. "That was the first shot I ever had, then Wacey shot that man in the head. How'd you do that?"

Wacey tried not to choke on her last bite, then hid her smile behind her napkin.

"I love tequila!" Tallulah continued, unabashed. "It feels so warm goin' down."

"Hey, Planet Clueless," said Matt, softly nudging Tallulah under the table. "What?"

There were looks around the table, then soft laughter, as chairs pushed back and plates began to clear.

"Okay, so road trip to the Puncher Dome," said Archie, clapping with excitement. "Friday Night Lights and fresh clover honey. *Puro Tejas* on tap!"

AFTER A CIVILIZED SIESTA, THE REUNITED CLAN ALL PILED IN THE Cougar Red Cadillac and enjoyed an absolute drama-free road trip. First, to the Coleman beekeeper, where Sister Ernestine purchased a fresh case of honey, then straight to the Mason City Park.

The Puncher Dome anchored the east end of the beautifully landscaped acreage. And was that stadium ever a sight to behold, filled to the brim with loud, proud Masonites. Of course, the Puncher Dome was no dome at all. More like a modified pole barn, covered on top with sheets of corrugated zinc with the home bleachers crammed inside and a press box piled on top.

The home-field advantage came from the noise level, which for a 2A crowd, rivaled much larger venues by virtue of its uncanny concentration of Puncher Dome cacophony blasting out over the field—wave after wave of Hill Country caterwauling that always unnerved the opponents.

Archie was so happy to show his people some genuine high school sacred ground. He had no intention of betting on the game, but did allow Tallulah to wager a crisp Benjamin with a fast-talkin' fence-hugger in a blue corduroy FFA jacket.

After some fairly conspicuous flirting, and a quick consult with Archie, Tallulah sauntered back to the rancher's son and offered him Junction +28.

"Four touchdowns!" he said, then let fly a full-length of Copenhagen spit. "Hells bells girl, I'm all over that!"

Final score: Mason 49 Junction 7.

Tallulah found him right where she'd left him—on the fence.

"How ya feelin' now, Mr. FFA?" said the suddenly confident gambler, thumbs in the loops of her distressed denim hip-huggers.

"I tole you," he explained. "I ain't got no hundred dollars."

"Your Daddy's got a hundred dollars," said the Sheriff, stepping up to the fence. "I just handed it to him."

"Say what?" asked the Future Farmer, shrinking a little in the shadow of the Sheriff's height, weight and tobacco-soaked voice. "I mean, Mister. Mr. Sheriff."

"Go on," said the Sheriff, stuffing his hands in his jacket to ward off the chill. "Your Daddy didn't raise no cheat."

"Cheater, cheater, pumpkin' eater!" sang Tallulah, sticking her tongue out for good measure, as the FFA man adjusted his camo Arctic Cat hat.

"Aw, shut up," he muttered.

"Go on, son," said Archie, who was also keeping an eye on the transaction. "Bring her back the hundred dollars she won fair and square."

"Hells bells," muttered the boy, adjusting his cap for the tenth time. "Don't seem right if Mason won."

Tallulah and Archie exchanged knowing glances.

"That's called the point spread," said Tallulah. "Dumbass."

"How come y'all let her talk like that?"

He looked up to find Archie and the Sheriff—the twin definition of serious face.

"Y'all need to put a bit in that mouth," he complained, shaking his head.

Archie and the Sheriff chuckled as the muttering young man wandered off.

"I'll be glad to get that money back," said the Sheriff, "Only reason I bet on Junction is they're the Coyotes; same as my Borden County boys."

"Well, you got the town right," said Archie, slapping the Sheriff on the back of his Borden County windbreaker. "It's the Junction *Eagles*."

"Aw hell," said the Sheriff.

"That's okay, Chuckster," said Tallulah, pat-patting on the Sheriff, basking in her gambling glory. "I got your back."

"Oh, I know you do," laughed the Sheriff, as his third orphan rescue pogoed around him in a jumpy circle. "That's what keeps me up nights, Tallulah Belle."

On the drive back, in a thickening fog, through Menard to Eden to Sterling City, Archie tried to talk everybody—actually anybody—into a little boot-scootin'. "Jody Nix is playin' at The Stampede tonight."

There was great enthusiasm at first, but by the time they dropped off Matt and Tallulah at Roger Tedesco's well-attended house party, and left Sister Ernestine and the Sheriff with his truck outside the First National Bank of Sterling City, it was just the two of 'em.

"It's gonna be past eleven by the time we get there," said Archie, looking at the Cadillac's glowing navigation screen. "If we're lucky."

"Stampede closes at midnight," said Wacey, not bothering to stifle a yawn. "At least it did a hundred years ago."

"Probably still does," said Archie, flipping from high to low beams, ripping through the swirling fog enveloping Highway 87. "I wonder if it's still BYOB?"

By the time they got to Big Spring and eased down Gregg Street, boot-scootin' was out and a twelve-pack was in. Archie pulled into the new Buck Easy's C-store; promised his bodyguard he'd be back in a jiffy.

As he fast-walked back to the beer coolers, he spied one of his ex-Keep On Truckin' drivers hanging out by the hot dogs. Archie cussed himself for forgetting names so fast—if he didn't *literally* see people on a daily basis, their names evaporated. When he got up to the cash register, there was some distance between him and the man with no name, but not enough.

"Hey Boss," said the twentysomething, in greasy jeans and a tattered jacket with insulation oozing out where the Keep on Truckin' patch used to be.

"What's up, brother?" he said, setting down his twelve-pack of Lone Star and a bag of Chili Cheese Fritos. He soul shook the driver's outstretched hand. The hand brought him in for a tepid bro hug.

"Still got your jacket, huh?" said Archie, trying not to stare at the young man who looked like he'd been rode *real* hard. "Gettin' cold out there, ain't it?"

"Yeah, I was trying to get on with another outfit; outta Midland . . . didn't work out," he said, by way of explanation. "Kinda messed up my jacket."

"Long as it keeps you warm."

"Hey, I been reading about you in the *Herald*," said the man, whose face appeared to be sandblasted in places. "Pretty crazy stuff over there in Dallas, huh?"

"Pretty crazy," Archie repeated, handing twenty dollars to the young lady behind the register. "I'm sorry about the job. Price of oil feels like it's goin' to the bottom again."

"Yeah, no, that's okay. That place I's lookin', it shut down too," he said, eyeing Archie's money; scratching at his neck. "Yeah, I read about you and a bunch of murders in Dallas. I couldn't believe it."

"It was a mess."

"I'm kinda seeing her." He nodded at the Latina making Archie's change.

"That's nice," said Archie, smiling at the *señorita* who didn't look a day over eighteen.

"Yeah, I couldn't believe it, my Boss mixed up with a buncha murders. But there you was in the *Herald*, with your picture and everything," he said, as the girl bagged Archie's beer and chips. "Said a girl shot a man right between the eyes at some fancy motel."

"That's a fact," said Archie, taking his bag by the loops.

Archie smiled at his nameless driver, while the nameless driver smiled at the clerk.

Finally, the name came.

"How you been doin, Daryl? Besides the no job thing?"

"Pretty good," he said, scratching at his sparse red beard. "Better when I got a little smoke to take the edge off."

"I hear ya," said Archie, fingering the bills in his pocket. He wanted to give the poor guy a twenty; but came up with two singles, which he pushed down. "Hey man, gimme a call next week. See if we can rustle you up a drivin' job."

Archie shook a man's hand, patted him on the shoulder. "It's good to see ya, Daryl."

"You too, Boss." He couldn't look Archie in the eye; just raked a hand through his lank hair; stared at his flip flops.

Coming out the door, Archie saw Wacey, eyes fixated on her phone, and thanked the Lord. He guessed co-dependence was a good thing (Sister Ernestine had recently introduced him to the term). All he knew was that he was glad to have a bodyguard-girlfriend.

And he was glad that 'ol strung-out Daryl had a friend, too.

West Texas could get you down quick without some kind of partner.

FULL MOON FRIDAY THE THIRTEENTH

EL PASO, TEXAS

NOVEMBER 13, 2015

As fast lanes go, Big Spring and Garden City didn't even break the speed limit.

All the same, Archie was glad to be slowing down—with Wacey. They were getting along famously in their twin shotgun houses in Big Spring, taking breakfast or lunch at his house and dinner at Wacey's.

At the Garden City compound, to which they retired almost every weekend, Archie and Wacey weren't comfortable sleeping together. So, they didn't. He stayed in his old room and Wacey stayed with Tallulah.

As winter set in, Wacey and Tallulah were practically inseparable, dishing on their favorite reality shows and bouncing off each other's peculiar personalities. Archie was grateful that Wacey'd taken Tallulah under her wing; especially since the gifted striker stood her ground on *not* playing volleyball at Tarleton.

After their court-ordered stretch of small-town house arrest, Archie and Wacey were flabbergasted that the Sheriff agreed to let them go to El Paso, unchaperoned.

"Y'all are grown folks," said Chuck. "Just keep your nose clean."

The downtime had given Archie a chance to get in the point spread zone. The result was a sneaky-good two-week run. After winning $25K off the Dimmitt cotton magnate and $25K off the dearly departed DC!!!, Archie had quietly cobbled together a combo Coahoma-Ackerly Sands win, and the next Friday, an extra-special Forsan victory. It was the first time Wacey'd been back to her alma mater since running away from home.

His cumulative winnings: $100K. A long way from $650K, but solid black.

So, on a daybreak Friday they loaded up the car with Yetis filled with French press and a basket of homemade ham, cheese and jalapeno jelly croissants and drove the breadth of the Big Empty in less than five hours. I-20 to I-10; due west across the Trans-Pecos wilderness at a hundred miles per hour—340 easy miles with the Cougar Red Cadillac barely breaking a sweat.

Archie'd also enjoyed a good run of exercise. Close proximity to triple murders made a man wary of sudden endings and the former slot receiver wanted to go out at his playing weight. He was glad to have stacked three weeks of five-days before he stuck his hand in Sister Ernestine's overflowing picnic basket.

"Did I just eat two entire croissants?"

"You did," confirmed Wacey. "I don't know where you put'em. Your Mom's cookin' sticks to me like glue."

An hour out, Wacey called the Hotel El Paso and found out the room wouldn't be ready until 3 p.m. The delay provided Archie with a perfect opportunity to show his new girlfriend the one (and only) scene of Weesatche glory as a Cougar footballer.

"Let's swing over to UTEP," he said, visions of an epic touchdown catch and run bouncing off the back of his eyelids. "We can grab some lunch on campus and I'll show you the Sun Bowl—the second prettiest stadium in the state."

"No lunch for me," she groaned. "Your Mom's makin' me fat!"

"I'd call it curvy."

"Of course you would."

As luck would have it, UTEP's world-class cross-country team was running the stadium steps when the Cougar Red Cadillac rolled to a stop in the shadow of the Franklin Mountains. The stadium gates were open and Archie and Wacey were soon sitting at the tippy-top of the sun-drenched Sun Bowl. They stretched out on the empty bleachers and watched the string-bean runners climb up and down the steep rows.

Archie cleared his throat. "Okay Ms. Foyt, prepare to be dazzled by the briefest bit of Weesatche glory," he began. "This is the site of my one and only touchdown. Senior year against the Miners."

"The Miners?" said Wacey, happily playing along. "What do they mine?"

"I could Google it, but I know you're dying to hear this story."

"Oh yeah," she said, pat-patting his hand. "I'm all ears."

"Check it out," he said, pointing down to the field at his imaginary self.

"Archie Weesatche, fifth-year senior from 6-Man Garden City, is lined up on the Cougar thirty-yard line. Klingler takes the first-down snap, rolls left, looks, looks; buys some time, he's runnin' out of real estate. Klingler slings a sidearm bullet; hits a streaking Weesatche in stride at the fifty-yard line. Weesatche is on his horse. Weesatche is pulling away. It's Weesatche, untouched, into the UTEP end zone for a seventy-yard Cougar touchdown. Way to go West Texas!"

"Wow, I can actually see you doin' that," said Wacey. "That's really cool."

"I kinda memorized that call," he agreed, squeezing his girlfriend's hand, so pleased that she looked a little impressed. "I haven't been back here till this very day."

"That's so cool," she said, basking as the sun peeked out from behind puffy clouds.

"Yeah, yeah. Enough with the faded glory," he said, raising up on the bleacher. "Where'd you learn to shoot? In CJ?"

"I learned to rope before I learned to shoot," she said, shading her eyes from the bright sunshine. "I got a good calf ropin' story."

"Do tell."

"The day all the *machos* fell in love with the *gringa*," she said, noticeably excited.

Wacey elaborated on a narco all-nighter at the rancho in Santa Elena where the first OJ Plaza Boss, Pablo Acosta, hid the purloined $6.5 million. Quite the little fiesta with *carne asada*, *cabrito* and lots and lots of cocaine.

While the villagers prepped long picnic tables and ranch hands lifted roasted meat off spits, Don Pablo's crew of dope runners and *sicarios* shuffled around the perimeter of a crude horse pen. Josy and Wacey were watching a few of the older *vaqueros* ride and rope when a younger hand brought in a roping calf. Despite Don Pablo's vocal urgings, none of his crew volunteered.

"I climbed over the fence, hopped on a horse. I ran that little sucker down quick," she said, "And threw him, too."

"Damn girl, I've heard of girls throwin' goats," said Archie. "But not full-grown calves!"

"He was a scrawny little thing," she continued. "My dad taught me on big calves. So anyway, they didn't give me a piggin' string, so the calf got away, but man, those *machos* were impressed. They'd never seen a girl ride and rope like that."

"No, no, I bet you were the belle of that fiesta."

"I had a hard time keeping Don Pablo off me after that," she said, shaking her head. "And Rudy flat out left Josy. Brought me from CJ to OJ, and the rest was history. Until Josy got her hooks back in me with that buried treasure."

"Yep," said Archie, enjoying Wacey's happy smile. "We're still chasin' that pot of gold."

BY TWO THIRTY, ARCHIE WAS SIPPING A CUBA LIBRE (WITH MEXICAN COKE!) under the Hotel El Paso's spectacular Tiffany stained-glass dome that crowned a hacienda-style bar. Their room was still being prepped, giving Archie time to punch in directions for El Paso High, a highly-recommended Tex-Mex joint called the L&J Café, and a dive called the Pershing Inn, or the PI, as it was known to the soldiers who flocked there from nearby Fort Bliss.

"Now that's as fine a Friday night as I can imagine," he said, pocketing his phone and hailing the bartender for a second Cuban. "You're not going to believe this high school stadium. I swear it looks like something out of ancient Rome."

"I can't believe how many football games you're draggin' me to," allowed Wacey, occupying herself with a *Topo Chico*.

"You bummed we're not goin' to the Kentucky?"

Archie might cross over to Juarez in broad daylight, but he wasn't about to try his luck on a late Friday night.

"Naw, I'm not feeling CJ, right now."

The *Rio Bravo*/Rio Grande Sister Cities—*Ojinaga*/Presidio, *Ciudad Acuña*/Del Rio, *Piedras Negras*/Eagle Pass, *Nuevo Laredo*/Laredo, *Reynosa*/McAllen, and *Matamoras*/Brownsville—were all basically war zones with intermittent cease-fires. When the cartels were battling for turf, the violence was horrific. Had been for the better part of two decades. But *Ciudad Juarez*/El Paso had it far worse. Sheriff Fuchs allowed that more drugs, guns, and money flowed across the four EP/*CJ* bridges in one day than all the rest of the Texas/Mexico border crossings, combined.

When the room was finally ready, they weren't disappointed. They walked straight to the fifteenth-floor floor-to-ceiling window and marveled at the Chihuahua Desert moonscape and *Ciudad Juarez's* crazy urban sprawl.

"What a wild city!" Archie cried, taking in a horizon full of rugged *Sierra de Juarez* mountains. "And look at that cool sculpture. It's a big red X."

"El Paso's awesome," Wacey agreed. "I had some good times here, that's for sure."

"Mighta' had something to do with being nineteen and bullet-proof."

"Maybe," she said, hugging his back. "I'm just glad I made it out."

"Me too," he said. "It's nice to have a partner on these long-ass drives."

"I'm startin' to feel half-normal, I think," she said, exhaling a lovely sigh. "I swear it's hangin' around your family. I guess I never knew what normal was."

"I know. I can't think about it too much," said Archie, turning to face her. "Sister Ernestine and Chuck are miracles. I mean where the hell did they come from?"

"France and Borden County," she said, laughing. "Last I heard."

"Exactly!" he said. "Who the hell is from Nice, France, and Gail, Texas? And lives in Garden City?"

"Us."

She kissed him full on. Then started down his neck.

"Lucky us," he said, taking the curvy measure of Wacey's full hips in his hands.

"Lucky you."

"Yes ma'am," he agreed, as she tugged on the silver tip of his ranger belt. "All day."

THE SUN WAS SETTING AND FRIDAY NIGHT LIGHTS WERE GLOWING ACROSS THE city.

The El Paso prize was a $25K wager with the "Implant King" of *Juarez* (dental, rather than breast, much to Archie's surprise). Doctor Hector Quiroga, was a 1980 graduate of El Paso Andress and the entrepreneurial genius who'd single-handedly created the "Golden Bridge," *Centro de Implantología Oral*, the richest practice in Chihuahua.

As Archie and Wacey waited below the majestic stadium side of El Paso High, he remembered Okinawa saying that Dr. Quiroga always dressed sharp. And sure enough, there he was, a tiny *norteño*, in an immaculate black pin-stripe suit, black ostrich boots and a black felt Stetson. And not only handsomely tailored, but the good doctor also flashed an absolute Farrah Fawcett smile.

"Hey Dr. Quiroga," said Archie, shaking the Implant King's strong hand. "I'm Archie Weesatche. This is Wacey Foyt. Thanks so much for inviting us to the game!"

"*¡Señor Huizache!*" he said, shaking a man's hand, then kissing Wacey's. "*Y Señorita. ¡Encantada!* The pleasure is mine."

"I told Wacey this is the prettiest stadium in Texas," he said, stretching his arms out wide. "And how 'bout this weather? How 'bout a starry, starry Friday night."

"*Señor* Okinawa didn't tell me your husband is a romantic," said Dr. Quiroga, finally letting go of Wacey's hand. "Yes, yes! I take it for granted, our stadium is *muy bonito*."

They all smiled at the valley below as the aurora of urban lights paled beneath the twinkling West Texas cosmos.

"Okinawa sends his best. You ready to bet on some EP football?" said Archie, uncharacteristically throwing his arm around Wacey's shoulders and pulling her close. "I assume your takin' Andress."

"*¡Por supuesto! ¡Mi alma mater!*" he cried, pulling out a rubber-banded roll of cash.

"Oak said you were giving me El Paso High and six," said Archie, uncuffing Wacey to pull out his own wad of bills. "That's the spread on MaxPreps."

"That's all you want? Against *mis Aguilas? Seis puntos solo?*"

"Against *Los Tigres*," said Archie, puffing up with good cheer. "*¡Seis puntos es perfecto!*"

"I think you may be *los tiburones*," kidded the good doctor, thumbing his Benjamins.

"*¿Que es tiburones?*"

"Sharks."

"Ay, sharks!" they cried.

Wacey was pleased indeed when the suave Dr. Quiroga suggested that she hold the money in her new Valentino handbag.

And just like that, another $25,000 bet was on. On a high school game!

Outrageous, thought Archie. Okinawa hadn't given him any actionable intel on either Andress or EP High, but had talked about this game—this bet—all year.

And was Okinawa ever right.

Dr. Hector Quiroga was pure. As golden as hometown boosters get—a rich, cheerful, former cheerleader from a city that didn't celebrate men with megaphones. As the teams lined up for the kickoff, Archie chuckled when Dr. Quiroga, again, kissed Wacey's hand. "Let's settle up on the same spot."

"Yes, enjoy the game *Señor Huizache*," he said, fluttering his elegant lashes at Wacey. "The night is almost as beautiful as *La Palomita Blanca*."

"You're adorable," said Wacey, extending her hand for the third time. "We should introduce him to Sister Ernestine?"

Dr. Quiroga stared at Wacey, baffled, for a split-second, then smiled at Archie.

"*¡Viva Los Tigres!*" shouted Archie.

"*¡Vivan las Aguilas!*" replied the doctor, his elegant fist flying up in the air.

The football, unfortunately, wasn't nearly as pretty as the setting, but the boys from El Paso's oldest public schools played a hard-fought game. The soccer-style kickers for both teams were impressive. Each blasting Division I-worthy field goals in the first and second quarters. Each team finally got untracked in the fourth quarter, scoring early touchdowns with the kicker from EP High inexplicably shanking his extra point to keep EP Andress ahead, 10–9.

"Maybe *he's* got money on the game," said Wacey, eyes locked on her Instagram feed.

Impressed that she even noticed, Archie assured her that El Paso High would prevail. "I'm still up five points, with three minutes to go."

"Oh yeah," she said, "I forgot you're the point-spread whisperer. How come you only bet twenty-five?"

"I bet Dr. Quiroga would've bet *you* fifty thousand."

Wacey beamed. "He likes me."

"We all love *La Sicaria*," said Archie, shocked when the Andress quarterback connected on a rare pass to keep the clock running.

"I'm not diggin' this *Sicaria* stuff," said Wacey, frowning at her phone. "Tallulah's better with nicknames."

As the clock ran down to five seconds, a cherry bomb exploded in the stands. In spite of the commotion, the EP Andress kicker split the uprights with a thirty-three-yard field goal.

Final score: EP Andress 13 El Paso High 9.

Dr. Quiroga's alma mater won the game, but Archie won the bet—by a slim two points.

True to his reputation, the Implant King stepped right up. Players and families from both sides mingled around them in the cool Trans-Pecos evening, everybody side-eyeing the cash exchange. When the count was clean, Dr. Quiroga handed Wacey his golden "Golden Bridge" business card with a wink.

"I thought I won," said Dr. Quiroga, charmed by the way Wacey was fanning his cash. "I forgot about the *pinche* point spread."

"I sure appreciate your graciousness, Dr. Quiroga," said Archie. "Last guy I bet with wasn't nearly as nice. Can I buy you a drink?"

"*No, Señor Huizache. Gracias a usted,*" said the doctor, reaching yet again, for Wacey's hand. "I have appointments to attend to. *Buenas noches, señorita.*"

"*Buenos noches, doctor,*" said Wacey, in surprisingly natural Spanish—an accent he'd never heard.

"I don't mean to be disrespectful, but is it okay to get a margarita at the Kentucky?"

"The Kentucky Club? In Juarez? No, no," said Dr. Quiroga, smiling at Wacey, then leveling his gaze on Archie. "*Solo,* perhaps. *Con este palomita, no, no. Es mejor, no.*"

"*Si, yo se,*" said Archie, sliding his hand around Wacey's waist. "We'll come back for El Paso High's hundredth anniversary."

"Yes, yes!" exclaimed Dr. Quiroga. "I will personally take you to *Juarez.* I have no problems. I give all the narcos' girlfriends beautiful smiles."

"And if you're ever in Garden City," said Wacey, with a cute smile of her own.

"Yes, actually, I know this town!" said the good doctor. "I have *a pequeño* oil and gas interests in Glasscock County."

I bet you do, thought Archie, trying not to roll his eyes when Wacey's hand was kissed, for the tenth time.

"*¡Vivan Aguilas!*" shouted the doctor, fist raised, as he strode across his hometown field.

WITH ANY HOPES OF A QUICK JAUNT ACROSS THE BORDER DASHED, ARCHIE escorted Wacey back to the Cougar Red Cadillac glowing gloriously among the dinged-up student jalopies—all practically flying out of the parking lot. The love birds had not gotten around to eating after an afternoon in bed. They decided on a quick drive down Missouri Avenue to the L&J Café. They found the dining room shuttered when they arrived.

"Can we still get some enchiladas?" asked Archie, slipping a twenty to the hostess, who smiled through her fatigue. She nodded, then led them down a narrow alley of empty tables to a bar where the Cowboys-Texans football game was on two big screens. It was a special Friday Night edition of Thursday Night Football and every table was full. The margaritas and beer had clearly been flowing based on the rowdy vibe. The room was full of mostly young Cowboy backers, dressed in full regalia—ball caps and jerseys for the men; T-shirts for the women. One guy wore face paint and shoulder pads.

Archie hated Thursday Night Football. He'd all but given up on the pro game after the Oilers moved to Nashville in 1996. He still watched the Cowboys, but the NFL was getting pretty sick. Gladiatoresque in its brutality. El Paso High versus EP Andress, under the stars, on a Friday night—that was football.

"We should've gone to the Kentucky," he yelled over the crowd noise.

Wacey shrugged, studied the menu, perked up when a fresh basket of chips and salsa arrived. They were seated next to a particularly obnoxious table; all loud-mouthed, oversized Anglos squeezed together on a banquette, the girls drunkenly gossiping.

Wacey absently reached for a bottle of Tabasco at the edge of the rowdy's table.

"Bitch! Don't be stealin' our shit," yelled a cowgirl, reaching for Wacey's wrist.

Wacey snapped up the bottle, then looked at Archie to confirm the girl's outrageous behavior.

"What the hell?" said Archie, looking the drunk girl in the eye, "There's no call for that."

Before she could respond, Tony Romo threw a Cowboy touchdown. Everybody went back to yelling at the TV.

A young, broad-backed bouncer, who'd observed the Tabasco exchange, leaned in close to Archie. "Would y'all mind moving to another table?"

After a moment's hesitation, they did just that.

The table of drunks was still in ear-shot, but Wacey and Archie decided to play it cool. They wolfed down a delicious enchilada dinner, and actually enjoyed their meal, if not the company. Wacey wasn't paying any attention, but Archie could hear the drunk girl continue to mouth off.

Finally, after paying the tab, leaving a good tip, and with Wacey in the bathroom, Archie sidled up to the rowdy Cowboy's fans. "Y'all need to learn some manners."

"Really, old man," sneered the cowgirl. "Fuck you!"

Archie looked at her and smiled.

"No," he said, casually firming his grip under their table. "You really do."

Archie lifted the table and proceeded to dump every plate, every mug, every pitcher of beer into their laps.

"Whoa, whoa, whoa, what the . . . HELL!"

As the drink-drenched idiots scrambled, Archie then squatted low, shoulder-pressed the entire table, and turned it upside down on their ill-mannered asses.

While Archie admired all the hell breaking loose below his feet, Wacey grabbed the back of his shirt and started pulling him toward the exit. Before they could make a clean get away, a muscled-up, warlock-looking Cowboy fan launched himself from under the table, straight into Archie's midsection.

Archie instinctively stiff-armed the warlock, but momentum took them to the floor. Somehow, when they hit the linoleum, Archie's right ring finger lodged in the warlock's mouth, and the sumbitch bit down. Hard.

Archie instantly began to fist bash the warlock's melon head; finally, hard enough to dislodge his finger which unleashed an ungodly torrent of blood. Wacey kept pulling on Archie's shirt till she cleared him. Then the bouncer rushed in, put the warlock in a chokehold, and squeezed on the little bastard till he blacked out.

In a split second, Archie and Wacey were out the door, in the Cadillac, and on the street. Blasting down Missouri Avenue and up Arizona, until Archie realized that he needed to slow the hell down. Meanwhile, blood was pouring all over the steering wheel, the seats, the console. Wacey grabbed a bunch of McDonald's napkins out of the glove box and slapped them on his hand while Archie asked Siri for directions.

Miraculously, the navigation screen lit up with precise coordinates to the hotel, and Archie and Wacey were again, at the lobby, up the elevator, and in the room, in record time. All instinct; nothing but.

"Good god! What the hell just happened?" he said, calming down, moving from the bedroom to the bathroom to check the damage to his right ring finger.

"What were you thinking?" said Wacey, as she ran hot water in the sink. "I've never . . . You never . . . what in the world, Archie?"

"Well," he said, unwrapping blood-soaked napkins and letting the warm water rain red down the drain. "I guess I had enough."

"You think?"

No, he thought, what saved me was football. The muscle memory of knocking the absolute crap out of a guy. That, and the counterintuitive fact that there was of no pain at the point of attack.

Back in the day, Archie'd gotten his ass kicked—bad—trying to box a street fighter down in Houston. The next time, and every time since, he waded in with pure rage, swinging and kicking and banging, then banging some more, till it was over. Big, small, one man, two men, gang; if you got in a fight—scorch the fucking earth. Keep attacking.

Worked in football. Worked in fights.

Worked even better with flesh-eating warlocks.

UNA HISTORIA DE VICTORIA

While Archie and Wacey were gallivanting around El Paso, fleecing Implant Kings and battling flesh-eating warlocks, Chuck Fuchs was flying to Laredo for a meeting with Josefina Montemayor.

While in the air, the Sheriff decided it was time to make a move; preferably a clean break. He was already in a foul humor, due to Sister Ernestine's announcement, during their weekly Friday lunch, that she was spending the weekend with her "friend" Sonny.

"You mustn't get the wrong idea, Chuck," she said, massaging the Sheriff's arthritic fingers between bites of pumpkin pie. "Sonny's eighty-eight, weighs three hundred pounds and smokes like a chimney. He's been asking me to visit his little ranch for years. As much money as he's made me, it's the least I can do."

"I've made you a fair amount of money," replied Chuck, extracting his arthritic fingers to fork some pie. "Deeded you all the land he found that oil under."

"And you know how much I appreciate that," assured Sister Ernestine, letting her boyfriend's hands well enough alone. "Do you still own your half of the minerals?"

"Oh sure."

"Not to mention what you've done for Archie, Matt and Tallulah."

The Sheriff finished his coffee, gave his fellow saver of souls a quizzical look.

"Yep, there's that."

"Oh Chuck, there most certainly *is* that," she continued, taking his plate and coffee cup to the sink. "How can Sonny Greene possibly compete?"

Chuck Fuchs couldn't imagine.

He sat a minute more, dug out a hangnail with his penknife, then stepped up behind Sister Ernestine as she rinsed the dishes. "If you want to spend your weekend with that old blowhard, fine by me."

"*Merci beaucoup, Sheriff,*" she said, exaggerating her lovely accent. She turned and put her warm, wet hands on his wind-tooled face and gave him an extra-long French kiss.

JOSEFINA MONTEMAYOR WAS SITTING IN DIM CANDLELIGHT AT A TINY TABLE IN a tiny cantina off a tiny brick-paved alley in *Nuevo Laredo*.

"Hello Chuck," she said, removing a pair of wildly expensive sunglasses. "Miss me?"

The lawman smiled at his sassy underboss, adjusting to the cantina's one-window gloom. *Bar Gato Negro* appeared empty, except for a skittish bartender, but Sheriff Fuchs knew that was incorrect. Ms. Montemayor always kept security close at hand.

"We all miss you, Josy," he said, eyes adjusted, moving toward the beautifully manicured hand offering him a seat. He took off his Stetson, sleeved the mid-November sweat off his brow. It was in the low fifties when he caught his Southwest flight out of Midland. It was in the high eighties on the Mexican border.

"Is this about the Hondurans? We got eyes on 'em," said the Sheriff, sitting stiffly in a cane chair. "They're trying another end-around."

"There's been a change in timing," said Josy, motioning for the bartender.

"What's that mean?"

"We need Archie's money now," she said, directing her attention to the hustling bartender, instantly at her side. "*Dos cervezas; y dos vasos frio.*"

"*Lo siento señorita. Pero no hay vasos helados.*"

"*Esta bien, joven.*"

The Sheriff settled into his seat. "Before we get into that, can you please explain why Rudy killed Archie's lawyer friend? The cops in Dallas are real curious."

The Sheriff nodded to the flustered bartender as he set down two bottles of *Bohemia*.

"The unfortunate Attorney Tuck," said Josy, sweeping her hair. "He knew too much."

"I know too much," said the Sheriff. "Wacey knows too much. How's that work?"

"Chuck, please," she said. "We both know why Wacey killed Rudy. He had it coming, no?"

"For a long time," agreed the Sheriff, slightly startled by the bartender's quick return with two small glasses. "Since the night he put that pistol in her mouth."

"So, there's your answer—Tuck talked too much," said Josy, smiling sweetly as the bartender poured their beers. "That's not a best practice."

"That's not an answer," said the Sheriff, raising his glass. *"Salud."*

"¡Salud! Tuck had a death wish. Rudy knew he was talking to the Hondurans again," she said, shooting her beer. "Have you talked to Sister Ernestine about a bridge loan?"

"Didn't know I was supposed to," said Chuck. "Archie's doin' all the good. He won another one last night."

"In El Paso. I know," said Josy. "Good for Archie. How's Wacey?"

"Good. Far as I know," said the Sheriff. "She still on your payroll?"

"Por supuesto," said Josy, pouring herself more beer. "If she behaves. Wacey's talented, but very impetuous."

"You make people impetuous," said the Sheriff, watching a pearl of sweat slide down his glass. "Have you noticed that?"

Josy ignored him. "The banker says he needs to get started. Too many banks and not enough time. He wants to start the process now; have it done by December thirty-first."

The Sheriff couldn't get a handle on Josy's mood—even more agitated than usual.

"Not much of a banker, is he?" said the Sheriff. "Unless he's puttiing the money to work, he's just a money launderer; plain and simple."

"*Ay Chuck*! He *is* a money launderer," she sighed, crossing her legs in a beautifully tailored mauve pantsuit. "You sound like my father."

"Good," countered the Sheriff. "He's ninety and lives like a king."

"Eighty-eight," said Josy, snapping her fingers at the bartender. "*Mezcal!*"

"I prefer not to drink on the job," said the Sheriff, plopping his jean-clad leg atop a knee. "Unless you insist."

"Oh, I do insist," she cooed. "And because you're such a good boy, I'll tell you a story."

"A story!" crowed the Sheriff.

"*Una historia de Victoria*," said Josy, directing the puppy-dog bartender to pour the shots. "For the old gringo. Do you read Carlos Fuentes?"

"Can't say that I do," said the Sheriff, turning in his chair to watch a street dog leave some fresh DNA on the door jamb. "But I am an old gringo."

"You are the *best* gringo," said Josy, raising her shot. "*¡A familia!*"

The Sheriff drank up, "*¡A famila!*"

"Family, loyalty, liberty," said Josy, clinking her shot glass with the long-time saver of souls. "My Holy Trinity."

"Sounds about right," said the Sheriff, trying his best not to stare at the provocative vent in Josy's starched white shirt.

"*Ahora, le cuento, una historia de Victoria*," said Josy, pulling a Kindle from a gorgeous calfskin, metal-studded handbag. She leaned back in the crude, straw-bottomed chair and began to read from the backlit tablet, "And I quote:

Mexican independence from Spain, gave Martin De León, [my great-great-great *abuelo*] a chance at settling a colony in Texas. He petitioned his government to bring forty-one Mexican families to Texas and was approved in 1824. The colony was funded in part by his wife Doña Patricia, [my great-great-great *abuela*] who provided $9,800 cash, horses, cattle, and pigs inherited from her father. Together, Patricia and Martín De León founded the town of Guadalupe Victoria—the only Mexican-majority colony in Stephen F. Austin's Texas settlements."

"Mind you—this is straight from Montemayor family history and veri-fied by the Texas State Historical Commission," said Josy, looking over a pair of tortoiseshell readers. "My father is consumed by this. All he talks about."

"So, how's he doing?" asked the Sheriff, with genuine interest.

"He's dying," she said. "COPD. Congestive heart failure. It's awful"

The Sheriff fingered the beer bottle's golden foil. "I'm sorry to hear that. Please."

Josy adjusted her readers:

"Nine years later, Martín De León died during a cholera epidemic leaving Patricia to head the family and an estate worth half a million dollars. In 1835, she received, from a grateful Stephen F. Austin, an additional five labors—888 acres—the balance due for fulfilling De León's empresario contact.

"Although an aging widow, Doña De León fully supported the Texas Revolution. Despite their well-known role in aiding the Texian cause, the De León family suffered greatly after the Texian's victory at San Jacinto. Fear, bigotry, and discrimination were rampant in the Republic of Texas.

"In fact, the De León's, the founding family of Victoria, were forced to abandon their livelihoods and possessions and flee the very country on whose behalf many had just fought. Doña Patricia re-settled in New Orleans and was quickly forced to sell 25,000 acres of land in Victoria County to support her family. The youngest De León son, Agapito, refused to leave the ranch in Victoria and was murdered by thieves raiding the family's cat-tle. Her second-eldest son, Silvestre, attempted to return to Texas, after six years in New Orleans, but he too was robbed and murdered."

"Damn," said the sheriff, who was well acquainted with the cruelty of his own Borden/Fuchs clan. They'd slaughtered dozens—maybe hun-dreds—of Comanches, Lipans, and Apaches during their days as conquer-ors of a *Comancheria* that once spread as far north as Idaho and as far south as Zacatecas.

The Borden/Fuchs clan had also lost a lot of kin. Many in unimagin-ably torturous ways.

Josy folded her reading glasses, shoved the Kindle back in her handbag. "And guess who the leader of the Victoria Anglos was?"

"Do tell?" asked the Sheriff.

"Seamus Callahan," said Josy, leaning over the table.

"Kin to Archie's old fiancée," said the Sheriff. "Patti Callahan, if I'm not mistaken."

"*¡Exactamente!*"

"I think they pronounce it Shay-mus, by the way," said the Sheriff. "Must've been Old Man Callahan's granddaddy."

Josy stared at the Sheriff, the picture of petulance. "Do you know how to pronounce, *venganza*?"

The Sheriff poured himself some more beer. "Sounds like vengeance."

"Really, does it?" she sassed. "Now *you* can explain something. Why do you hate to speak Spanish? At least Archie tries."

The Sheriff filled Josy's glass and then his own with beer; took a sip.

"My Spanish is fine, Josy. That's an interesting story," allowed the Sheriff. "My granddaddy used to talk about the Comanche raids all the time. Scared us to death."

"Did you ever talk to a Comanche? To a Native American?" said Josy. "To the families that your people slaughtered?"

"So, this is a crusade," he said. "Avenging angel Josefina to the rescue. Right all the wrongs; what, since Cortes?"

"Why shouldn't I?"

"Not really your style, Josy," he said. "Who's puttin' you up to this?"

"My father," she said, resigned.

"He's dying. Tell him what he wants to hear," he said, exasperated. "Look, I'm eighty years old myself, sitting in a bar in Nuevo Laredo because you asked me to. That's what partners do. Why am I here?"

Josy stood up, stretched her arms, cocked a hip. "I like you, Chuck. I do," she said, hugging herself, walking in a small circle. "But you can't protect anybody. Wacey's not a puppy. You can't put Archie on a leash and keep him safe."

The Sheriff scanned the dark corners of the bar again as Josy stepped up behind his chair and began to knead his shoulders.

"My father wants justice," she said, pressing against his broad back. "Callahan's men killed my ancestors—*¡mi familia!* —in cold blood!"

The Sheriff reached back, took Josy's hand, and guided her back to her chair.

"Josy, with all due respect to your father and family, this is no time for vendettas," he said. "We're trying to keep people safe, not get 'em killed."

"*¡Ay, cabron!* Mexicans love death!" said Josy, pushing away from the table. "We embrace it. Back to the Aztecs—centuries of human sacrifice. We don't fear it! Not like you pious gringos who want to live forever. You said it, you're scared to death."

"You want to take on the Callahans—two hundred years later!"

"You're all disrespectful," she said, putting on her shades. "Americans, *gringos*, fucking Texans. *¡Mamones!*"

"So, *all* the gringos pay for *all* the sins. Is that it?" replied the Sheriff. "That's why we fought the Mexican-American War, Josy . . . your boys lost."

"Lost," she said, "Your entire pathetic country is lost!" she cried, then slammed the rest of her beer. "But we're winning your precious War on Drugs, aren't we?"

"Whose we?" said the Sheriff, dumbfounded. "Where's your dad? Does he know you're here? In Laredo?"

"He's wants vengeance, Chuck," she spat. "And so do I."

"Come on, now! You're just talkin' in circles," he said, backing his chair from the table. "I tell you what, Josefina Montemayor."

"What, Chuck Fuchs? What are you going to tell me?"

"You want to talk about vengeance? About revenge? Take it up with Sister Ernestine," he said, standing like a *Yanqui* colossus. "Did you know that Sister lost four family members in World War II?"

"No."

"Didn't think so," said the Sheriff, squinting to see who was lurking behind Josy. "Let's see how you handle a French Jew who's seen more human sacrifice than you'll ever know."

"Maybe I will," she declared, staring down the Sheriff. "Sister Ernestine likes me."

The Sheriff simultaneously reached for his Stetson and pulled a Glock from the small of his back. He sensed something, someone, in the black-ened corner of the bar.

"Really," said Josy, raising her hands with maximum theatricality. "Don't shoot."

He backed out slowly toward the door, one hand touching the bar stools; one finger on the trigger. "And don't bother callin' any more. I'm done playin' phone tag."

"¡*Largate!*" she said, waving him off. "Run home, momma's boy."

ENTER SAND QUEEN

After a painful Sunday return from El Paso, the Cougar Red Cadillac blew into Big Spring at a high rate of speed. Archie's entire hand was angry red, hot to the touch and swelling by the minute. At Wacey's insistence, he agreed to medical attention.

Fortunately, the Scenic Mountain Hospital ER was manned by a Viet Nam-era army doc who immediately put Archie on IV antibiotics. The soft-spoken combat surgeon examined the wounds with keen curiosity. He muttered about tendons and blood vessels as he peered at the mangled ring finger. Finally, he dunked Archie's hand in an iodine bath and kept it there.

"Nasty stuff, human bites," said the doc, who turned out to be related to Okinawa by marriage. "Cats are the worst. But human bites are almost as bad because of all the bacteria. Who knows what that fella had going on in his mouth—staph, strep, syphilis, HIV—ain't no tellin'."

The speculative list got Archie and Wacey's attention as the doc's assistant began to clean the wound, much to Archie's discomfort. Archie looked at Wacey, as the doc began to suture the finger, as if to say, This is serious.

After the assistant wrapped the loosely stitched wounds in cohesive bandage, Archie received another bit of apocryphal news. "I'll be honest; you might lose that finger."

Archie wished the doc was a little less forthcoming but appreciated his expertise.

"First thing in the morning you drive straight to Steve Harris's clinic in Midland. I'll set up the appointment, but you gotta go."

"Yes sir, you can count on it."

"Best hand surgeon in West Texas; probably the whole state. You wouldn't believe how many roughneck's hands he's saved. The guy's a machine."

"You meet him in the army?"

"Naw, he's a young guy; half my age," said the doctor, eyeballing his young assistant's bandage job. "Put some more CoBan over the top; case he bangs it around."

Archie hadn't visited an emergency room since his move back to Big Spring. He hadn't had surgery since a hernia at age six. Archie was all good with self-inflicted pain, the kind you dealt with in football and track, or lifting weights. But this human bite business was a whole new level of pain—sharp, searing, and acute—super acute.

As Wacey drove them back to Garden City, they debated how to explain the "incident" to Sister Ernestine and the Sheriff. They decided the bar fight/human bite scenario was just too weird. Especially after the Sheriff's admonishment to stay out of trouble.

"I'll just tell'em I smashed my finger in the trunk," said Archie, proudly recalling the shocked look on the girl's face when he flipped the table on her loud mouth. "I had no intention of fighting—for the rest of my life. I couldn't believe that girl was talkin' to you like that."

"I had no intention of shootin' Rudy, either," said Wacey, eyes focused on the narrow two-lane highway to Garden City. "Shit happens."

"Well, I'm *not* losing this finger," said Archie. "I'm gonna be the best patient that combat doc's ever seen."

Not.

After five days of excruciating wound care, two things were clear: Wacey Foyt would make a fine battlefield nurse and Archie Weesatche was no soldier. The best he could manage during Wacey's twice daily, laser-focused meatpacking was closed eyes, dead silence, and white knuckles death-gripping a wooden spoon. The morning/evening triage, at Sister Ernestine's kitchen table, had a way of clarifying the relationship.

"Are you okay?" Wacey would ask, after each meticulous application of medicated packing wrapped in blue CoBan.

"Yes. Thank you," Archie would say, then head straight to the door for a long, convalescent walkabout. "Thank you to the moon."

The first surgery, by the miraculous Dr. Harris, removed all of the necrotic flesh on the upper half of the finger. A second corrective surgery, sutured synthetic skin grafts over his (finally!) infection-free finger. Archie was anxious—an impatient patient. It was hard to clear his mind of warlocks who bit instead of hit.

"It's friggin' Un-American," groused Archie, on yet another walk around the Garden City High School track. "What kind of tool bites your finger in a bar fight?"

"A ratchet Zombie tool," said Tallulah, bouncing lane-to-lane alongside Archie.

Tallulah was the perfect tonic to Uncle Archie's blues, and of late, an unexpected source of new betting action. She'd been flirting—apparently all fall—through texts and SnapChat with a girl she'd met during her single week in Stephenville—a Tarleton student manager for the volleyball team named Ruth Bishop.

Miss Bishop turned out to be richer than Boone Pickens (not really, nobody's that rich). One of eleven children of a new billionaire from Rising Star, Texas—population 835.

The Bishop family fortune was in sand.

Not the Saudi kind filled with oil. The fracking kind filled with cash.

According to a *Forbes* article that Tallulah read as they walked, the Bishop's sand was mined by the metric ton from pits in Eastland County and used by service companies such as Halliburton, Baker Hughes, and Schlumberger to crack open the microscopic fissures in the Permian Basin and Eagle Ford shale. Heretofore worthless flash-flood creek beds were now worth millions, and finally, billions, after a hedge fund in Singapore snapped up the Bishop family company, SandTech, for a cool $1.6 billion.

For sand!

2

Eastland County now claimed a second famous son—Big Bill Bishop—joining the hotel magnate Conrad Hilton, who was from nearby Cisco. Archie could feel the football cosmos magically aligning in the form of new money—new BIG money—needing a respectable way to be spent.

"She's a total powdered donut, Arch," said Tallulah, marching backward as her brother grimly trudged around the track. "Totally lesbonic."

As always, Archie was enthralled by Tallulah's patois. "Tules, I love the sound of lesbonic, but what's up with the powdered donut?"

"She's so bad, March," squealed Tallulah, high knees pumping. "Ruth taught me two things in one week: girls kiss way better than boys and I love powdered donuts!"

Archie surmised that powdered donuts was too big a reveal. Tallulah sprinted away at top-speed into a round off that launched an impossibly high, impossibly graceful, extended–leg backflip.

"Good lord, girl," shouted Archie, trying to sprint his ownself. "We've *got* to get you on a volleyball court."

The newly pan-sexual teenager was having none of it.

"She's a super-hot mess, Arch," said Tallulah, giggling as she caught her breath.

And there was more.

Tallulah fell for the smooth-talking Ruth first, because she was the best ankle-taper she'd ever seen, and second, because they both hated their parents' crazy cults—Pentecostal and Mormon offshoot, respectively. After she and Ruth simultaneously dropped out of Tarleton, five days before the first volleyball game, Tallulah engaged the Sand Queen in marathon text sessions, soon discovering the secret to the rich girl's disposable income.

Cyber-hacking was Ruth's gig.

In fact, the young hellion from Rising Star was so adept at plundering her daddy's "Sand Money" accounts, of which there were so many, in so many small-town banks, that none of Big Bill's legion of financial consultants had a clue about the daughter's brazen larceny.

Ruth pilfered small amounts from myriad accounts that accumulated into spectacular wads of cash. Money that she promptly unloaded on unsuspecting college bars in Stephenville, barbecue joints in Brownwood, and boutiques in Ft. Worth. Ms. Bishop kept a high profile in low places. And the bigger Miss Rising Star's account grew, the more obnoxious she got.

Of course, Archie had other plans for the Sand Queen's cabbage.

In Texas, there was no more proper way to burn cash than supporting your hometown football team. Archie immediately proposed a bet on the perfect Six-Man slugfest—Rising Star versus Sterling City. A genuine Big Country throw-down featuring two of the hottest tailbacks in all of small ball—Tallulah's boyfriend, Ramblin' Roger Tedesco of Sterling City and Rising Star's one and only Battlin' Billy Bishop.

As they walked back to the Nice House, Tallulah was already on the job. "Look!" she screamed, shoving her phone in Archie's face:

> tell ur Big Shot Uncle 10K says my baby brothers gonna kick
> your boy toys ass. Can't wait to EAT UR PEACH !!!!

"Sounds like we got a live one, Tules," said Archie, with visions of huge paydays and powdered donuts dancing in his head.

THE WEESATCHE TEXAS TOUR RE-STARTED FIRST THING FRIDAY MORNING WITH breakfast at Sister Ernestine's big kitchen table featuring bowls of jalapeno-flecked scrambled eggs, plates of crispy bacon and simmering deer sausage. Pitchers of orange juice and milk were passed followed by plates brimming with berries and fresh-cut fruit. Sister Ernestine soon arrived from the stove with a tower of flapjacks and grits laced with cinnamon.

"Fine spread, Ms. Ducornet," allowed Sheriff Fuchs, safely home from his quick trip to Nuevo Laredo.

"I-G-G-Y! Ruth's in for twenty-five K!" screamed Tallulah, reading a text message over her stack of pancakes.

"She must've hacked a new account," said Archie, washing down his third cup of French roast. "And since she's such a sport, we'll bet straight up; no points. Best tailback wins."

"Green fucking salad!" gushed Tallulah. "Can I give Roger some if you win?"

"What exactly do you mean by *give Roger some*?" said Matt, piling his plate with mounds of sweet and savory.

"Matthew, we'll have none of that suggestive talk," scolded Sister Ernestine from the stove, now busily prepping one of her fabulous apple pies.

"Ask Iggy," whispered Tallulah, giggling into her glass of juice.

"This Ruth girl better behave," said Wacey, fully aware of—and not happy with—Tallulah's new BFF. "I'll shut her down."

"Ooh *Mami*, don't say that," said Tallulah, mooning at Wacey, as she passed the pancakes. "She likes it rough."

"Tallulah," said Sister Ernestine, walking up to her well-fed crew. "You're getting to be quite the *provocateur.*"

"Is that good?" she asked, stealing a look at Matt. "It sounds fun."

"It sounds," said the Sheriff, "like you might want to slow down with this Ruth girl."

Several sets of eyes exchanged glances. Followed by a torrent of Tallulah giggles.

"Okay, so seven o'clock kickoff," said Archie, seizing the opportunity to finalize his escape after another week of grueling finger rehab. "Oak says Sterling City's got the serious red-ass about losing to Garden City last week. How's Roger's hamstring, by the way?"

"What's a hamstring?" asked Wacey and Tallulah, simultaneously.

"Matt. Definition, please," said Archie, stabbing a final slice of deer sausage and dredging it through a puddle of pancake syrup.

"Hamstring—muscle group; back of knee to buttocks," he recited, from personal experience. "Problematic when tweaked; career-threatening when torn."

Tallulah raised her hand, classroom-style.

"Attention please! Six-Man intel: Rising Star is undefeated, seven oh. Ranked sixth in the state," she read from her phone. "Number five is Motley County, number four Borden County, number three Balmorhea, number two Follett, and top-ranked Richland Springs, is going for their seventh Class A Division II state title."

"Excellent update, Tules," said Archie. "Okinawa wants to hire you."

"He does!"

"No. He wants to hire me," said Matt. "And that's pronounced, Bal-more-ray."

"Okinawa should hire you both," said Sister Ernestine, pouring lush apple cinnamon filling into the crust. "The *Herald* needs some new blood."

"My Coyotes are playing some good ball," added the Sheriff, wiping latte foam off his push broom of a silver mustache. "I got a Deputy says we'll take state if the boys stay healthy. His son's the center. Big 'ol boy— runs about two fifty."

"Two fifty! In Six-Man?" said Archie. "Dude!"

"Borden County, Balmorhea," sang Sister Ernestine, busy finger-denting her pie crust. "Names that sailed me across the Seven Seas. Tales of Texas swirling in my head."

Sheriff Fuchs let out a hoot. "Bet you were sorely disappointed when I came bustin' through your door with ol' gambling man, over here."

"One of the best days of my life," cooed Sister Ernestine, walking over to wrap Archie and the Sheriff in an apple-infused hug.

A SIZABLE CROWD WAS ALREADY SWARMING THE STERLING CITY STADIUM WHEN Archie, Tallulah, and the Cougar Red Cadillac rolled in amongst a fleet of mud-spattered ranch and oilfield trucks. Sheriff Fuchs and Wacey were in Borden County on law enforcement business. Some trouble north of Gail about which the dynamic duo was tight-lipped. Matt had opted for a Kurt Vile concert in Lubbock. Sister Ernestine was holding down the Nice House with her apple pie. And maybe, Sonny Greene.

The news of the parking lot was the local Frito-Lay delivery man in a ditch with a busted axle out toward Water Valley. The Sterling City folk were fitted to be tied.

"Hell you say!" gruffed an old-timer. "What kinda sorry outfit runs outta Fritos for the Frito Pies?"

As the Sterling City and Rising Star players finished their warmups, Archie joined the fence huggers. Tallulah immediately spotted Roger and ran to give him some good luck sugar. She puckered up right in front of the Sterling City head coach, who clearly wished Tallulah was playing wide receiver for him.

"Hey Weesatche!" came a voice from above. Archie looked up into the bleachers, instantly blinded by the next-to-last sunset of Daylight Savings Time.

"Hey yourself," he said, shielding his eyes. "Ruth Bishop?"

"The one and only," said the voice, still a red-rimmed blur in Archie's watering eyes. "Got some Johnny Wadd burning a hole in my pocket."

"Some what?" said Archie, stepping into the shade.

"Tube Steak Boogie, baby!" answered the voice, clomping down the bleachers.

Archie laughed, "Come on down."

He watched the stout girl stomp past the football moms and young-sters, oozing attitude. She was game-ready in dyed black Wranglers with a black T-back peeking under a shirt of untucked flannel. Her hair was shoul-der-length and jet black with shocks of purple, professionally applied. Her face was wholesome and round but with crazy-cool makeup. The smile was pure cocky. And upon closer inspection, Ms. Bishop was seriously packing, nothing poochy about her.

"Welcome to SC," he said, gingerly bumping fists with his blue-ban-daged hand. "And I don't mean Southern Cal."

"No shit," she said, tipping a pair of state-of-the-art Oakley's at Archie's hand damage. "Course, I can't talk; Risin' Star's the size of a Porta-Potty."

"Had a little incident in El Paso," he said, by way of explanation.

"Tallulah told me," she said, smirking. "You look pretty clean cut to be startin' bar fights."

"Endin' bar fights is what I do," said Archie, with a smile. "Defending my girl's honor."

"That'll work."

"So, you ready for some football?" asked Archie, stepping into a semi-quiet spot under the bleachers.

"Damn straight," she said, arms crossed under her ample chest.

As Archie extracted a fat envelope, he took in the girl from Rising Star's full measure.

"We gonna bet, or stare at my tits?"

"Uh, both," he ventured. "I guess."

Ruth Bishop laughed and slapped his shoulder. "Double D's, in case you're wonderin'."

"Nope. Yep. Hell, I'm sorry," he said, blushing like an altar boy. "The bet's twenty-five thousand; no points. Best tailback wins."

"How 'bout fifty?"

"On Six-Man?"

Ruth Bishop didn't flinch; held her cocksure smile. "Come on Gamblin' Man, Tallulah says you're some kind of Six-Man guru."

"Let's do it," he said, wondering about the extra $25K. "You take a check?"

"Nope." she clucked, firming her shades. "If I win, you'll find the cash. I guarantee."

"Oh yeah," allowed Archie, re-tucking the tail of his starched, monogrammed shirt into his Levi's. "Cash is king."

And then, a funny thing happened on the way to the end zone—a three-hour, back-and-forth Six-Man free-for-all.

Archie couldn't imagine what Tallulah's pre-game pep talk entailed, but Ramblin' Roger Tedesco was some kind of motivated—to the tune of nine touchdowns and twenty-seven tackles, motivated.

Final score: Sterling City 94 Rising Star 86.

As the entire population of Sterling City emptied from the stands, Ruth Bishop ambled down from the tiny visitor's bleachers and on to the eighty-yard field. She cuffed her little brother around his thick neck; told him good game.

Archie watched them from the end zone, not exactly anxious to collect from someone so certifiably certifiable. Fortunately, as he walked up, Battlin' Billy Bishop launched into a curious soundbite for a female sportswriter out of Abilene.

"I gotta be more physical," said the junior running back. "I want to get big underneath the line, keep my pads low, and keep God in the center of the game."

Archie raised an eyebrow. "You teach him to talk like that?"

"Fuck off," said Ruth. "Let him be Pentecostal if he wants."

Archie took that in stride and waved for Tallulah to join them. "How 'bout them, Sterling City Eagles!"

"Aw, shut up. You're luckier than goddamn Lucifer," yelled Ruth, fishing a wallet-thick wad of bills out of her Wranglers. "How 'bout double or nothin', Big Shot?"

Archie smiled at his Red Wings, waved at Roger Tedesco. "Helluva game, Roger!" he shouted, as the gridiron hero gave Tallulah a big sweaty kiss and hustled to the locker.

Archie re-focused. "Ruth, you *really* wanna bet a hundred grand?"

"I knew you were all talk," she said, waving him off.

You're the damn talker? he thought, trying to buy some time. "You really want to dosey doe with the Six-Man Devil?"

"Pick the fuckin' game," said Ruth, wiping her hands like a blackjack dealer. "I'll spread deviled ham on your ass and let the big dog eat!"

Just that instant, Tallulah walked up. Archie was thanking God.

"Are you being bully, again?" said the volleyball goddess, hooking a thumb in her new BFF's belt.

"Callin' bullshit is what she's doing."

"You got that right," said Ruth, slapping Tallulah's palm high and hard.

Tallulah snaked her hand into Ruth's pocket, tugged on the wad of cash.

"Go on, girl. Take that cabbage."

Tallulah did just that. Then fanned the bills into a thick green crescent.

"You won this?"

"Maybe," answered Archie, "Might be doublin' down. If your girl's got the sand."

"Oh, good God, do I ever have the sand," she said, folding Tallulah's fan and handing the bills to Archie. "Let me know, hustler. A hundred K, all day."

Archie took the money from Tallulah and tucked the stack of bills long ways inside his Carhartt. "I'm headed down to Round Rock next weekend."

"Who's playin'?" said Ruth, distracted by Tallulah nuzzling on her neck—a source of great concern to the gaggle of football moms eavesdropping, steps away.

"SPC Championship. Coupla Houston privates," said Archie, marveling as the Sand Queen melted beneath Tallulah's touch. "Got some new Eagle Ford money betting fifty K on his boy."

"I'll bet all that money in your pocket," said Ruth, basking in Tallulah's attention. "That your Eagle Ford man pays SandTech a million a month," she said, pushing her shades up and giving Tallulah a full-on kiss. On the fifty-yard-line!

The hovering football moms had an absolute conniption. "Well, I never!" they hissed.

"You're probably right," said Archie, handing her the stack of cash. "How 'bout you hang on to this, till Friday after next."

"Seriously?" Ruth Bishop didn't hesitate to take her money back. "Awright then, you lemme know what's next."

"I'll keep an eye on it for you, Uncle Archie," said Tallulah, breaking into a set of flawless cartwheels.

Ruth and Archie stood and admired a final, effortless Tallulah backflip.

"Good Lordy girl, I need to show you *off!*" said Ruth, ogling her friend's long, long legs. "Hey, we're partyin' in Angelo tonight. You wanna come?"

Archie paused a beat. Smiled at his new rival. "Nah, I'll leave y'all to it," he said, pleased to be making a little headway with Ruth. "But thanks for askin'."

"Let's get!" said Tallulah, hop-skipping a few steps toward the track, then turning back. "My boyfriend played good, didn't he?"

"Not as good as I'm gonna play you."

Archie swiped the Sand Queen's sassy ass as they exited. "Y'all be careful, now."

Ruth shot him a hard look, but didn't miss a beat, trotting after her prize filly, sing-songing, "Kiss my ass and a rattlesnake cake!"

Of course, Archie strenuously objected to Tallulah having anything to do with this money-whipping piece of work, but was powerless to intervene.

Besides, it was crazy to think that Tallulah would do anything but take care of herself.

On cue, Tallulah waved and smiled, the picture of teenage bliss.

Ruth Bishop waved, then shot him the bird, way up high.

"Bye-bye, crazy," said Archie, waving at his future $100K payday. "Watch out for the DPS. By the State School."

WALTZ ACROSS TEXAS

Archie was all by his lonesome.

As he drove back home to Big Spring, Six-Man stats swirling in his head, the Cougar Red Cadillac rushed past one of TXDOT's new retroreflective road signs: **MONAHANS 60**

Oh man, he thought . . .

That night.

That life-changing night.

Forty years ago.

It all came rushing back.

Not that Archie remembered much—he was only five years-old. And no matter how many times he asked, nobody had the heart to tell him the truth about that night.

Not brave Sheriff Fuchs, first on the scene in the sandhills south of Wink.

Not soothing Sister Ernestine, on the many restless nights when Archie asked after his mom and dad. Where'd they go? What are they doing?

For years—his entire childhood—Archie wondered if he'd done something wrong. Or not done enough. Knowing better, as he grew older, that something was up.

How could Big Arch and Bunny just disappear? Surely, they were coming back.

No.

And yet, Archie could not blame his parents. Would not. He idolized his handsome Daddy. Adored his sun-kissed Momma.

But still.

Archie always wondered why? Why his parents were gone? Why?

Little Archie Carter, the fortunate foundling from the Big Empty, needed to figure out what that awful night meant. How he could make sense of it, and move on.

Finally, his senior year at the University of Houston, with the timely assistance of a resourceful Student Services counselor, Archie got the help he needed. He enrolled in a senior-level fiction writing course in UH's nationally-renowned Creative Writing Program, where he was promptly taken under the psychoactive wing of Antonya Boswell and Robert Nelson, a pair of wild-child visiting professors.

The unconventional husband and wife team were terrific teachers. And uber-talented writers. They showed their willing pupil how to plot a simple story, then encouraged Archie to focus on how his people talk.

The fiction class proved to be a godsend. The one truly meaningful academic experience of his undergraduate career. And the one story that he actually completed. Not to mention the only A the committed jock ever received at UH.

On the Monday after Thanksgiving, his football career bitterly concluded after losing a last, hard-fought game to rival Rice (in the Astrodome!), Archie holed up in his cubicle at the MD Anderson Library. And didn't come out until he was finished.

Archie wrote his own damn origin story.

And stuck to it.

Waltz Across Texas

by Archie D. Weesatche

The stars at night are *big and bright.*

Deep in the heart of Texas.

They most certainly were in the heavens above Big Arch Carter.

After graduating from the University of Texas's exalted Petroleum Geology pro-gram, the lanky Longhorn was celebrating America's Bicentennial and his tenth year as Drilling Supervisor for Falcon Seaboard Drilling. Nicknamed "The Only Needle with Two Eyes" during his days as a two-sport star for the Brownwood Lions, Big Arch had put on a few pounds since his wide receiver/power forward days but still fit loosely in pressed khakis and a monogrammed Hamilton shirt. He cut a classic oilfield figure in a short-brim Stetson and polished ranchers leaning against the guard rail girding the floor of his massive drilling rig.

This particular rig "Old Ironsides" was currently leased to Mr. Perry Bass of Fort Worth. He was drilling a confirmation well for a bold new step out, a deeper Wolfcamp extension of the Spraberry Trend, originally discovered by Mr. Bass's uncle, Sid Richardson, back in the early 30s.

Mr. Bass was anxious to reach the well's total depth before Memorial Day. The cagey wildcatter was keen to spend the first holiday of summer on San Jose Island in peace; at his leisure. Secure in the knowledge that the Bass family tank batteries were filling with fresh torrents of Permian crude.

This latest string of pipe, equipped with Hughes Tool's finest diamond bit, was grinding away at 13,000 feet, headed for 14,522. Arch had seven days to reach Total Depth. His calculations had Halliburton shooting the casing in four days.

It was 8:00 p.m.—Night Tower shift change—and Big Arch was mildly amused by all the ass-draggin' up to the rig floor. The night was breezy and cool—about as nice a time of year as it got in the sandhills south of Wink. Night Tower was, to a man, moaning about not dancing with their darlings on an oilfield Saturday night.

"You boys can't two-step to save your ass," opined Arch, as the floor hands slapped on hard hats and readied a connection. "No dancin' buncha reprobates."

"Hell you say, Boss," crowed Sonny Sustaita, a forty-year-old from Goliad down on the Coastal Bend. "I can sure as hell two-step to some Freddy Fender."

As soon as the thin-muscled tong man, dressed in blue Dickies coveralls, spun the pipe threads tight he danced a jig with the greasy joint as it eased down the hole. Singing Wasted Days and Wasted Nights at the top of his lungs.

"Come on Arch, I can waltz across Texas," announced the driller, Eddie "Mutt" Matula, a sausage-legged Czech with impressive skills on the brake handle.

"Yeah, yeah, Mutt. You and Sonny need to work on your night moves, brother," said Big Arch, stepping across the rig floor to the rotary table to see that all was turning smooth.

"Orale, Matula!" taunted the tong man, double pumping in the driller's face. "You want some of this, chico?"

"Hey, honyak! Don't make me chain the brake," warned Matula. "I'll whip the brown power right out of your ass."

"Bring it, you pinche . . ." hissed Sustaita. "Kolache-eatin' cabron!"

"Hey now! What the hell!"

Big Arch gave Sustaita the serious face and side-eyed Matula. He didn't often get in the middle of his crew's macho crap, but his tool pusher, a ramrod from the rice fields of El Campo named Alton Kohoutek, was currently on the banks of the mud tank checking the well's flow back.

Matula smirked and Sustaita grabbed his crotch, both loving Big Arch's cocky vibe as he shouldered past and strode down the catwalk waving a middle finger behind his short-cropped head.

Big Arch loved the oilfield.

Learned it from his own daddy, Charlie Carter, who'd marched down from the Ozarks to train for World War I in 19 and 17. Fortunately, armistice was signed, and Arch's dad found himself in the middle of an oil boom in Ranger, Texas. The enterprising young man from the Show Me State promptly worked his way up from roustabout to roughneck to pushing tools by the time he was 25. Old Man Charlie Carter worked for Falcon Seaboard for 40 years. Made each of his three strapping boys swamp, roustabout, and roughneck—every summer; every holiday.

As such, Arch, the oldest Carter boy, knew his way around a rig like it was home—every tool, every instrument, every diabolical downhole trick Mother Earth could throw at him. Big Arch Carter was good to go and pretty damn clever with his problem-solving.

Big Arch also knew his way around a crew; when to get tough and when to back off. How to suss a legitimate concern from bellyaching. He'd learned early that there was no shortage of complaints from hands who were tired, lazy, or just plain dumb.

But as long as Big Arch's crew was on time and worked safe, he kept 'em paid in *full, running good equipment and enjoying high praise for hard work. He didn't give a damn about their hair, their politics, their girlfriends, or boyfriends for that matter.*

Big Arch loved his boys. And he let'em know it, plenty.

But just this minute, now that the pipe was turning to the right, he couldn't wait to escape to his company Ford, light up a Travis Club, and enjoy some early season baseball. As soon as Arch got down to his late-model LTD, he cracked his window, lit that cigar, turned on the Rangers-Angels and pulled his Stetson down over an un-furrowed brow.

The cantankerous owner of the Rangers, Mr. Eddie Chiles, was telling folks, "If you don't have an oil well, get one – you'll love doing business with Western!"

"Come on Eddie, I thought you were mad as hell."

"Am not," answered a low, soft voice.

Big Arch looked up just in time to be arm tackled by Justine Plunkett, all of twenty years old and damn near busting out of her knot-tied gingham blouse.

"Good Lord, girl," he said, pleased indeed that the prettiest young thing in the Permian Basin was paying a visit. "You scared hell outta me."

"Did not."

"Well, it's great to see you, but . . ."

"But what?" she cooed, covering him up with kisses.

They made out for a minute before she grabbed him by the shirt sleeve. "I got somethin' to show you."

"I bet you do."

Big Arch got out; peered around the doghouse and saw'em all—Kohoutek, Matula, Sustaita—the whole crew, up on the floor, watching the pipe go 'round and 'round.

Justine, a genuine Kilgore Rangerette, with the wheels to back it up, made a break for it. "Come on!"

"What you got, Justine?" he said, following her tan lines through the shinnery. "One of them Mary Jane cigarettes?"

Big Arch shook his head, but couldn't quit smiling, as they side-stepped prickly pear and slid under thick branches of mesquite.

Justine was going to make somebody a fine wife, in a year or two. After she high kicked her way into the heart of some West Texas wildcatter or an East Texas timber baron. She'd have her pick.

The shameless pair stumbled through the half-dark till they came to a ranch road where a brand-new, lemon-yellow Mustang convertible sat with the top down. The paint job practically glowed in the moonlight.

"Isn't she gorgeous?"

"Damn," said Big Arch, running his hand over the smooth curves of sheet metal. "What's the occasion?"

"Got my dental hygiene degree," she gushed. "Finally!"

With that, Justine struck a pose on the hood. Angled a long Rangerette leg against the nighttime stars in what Arch imagined were, quite possibly, the world's shortest cutoffs.

"Hell girl, that's big-time," he said, trying to snap straight, calculating how many paychecks he'd have to fork over to buy his wife, Bunny, a brand-new Mustang.

Justine didn't have to worry about paying for much. Daddy Plunkett owned the biggest lumber yard in Andrews.

"Come on Arch," she said, pushing her short shorts off the hood and into his hips. "Let's break it in."

Big Arch tried to resist, but failed miserably, when Justine started stripping off. "Whatcha waitin' for?"

Big Arch whistled through his teeth. Looked back at the rig.

"Justine," he said, tossing his hat on the gear shift; shucking boots, pants, and shirt as fast as he could. "Damn girl."

"Come here, you," she purred, curling a finger as she adjusted a plump car pillow behind her head. "Come to Momma."

"Hang on . . ." he said, high-stepping from front to back, easing his 6'6" frame down into the finest bunch of new car smell, maybe ever.

• • •

Not twelve hours previous, Bunny Carter, a world-class fireball from Burkburnett, sent Big Arch, her hard-working husband, back to his Falcon Seaboard rig with a smooch and a giggle. The couple's mini-vacation in Monahans had been unexpectedly successful. Room 7 at the Starlight Motel was almost romantic. She just knew she'd bought herself some time to talk about a new career path.

Bunny had just finished up her first year as first-grade teacher at Devonian Elementary. She planned to tell Big Arch it was her last. But they'd had such a good steak at the Bar H, and were pawing at each other on the way back to the motel, that she didn't want to spoil the mood. Andrews ISD paid their teachers more than most— all that oil money sloshing around—but teaching was hard. Bunny wanted to be a full-time Mom.

After a lovely afternoon at the Andrews Country Club, watching little Archie swim, and drinking a few rum and Cokes, of course, Bunny took her only child down to Bliznak's for some fresh-baked gingerbread men.

Unfortunately, she ran into two of the town gossips picking up a birthday cake.

Bunny tried to avoid them, but the little witches stepped right up. "Hey Bunny, we heard that Plunkett girl was flirting with your man."

"Who'd you hear that from, Margo?"

"Oh, a little bird," trilled the tart, tragically mismatched in a peasant blouse and patent leather mini skirt—with big ugly zippers!

Bernice, the bovine friend, weighed in: "More like a little tramp."

Bunny lowered her sunglasses to Bernice; lifted her chin. "Takes one to know one."

As her tormentors stood cow-mouthed, Bunny handed the baker a ten-dollar bill. "Thank you, Mr. Bliznak."

She turned on her heel and walked out of that bakery without a word, or change.

"Thanks, Mr. Bliznak," said Little Archie, waving a headless gingerbread man; barely resisting the urge to stick his tongue out at the mean ladies.

When they got back to the car, the sun was sinking below the Andrews County Courthouse. Bunny frantically searched for her keys. She knew better . . . knew those women were just awful wanna-be's . . . but, they might know something.

"Hey, Booger Bear, let's go surprise your Daddy," she said, opening the car door for her five-year-old. "Don't you think he'd like that?"

"We can take him some gingerbread men," agreed Archie, checking the bag to see how many were left.

And that was that.

After sprucing up a little bit, and a few more cocktails to fortify her courage, Bunny set up her little man in the back seat with pillows, quilts, and a half-dozen comic books. Belted him tight for a nice evening drive.

And as mom and son zoomed south, plowing across those crazy, landlocked sand dunes, the Lizard King chanted his come-hither chorus on the Mexican radio:

Come on baby light my fire,

Come on baby light my fire,

Try to set the night on fire!

. . .

Back in the boondocks, it was time for a cigarette.

Neither Big Arch, nor Justine, noticed the plume of dust rising in the moonlight. A diaphanous cloud of caliche floating above the lease road like Comanche smoke.

A Ford station wagon was coming hell-bent down the scraped lane, bouncing all over the washboard road. Behind the wheel, Bunny was having second thoughts, but only slowing to sixty in the pitch dark.

"I ought to turn around," she mumbled, gunning for the light-ringed rig.

Little Archie sat stock still, clutching his comic books, wishing his mom would slow down. "Why are we goin' so fast, mom? Dad's right there."

"He better be."

. . .

"Aw hell."

Big Arch knew it was trouble; knew it in his gut. Knew it when he heard, then saw, a station wagon flash by. The taillights slowed to a stop, backed, swiveled at the T, and headed down the ranch road.

"I gotta . . . get dressed, Justine!" he stuttered, pulling and buttoning and buckling as fast as he could.

"Where you goin'?" she yelled at the shirttail hustling out the back and up the road.

"Crazy ass woman . . . coming out here . . . what the hell?" grumbled Big Arch, tucking in his shirt, watching the station wagon engulf him in headlights.

Big Arch was talking tough, but he knew it was going to get bad, and get bad in a hurry, if it actually was Bunny. He wished Justine would haul her fine ass, and her fine Mustang, the hell out of there.

And from the minute Bunny skidded to within an inch of her husband's raised hands . . .

"STOP!"

. . . it was nothing but Fist City.

Yes, there was nothing quite like the sight of Bunny Kolb Carter on the war-path, launching out of that station wagon in her cat-eye glasses and blonde bouffant. Looking like five-foot-three inches of blasting cap, packed tight in a pair of white Capri pants; moving right up in Arch's grill in her pink espadrilles.

"Dammit to hell, Arch Carter, I'm gonna . . . I'm gonna kill you!" she screamed, spying the Mustang. "Who's out there? Who is that?"

"What in the world, Bunny? What the hell?"

"I can smell it all over you, you cheatin' sonavabitch," she screamed, trying to pull loose from Arch's grip.

"Dammit Bunny, stop!" he pleaded. "You're gonna get me fired."

"You deserve to be fired, you sonavabitch! Who's in that car?"

"I am," announced Justine, rising straight up from the back seat with black hair matted and makeup smeared. Wearing nothing but Arch's Stetson and the glow of good sex. "Who the fuck are you?"

And boy, that's all it took.

Bunny tore loose from Big Arch and dove straight across the Mustang's trunk into Justine's solar plexus. Mrs. Carter then proceeded to pound the living hell out of the unrepentant slut, who, of course, didn't just sit there, but retaliated like a Tasmanian Devil; throwing her share of punches and landing quite a few upside Bunny's beautiful head before Big Arch got hold of Bunny's ankles, and finally Bunny's waist, and pulled her clean out of the car into the bar ditch.

Justine jumped into the driver's seat while the Carters wrestled around in the dirt.

Meanwhile, Kohoutek and all the hands were raising cane up on the guard rails, waving and hollering. Really enjoying the show from the sound of it.

"Dammit Bunny, what the hell?"

"What do you mean, what the hell?" she screamed, panting fiercely, bent at the waist. "Who is that? Who is that woman?"

"Just calm down, Bunny. Please!" he pleaded, finally half-manhandling her

back to the station wagon. Just as he was getting her calmed down, Justine roared past, honking and cussing; lofting Big Arch's Stetson into the Mustang's slipstream.

Instantly, Bunny chased down the hat; two-foot stomped it, then waded back in, fists flying. Big Arch slipped a wild right, came up out of his crouch, only to lock eyes with— Little Archie.

"Jesus, Bunny" he cried, as his son sat bug-eyed in the backseat of the station wagon. "You brought . . . Jesus, Bunny."

"Don't you Jesus Bunny me," she screamed, scurrying around the front of the station wagon, throwing the passenger door open.

Big Arch opened the back door and smiled at his son; his pride and joy.

"Hey, bud. How ya doin'? You keepin' your mom company?" he said, reaching to shake a man's hand.

Little Archie sat motionless.

"Hey, how 'bout runnin' over to the doghouse. Tell Sustaita to get you a Delaware Punch. You remember Sonny."

Bunny reached over the front seat and punched Big Arch's skull, "Cheatin' bastard!"

He grabbed hold of Bunny's wrists. "Dammit Bunny, stop!"

"Dad?"

"It's okay, son," Big Arch said, as Bunny threw herself across the front seat, wailing.

"Just go on over to the rig, son. Sustaita'll get you somethin' to drink. And Matula's got Baby Ruth's in the doghouse cooler. He's got all kinds of candy."

"Okay, Dad."

As soon as Little Archie disappeared through the brush, trotting toward the rig, all hell broke loose. Big Arch fended off blows as best he could; started the engine, threw it in Drive, determined to get his crazy wife out of earshot.

But Hurricane Bunny wasn't going out like that.

Bunny grabbing shirt, Bunny grabbing hair, Bunny punching ear, nose, and throat. Big Arch fended off fists, elbows, and kicks. "Bunny you have got to calm the hell down," he pleaded, tires furiously spinning in the dirt . . . eyes off the road, and . . .

BAM!

The Ford station wagon's big chrome bumper plowed straight into 2,000 pounds of bolt-anchored gas well. High-centered at a dead stop, engine racing . . . then

BOOM!

Zippo flash; hellfire ignition. 30 feet of flame exploded up from the ruptured well. Totally engulfed . . . every single thing.

Raging combustion, all-consuming fire—turning flesh to ash and sand to glass— nothing but melted iron; melted plastic, melted rubber. And not an eyelash trace of Little Archie's parents. Not even a scream.

Big Arch and Bunny Carter never knew what hit'em.

And their only son?

Watching. The whole thing behind the smudged glass of a doghouse window.

Watching.

Waiting.

Wondering . . . not quite believing . . . not even realizing he was safe in the arms of Sonny Sustaita.

The tong man held the little boy tight; then tighter still. Whispering sad Spanish.

• • •

Red Adair and the Hellfighters were on the way.

As soon as Elton Kohoutek explained the situation to Mr. Bass, Mr. Bass called Mr. Adair, directly. With the rig shut down, and their beloved boss gone, all the crew could do was wait, and wonder.

They stood around the doghouse, dumbfounded, listening to a motor-mouth lawman.

"Nothin'. Never seen nothin' like it," allowed the string bean of a DPS trooper, explaining the scene by the light of the still-raging fire. "Station wagon done run plum over the gas works! Time I got here, everything big enough to burn was pure D melted. Every gawl-durn thing. Including them two lovebirds. Darndest mess I ever seen."

The excitable trooper was addressing Archie's guardian angel, a veteran Sheriff out of Borden County named C. W. "Chuck" Fuchs, who, five hours later, would deliver a bucked-toothed boy to the love of his life, Sister Ernestine Ducornet.

The Sheriff and the Sister were earthbound angels. Soul Savers.

Archie was their first.

But let's get something straight.

At the time, Little Archie Carter knew no such thing, about no such people.

The boy had no idea that he'd call Sister Ernestine and Sheriff Fuchs—mom and dad—for the rest of his life.

No, the best the shivering little red-eyed creature could do for the remainder of that fitful, fateful night was lay down and sit up. Eyes closed; eyes open in the cavernous cab of the Chuck Fuch's F-250. Listening to the solemn voices of authority drone on the two-way radio. Listening to the whine of rubber on an endless stretch of road. Trying to forget the twisted sound of metal-on-metal; the fireworks explosion. Watching the black dark of 3 a.m. The twinkle of far-away farms, fast asleep.

Little Archie sat there, trying not to cry. Swaddled in a pile of dope-stained sweatshirts. Shivering in the backlit dark; swatting unwelcome tears, sniffling his runny nose.

He leaned into the cool window glass. Using his daddy's Falcon Seaboard windbreaker for a pillow. Thinking about his hopping-mad momma and gingerbread men.

All alone . . .

. . . but only for the moment.

• • •

On that terrible Saturday night, turned Sunday morning, the Sheriff of Borden County stepped up. The San Angelo State School's weekend administrator directed him to Sister Ernestine's spartan single room.

He knocked on the door; asked to come in.

"Yes," said Sister Ernestine, reaching for her eyeglasses. "Who is it?"

Sheriff Fuchs booted the door and slowly entered arms loaded with little boy fast asleep from the longest day of his life. The childless French mother flew out from under the covers, fully dressed in a maroon and white habit, as was her habit.

"Oh, sacre dieu!"

The Sheriff laid Little Archie Carter gently on the bed.

They watched him; never an eye open, barely moving, as mourning doves cooed and the sun rose pink, then red, then orange, outside the window.

Finally, Sister Ernestine looked into Chuck Fuchs' eyes. Her admirer, her champion, standing there, arms crossed, stoic, heroic. Stout as a cistern.

"He's yours if you want," said the Sheriff. "Orphan, as of last night."

And in that instant, Sister Ernestine fell furiously in love with her Texas Pieta— this nut brown, loose-limbed boy with sand-blond hair and a sweet, buck-toothed smile.

"Merci, beaucoup! Oh, Sheriff! Merci! Merci! Merci beaucoup!" She climbed the lawman's shoulders. Kissed his cheeks, leaking tears, crying for pure joy.

And there they were. The dutiful lawman, the self-made Sister, and the future Garden City Bearkat—come together, bound forever. In the summer of '76, a lucky American lad was born again—officially adopted and adored—with a new name all his own:

Archie Ducornet Weesatche.

SHARP-DRESSED LOBO WITH AN RPG

Wacey was surveilling high above the Staked Plains of Borden County.

Sheriff Fuchs assigned her to watch for two late-model SUVs packed with Hondurans and methamphetamines. He'd received a heads up from Texas DPS that a caravan of rogue smugglers was trying—again—to by-pass the Ojinaga Plaza and establish a new distribution channel for the lucrative Permian Basin oilfield market that stretched from Abilene to Albuquerque, north to the casinos in Oklahoma; south to Eagle Pass.

The federal and state intel was sketchy, but indicated that the vehicles were being driven by the same knuckleheads from Tegucigalpa that the Sheriff intercepted in 2014 trying to open a new route through Big Bend. With Rudy dead, and the Ojinaga Plaza in transition, the Central Americans were back—snaking their way up through Mexico, and now Texas.

Texas DPS first spotted the two cars carrying the Hondurans north of Dryden, using extreme back roads; some Farm-to-Market, but mostly private ranch and farm roads. As a result, the state troopers lost track of the armored trucks after their first stop at a safe house in Noodle, Texas, in rural Jones County. The Hondurans were re-engaged in Fisher County, according to a radio intercept, headed to Lubbock by way of Borden County.

Wacey had climbed up the cell tower maintenance road bulldozed by Clayton William's old ClayDesta Communications and was sitting amidst a bristling array of telephone equipment. In spite of being surrounded by cell towers, she'd been instructed to use the Sheriff's satellite phone as she perched atop Gail Mountain. The semi-circular butte overlooked every bit of the county's infrastructure: the sprawling Borden County K–12 campus, the Borden County Courthouse and the Borden County Post Office with clear views of the county's only paved roads—FM 669 and State Highway 180.

Naturally, a norther was blowing in.

It had been flat-out hot during the climb up, but now Wacey wished she'd dressed a little warmer than a camo hoodie and jeans. As the evening shade turned dark, Wacey settled in at the summit with her dove-hunting stool, field glasses and canteen.

Down below, the football stadium was packed as the Borden County Coyotes kicked off to their Six-Man rivals from Jayton. Through her binoculars she could see Sheriff Fuchs doing his PR thing. Every registered voter in the county was probably in attendance. At population 641, Borden County was one of the least populated in Texas. But everybody loved their Coyotes, especially when the rival Blue Jays were in town.

Wacey was confused when the satellite phone began to ping. It wasn't the Sheriff; she was looking at him, standing on the fence line, yukking it up with a herd of Stetson-wearing ranchers and their adult sons.

"*Hola cariño. Como estas?*" said Josefina, back at *Hacienda Montemayor* after her whirlwind trip to Laredo to meet *Lobo Loco*, the new Plaza Boss of Ojinaga.

"*Hola* yourself," said Wacey, instantly recognizing Josy's voice, but leery of her sexy salutation. "How come you're using Chuck's super-secret satellite phone."

"Because it's *my* super-secret satellite phone."

"Oh," said Wacey, baffled.

"Are you ready, *hermosa*? This is it," asked Josy. "The Hondurans take out *Lobo*, and we're home free."

"You're sure about these guys?" Wacey asked, scanning the darkened pastures below. "What if Chuck knows . . . knows you're setting up *Lobo*."

"*Nombre!* Chuck thinks *Lobo* is wiping out the Hondurans," spat Josy, "*Mira*, these guys are ex-military. *Lobo* screwed them in 2014 and they want payback. It's going to work."

"You sound like Archie."

"I don't need luck, *chiquita*," assured the underboss. "I plan. You watch."

"Oh, I'm watching," said Wacey, following the Sheriff with her binoculars as he took a seat on the fifty-yard line. "You better take me to Cabo. We deserve it!"

"God Cabo . . . Let's go!" said Josy. "We're so close, *linda*."

"I know! Plus, Archie's really doin' good. I just talked to him," Wacey said. "He won fifty grand from some super-rich sand girl and the dumb bitch wants to double down."

"He's probably sleeping with her," said Josy, sucking up the last sip of a blood orange and tequila. "Archie's a hoe. *Le gustan todas*."

"*En serio?*" said Wacey. "You're the hoe."

"What? I can't keep him out of my bed," she crowed. "He loves my *chichis*."

"Everybody loves your *chichis*!"

"*Es verdad*," she bragged. "*Ay*, I miss you, Wacey."

"Quit it," she whined. "I got to stay focused."

"You worry too much," said Josy. "Enjoy the show."

Please, thought Wacey. Enjoy the show. Says the woman eating *pan dulce* by the pool. She put her binoculars on a pair of headlights, far in the distance, slowly moving up the Snyder Highway.

"So, where exactly are you?" asked Josy. "I'm confused."

"On Gail Mountain. I think I see'em." said Wacey, focusing the lens. "It's two SUVs. Jacked up. Looks like armor plate? Black and red?"

"Yes!" she said. "That's them."

"And *Lobo's* out there?" asked Wacey. "I can't see'em!"

"Good. They're there," said Josy. "I gotta go. Stay safe. Love you, *hermosa*."

For five years, the "phone" had been an integral part of an arrangement with the Sinaloa bosses. A deal, beautifully brokered by Miss Montemayor, that had indeed removed the barrel of Rudy Leos's Desert Eagle from Wacey's mouth.

And compromised the Sheriff's professional life, greatly.

While Sheriff Fuchs was not at all pleased with his Josy/Sinaloa predicament, his colleagues at the DEA saw it as an opportunity to witness, first-hand, the marriage of the heretofore untouchable Montemayor family with the ambitious and increasingly powerful Sinaloa Cartel.

So far, Chuck Fuchs had had to answer the "phone" only twice. First, in 2012, for transportation and security of a captured Zeta *sicario* from Presidio to El Paso. Second, in 2014, for assistance with the interception of an unauthorized shipment of meth being muled through the Big Bend moonscape by a rogue cell out of Tegucigalpa, Honduras.

Now, the Hondurans were back for a second Permian Basin end-run.

After she hung up, Wacey trained her field glasses on the two armored SUVs, cruising through Gail's single-block city limits. She followed them, walking out to the edge of the bluff, all the way out of town.

Suddenly, a firestorm of muzzle flashes lit up between the open pasture and the highway. A hail of automatic weapon's fire opened up on the convoy, bringing the SUVs to a stop in the middle of the road.

From Wacey's vantage, it looked like a scene from Afghanistan. As *Lobo Loco* and his Ojinaga soldiers continued to attack the Hondurans with withering AR fire, she hunkered down behind an outcrop, then scrambled back to the satellite phone when the shooting suddenly stopped. As she dialed, Wacey heard the whoosh and scream of a Rocket Propelled Grenade.

Sheriff Fuchs picked up on the first ring, hustling down the stadium aisle. "I heard it! What the hell?"

"RPG!" Wacey screamed, rushing back to the ledge, in time to see a pair of .50-caliber barrels poke from slits in the SUVs. A ten-second burst from the Honduran's machine guns completely obliterated *Lobo's* truck.

"Oh my God! Jesus, Chuck!"

"Get off that mountain. Now!" said the Sheriff, "Straight down, do *not* use the road."

"Hurry, Chuck!" she said, already picking her way down a steep incline. She quickly gave up standing and slid down the talus on the seat of her pants.

"Dammit to hell," cursed the Sheriff, fast walking out of the stadium to his truck.

As he sped out of the parking lot, Chuck Fuchs knew that fifty years of law enforcement wasn't going mean squat, if he and Wacey didn't deliver ten Honduran smugglers and two SUVs full of meth.

It was his operation. His show.

As the Sheriff sped away from the stadium, Wacey was taking huge, gravity-assisted steps, bounding toward him from the base of the mountain. He flashed his lights, rolled down the passenger window.

"Grab the AR and climb in the back. Be ready to lay down cover."

Wacey took the rifle off the back rack and hopped in the truck bed. It didn't take two minutes to round the bend to the scene of the firefight. But when they rolled to a stop, there was no scene at all. No SUVs. No bodies. Just empty highway with shards of safety glass glittering under the headlights.

The Sheriff jerked to a stop in the middle of the empty road, lights flashing. He scanned the asphalt and bar ditches. As Wacey joined him, they heard a barely-perceptible moan coming from the pitch-dark pasture.

The Sheriff drew his pistol.

"Get back up there," he whispered. "Scope back behind us. And stay down!"

Sheriff Fuchs retreated behind his driver door, then cracked two glow-sticks and threw them on the road. The green light revealed a scatter of spent ammunition. The Sheriff reached down to inspect a full metal jacket next to his boot.

"Fifty cal," he said, pocketing the shell. "See anything?"

"Nothing," said Wacey, slowly scanning the blackness.

"Hang on," he said, reaching under the dashboard. "I'm gonna hit the floods."

The spotlights revealed, over two hundred yards away, a shot-to-pieces pickup with Chihuahua plates. The only sound was wind blowing and the muted cheers of Six-Man football.

And then, a telltale report.

"Shots fired!" Wacey cried, sliding along the truck bed, training her scope on a man gingerly picking his way through the uneven terrain. She clicked the laser. "On target."

"Don't shoot!" screamed a terrified man, hands up, sharp-dressed in a black and red camouflage uniform. He threw a gun in front of him. "It's me, Arturo. Don't shoot!"

"Stand down, Wacey," said the Sheriff, moving around the car door toward the approaching man. "Stand down. I got this."

The Sheriff kept his gun trained until the man stopped, and turned in a slow circle, showing the Sheriff that he was completely unarmed.

"Arturo!" he called out. "*¿Que pasa, hombre?*"

"*¡Sherif!* Chuck!" said Arturo Villalobos, also known as *Lobo Loco*, and quite decidedly unknown as Sheriff Fuch's latest undercover recruit. The forty-year-old former Gulf Cartel accountant turned Ojinaga Plaza Boss was muttering, visibly relieved. "*Ay, mios dio. Gracias, Sherif. ¡Gracias!*"

"What the hell happened?" said the Sheriff, looking back at Wacey, who was scanning the opposite pasture.

"We had'em, *jefe*. We tracked them for two days. We had'em. Right here. The RPG missed. That's all I remember," said *Lobo Loco*, pointing back at the Chihuahua pickup. "We only got one shot. They opened up on us. I can't believe I'm alive."

"Where are their trucks?" asked the Sheriff, "Where the hell'd they go?"

"*No sé*," said *Lobo Loco*, still visibly shaking. "I can't believe it, *Sherif*. I was behind the truck and then all this shooting. I tried to make myself small."

The Sheriff kicked another .50-cal shell with his boot, sizing up the scene.

"How many?" said the Sheriff. "How many'd you lose?"

"Two. Young guys." said Arturo, running both hands through his thick black hair. "Teenagers, *jefe*. I don't know why I'm alive."

"The Hondurans were loaded for bear this time," said the Sheriff. "And I guarantee, they've got intel. Driving through West Texas like they own the goddamn place."

Wacey joined the Sheriff as he walked Arturo to the passenger side of the truck. Before he opened the door, he put his hand on the short man's shoulder. "You fire a shot?"

Arturo looked up at Chuck Fuchs, pensively. "He was suffering. His jaw was gone."

"Ever killed a man?"

"No," he said, looking at his savior with wet, sorrowful eyes.

"Won't be the last time," said the Sheriff. "Go get your gun, Arturo."

FALCONS FLY!

ROUND ROCK, TEXAS
NOVEMBER 27, 2015

As usual, Archie made excellent time.

He easily located Dragon Stadium, the pride of Round Rock ISD, a prosperous Austin suburb up I-35 North and host to the 2015 fall sports championships for the Southwest Preparatory Conference. The final event of the season was Large School Football—a state championship re-match between Houston Kinkaid and Bellaire Episcopal.

When he pulled into the narrow parking lot across from the stadium, the tailgating was going full steam and fan-cy! Elegantly attired moms and sporty dads, all rigorously color-coordinated—purple and gold for Kinkaid; royal blue and white for EHS—were clustered around tricked-out Mercedes Sprinters and all manner of luxury SUVs. The smell of grilled meats filled the cool air; everyone stuffing face with catered Tex-Mex and hoisting libations at a furious pace. Archie figured his $50,000 date was milling among the well-dressed throngs, but he didn't want to stalk the man.

He'd only met Miles Mathis once, last spring, at a fortuitous encounter during the Houston Rodeo Lamb and Goat Auction, where Mr. Mathis purchased the prize billie. Archie'd made sure to stay in touch, for business reasons, more than gambling. Having the cell number of the biggest land owner in McMullen County—smack in the middle of the Eagle Ford play—would come in handy when Archie eventually got back in the hotshot business.

Archie got out of the car, but dove right back, when the winds of a blue norther, mixed with fine mist, hit him in the face. "Ooh, now *that's* some football weather."

He pulled out Matt's iPad, yet another attempt by his little brother to drag Uncle Archie into the twenty-first century.

Houston Prep Powerhouses Take Center Stage
Episcopal, Kinkaid return for third straight showdown in SPC finals

The headline was surely below the fold, but Archie couldn't tell as he scrolled down a list of *Chron.com* articles on the slick computer screen. Archie had "borrowed" the device knowing there was no way in hell an actual *Houston Chronicle* newspaper could be purchased between Big Spring and Round Rock. Despite the annoyance of *not* getting newsprint all over his hands, Archie was duly impressed that the SPC Championship rated such sizable coverage in the *Chron's* digital sports pages.

He'd been texting Mr. Mathis before the season even started, and kept close tabs on the Episcopal Knights and their three *USA Today* Top 100 Recruits—defensive tackle Marvin Wilson, offensive tackle Walker Little and wide receiver Jaylen Waddle. EHS had beaten Kinkaid 42–21 early in the regular season. And the Knights were rolling, 9–1 on the season, winners of eight in a row, and prohibitive favorites against the 6–3 Falcons. Archie needed at least three touchdowns if he was going to take Kinkaid.

"Guess it's time to send a man a text," said Archie, tossing the iPad into the passenger seat, a seat he wished was filled with Wacey Foyt. She'd begged off the road trip, explaining that a friend from Wink was coming to spend the weekend. Matt and Tallulah were watching Roger Tedesco and the Sterling City Eagles play in a regional playoff game in Crane.

Archie sighed. He was glad that Wacey was excited to host her first sleepover, but he missed his running buddy. He didn't want to wander alone through a bunch of rich people's tailgates, snooping around for a multi-millionaire who probably didn't want to bet $50,000 on a high school football game.

But Josy sure wanted him to. He'd finally talked to Ms. Montemayor on the drive down.

"I can't believe how good you're doing," she said. "Go for it, *Archito*."

Archie promised he would. "I got this one, the state championships in Houston, then Vegas for the clincher."

"Why don't you come here. Now," she cooed, cell phone static crackling between southern Tamaulipas and central Texas. "Come to the *hacienda*. My father wants to smoke cigars with you."

"I'd enjoy nothin' more," he said, fondly recalling the grand dinner at the Montemayor estate. "Doesn't get much better than smokin' a Cuban with your dad by the pool."

"Sure it does," Josy purred. "Come see me, *guapo*."

The line went dead.

"Come see me. Right," said Archie, forever vexed by the mercurial *Mexicana*.

IT WAS TIME TO LOCATE THE KING OF MCMULLEN COUNTY.

Miles Mathis, Sr., born and raised in Kingsville, Texas, a distant heir to a certain south Texas ranching family, and of late, one of the prime beneficiaries of the Eagle Ford shale boom. Not on the King Ranch, mind you, but on five thousand acres of his own, in McMullen County—a semiprofitable goat ranch he'd bought for pennies on the dollar in a fit of early-seventies anti-establishment pique.

An unlikely counterculture participant, Mathis decided, upon graduation from the University of Texas, that he didn't want to go to work for his family, or "The Man." Instead, he used his degree in Petroleum Land Management to raise goats with a hippie first wife.

And middle-fingered everybody else.

For two decades, the goat ranch provided excellent write-offs for his sizable trust fund. However, the trust ultimately didn't generate enough income to satisfy the first Mrs. Mathis, who quickly realized that only women in their twenties look good in tie-dye.

Miles was single for ten years until he met the second Mrs. Mathis, tubing on the Frio at Garner State Park. Turned out Melissa Severcek Monzingo was from Tilden, Texas, county seat of McMullen. But the best news was that the former Mrs. Monzingo was good to go with goats. And five years into a happy second marriage, a funny thing happened on the way to the Tilden Seed and Feed.

Schlumberger fracked one of Hilcorp's first horizontal Eagle Ford shale wells, on the aforementioned Mathis goat ranch, and the well came in a gusher. Suddenly, the second Mr. and Mrs. Mathis were the richest couple in the county, with royalty checks hitting six figures a month and climbing.

The windfall gave Mr. Mathis a chance to buy a new luxury condominium on Kirby Drive in Houston and the second Mrs. Mathis an opportunity to be close to her only son, Scooter, who was turning out to be a helluva athlete at Episcopal High School, or EHS, as the cool kids called it.

Mr. Mathis had never spent any appreciable time in the state's largest city but found Houston much to his liking. There were tons of things to do in Bayou City if you had a little Eagle Ford money to spread around. And Melissa was thrilled that her husband, never an athlete but a true sports fanatic, seemed to so genuinely enjoy watching Scooter during his all-state senior season playing wingback.

"Goodness gracious! This Weesatche guy won't give up," said Mathis, looking down at his phone between bites of prime rib, served on toasted brioche by the couple's driver/valet. "Sumbitch's been trying to get twenty-one points out of me all week."

"What's the bet?" asked a Mathis sycophant, wiping Dijon off his two-day stubble.

"I'm gonna give him plus seventeen for fifty K."

"Fifty-thousand!" spewed the friend, "Damn, son!"

"Hey, sweetie!" chirped the second Mrs. Mathis, resplendent in head-to-toe Tootsies including curve-perfect white skinny jeans and a white cashmere sweater overlaid by a blue leather jacket with an embossed paisley design. "You wouldn't believe what those Kinkaid people are sayin'; All *poor me* and '*y'all are gonna kill us*'; '*please have mercy*'. It's a little weird."

"What's weird is how quick we're gonna rip their throats out," boasted the sycophant.

"That's gross! It's high school!" replied Mrs. Mathis, side-eyeing her husband's friend from the Lamb & Goat Committee. She leaned in close to her husband and whispered. "Are you really bettin' fifty thousand dollars?"

"Hell, yeah," he whispered back. "You think I won't."

"Didn't we beat'em last game, like really bad," said Mrs. Mathis, cocking an eye at a much younger, much tipsier, trophy wife one tailgate over.

"We did. Eight weeks ago," he said, with a smile. "And did I tell you, you look hotter than a four-alarm fire."

"Thank you, sweetie!" she said, pressing her cashmere into him, careful not to tip his new plate of tamales and charro beans. "You ready for another scotch?"

"Fill'er up," said Mathis, shaking the ice in his empty cup.

He texted Archie to meet behind the north goalposts. That he'd be waiting on the track.

"Weesatche is a good guy. Almost sold his hotshot company for a couple of million, but the bottom dropped out before he could close."

"He must be rich if he's betting fifty thousand," said Mrs. Miles, dutifully taking the sycophant's cup—embossed EHS cups—the team moms special-ordered for the championship.

"Welcome to the E&P roller coaster," said the sycophant, pulling down his EHS cap. "Hell, I've been through at least six booms and busts."

Mr. and Mrs. Mathis smiled at their friend. Miles was grateful that his phone buzzed with a new text.

"Weesatche says he's good with plus seventeen," said Mathis, looking over his reading glasses. "All cash."

"Cash?" said Mrs. Mathis, "I don't think I've ever seen fifty thousand dollars in cash."

Mathis and his friend exchanged knowing smiles.

"Hell, our boys are gonna steamroll their silky asses?" crowed the sycophant. "I'd give him four touchdowns."

"That's why you aren't allowed to gamble anymore," said Miles, winking at his wife. "Although the Vegas line would be at least twenty-eight."

"Vegas doesn't bet high school football!" cried Mrs. Mathis. "Even I know that!"

"Sweetie," said Miles, pointing finger guns at the empty Styrofoam cups. "And make'em stout, *porfavor*. They gotta last till halftime."

ARCHIE STOOD ON THE TRACK BEHIND THE END ZONE, HIS BACK TO A BREEZE fresh from the North Pole. A wind with icy intent. But no straight-up rain yet. Miles Mathis walked up in a olive-green Orvis hunting jacket, pressed khakis, Lucchese ostrich skins and a smile—a confident smile.

"Hey Miles," said Archie, shaking a man's hand, then pulling two Keep On Truckin' envelopes containing $25K apiece. "You mind holdin' the money?"

"Not a bit," said Mathis, shoving both envelopes into the inside pocket of his coat.

"Heard your son's havin' a helluva year in the slot," said Archie, glad that the transaction was seemingly complete.

"Step-son. Yeah, they got Scooter at wingback this season," said Mathis, shifting his back to the wind. "He's done some damage over the middle."

"That's tough duty," said Archie, remembering his days of running slants over the middle. "Got my clock cleaned a few times at UH."

"You play for UH?"

"For Coach Yeoman," admitted Archie, with a proud smile. "Tail end of the Southwest Conference days."

"Man, those were some good years; good teams," said Mathis, with a whistle. "Yeoman, Darryl Royal. Grant Teaff."

"Jackie Sherrill, Frank Broyles, Spike Dykes. Didn't know how good we had it," said Archie, trying to wrap up the small talk. "I 'preciate you givin' me seventeen. I'll need'em all."

"I heard Kinkaid had some good players out the first game," allowed Mathis. "And this weather and all."

"That's why they play the game," said the sycophant. "Can't be a champion till you win the championship."

Miles and Archie stared at Mr. Obvious, shook hands, and headed for their respective sides of the stadium. "Go Falcons."

"Go Knights," answered Miles, with a thumb's up.

Archie lingered in the throng of cheerleaders, dance teamers and students clogging the track. The players were still in the locker room, undoubtedly listening to fiery pre-game speeches and praying for a championship.

Archie remembered.

When he was a senior, Garden City lost the state finals to Jayton, 78–70.

Beat fair and square, but it still hurt. Nobody remembers a runner-up.

As he climbed the bleachers, he was glad to be wearing a down vest under his Carhartt—the wind was cutting. He smiled at the mom's waving their poms; waved to the dad's raising Cain with their cowbells. It was good to see—rain or shine—how much Texas loved its high school football.

Archie picked a spot close to the top; set up his stadium chair and took a seat with his back against the press box. He took it all in; all the school spirit, all the teenage energy, and old-time nostalgia. He wondered what Texas would do without football. It was getting' too damn dangerous. Kids were getting too big and too fast—hell, he watched two two-hundred-pound backs in *Six-Man*, the week before last.

All the same, Archie couldn't imagine how small-town Texas would survive without it. Small-town Texas was going to survive—anything and everything— but it was going to be sad if they ever drove old Friday Night Lights down.

On its very first play from scrimmage, Kinkaid threw an interception.

"Aw hell," Archie cussed, knowing his streak was over. "Plenty of time left."

And sure enough, after playing through some very noticeable first-quarter jitters, Kinkaid turned out to be an underdog with bite.

Thanks to flawless execution on *five* on-side kicks and a spirited defense that shut out the hell-bent Knights during a crucial fourth quarter, Kinkaid pulled off an upset for the ages, surviving 31–27 with a game-saving interception as time expired

"Holy moley!" said Archie, jumping and hugging and high-fiving the

Falcon parents all around him. "What a game!" he said, over and over. "What a friggin' GAME!"

It was sheer pandemonium on the field. Kinkaid's kids crying for joy. The EHS kids wailing—still not believing they got beat; even after the final whistle faded.

Never happens.

And then it does.

The Kinkaid Falcons were SPC champs. And Archie Weesatche was the luckiest sumbitch in the continental United States.

Now he was wondering if he was going to collect a single dollar bill after such a crazy game. Miles Mathis was bound to be as upset as his step-son Scooter, who was—literally—crying his eye-blacked heart out.

Archie picked his way through the spent husks of players, coaches, students, faculty, parents, fans, all manner of prostrate people laying on the field, jumping in arms, slapping heads, weeping openly, slamming helmets, knees-bent to God in prayer.

He saw the Kinkaid coach in the middle of a purple and gold swarm, drenched head-to-toe from his Gatorade victory bath. He would have liked to shake Coach Larned's hand; congratulate him on pulling off one of the biggest upsets he'd ever seen, but his payday was walking.

"That was somethin', whatnit?" said a pleasant voice. Mr. Miles Mathis, gentleman that he was, stepped up with a wistful grin and four envelopes— two KOT and two Mathis Production Company.

Archie didn't even count it. He wordlessly stuffed the envelopes in his jean jacket. "You ever heard of an outfit called SandTech?" he asked, buttoning up against cold.

"Sure," said Miles, stuffing his hands in his pockets. "SandTech's got good sand. Made me a ton of money. Frackin's made a ton of money for lots of people."

"Lucky dude, huh?" said Archie. "Sold his company for $1.6 billion. For sand!"

"Lucky! Look who's talkin," laughed Mathis, rubbing his hands together, stomping on the AstroTurf to stay warm.

Archie stomped his boots, then extended his hand. "Your boy played a helluva game; caught some tough one's over the middle. That wheel route was a thing of beauty."

"Thanks," said Miles, shaking Archie's hand. "Tough way to lose his last game."

"Yes sir. Nine times outta ten, EHS wins that game," said Archie, laying a hand on the round of Mr. Mathis' shoulder. "Thank you."

"You're welcome," said Mathis, looking Archie in the eye. "Drive safe."

DIAMOND DAVE IN THE HOUSE

"Guess who this is?"

There were few things Archie found more annoying than an unknown caller insisting on being identified. His instinct was to spew a string of expletives and hang up, but the bourbon-over-gravel voice gave him pause.

"How 'bout you guess what town I'm driving through?"

"Somewhere in bumfuck," said Diamond Dave Roth, decidedly NOT the former lead singer of Van Halen, but just as cocky.

"Diamond Dave! My man! I'm in Llano," said Archie. "About to stop for a pork chop the size of your head. Whattup?"

"Stop stealing my money."

"Roth, I have no idea what you're talkin' about, but I'd steal you blind; on principle," said Archie, smiling as he rolled up to Cooper's, one of the true Texas meccas of smoked meats. "And whaddaya mean, one of your clients?"

"I mean Miles Mathis," said Dave. "*My* golden goose, not yours."

"Aw hell, Mathis is one of your boys?" said Archie, laughing. "Nice guy. And rich as Croesus from what I gather."

"Come on, Weesatche—fifty grand!" yelled Dave. "On a high school game!"

"Totally legit, brother," replied Archie, who was trying to remember the last time he'd seen his former roommate/teammate at UH. "Met your man last year at the Houston Rodeo; at the Lamb and Goat auction. Been talking to him all season."

"Seriously, Weesatche," said Dave. "Stay away from my money."

Archie knew it'd been at least ten years since they'd last spoken, and much longer since their junior season when Diamond Dave got his teeth kicked in on a Cougar kickoff. After UH paid for his dental reconstruction, Mr. Roth, officially retired from kamikaze special teams duty, and ran the liveliest sportsbook on Cullen Boulevard. In fact, Roth was so successful that he was eventually expelled from school due to too many booster's sons losing too much money.

Young Roth's unceremonious removal from UH also had something to do with his use of Cougar lineman as enforcers. Okinawa Watkins, in early rehearsal as Keep On Truckin's fiercest repo man, liked to lift scrawny frat boys by their button-down throats.

Archie didn't know for sure, but he'd heard that his former wedge-busting friend's gambling issues got worse, before they got better. Apparently, Diamond Dave finally swore off gambling in 1998, put his degree in accounting to positive use, and was now a successful wealth manager in Houston—not Fayez Sarofim successful—but quite comfortable.

"Okay, I promise I will never bet Miles Mathis again in your lifetime. Exceedingly good man, by the way," said Archie, crushed that his Cooper's victory chop was locked up tight for the night. "I hope you keep Miles, and the extra-lovely Mrs. Mathis, in high cotton for the rest of their long lives because he is never going to experience a more gut-wrenching loss than he did tonight."

"Yeah, yeah," yapped Roth. "How gut-wrenching is it to cash six-figure royalty checks every month?"

"Was he weeping?" asked Archie. "His son Scooter was. I mean ballin', in the fetal position, in the end zone."

"Yeah, he was pretty upset," said Roth. "About the game; not the money."

"Seriously Dave, I just witnessed the finest display of high school game-plan execution, ever. These kids converted three of five onside kicks and ball-controlled a bunch of D-I talent to death. Never let'em on the field. Kinkaid ran like seventy offensive plays to thirty-six for EHS. And the defense shut down the best collection of high school skill players I've ever seen, bar none. Sealed it with an interception with like thirty seconds to go. Remember Antonio Armstrong, that badass d-end from A&M? His kid saved the game; goes up and steals a touchdown pass in the end zone!"

"Damn! That *was* a good game."

"Roth, that's how you win fifty grand," Archie continued. "Those Kinkaid boys played it to perfection. I mean flawless."

"Wow, okay. Calm down," said Dave, with an exhale. "Mathis loses fifty K fair and square. I get it."

"And how 'bout ol' Tom Herman and the Houston by god Cougars!" said Archie, clearing the Llano city limits and inching up to his nighttime speed limit of seventy-five.

"Yeah, you're always yappin' about West Texas talent. Let's talk HISD," said Dave, a proud Houston Waltrip grad. "Mr. Tom Terrific, comes in, sight unseen; has no time to recruit; takes Tony Levine's local boys and goes 11 and 1. That's some damn mojo!"

"I saw Herman at the Touchdown Club in August," said Archie, digging through his console. "Dude, I was ready to run through the drywall. The guy is crazy smart."

"Thanks for callin'," jabbed Roth. "You comin' to the AAC championship?"

"Hells yeah," said Archie. "Get me some action, Jackson!"

"I might have a live one for ya," said Dave, "Pa. boy. Lives in Austin and loves Temple. Made a ton of money with Dell."

"You manage his money?"

"Of course."

"Let's make it fifty K!" said Archie, patting his jacket to see that the Mathis cash was still bulging. "I'm on a righteous roll!"

"How much?"

"Hundred and fifty."

"No way."

"Every bit of it; on five games and a push. And that's startin' ten grand in the hole after my Steers got castrated in Sweetwater," he said, flipping his high beams on a big-eared jackrabbit scurrying across the blacktop. "So how much can I rake off this Dellionaire?"

"Five," said Dave. "Maybe, ten if you'll give him eight."

"Eight points!" barked Archie. "Temple's tough, man! I know we're playin' at home, but they got a crazy good quarterback; plus, they run the ball."

"Coogs got a crazy good defense," countered Dave. "Give him eight. Greg Ward's gonna take care of business."

"Come on now, one time for your old roomie," said Archie. "I'll give him nine for fifty and I'll see y'all at, what is it? TDU Stadium?"

"TDECU," corrected Dave. "Texas Dow Employees Credit Union. Can you believe that? A friggin' credit union payin' fifteen mil for naming rights. God bless petrochemicals!"

Suddenly, the dashboard screen announced an incoming call from Josefina Montemayor. "Hey, I gotta run. We'll be talkin'. Go Coogs!"

Archie let it ring three times, thought about letting it go to voice mail, but couldn't help but brag to his underboss.

"So, did you win?" asked Josy's stereophonic voice.

"Yes, *we* did," said Archie. "And when I wire the entire six hundred and fifty to the Happy State Bank, *we're* gonna be six and a half million dollars richer?"

"*Exactamente, guapo. ¡Asi es!*"

"Excellent news," he said, holding the steering wheel with his knees while he located the one-hitter and ground a tiny hit.

"*Ay, Archito*, where are you?"

"Lost in Space," he said, pausing to light, puff, and exhale.

"Come to Mexico. You need a break," she pleaded. "I'm worried about you."

"Come on, Josy."

"What?" she asked, almost in a panic. "Let me send the plane for you. Come rest."

"I'm fine. I'm lovin' it! I'm driving around Texas betting on high school football," he said, peering into the black night, not a car in sight. "I'm in heaven."

There was a long silence, and then a long sigh. "*Te amo guapo*. I love you." The call went dead.

Archie stared into the halogen-lit blackness, gently tisk-tisking.

"No, you don't," he said. "You love something. Ain't me."

JOSY'S FATHER, DON JOSE, WAS SO FAR GONE—PRACTICALLY IN A COMA—THAT she was able to commandeer the G-5 and fly direct to Big Spring. A car and driver picked her up at Big Spring's former Webb Air Force Base and drove her to the Hotel Settles where she'd reserved a nice tenth-floor suite. After her days of slumming in Wink, one of the wealthiest woman in Tamaulipas knew all about dicey accommodations in West Texas. She didn't need to *stay* at Wacey's, but on the short drive from the Settles to the Gregg Street bungalows, Josy was eager to see her potential new sponsor, Sister Ernestine.

"Sister Ernestine!" said Josy, wrapping her future funding source in a hug while Wacey put Sister's casserole dish full of French Onion Mac and Cheese in the refrigerator. "The casita is so cute! You and Wacey have done such a great job."

Wacey took Sister Ernestine's heavy coat and hung it in a tiny closet. "Where'd Matt run off to?" she asked, thrilled to play hostess. "Thank you so much for the Mac and Cheese. It looks amazing!"

"Oh, you're welcome. Matt says hi. He's playing basketball at the Y," said Sister Ernestine, walking into Wacey's newly redecorated living room and taking a seat on the sofa, recently re-upholstered in an off-white tufted fabric.

"Oh good," said Wacey. "I don't think he's been here since we fixed the place up."

"Your sports-crazy boys, Sister," said Josy, cozying up next to her on the couch. "Archie and *Mateo* stay in such good shape. My brother *Ricardo esta flaco, flaco*, but only because he never eats. It's not healthy."

"Send him to Sister's," said Wacey, rubbing her flat belly. "She's fattened me up, good."

"You look wonderful, Wacey," said Sister. "I'm still mad at Chuck for keeping you cooped up in that awful duplex."

Wacey raised her eyebrows at Josy.

"My place after Windi's," she explained, then caught Sister's Ernestine's eye. "Josy and I lived together at a friend's place in Wink. They're big alfalfa farmers."

"That sounds nice, although Wink is a little remote," she said, before catching herself. "This coming from the woman who lives in Garden City, Texas, for goodness' sake."

"No, Sister, Wink is the end of the world," cried Josy. "*No hay nada.*"

They all laughed like sorority girls.

"At least Garden City is kinda close to Midland," agreed Wacey. "Wink's a million miles from anywhere."

"And where's Windi, now?" asked Sister Ernestine, delighted with the conversation.

The girls looked stricken.

"She passed away," said Wacey, taking a seat in an elegant curved chair covered in green velvet. "It was sad. She was a little older, but only like forty-five."

"What happened?"

"Massive stroke," said Wacey. "In the middle of the night."

"We found her in her room! In the morning. It was awful," exclaimed Josy. "We drove straight to the emergency room. Where, Wacey?"

"Kermit."

"Oh no, poor thing," said Sister Ernestine, the former nurse, well aware of the difficulties of rural emergency care.

"They transferred her to Midland," said Wacey. "But it was too late."

"She lasted ten days," added Josy. "But not conscious."

"Could she understand when you talked to her?" asked Sister.

"I think so," said Wacey. "She couldn't talk, but I think she could hear us."

"She squeezed my hand," said Josy, starting to tear up.

"Oh goodness, her quality of life . . ." said Sister Ernestine. "It's just so hard to get someone the proper care out here. It's the downside to all these wide-open spaces."

"I know, I worry about my father," said Josy. "We have round-the-clock nurses, but the best hospital is at least an hour away; maybe more with traffic."

"I'm sorry to hear of your father," said Sister Ernestine, "Archie told me he's been ill."

"*Sí*, COPD."

The girls went silent.

"Well, let's not dwell on maladies," said Sister Ernestine. "You like what we've done with Wacey's little house? I know Archie's thrilled to have you next door."

"Very elegant, Sister," gushed Josy. "Like the houses in Mexico. You never know it from the outside."

The girls continued to gab, then toured all the rooms with glasses of wine. They were shocked how quickly the time had passed when Matt came bounding through the kitchen door.

"Sorry I'm late, Mom," he said, glistening head-to-toe. "We had enough people to play full-court. It was great!"

"That's wonderful," said Sister Ernestine. "Does Archie ever play with you?"

"No. Remember, he tore his Achilles. Hasn't played since," said Matt, bouncing on the balls of his high-tops. "The old gym rats say he was good."

"Oh, that's right! He was so mad. The doctors wouldn't even let him jog," said Sister Ernestine. "But that's when he got serious. Archie wrote a business plan for Sonny Greene, and off went Keep On Truckin."

"I love your optimism, Sister," said Josy, reflexively pouring Matt a glass of cold water. "I know where Archie gets it."

"But he's *soooh* optimistic," Wacey agreed. "It's taking me a while to get used to."

"You're practical, Wacey," soothed Sister Ernestine, moving to take her hands. "Lord knows Archie needs a practical girl."

"And what about you, *Mateo*," said Josy, sidling up to the young baller. "What does the future hold for the talented Mr. Matt?"

"Still sortin' it out," he said, as always, magnetically attracted to Ms. Montemayor's ample charms, discreetly covered at the moment, with a black cashmere shawl and heavy wool pants. "I think Uncle Archie's 'bout to talk me into being a truck driver."

Sister gave Matt a look. "We can't keep you and Archie off the road, can we?"

"He was driving somewhere—*Llano*, maybe—when I talked to him tonight," said Josy.

"You did?" said Wacey. "Where?"

"He's doing so good with his games," said Josy, ignoring Wacey's glare and Sister Ernestine's frown. "Who knew high school football could be so lucrative, no?"

"Archie and Okinawa are like Ph. Ds in Texas sports," said Matt, watching Sister Ernestine walk to the closet.

"Matt, you're going to catch your death in this cold," she said, returning with her overcoat.

"I'm good," he said, helping his mother with her coat, then remotely starting the engine of his four-wheel-drive F-150, a graduation present from his parents. "It'll be nice and toasty when we get in. I love my new truck, by the way. Thank you, Mom."

"Oh, you're welcome," said Sister Ernestine, gladly accepting Matt's kiss on her cheek. "We're very proud of you."

"I know Matt, that's great," said Wacey. "I wish I'd gone to college."

"Okay, well, I guess it's hi and bye, *Mateo*," said Josy, coming in for a two-cheek kiss. "Come see us in *CV*. *En mi casa* there is always room for you."

"I'd love to," said Matt, as Wacey and Sister Ernestine herded him to the door.

After they said their goodbyes, the old friends poured another glass of wine and took it to the living room.

"You're so over the top, Wacey," scolded Josy, throwing herself on the couch. "It's not like I'm making a move on *Mateo*. I'm effusive. I'm Mexican!"

"Girl, please," said Wacey, putting an Amarillo College coaster under Josy's wine glass. "You want to own everything you see. What were you talkin' to Archie about?"

"Business," she said. "Why? Do you think he's your boyfriend now? He doesn't even sleep with you."

"Really? You're goin' there?" said Wacey, side-eyeing her friend. She took a seat and a slow sip of wine. "*Pobre viejita*. Archie probably thinks you're going through menopause."

Impertinence that promptly induced a full Josy spew across the coffee table."

"Girl!" Josy cried, running to the kitchen. "See what you made me do!"

Fortunately, the marble table was completely devoid of knick-knacks and magazines as they wiped up the mess. Wacey'd decided early in the redecorating process that she preferred clean lines to clutter.

"Go! Right now! Go get Archie's *mota*," said Josy, popping Wacey's leg with the wet dishtowel. "If you're going to talk crazy, go get us some weed. *¡Andale*, girl!*"

"Fine! Whatever, Miss Menopause," said Wacey, leaping away from the towel. "You need to quit messin' with my man."

"*Your* man!" Josy scolded. "*Porfavor*, you can't compete with *La Princesa.*"

"*Princesa!*" said Wacey, throwing on a coat. "You're a hoe!"

"Says the horniest toad in West Texas," she cried, popping Wacey's backside again. "You're just jealous! Your men can't keep their hands off me."

The back door slammed, but Josy could hear Wacey's laughing voice, "Whatever, hoe!"

Wacey's returned with a full dirt-weed dugout.

"You need to take me to Cabo," she said, lighting and hitting the one-hitter.

"God Cabo. Please, yes!" said Josy. "But my father's so sick. We're all just waiting."

"I'm so sorry. That sucks," said Wacey, grinding a hit for her friend. "I remember when my Daddy got sick. He didn't last long; like two days in the hospital."

"My father's too proud to die," Josy said, inspecting the little pipe. "And my idiot brother is like a vulture. It's disgusting"

"So, you're stuck at the house?"

"*Papi* wants me home since all the trouble in Dallas," said Josy. "But I took the plane this weekend. Ricardo's *en El DF*. And poor *Papi*, he doesn't even know I'm gone. How do you work this thing?"

"Light it like a joint," she said, getting up to retrieve the bottle of Pinot Grigio. "We've got to get that money out. We're too old for this gangster shit."

Wacey traded Josy a glass of wine for the one-hitter, then demonstrated correct toking technique. After a deep inhale, she leaned down to give Josy a slow, smoky shotgun.

"*Gracias, chiquita,*" said Josy, a bit wide-eyed. "What a gracious hostess."

Josy got up to inspect a framed photograph of Billy Tuck, Archie, Wacey, Matt and Tallulah at Joe. T. Garcia's in Fort Worth. "I feel so bad about poor Tuck."

"Why?" asked Wacey. "You ratted him out. What did you expect?"

"I didn't expect you to shoot Rudy," Josy said, looking over shoulder with a devilish smile. "Maybe in the knee, no?"

"Bitch, please," said Wacey, joining her to look at the picture. She smacked her friend's backside. "Did you know that Rudy was going to steal our money."

"Was not. Really?"

"Yes, really," said Wacey, "You remember that bad fight we had at Wendi's? That last week, when we we're all tweakin'?"

"Worst week of my life," said Josy. "First you leave, then Wendi has a stroke. Ten days later, she's dead. That seems like a million years ago."

"I was so mad at you," said Wacey. "I drove straight to Rudy's place in OJ and blabbed and blabbed and blabbed."

The two old friends settled back on the couch enjoying their wine and weed.

"Rudy was going to get that money, one way or the other," Wacey continued. "He was going to kidnap the banker. And if that didn't work, he was coming after us."

"He was acting so weird in Dallas," cried Josy. "Why didn't you tell me?"

"I was mad at you! You can be really mean," said Wacey, swatting her friend's leg. "And you're welcome. Rudy didn't care about us."

"*¡Estoy harta!* I'm so tired of these machos," said Josy. "And this *Lobo*

Loco guy, he's so weird! All sharp-dressed. I don't know who he thinks he's fooling."

"Gimme the word, *mami*," Wacey said, leaning her head on Josy's shoulder.

"I will, *hermosa*," said Josy, closing her eyes, luxuriating on the cushions. "Let's get our money out of Texas and into Caymans. Now."

"You mean *your* money," said Wacey, reaching for her wine. "I'm just on your payroll."

"Exactly *chiquita*," said Josy. "I'm not paying you to sleep with Archie. I'm paying you to protect him."

"Archie's been pretty nice, actually. He's probably changed a lot since y'all dated."

"Dated! Please! He was cheating on his fucking fiancé!" said Josy, pulling Wacey deeper into the pile of pillows. "Men want one thing, *chiquita*."

"Is that right?" said Wacey, stretching her legs out on the sofa. "Then how come we give'em so much of that good stuff?"

Josy knew why.

"Archie's sweet. But he won't change," she said. "He'll break your heart."

"Maybe not."

"*Ay chiquita*, maybe so," said Josy, taking Wacey's hand, gently massaging her long, strong fingers. "Archie's never going to be a forever man. You're better off with me."

YOU KNOW IT'S GONNA END SOMETIME

WACO, TEXAS
DECEMBER 4, 2015

Ruth Bishop wanted to double down. And double down hard.

Two hundred K. Insisted.

Archie took the bet.

And did some insisting of his own: Austin Westlake +10 against Allen.

And just like that, on a chilly evening at a packed Waco ISD Stadium, the schoolboy cosmos came into perfect alignment during the Texas 6A Division I semifinal. Allen High's epic fifty-seven-game win streak came to a close with a Waco whimper, after Austin Westlake held off the Eagle's furious fourth-quarter rally to win, 23–14.

"You know it's gonna end sometime," Allen head coach Tom Westerberg told *The Dallas Morning News.* "You don't want it to, but you know it's gonna end."

"YOU SUCK BALLS, WEESATCHE!"

Ruth Bishop, with Tallulah in tow, stomped up to Archie, who was leaning casually on the grille of the Cougar Red Cadillac. Legions of faithful Allen fans were clearing the stadium parking lot—fast—headed back to the Metroplex.

Archie didn't mind lingering.

"Hell Ruth, I didn't even need the points," he said, twisting the blade, while Tallulah pulled five banded stacks of Benjamins from her girlfriend's

Yves St. Laurent quilted leather handbag. "Who am I again? The Six-Man Whisperer. 6A Whisperer?"

"Just suck it," spat Ruth. "You and your Cougar Red ghetto cruiser."

"Ruth, that's ratchet," said Tallulah, handing Archie the fat stacks. "I'm not goin' to like you anymore if you keep being so racist."

"I am ratchet, goddammit!" she yelled, kicking parking lot gravel on Tallulah's new Jimmie Choo's. "Mormons are big-time racist. What's your Mormon name?"

"Brittany Jeffs," answered Sheriff Fuchs, stepping into the circle of three, backlit by streams of car headlights.

"I wadn't askin' you."

"Well, I'm telling you," said the Sheriff, shaking out a Lucky Strike from a soft pack in his jacket pocket. "Tallulah's daddy's doing life plus two forty over in Palestine."

There were suspicious glances all around when Ruth lit the Sheriff's cigarette with a quick-handed Zippo.

"Appreciate it," he said, keeping a close eye on the flame.

"I'm good people," announced Ruth, flicking the lighter closed. "I just hate to lose."

Archie accepted the banded bills from Tallulah.

"Ruth, how 'bout if we put this two hundred thousand dollars to work."

"What? Double down on the Cowboys?"

"NFL is for suckers," said Archie, meeting the Sheriff's surprised expression with an unspoken appeal for calm. "Although, the Cowboys *are* gonna kick the Redskin's ass."

"Whatever," she said, eyeing Tallulah, as her about-to-be ex-girlfriend pogoed in place. "Whatcha got?"

"Straight trade. Your two hundred K for equity in our new company," said Archie, slapping the bundles. "And a good word with your dad when the time comes."

"Comes for what?" she shot back.

"For Weesatche Transport to truck gasoline, diesel and LNG from Texas to Mexico. For ten years," added Archie. "Monthly contracts guaranteed by the Mexican government."

"For fuck's sake, the Mexican government!" she said, folding her arms across her chest. "Last I heard, cartels are runnin' that country."

"That's why we've got cartels providing security," said the Sheriff. "We got protection on *both* sides of the border."

Ruth Bishop side-eyed Archie, then the Sheriff. "You're gonna give me two hundred thousand dollars back?"

"We're nice people, Ruth," said Tallulah, leaning down to kiss her cheek "You should try it sometime."

Everybody stared at their shoes while Ruth Bishop grabbed Tallulah around the neck and planted a perfectly sexy kiss on her. "Fine. Whatever. I'm in."

"Really?" said Tallulah, reaching for the Sand Queen's money. "For me? To keep?"

Suddenly the fat stacks were on the move. Archie, the Sheriff, and Ruth stood smiling as the irrepressible orphan ran pell-mell through the parking lot. None of them had a clue what Tallulah was up to.

"How's that for nice," said Ruth, as her volleyballing bandit turned to blow a kiss.

"Nice and crazy," said the Sheriff, grinding the last of his Lucky under heel. "We'll put you down for two hundred."

"Put me down for a million," she said, pulling her own smoke—a super-fat blunt—out of her purse. "And a peace offering for my new partner."

"Don't mind if I do," said Archie gladly pocketing the blunt and shaking his new partner's hand.

Ruth, with a mischievous grin, retrieved the blunt from Archie's pocket.

"Look it," she said, lighting, puffing, and passing. "I *am* good people. You do me a solid; I'll do you ten, if I can."

Archie avoided eye contact with the Sheriff as he reached for the finger-sized spleef. "Right on padna." He knew better than to take more than just a nip of whatever Ruth was smoking. "Damn, that's tasty."

Tallulah returned, breathless from her victory lap. She waved off Archie's cupped hand. "I'm a dirt weed girl."

"You're a no weed girl," said the Sheriff—asking for and receiving—the fat stacks without a peep from Tallulah. He stuffed the money back in Ruth's bag.

"Get me some paperwork," she said, stubbing the blunt on the sole of her custom Tecovas. "Dad's big on contracts. He reads *all* the fine print."

"Weesatche Transport LLC will be legal next week," said Archie. "We'll have the business plan to your dad by the end of January."

"Maybe sooner," added the Sheriff. "If I can get him to quit smokin' all that dope."

"Aw, don't do that," said Ruth, jabbing Archie's ribs. "He's cute when he's stoned."

"So y'all are going into business?" squealed Tallulah. "For real."

"Puttin' money to work's better than losing it," she said, wrapping an arm around Tallulah's waist. "I never *heard* of luckier fucker than your uncle, much less seen him."

"It's a good investment. Thank you," said Sheriff Fuchs, shaking Ruth's hand, then starting his truck with a keyless remote. "Come on Tules, if you're comin'."

"I'm comin'," she said, kissing the top of Ruth's head, whispering, "Thanks, sweetie."

"That's all I get!" cried Ruth, hanging on to Tallulah's hip huggers for dear life. "Come back here, girl. I'll introduce you to Chip & Jo over at the Magnolia."

"Really," said Tallulah, stopping in her tracks. "You know'em, like in person?"

"Hells yeah, they just finished a barndominium for dad over in Ranger," she said, turning the motor over on her new tricked-out Shelby Mustang with a keyless remote.

"Can I?" asked Tallulah, looking first at Archie, then the Sheriff.

Archie laughed, watching Ruth Bishop's off-the-charts swagger. "Sure."

"Y'all be careful. Lots of law in this town," said the Sheriff.

"Lots of Baptists, too," said Archie. "In case y'all were thinkin' about sinnin'."

"Sinnin's all I do," allowed the Sand Queen. "Let's go, Pogo."

Tallulah let out a squeal, kissed the men, then hopped in the Mustang while the rough, tough Ruth Bishop actually held her door. As the ladies joined the procession of Austin Westlake cars honking and slow-rolling out of the lot, Archie followed Sheriff Fuchs to his truck.

"That worked out pretty good," said Archie, throwing a hand up on the Sheriff's broad shoulder. "Don't you get tired savin' the day?"

"Come on, now," he said, unlocking the driver's side door. "You're the hookin' bull on this deal. I'm just helpin' with security."

"And Ruth's Dad is hell for stout," said Archie. "He'll be a game-changer if he likes what he reads about Weesatche Transport."

"Then make sure he does," said the Sheriff, chuckling at a carload of Westlake teenagers hangin' out the car windows, laughing and screaming.

"Miles Mathis swears this deal is solid," Archie agreed. "As long as MexGas and your Arturo guy keep their word."

"I got *Lobo Loco* right where I need him," said the Sheriff, stepping up on his running board. "The Sinaloans are solid. This new bunch in Ojinaga wants to get legit."

"You really trust 'em?"

"I trust money," said the Sheriff. "We give the Sinaloans a big chunk of that buried treasure; they'll see it through. How's that going, by the way?"

"Workin' on it," said Archie. "Big week in Houston."

"What you got goin'?"

"Five championship games on Wednesday, Thursday and Friday," said Archie, rubbing his hands together. "Then UH-Temple on Saturday. And a 6A final on Saturday night."

"Damn!" said the Sheriff. "You got action on all those games?"

"Just about," Archie affirmed. "Lifetime in the makin', down to one weekend. I even got Patti's Callahan's third husband in on Refugio."

"Old Man Callahan's daughter's husband?"

"Shane Hrdesky," said Archie, laughing. "KOT delivered a ton of Eagle Ford pipe for him the past coupla years out of the Victoria yard."

"Is it Callahan's company?" said the Sheriff. "Your ex is liable to have a long memory."

"This is strictly me and Shane. I'm not gettin' within five miles of Patti Callahan," Archie explained. "Shane played with Willie Mack Garza on those Refugio state champion teams in the mid-eighties. Huge Bobcat booster."

"Sounds good," said the Sheriff. "You gotta replace Ruth's two hundred thousand."

"Yep," said, Archie, shaking his head. "Good problem to have, but I'll need a coupla more bets down Houston way."

Both men scratched at the gravel, lost in thought, while the last caravan of delirious Austin Westlake fans headed back to the Hill Country.

"Alright, I gotta relieve my jailer," said the Sheriff, climbing into his truck. "I'd get a room in Waco, but he's been workin' straight through since Wednesday."

"How far is it to Gail?"

"About three hundred," said the Sheriff. "I can make it in four, four and a half."

"You came all the way to Waco to keep an eye on Tallulah," said Archie, making the Cougar Red Cadillac's lights flash with his remote.

"And you," said the long-time saver of souls. "Makin' sure ol' Sand Queen paid up."

"She sure did," said Archie, stretching for a handful of stars. "We get SandTech money behind us and Weesatche Transport gonna be a goin' concern."

"No place but Texas," said the Sheriff, as the last Westlake SUV streaked across the lot.

FULL COURT PRESS

Archie wracked his brain.

Exploring Okinawa's Booster Book, searching for deep-pocket locals with a team in the upcoming state championships. He studiously scanned the ancient piece of black leather technology as the Cougar Red Cadillac's capacious tank filled to the brim.

Over his shoulder, the slopes of Big Spring's Scenic Mountain were bathed in pristine dawn. The morning breeze was brisk, not bitter. Just right for a slow Tuesday roll to Houston for Texas High School Championship Week and the first-ever American Athletic Conference championship.

Big Spring to San Angelo to Brady to Llano to Columbus to Katy to Houston—516 miles of righteous road trip. Archie was grateful to be tracking a sinuous path through the Texas heartland. Pleased indeed for the opportunity to introduce Wacey to his favorite city and its many under-reported pleasures.

"Go Coogs!" shouted Archie, at a large roadrunner gorging on a garter snake at the edge of the convenience store's concrete apron. Much fiercer than his cartoon brethren, the raptor cocked his head at Archie, thrashed the garter for good measure, then darted into the chaparral with his breakfast.

"Good sign," he said, topping off his twenty-five-gallon tank. "Gots to be."

ARCHIE AND WACEY MADE EXCELLENT USE OF OKINAWA'S METICULOUS twentieth-century technology as they blasted through the High Plains and Hill Country. Wacey played admin, and after three dry calls to boosters from Converse, Cuero, and Iraan, she dialed up a winner, Leland Dupree, a stockbroker/arbitrage specialist from Albany, who now lived and worked in Fort Worth.

"Hey, Leland, how much you makin' on that Howard Resources deal?" said Archie, hoping to impress his stock broker with some oilfield intel.

"Archie Weesatche, as I live and breathe," said Dupree, perched high atop Ft. Worth's Sundance Square in a corner suite of cutting-edge glass and steel. "Those boys in Big Spring are asking too much for that condensate. Salad days are over in the Permian."

"I hear you," said Archie, giving Wacey a wink. "I didn't get out at the top, but at least I got out."

"No! You sold Keep On Truckin'?" cried Dupree, with his distinct Red River accent.

"Cashed out, signed a one-year non-compete, and hit the road," said Archie, setting the cruise control at a modest seventy-five. "Been bettin' on games all over the state: Presidio, Sweetwater, Lamesa, Sterling City, El Paso, Round Rock, Waco. I'm headed down to Houston, right now. For the state championships."

"Damn, Weesatche that sounds like fun," said Dupree, above the din of furiously ringing brokerage telephones. "Albany made it to state again."

"I know! The Lions are rollin'."

"Who are they playing? That team that starts with a B?"

"Exactly. State final repeat with Bremond," said Archie, ready to set the hook. "You interested in a little alma mater action?"

"Whatcha got?"

"Albany and a touchdown for ten K," said Archie.

"Is that right?" asked the broker, clearly mulling his options. "How 'bout you give me Albany plus ten for twenty-five K, and if I lose, I'll put the twenty-five in your new retirement account."

Archie loved the look of Wacey's jaw dropping.

"Deal."

"Deal!" shouted Dupree. "Hey, I gotta run, Arch. We'll be in touch. Go Lions!"

"Yessir! Go Albany!" cried Archie, beating the console with a happy fist. "Thanks, Leland. We'll be talkin'."

He hit the end call and high-fived his elated assistant.

"One down, four to go!" he cried. "Who's next?"

"Okinawa sure writes little for such a big guy. I can barely make out his handwriting," said Wacey, the Booster Book close to her nose. "Looks like, Shane Hrdesky, Owner/Callahan Pipe, Victoria, Texas. Wasn't your ex a Callahan?"

"It's Ra-des-key. I've already got him down for ten grand," he corrected, with a sly smile. "And yes, I was engaged to Patti Callahan. Until I met Josefina."

"I know the story," said Wacey, looking straight ahead. "Ida' killed you both."

Archie took that under advisement, gratified to be upgraded to "worth shooting."

"Shane is Patti's third husband," replied Archie "I met him when we opened the KOT yard in South Texas. He's perfect for Patti, and us."

"Why?"

"Because he gives two fucks what Patti thinks about his gamblin'," replied Archie, "And he's a state champion linebacker from Refugio who are playin' Canadian in the Two A championship. Tomorrow."

"Does Josy know you're screwing your ex?"

"What? Nobody's screwing anybody's ex," pleaded Archie, slowing to pull over into a bar ditch covered in tan winter grass. "How 'bout we stretch our legs a bit."

"I'm fine."

"You mind if I confirm with Shane outside?"

"Go for it," she said, pouting. "Can you hurry? I'm starving."

"No worries," said Archie, grabbing his phone. "We're about ten miles out of Llano."

"Are we going to eat barbecue again?" she asked, to his exiting backside.

Archie leaned back in the open door. "I am."

"Fine. Go!" she said, shooing him away.

Archie gingerly closed the door, mumbling under his breath. He did a couple of jumping jacks in the bar ditch, then settled up against the trunk.

"Hey Shane, this is Archie Weesatche. I'm just callin' to confirm our bet."

"Hey Arch," said the man who always picked up on the first ring. "Damn, I forgot all about that. How you doin'?"

"Oh, fair-to-middlin'," said Archie. "You headed to Houston for the game?"

"Absolutely!" said the fifth-generation Texas Czech. "Cats are gonna kick those Yankee's ass."

Archie had to laugh. A lot of old-timers in South Texas claimed anybody living north of Waco was a Yankee. When he moved to Victoria, he didn't think the locals were serious, but quickly learned better.

"I got you down for Refugio plus fourteen for twenty-five."

"Twenty-five!" he screeched. "Thousand?"

"Yeah, I'm running a pretty healthy state finals pool."

"Hell, I 'magine," he said, sounding skeptical, but still on the line. "How many points?"

"Refugio plus fourteen," said Archie. "I talked to you about it a couple of nights ago."

"Hell! I's drunk as a skunk two nights ago," he said. "Whatever. Sign me up! Fuck it. Ain't my money."

"Excellent!" said Archie, pumping his fist, bounding over to Wacey's window. "Got it. Shane Hrdesky – Refugio plus fourteen for twenty-five thousand dollars."

"When's the game start?"

"Early," said Archie, knocking on Wacey's window. "Ten a.m."

"Alright, Weesatche," said the pipeman. "I'll see you at NRG bright and early."

"I'll be there," said Archie, giving his unresponsive girlfriend the gas face. "Give Patti my best."

"Guess I won't," he said, with a laugh. "She hates your guts."

"Sounds about right," said Archie, wondering how he could be so stupid. "Alrighty Shane, see you tomorrow. Drive safe."

Fifty thousand dollars on the Wednesday games! Archie was so pumped that his grumpy girlfriend agreed to let him stop for barbecue.

And, as always, Cooper's did not disappoint. Steering with one hand and eating with the other, the peppery sausage, beautifully barked brisket and succulent pork ribs were gone by the time they hit the interchange in Columbus, joining the bumper-to-bumper nonsense that masquerades as traffic flow on I-10 East.

As the Interstate widened to a world-record eighteen lanes in Katy they picked up speed and, as planned, did indeed beat the infamous Houston rush hour—door to door in a zippy, seven hours and thirty minutes.

"Welcome to Hotel ZaZa," said a nattily attired bellman. "Checking in?"

"Yes sir," confirmed Archie, exiting his BBQ-infused space shuttle. "Five nights in the Space City Special."

"Ah, yes sir," said the young man, "One of our best."

"Outstanding," said Archie opening the trunk, then ushering Wacey up the polished stone steps into the ZaZa's spacious lobby.

"This is nice," purred Wacey, turning a heel on the gleaming marble floor, holding Archie's hand as they approached the front desk.

"Archie Weesatche," he announced, handing the immaculately groomed front desk clerk his driver's license and credit card. "Checking in."

"Of course, Mr. Weesatche, we're so pleased to have you with us."

"Glad to be here," he said. "Place looks spectacular."

"Thank you, yes, welcome to Hotel ZaZa," said the clerk, running Archie's credit card. "It was the Warwick, when you were with us last?"

"Afraid so; late nineties, I think."

"Well, the *grande dame* has undergone a complete renovation, top to bottom," said the young man, fingers flying, never looking up from his keyboard, until he fixed Wacey with a dazzling smile. "And you, young lady, are going to love it!

"I already love it!" she said, much to Archie's delight. "Houston's so big."

The clerk's eyebrows rose in Archie's direction.

"She's adorable," the clerk said, motioning for a bellman. "Okay troops; relax, freshen up, but no napping. We have pure fabulosity right here in the lobby bar. Our jazz combo plays its first set at six."

"I was thinking about catching a sunset over at Rice; I hear it's beautiful."

"Look at you, Mr. Romantic," said the clerk. "And yes, Turrell's Twilight Epiphany is to die for. Even better now that Houston's ten days of winter are upon us."

"See who's workin' the full-court press," said Archie, easing a hand around Wacey's hip, pleased with this big city chat.

"And five nights; well done," said the happy clerk, clasping his hands. "There's no telling what Mr. Weesatche has in store for you."

"True that," said Archie, grateful to see another couple swirl in through the revolving door. "Lots of stops on the UH Nostalgia Tour."

"So, you're a Cougar," said the clerk, cutting his eyes at the approaching elders.

"Do I look like a Cougar?" said Wacey, jutting a hip just so.

"Oh no, honey!" cried the clerk, bouncing from behind the desk. "You're a rock star."

"Welcome, welcome!" said the genial host to the newly arrived guests. "It's so good to see you again, Mr. Pickens, ma'am. Are you in from Amarillo?"

"Dallas."

Archie did a double-take. It was indeed, that man, T. Boone Pickens.

Wacey followed the bags to the elevator, but Archie lingered.

"And what brings you to Houston, Mr. Pickens?"

"The beautiful women," said the silver fox. "And an oil company that needs savin'."

"Oh hush, Boone," said his extravagantly wardrobed lady friend, gently swatting his arm. "You know the best-lookin' girls come from Dallas."

"Shoosh!" said the clerk, finger to his lips. "Don't tell."

Ah, the sweet sound of billionaire banter, thought Archie, as the ding of an arriving elevator called him away.

AFTER A QUICK INVENTORY OF SEVERAL NIFTY NASA ARTIFACTS, AND AN EVEN quicker cat nap, Archie willed himself not to be lazy; to resist the re-rack, to get moving.

He and Wacey laid on the super-cozy King-Size, taking in a mellow winter sun through a bank of picture windows that framed sprawling Hermann Park, Mecom Fountain and the wide Museum District boulevards that Bob Hope once bragged were as "pretty as Paris."

"Welcome to Houston!" he said, leaping from the bed and dramatically opening the curtains to reveal the towers of the massive Texas Medical Center. "We'll pay our respects to Sam Houston, stroll to the Skyspace, then call it an early night."

"Perfect. Thank you for being so patient with the little bitch this morning."

"*My* little bitch," Archie said, rolling over for a kiss. "It's all new. We're working on it."

"It *is* new," she agreed, luxuriating on the snow-white duvet. "For a Forsan girl."

"I love Forsan girls," said Archie, stealing another kiss on his way to the mini-bar.

Presently, Archie and Wacey slid past the packed lobby bar, saluted General Sam astride his giant bronze steed, then navigated the crushed granite paths beneath an amazing live oak canopy spreading across the breadth of the lush Rice campus.

There was a full crowd assembled for sunset at Mr. Terrell's stunning landscape installation, an artwork designed specifically to capture the rays of dawn and sunset.

"This is wild," said Wacey, squeezing Archie's arm, as they settled in with a gaggle of undergraduates on one of four stone benches. All around, the sky grew darker until the remaining light squeezed through an oculus filling a precisely positioned metal canvas with vibrant orange. Suddenly, as the sun dipped below the speckless grass berms, and the colors became unbearably beautiful, the lucky participants erupted in applause.

Archie hugged on Wacey's shoulder as they stared overhead at the sublime blend of cosmic color and artful refraction.

"No way," said Wacey, ogling the otherworldly display.

"Yep," assured her faithful guide, delighted with the start to their metropolitan sojourn.

EIGHTEEN HOURS LATER, AFTER THE REFUGIO BOBCATS LOST 60–21 TO THE Canadian Wildcats, Archie was face-to-face with his former fiancé.

"Hey Patti," he said, instinctively bending to kiss her cheek. "You look great."

"Oh hush," she said, clutching his shirt sleeve, obviously pleased.

Patti Callahan did, in fact, look a lot better than Archie predicted. Nicely turned out in classic rancher chic—draped head-to-toe in dove grey ultra-suede and working a full head of big, highlighted Texas hair. Archie wished the occasion didn't include collecting twenty-five thousand dollars from her husband, but there it was.

"Patti, this is Wacey Foyt," he said, trying not to grimace, when Wacey chose not to shake the heiress's jewel-encrusted hand. Curt smiles and minimal eye contact ensued.

"Hey Shane," said Archie, shaking a man's hand. "Bobcats had their hands full. That's thirty-one in a row for Canadian."

"Pick six on the first drive," he said, tipping his silver-belly Stetson back a bit. "I knew it was gonna be a long day."

"Oh, did you lose a bet?" inquired the curious Patti.

"Just a gentlemen's wager," said Archie, quick to give Patti his best little boy smile. Although twenty years had passed since the Thanksgiving Archie was sent into deep West Texas exile, she remembered well his devious ways.

"How much of a gentlemen's wager?"

"Why the hell do you care?" asked Shane. "Refugio got beat. Let it alone."

A long moment passed as the huddle of four stood, heads down, buffeted by throngs of small-town fans exiting the cavernous NRG Stadium concourse.

"Y'all staying in town tonight?" asked Archie, desperate to wrap it up.

"Not me," said Shane, giving his wife the stink eye. "I don't know what she's doin'."

"Oh, get over it, Shane," said Patti, crossing her arms defiantly. "Refugio lost, big whoop. I'm goin' shoppin'."

"Yeah, you're good at that," he said, staring her down.

Archie shot Wacey a look. He knew Shane was good for the money. It was time to bolt. "Well, hey, we're meetin' some folks for the Bremond-Albany game," he said, snaking an arm under Wacey's. "Great to see you, Patti. Shane."

"It's nice to meet you," said Wacey, smiling at Patti and shaking Shane's hand.

They walked away from the awkwardness with seconds to spare. Archie couldn't pull Wacey up a near-by escalator fast enough.

"Are we clear?" he asked, eyes straight ahead.

Wacey looked over her shoulder as they ascended the rolling stairs to the Suite Level. "Oh my God, they're screaming!" she said, pointing at the highly-verbal combatants.

Archie pulled her arm down and snuck a peek at the pair, red-faced and toe-to-toe.

"Man, that girl's *all* growed up," he said. "She'd kick my ass all the way back to Big Spring."

"I bet you could handle her," she said, playfully punching his backside. "At least you'd be rich."

"Rich. And pushin' daisies," Archie said, glancing at the combatants, glad not to be in Shane's shoes. He leaned down to kiss his bodyguard's cheek, relieved to be exiting the early playoff games a winner.

Archie was rolling. Of this, there was no doubt.

But he was still $150,000 shy of what he needed for Vegas.

H-TOWN TAKEOVER!

The Thursday championships games came and went—unwagered—victims of a fierce round of post-game celebration after Bremond put a beating on Leland Dupree's Albany Lions, 35–20, to extend Archie's win streak.

Not that the luckiest man in Texas had any high-level intel on the Thursday 3A games. Waskom beat Franklin for back-to-back state titles in Division I. Brock blasted Cameron Yoe in Division II. He would have bet on Cameron Yoe, a perennial 3A juggernaut.

At this point in the streak, even Archie's omissions were fortunate.

By the light of a Houston dawn, amidst furrowing fog banks in moss-draped Hermann Park, Archie searched for marks. Searched for three clear bets. Okinawa's Booster Book yielded no leads. So, as Wacey snoozed away an impending hangover, Archie decided it was time for a call.

The call.

The one he'd been saving up all fall, to the Roznovsky Twins—the oldest, richest bookies in the Coastal Bend.

Nestled behind the so-called River Cane Curtain, along the banks of Carancahua Bay, Nancy and Samantha Roznovsky started their highly-successful enterprise in the mid-seventies at the old Sharkskin Palace, then moved to Houston during the Austin Chalk boom. With-Energy Capital of the World's economy ever-soaring and football always king, the highly competent Roznovsky Twins grew a steady clientele over the next four decades.

"My goodness, Archie Weesatche!" gasped Nancy Roznovsky, as sibling Sam hooted in the background. "I thought you were long gone."

"Yes, ma'am. Old Man Callahan sends you packing, you best stay disappeared," said Archie. "Hey, y'all taking any action on Championship Week?"

"Coupla North Shore bets is all so far," said Glenda. "Whatcha got?"

"Well, it's a little pricey," said Archie, feeling his way.

"C'mon Arch," she assured. "Gosh, it's good to hear your voice."

"Yours too. Is this Nancy or Sam?" said Archie.

"This is Nancy," she said, laughing. "Silent Sam's totin' up the dailies."

"Okay then, how 'bout a South Texas Special," he ventured. "Straight up. No points."

"I'm listenin'."

"Three-team parlay; West Orange-Stark over Celina, Friday morning; George Ranch over Mansfield Lake Ridge, Friday night and Katy over Lake Travis, Saturday night."

"That's a fair bit of action," she said. "What about North Shore?"

"No ma'am," he said. "Westlake won me a big game last week. Can't bet against'em."

"Alright, just checkin'," she said. "Hey, let me text you back. We're takin' a ton of action on the college games this weekend. Lemme see if I can lay some off and get right back to ya. Can you wait till ten?"

"You bet," said Archie, "I appreciate you takin' any of it, on short notice."

"Darlin', that's what we do," said the veteran bookie, who had to be pushing seventy-five, maybe eighty-five. "I bet you're a sight for sore eyes. Can't remember how long it's been."

Archie was in his early twenties last time he'd seen the Roznovsky Twins, but recalled fondly their demure attire and expert bookmaking in decided contrast to the Sharkskin Palace's daily display of non-stop flesh.

He exchanged a few more pleasantries, and the tale of mutual-friend Billy Tuck's tragic demise, then re-confirmed the parlay details. When they rang off, Archie knew the bet was solid.

By the time Wacey lifted out of her luxurious ZaZa cocoon, Archie'd eaten breakfast, downed a full pot of coffee, and read all four sections of the *Houston Chronicle*, including a front-page story touting the Cougar's "H-Town Takeover!"

"Hey there, sleepyhead," he sang. "You ready for some *more* football?"

"Believe it or not, I am," said Wacey, sounding chipper, despite the previous evening's boatload of Tito's and cranberry.

Archie got up from two hours on the sitting room couch and slid over to the bed for a wake-up kiss. "What can I get you to eat, drink, or both?"

"That orange juice looks nice," she said, pointing at the room service cart. "And maybe a little toast."

"All good. It's goin' on nine thirty for a noon kickoff," he said, unwrapping the cellophane from the top of Wacey's juice. "Take this with you and I'll bring you some toast and jam. And a little crispy bacon. And a lot of Goody's."

"Yes!" she said, rubbing the sleep out of mascara-clogged eyes. "I can get ready in like thirty minutes."

"No rush. Take your time," said Archie, reading an incoming text. "Roth's software man's driving in from Austin. He wants to meet at eleven thirty. We're ten minutes from the stadium. Enjoy your shower."

As he leaned in with the juice, Wacey took Archie's face with both hands and laid a big one on him.

"Yes ma'am!" he said, coming up for air. "Go Coogs!"

HAVING TAKEN BACK ROADS FROM THE MUSEUM DISTRICT TO AVOID THE nightmare traffic on I-45, the Cougar football carnival was in full swing when Archie and Wacey arrived in Third Ward. The Cougar Red Cadillac felt right at home as they rolled into the Holman Street Garage with minutes to spare. They walked across the vibrant stadium complex, thrilled to be a part of the red and white throngs.

The wealth manager and the Dellionaire had been waiting below the splendid new statue of Coach Yeoman for a full thirty minutes.

"Diamond Dave!" yelled Archie, giving his noticeably thinner roommate a vigorous soul shake/bro hug. "Dave, this is Wacey Foyt of Forsan, Texas, straight shooter and born-again Coog!"

With a little morning marijuana in full effect, Wacey gave the boys a twirl in her new UH outfit featuring a red mesh Case Keenum jersey/turtleneck combo paired with white stretch jeans, black knee-high boots and a pair of wraparound shades that glowed with gasoline iridescence.

And Wacey was having a *real* good hair day.

Big Winner Weesatche had driven straight to the Galleria after Bremond made him $50,000 richer. He wanted to make sure his bodyguard was high-stylin' for the Coog's big game. The personal shoppers at Neiman-Marcus did not disappoint.

"And Mr. Craig, I presume?" Archie continued. "The Pennsylvania gentleman."

"Yes, sir! Riley Craig!" said the big man with the big smile and a firm handshake. "Nice to meet you."

"Nice to meet you!" said Wacey, stepping up to give the towering former pulling guard a proper Texas hug. "Welcome to Texas!"

"Well, I've been here about fifteen years," he replied, as Wacey clung to his big frame. "Guess they're right about Texas being The Friendly State."

Diamond Dave and Archie couldn't agree more as Wacey preened and the Spirit of Houston Marching Band came blasting up Cullen Boulevard. It felt like the entire neighborhood was surrounded with tailgates and tents, keg beer, and full bars, all pulsating with mobs of trash-talking Coogs. The band was followed closely by the players, coaches, and staff all woofing and jiving with the masses, everybody so proud of their new on-campus stadium. As the football entourage slowly snaked through day-drinking multitudes, it was clear that the UH fans were beside themselves about the 11-1 Cougars and their new head coach, Tom Herman.

"Mr. Craig, rumor has it you're gamblin' man," said Archie, as they made their way into the stadium, and more importantly, into the shade.

"It's Riley. And yes, I have permission from my wealth advisor to bet anything I like."

"Hells yeah!" yelled Wacey, bouncing from one hug to another for Diamond Dave. "It's fun to bet on football."

"Dave said you'd give me six points for ten K," said Riley, showing off his professionally whitened smile for Wacey. "Give me eight and I'll make it twenty-five."

Roth did a double-take.

Archie did a quick calculation.

The Vegas spread was a hard six. And Temple was a damn good team with a quicksilver quarterback and a running back who could control the ball if the Owls got an early lead.

"Eight for twenty-five it is," said Archie, shaking a man's hand. "And thank you so much for driving down from Austin on this fine football Saturday."

"Beats watching UT," he said, accepting yet another hug from Wacey. "I never thought I'd say it, but I'm pretty sure Temple could beat UT this year."

"UT sucks, right?" added Wacey, accepting a Red Solo cup from a total stranger.

"Easy there, Cougar," said Archie, gently taking the spilling beer and helping himself.

"Those chicken shits won't schedule the Coogs in a hundred years," added Roth, quickly surmising why Archie was so smitten with his bodyguard.

"Alrighty roo," said Archie, kissing Wacey for no apparent reason. "Let's go watch us a championship!"

Diamond Dave had great seats on the visitor's side, about four rows up from the Temple bench. The stadium was still filling, and to nobody's surprise, there was only a smattering of maroon and white in the stands. Temple was famous for basketball, not football. Not to mention Philly was a long, long way from Houston.

As luck would have it—and Archie knew it was luck, *not* his incredible sports wagering skill set—Houston jumped out to a 17–0 lead.

It helped that forty thousand plus Coog fans were losing their collective minds and the UH defense—the Chain Link Posse—were ranging from sideline to sideline, resulting in two crucial turnovers. One that set up a forty-seven-yard touchdown run.

Temple, who'd won ten games for the first time in school history, had a chance to get within a touchdown early in the fourth quarter, but UH knocked down a pass in the end zone and the Owls settled for a field goal to make it 24–13.

Temple had two more chances to cut the deficit—chances that had Archie about to soil himself—but the UH defense came up big, stuffing the Owls on fourth down, *twice*.

After the final whistle—unleashing a tsunami of students celebrating UH's first conference championship in ages—Archie was in heaven, watching the Coog ballers dance and hug and high five in a frenzy of feel-good. Archie knew he couldn't keep it up, betting all this crazy money on football games. And winning. He also knew he *had* to keep betting as long the streak was alive.

But damn.

Wacey was dumbfounded. Especially when Archie pocketed an old-fashioned paper check for $25,000 from the best-natured football fan in the history of Philadelphia.

"Best season the Owls ever had," said Craig, handing Archie the check with a wistful smile. "Temple doesn't even have a football history."

"How many shares of Dell is that worth?" asked Roth.

"Oh, about twenty-five hundred."

"How many you own?"

"About two hundred thousand," said Craig, now grinning from ear to ear.

"Are you doing the math, Weesatche?" said Roth, punching his absurdly lucky friend.

Archie squinted, "Roth, I failed calculus, twice."

"I'm doin' the math?" said Wacey, perking up after three and a half *long* hours of football. "That's a lot of zeros."

"Yes ma'am, that's the number twenty, followed by six zeros," said Roth, high-fiving the fattest of his many golden geese.

Wacey looped her arm through the rugged Pennsylvanian's. "How's your bodyguard situation?" At six-foot-four, and lineman stout, Riley Craig didn't exactly need a security detail.

"You're looking at it. Why?"

"Just sayin'," she said, squeezing his bicep. "Good to have someone watching your back."

"Is that what you do?" he asked, amused.

"Handles her nine like Mission Impossible," bragged Archie, wondering how Wacey had avoided the stadium metal detectors.

"Damn," said Craig, stepping back as she loosened her grip. "You packin' right now?"

"Maybe," she said, with a wicked grin.

"Would you have to kill me?" asked Roth.

"A jealous husband's gonna take care of that," she said, smiling over her shoulder as they started the long march up from the fan-clogged field-level.

Roth raised his eyebrows at Archie as she passed by. "Nice *chica*, Weesatche."

"Talented beyond your imagination," said Archie, following him close.

"Nothing's beyond my imagination," he said. "Except your winning streak."

"Yeah, thanks for the jinx, pal," said Archie, kidding—but not much.

Roth insisted on visiting the venerable West Alabama Ice House, a prime hangout during their UH days, for a post-game celebration. Riley Craig was not expecting to find such an Austin-esque setting in the middle of Houston. All he'd heard from his computer brethren was that the Bayou City was a petrochemical wasteland.

"Stick around and I'll take you down to the San Jacinto Monument," said Roth, ushering the group to a picnic table under trees and strings of bulbs surrounding an indoor/outdoor bar. "Biggest refinery complex in the world. Ground Zero when World War III starts."

For reasons entirely unclear, Wacey had strapped on her shoulder holster for the afternoon festivities and as soon as she sat down a super-skinny biker sidled up to their picnic table to check out her gun.

After Wacey reluctantly handed over her Glock, Mr. Straggly's first move was to draw a bead on a huge dude with San Jacinto High Roller stitched across the back of his vest.

"Hey, dumbass!" yelled a tiny bartender, from behind the bar, leveling a sawed-off shotgun. "Drop it! Now!"

"Hell Ramona, I was just funnin'," said Straggly, carefully laying the gun down and tip-toeing backward, arms raised.

"Jesus, Joseph and Mary," exclaimed Riley Craig.

"All good," said Wacey, quickly securing the gun in her holster. "All good."

The rest of the outdoor patio, packed with matrons, patrons and kids on a pretty winter Saturday, went dead still. Even the dogs were quiet. The only sound was James McMurtry singing an ornery Texas song.

"So much for open carry," said Archie, as the bartender racked her shotgun over shoulder. "¡Vamonos!"

By the time the foursome settled up and retreated to their respective cars, Riley Craig had seen about enough of H-Town. "I'm outta here. Hope UH beats the hell out some Power Five team."

"You gimme a call if you need some protection," lobbied Wacey, who doubled down with a tippy-toe kiss on Riley Craig's cheek.

Speechless, Riley Craig smiled at the kiss, saluted Roth, shook Archie's hand, and turned tail for his Corvette and the promise of a peaceful drive back to Austin.

AFTER WOLFING DOWN TWO EXQUISITE THIN CRUST SHAMROCK PIZZAS (CORNED beef and grilled onions) at nearby Kinneally's, and drinking pitcher after pitcher of cold Harp on the sun-drenched outer patio, the former Cougar teammates quickly ascertained UH's bowl game opponent: fourteenth-ranked Florida State, who beat the dog out of tenth-ranked Florida, 27–2.

"Peach Bowl! Man, I'd love to go that game," said Archie, signing his receipt and sticking twenty dollars inside the bill holder. "Wacey, you ready to go to Hot-Lanta?"

"I thought we were goin' to Vegas," she said, tearing her gaze away from her phone. "With the whole family."

"Yeah, I did say that, didn't I?"

"How 'bout them Coogs going to the Peach?" said Roth, toothpick in place. "Beats the hell out of playing Ball State in the Toilet Bowl."

"Yeah, I wasn't counting on playin' the 'Noles," agreed Archie. "That's big time!"

"How much you gonna bet on that one, hotshot?" said Roth, stretching in the late afternoon light as plumes of cigar smoke wafted out the open windows. "Florida State is a damn sight saltier than Temple."

"Might let the whole thing ride," he said, pulling a chair for Wacey. "If you promise not to jinx me."

"I did my part," said Roth, waving off. "Frigging twenty-five-K payday! Are you kiddin'?"

"Is he really that rich?" asked Wacey, gathering up her shades, phone, lip balm, and purse. She left the Glock in the car this time.

"Oh yeah, Riley Craig got in early during the software boom," said Roth. "I've made him a little money, but my main job is keeping the vultures away."

"Who you callin' a vulture?"

"Not you, darlin'," assured Roth. "You've got mad skills and a large firearm."

Archie smiled as Roth commenced crawdadding. "I'm talkin' 'bout these pencil-neck geeks with the next big idea. All they need is some venture capital and shazam! Everybody's a zillionaire."

"Bullshit artists."

"Yeah, kinda like you, Weesatche," said Roth, delivering a stiff arm. "'Cept you bet on high school football, and you're harmless. Start-ups are money pits. Burn rate, they call it. Big burn rates."

"He's definitely rich," said Wacey. "I'd lose my mind if I lost twenty-five thousand dollars on anything, much less a college football game."

Which reminded Archie about the last game of his three-team high school parlay.

He was two-thirds of the way there after the Friday games: West-Orange Stark smoked Celina 22–3 and George Ranch crushed Lake Ridge, 56–0. Now it was up to Katy to beat Lake Travis. A daunting task.

After Archie and Wacey bid adieu to Roth, and went to lay down in the suite for a nap, the week's festivities finally took their toll.

The quick nap turned into midnight room service. Midnight turned into 3:00 a.m.

Archie had to look.

He slipped out of bed and into the sitting room, picked up his phone, and said a prayer.

Katy 35 Lake Travis 14.

"Holy Moly!" he silently screamed, jumping up and down in the dark. "How 'bout them Katy by god Tigers!"

Archie enjoyed a glorious five-hour re-rack. Wacey nuzzled on his neck till he finally woke up, soft sunshine pouring through the curtains.

"We won."

"I know," she said. "Go Coogs!"

"I'm talkin' about the parlay," he said, smiling so big it almost hurt. "Katy did it."

"You won a hundred and fifty thousand?"

"We did."

Wacey laid back in a nest of pillows, crooked a lovely trigger finger. "Come here, you."

AFTER SECURING THE BEST BREAKFAST IN TOWN AT HARRY'S ON TUAM, ARCHIE'S personal H-Town Takeover was done. The massive plate of migas with a side of grits, crispy bacon, and two glasses of fresh-squeezed orange juice had a man ready for the road.

"Let's get you back to West Texas," he said, holding the passenger door.

"Where I belong," said Wacey, hiding behind her petrol-tinted shades.

Road trip returns were always the hardest. And then there was I-10 West. Four straight hours of stop-and-start Interstate brutality, punctuated by Wacey's irritable questions.

What exactly was he planning to do with all that money? Surely, he wasn't going to trust Josy and her crooked banker at the Happy State Bank?

Crickets.

And then, out of the clear blue . . .

"You know Rudy was goin' to kill you?"

At this point in the nine-hour drive, Archie was zoning out; somewhere in the pitch dark between San Angelo and Sterling City.

"Jesus," he said, wiping his face, trying to snap out of a heavy road fog. "No, I did not know Rudy was going to kill me."

"Well, he was," said Wacey, staring a hole through his right ear. "Why in the world do you think Chuck hooked us up in the first place?"

"No idea," said Archie.

Wacey snorted. "What makes you think Chuck's not working with Josy?"

"Who? The Sheriff?"

She didn't answer, but he could feel Wacey's impatient eyes. As if to say, hey peanut brain, wake the hell up.

There wasn't a single headlight, ahead or behind; only the twinkle of house light and barn light in the Staked Plains distance. The Cougar Red Cadillac was cruising seventy-five, but they were still an hour from Big Spring.

"So, what's up? What's your point?"

"Nothin'," she said. "Maybe you don't know Chuck as well as you think."

"I know Chuck Fuchs saved my life," said Archie. "And raised me like a son."

"All I'm sayin' is he *is* in with Josy," she said, finally taking her eyes off Archie and staring out at the shafts of halogen light cutting through the darkness.

"How?" he asked, trying to buy time. He didn't know what to say; he'd never thought about Chuck and Josy. Never knew he needed to.

"He loves you, Archie," she said. "Chuck's just tryin' to protect you."

Archie thought back to when Wacey arrived at his doorstep. Best thing that had ever happened to him. Lately.

"So, I'm supposed to be suspicious of Chuck?" he asked, incredulous. "Not happenin'."

"I don't know, Archie. You're a nice guy," she said, her face reflecting the soft glow of the instrument panel.

"Yeah, I'm super nice," he sighed. "Come on! What do you know, that I don't?"

"That I'm more interested in Josy's money than you are."

This was not good news. This change of attitude.

"How come you're telling me this now?"

"Because I like you."

"Hmm. How 'bout this weekend," said Archie. "How'd that go?"

"It was super nice," she said, reaching for his hand on the console. "Nobody's ever treated me this nice."

He let her take his hand over to her lap.

"Look, all I'm sayin'," she continued. "You're still a long way from getting what Josy needs. Right?"

Archie couldn't remember what he'd told her. Probably everything.

"I've got what I need for Vegas."

"And you think this is all gonna go down nice and easy?"

"Probably not," he said, trying not to sound defensive. "But so far so good."

Wacey harrumphed, then went quiet.

"I made a promise," he said, sticking his finger in his mouth, then wiping saliva across his dry eyes—a trick of the hotshot trade. "I'm stickin' to it."

"What's wrong with what you got in your floor safe right now?"

"I showed you that?"

"Yes."

"See how much I trust you."

"You were stoned."

"And?"

"I like you when you're stoned."

"I like you when you shoot people who want to kill me."

Archie let that sink in.

Beneath a sky-wide blanket of stars—the likes of which light-polluted Houston, Texas never sees—night drenched the badlands in indigo blue. In the distance, a Permian Basin drill site throbbed beneath coronas of rented light as a fleet of frack trucks pumped sand and slickwater down the throat of a shale well.

The Cougar Red Cadillac slipped by as Wacey weighed her options.

"What if *I* make you a deal?" she asked.

Archie popped the thick of his palm on the steering wheel.

"Absolutely! Make me a deal, girl," he said, snaking a pinkie finger back to tickle her palm. "Whatcha got?"

SISTER ERNESTINE SETS SAIL

BIG SPRING, TEXAS
DECEMBER 13, 2015

The deal-making had to wait.

Wacey and Archie were completely distracted by a momma feral hog and her prodigious brood crossing the highway outside of Forsan; a swerving near-miss. Before negotiations could resume, they were cruising down Gregg Street, with the sidewalks of Big Spring rolled up tight.

He hugged Wacey after dropping two bags on the floor of her spotless kitchen.

"Thanks for coming to Houston," he said. "That was a long haul."

"I'm tired," she said, throwing an arm around his neck and giving him a good kiss. "I'm gonna sleep like poured concrete."

Archie laughed at his funny girl. Wrapped his bodyguard in a tight hug.

"Hey, I'm thinking about what you said."

He gave her another kiss on the forehead.

"Don't worry about Josy. We're gonna be fine."

As Archie walked away, Wacey lingered at the door.

"Who's we?"

Archie turned and walked backward, "Me and you, pale face. Joined at the West Texas hip. Sweet dreams!"

WHEN ARCHIE WALKED INTO HIS LIVING ROOM, HE FOUND OKINAWA WATKINS snoring on the couch with Sunday Night Football blaring on the big screen.

"Say, brother. What up, Arch?" he said, rubbing the Sunday Funday out of his eyes. "Where's Miss Wacey?"

"Her place," he said, jerking his thumb over his shoulder.

"I forget she's next door," he said, straining to get his big body upright. "My old lady kicked me out, again. You mind if I crash with you?"

"Always, Oak," he said, throwing his duffel on the bed then heading for the fridge. "How'd you get in?"

"Key's in the shed," he admitted, sheepishly. "You showed me a long time ago."

"No. No. All good," said Archie, slumping into his armchair after the excruciating nine-hour and forty-five-minute drive. "You want a beer?"

"Got any of that hydro left?"

"In the Caddy," he said, digging for the car keys. "In the console."

As Archie tossed the car keys to his friend, Tony Romo threw an interception. "C'mon, man!" they harmonized. "Dog-ass Cowboys!"

Okinawa was back in time to watch the Eagles take a fourth-quarter lead.

"Forget the Cowboys, dawg. How 'bout them Coogs!" he said, handing the dugout to Archie. "I was lookin' for y'all. Great game, man. Coach Herman's got'em goin'."

"Oak, I love it, man. Those boys are solid ballin'!"

"Coach Yeoman used to fire us up," said Okinawa, grinding out a hit. "But this dude's takin' it next level. That sideline was jumpin'!"

"Made me a pretty penny, Oak."

"How much?"

Archie thought about his answer. A little wary after Wacey's warnings. "Twenty-five."

"Money, money, mon-ey!" sang Okinawa. "You ready for Vegas?"

"Ready as I'll ever be," Archie allowed, extracting two envelopes of cash and peeling off twenty-five hundred-dollar bills for his partner's cut. "Thanks to you."

To toast the Coog's first conference championship since 2006, Archie was up and back with a bottle of Maker's and the two hand-blown shot glasses—gifts from Josy slipped into his suitcase after their crazy disco night in Ciudad Victoria.

"Man, I was watching that game, in that pretty new stadium, and you know, I haven't been back to Houston in, hell, ever," said Okinawa, "How's Third Ward?"

"To the Coogs!" said Archie, raising a glass. "Beat the hell out of Florida State!"

"*Salud*, brother!" said Okinawa, clinking his shot, obviously enjoying the respite from marital reality. "Go Coogs!"

"Go Coogs!" said Archie, pounding the armchair. "Man, Oak, you're gonna love the new stadium. They should've built it on I-45, but other than that . . . cool architecture, good sightlines. All kinds of high-tech. Hey, and Roth said to tell you howdy. Brother hadn't changed one bit."

"Roth! That dude is a trip. Straight up hustler," said Okinawa, sucking so hard on the bat that his eyes bulged. "Hey man, this thing's clogged."

Archie hopped up to retrieve a paper clip from his antique partner's desk, the same one that'd damn near killed'em both when Okinawa helped him move back from Victoria.

"Gimme that thing," said Archie, plunging the business end of the paper clip down till the miniature pipe was clear. "No, Roth has not changed one iota."

"So how you and Wacey doin'?" asked Oak, grinding a clean hit. "Y'all pretty tight?"

"I don't know . . . I'm tryin' too hard," he said, chasing his shot with a cold sip of Bud.

"Naw Arch," he said, waving off. "That girl's buck wild. She's never had it so good."

"I don't know about that," said Archie, easing back in his chair. "I got nothin' for a woman in the long run."

"You preachin' to the choir, brother," said Okinawa, settling back into the couch. "My old lady's gonna kill me, man. I'm not sure I blame her; I gotta bad attitude."

"I've *had* a bad attitude, since 1998," said Archie, finishing off Okinawa's hit.

"Say, man, what about Josy?" he asked, "Maybe you need to be hookin' up with that rich *señorita*. Especially if you get her that money. She be owing you big time."

Archie did a tiny double take.

"That's not the way Josy rolls, dawg," he said. "According to her brother, I owe the Montemayors all that money, and more."

Okinawa looked at his friend, shook his head, perplexed.

"Appreciate you, dawg. You just saved my Christmas," said Okinawa, picking up his stack of Benjamins. "What about the cartels? Her family have trouble with'em?"

"Don Montemayor keeps'em under control, but he's not long for this world," said Archie, flipping the channel to an early Texas Tech basketball game during a Cowboys' timeout. "No tellin' what's gonna happen when he's gone. Josy says it's damn near impossible to keep the cartels outta your business. If they want a piece."

"Law of the jungle," said Oak, grinding another hit and offering it to Archie. "I don't like the po-lice; buncha quick-trigger motherfuckers. But I'll sure as hell take'em over the cartel. They straight-up savages."

"I try not to think about it," said Archie, passing on Okinawa's out-stretched hand, happy to be able to give the father of two adult girls a nice holiday bonus.

"Josy's got a place in San Antonio. I bet she moves there when her father passes. Her brother gets the *hacienda* and everything—all that primo-geniture stuff."

"What's primogeniture?"

"First-born inherits everything—bloodline," said Archie, pulling off his fresh new UH hoodie. "The Montemayors are Europeans, basically. Old World money." He took a final swig of Budweiser, glad he passed on the hit. "We'll see. I got a lot of money to win before she's off my ass."

"Dawg, I never even *heard* of a dude on a roll like you, much less seen it," said Oak, taking a long last toke. "No jinx. No jinx!"

Archie wanted so bad to tell Oak about his high school championship parlay with the Roznovsky Twins, but couldn't do it.

"No jinx, man. I going in huge with the Coogs," he said. "It's the only way."

"You talkin' parlay?"

"Two fifty to win six fifty," he said. "Coogs plus seven and over fifty-five—parlay for the ages!"

Okinawa took that in and whistled through his teeth.

"That's *strong*, Arch," he said. "You pull that off and you're straight-up legend. Hell, you're already a legend, in my books. I made more money with you this fall than a whole year at the *Herald*."

"Bingo, baby!" cried Archie. "Just a coupla solid citizens stimulating the local economy."

OKINAWA WAS OFF THE COUCH, SHOWERED, AND OUT THE DOOR BY SIX THIRTY the next morning. Archie ushered the Sports Editor out of the kitchen with a big cup of Community and bid him adieu as he walked across the street to start laying out the digital sports pages for the *Big Spring Herald*.

Archie thought about going back to bed, but never could. He knocked out his morning exercises. Even jumped rope for twenty minutes. That was the one piece of his Keep On Truckin' routine he'd kept up. Maybe not the Monday, Wednesday, Friday runs up Scenic Mountain, but the push-ups, sit-ups, and stretching got done; five days a week, come hell or high water.

On his drive to Garden City, for breakfast at the Nice House, Archie glided his window, enjoying the crisp morning breeze of yet another "blue norther." Suddenly, a call rang came through on the Cougar Red Cadillac's speakers.

"Mr. Archie, you need to come now. Your Mom. She's hurt," said a panicked voice, one that Archie immediately placed as Hipolito, Sister Ernestine's long-time gardener.

"Aw hell. What happened?" he asked, feeling his heart race and foot push the gas.

"She's in the hall, Mr. Archie," he explained. "I don't know what to do."

"What, passed out?"

"No! She's making noise."

"Don't move her, Hip. Put a pillow under her head," he said, looking at the car's clock. "I'll be there, in like, ten minutes. Just stay with her. Talk to her. Tell her she's okay."

"Okay, Mr. Archie. Hurry!" pleaded the gardener.

Archie called the Sheriff, who put him on hold, then quickly returned. "The goddamn LifeFlight's in Pyote; some roughneck drove into a sinkhole."

"Dammit! What'd y'all do this weekend?" said Archie, flying down the Farm-to-Market, grateful that the Cadillac weighed two tons and was low to the ground.

"She was in Midland," he grumbled. "With Sonny Greene. How far out are you?"

"Five; ten tops."

At 7:51, Archie crashed over the Nice House cattle guard and into the circular driveway. He was instantly at his mother's side, and it didn't look good. She couldn't talk, but recognized him.

"Hey Mom, how ya doin'? Hang in there," he said, on hands and knees in the hallway. "We're goin' to the hospital right now."

Archie and Hipolito hoisted her by ankle and under arm; hustled her out to the Cadillac. It was awkward lifting, but they finally positioned her head in Archie's belted lap. When Hipolito slammed the door, Archie didn't even wait for him to get in, just blew gravel all the way to FM 33.

About halfway to Big Spring, Sister Ernestine opened her eyes and smiled, tried to say something that came out a bubbly slur.

"You're good, Mom. Hang in there. You're doin' fine. Just breath, Mom. Breathe."

He took her gnarled hand, and squeezed, but couldn't risk a hand off the wheel.

His mother smiled, tried once more to talk, but could say no more.

She looked up at Archie; closed her eyes.

The Cougar Red Cadillac crossed the Big Spring city limits at 8:08, going eighty miles an hour down Gregg Street, honking, swerving, streaking through the minimal traffic.

By the time they hit the Scenic Mountain ER, Evangeline Ducornet's body was there, but Sister Ernestine was gone.

Sheriff Fuchs had called ahead. He and the EMTs were waiting with a gurney when Archie screeched to a halt at the ER entrance, one hand cupping his mother's blue-white chin, the other stroking her wiry grey hair.

The professionals pulled her off his lap and out the door in one fell swoop. When Sister Ernestine disappeared behind heavy doors, Archie finally exhaled.

He tried to walk it off in the parking lot, but ended up at the edge of the grass, gut-punched to a crouch, and finally, to his knees.

He couldn't quit crying . . . but had to.

It all happened so fast.

Dead of a stroke at eighty-six.

Sister Ernestine was gone.

MAMA TRIED

GARDEN CITY, TEXAS

DECEMBER 23, 2015

West Texas grieved.

Every newspaper, every television station, every radio station in the Permian Basin ran obituaries extolling the unending virtues of the exuberant nurse/educator and her proud immigrant story. They sang her praises for healing. They eulogized her extraordinary feats of education. The tongue-tied narrators tried to explain, in their curious country way, that Sister Ernestine Ducornet was as bright and fun as a red carpet at Cannes—a fine French whirlwind.

And every single, solitary person in Glasscock County showed up for the funeral.

Afterward, the best most could manage was to sit quietly in Sister Ernestine's Nice House, consoling their heavy hearts with mountains of food and buckets of drink brought to the family by mourners far and wide. The women dabbed at their eyes and puttered around the kitchen. The men drank. Thankfully, an endless stream of former students kept teary-eyed Archie, Matt and Tallulah from a collective meltdown with their endless Sister Ernestine stories.

Finally, as night descended on the wake—as if the heavens were sighing—the slate grey West Texas skies snowed a blanket of Christmas white.

It snowed and snowed. The night of the funeral. And freakishly, for many days after.

So, while the Staked Plains settled into an unnatural quiet, the Nice House rumbled with volcanic angst.

Chuck Fuchs remained his batholitic self.

But the orphans were restless. Only beginning to miss their incandescent Mother Superior—the sound, the touch of their savior, just out of reach.

Tallulah swung wildly between bouts of catatonia and angry mania. She cursed her phone; hid it under the pillows in her blacked-out bedroom. She crashed out of the compound and ran blistering quarter miles. Elegant, loping, full-out four hundreds on the high school track. But no rounds-offs. No long-legged flips or dizzying feats of flight.

Then, Tallulah discovered one of Wacey's old vape pens.

She stalked the perimeter of the property with clouds of cucumber steam blasting from her dragon face. So sulky was the dropout's funk, that she scared off Roger Tedesco *and* Ruth Bishop—a remarkable feat.

Matt was so pained, watching Tallulah's torment, that he broke out in shingles. As soon as his mother's ashes were released into the West Texas wind, the second orphan rescue suffered his own torment, misdiagnosed as a migraine.

All the bedraggled baller could manage was to gobble ibuprofen and guzzle Maker's and water—all day. Matt slept a lot. And then slept a lot more when he discovered a long-forgotten stash of Uncle Archie's dirt weed mellowing in an armoire nook.

Archie was the only orphan who half-way hung in there, seeking his solace in sweat. He'd made peace with Sister Ernestine's passing, though the drive to Big Spring still haunted him. Daily, on an endless loop. Not the replacement he had in mind for Big Arch and Bunny's Technicolor Dreamscape.

With Wacey gone to Marfa on another undercover assignment, Archie ran Scenic Mountain. He did push-ups and sit-ups and squats and lunges and leg lifts and more push-ups. He jumped rope. He even played basketball at the Y.

It felt good to sweat. To lose his mind in exertion. To *not* smoke pot or drink beer.

Finally, after unprecedented accumulations of snow-white blues, Archie Weesatche pulled his family out of their uncontrolled skid and around the kitchen table.

He cooked a huge breakfast, just like his mother taught him—scrambled eggs with diced jalapenos, crispy bacon, deer sausage, grits with butter and cinnamon, fresh honey dew and strawberries, croissants, tall glasses of fresh orange juice, and pots of *café au lait*.

He sat his brother, sister, and father down to feast—a bit bittersweet—but pleased indeed to have his beloved close at hand, feeding on a fine French breakfast.

As they passed the platters and began to eat, there was no talk at all. Only soft eyes and sad smiles. The clink of cutlery and the occasional slurp. The snow was over. A dazzling sun drenched the kitchen with winter light. Slowly, they warmed.

Archie looked over a forkful of pan-fried sausage at the chair where his mother never sat—such was Sister Ernestine's perpetual motion.

"Not quite as good as Mom's."

"It's better," countered Tallulah. "It's fucking delicious."

Archie took that in and decided, then and there.

"Let's throw a party!" he blurted. "At the Settles."

The Sheriff snorted; helped himself to grits. "Better than mopin' around here."

"I can DJ," said Matt, stretching in his cane back chair. "Dirges and disco."

"And a little Merle Haggard, I hope," requested the Sheriff. "*Mama Tried.*"

"Yes, she did," agreed Archie, reaching out for Tallulah's hand. "And you can spike volleyballs at all the guests."

Tallulah's eyes twinkled. "I'll split their lips! Ruth can hog-tie'em."

"Oh boy," sighed Matt. "Mom would love that."

Yes, they all agreed, Sister Ernestine would adore a raucous rave held in her honor.

SO, WHILE THE ORPHANS AND RUTH BISHOP PLANNED THE BIG PARTY, THE Sheriff fumed.

Chuck Fuchs was furious.

First of all, *he'd* planned on being the first one in the family to meet the heavenly call.

Not Sister Ernestine.

And now that he was NOT the first in the family to shuffle off this mortal coil, he vowed to pour eight decades of wiles into a *coup de grâce*—Weesatche Transport.

The U.S.'s fifty-year War on Drugs was an abject failure. Sheriff Fuchs readily admitted it. He knew that if he could help Archie and the next generation establish and maintain a legitimate US-Mexican import/export scheme, with cartel security, it would be a start. Maybe the War of Drugs would fade away for good if Weesatche Transport could lead the way. Show'em how bi-national trade could really work.

Pipe dreams aside, Chuck Fuchs was ripping pissed at Sonny Greene.

If he couldn't kill the fat bastard, for killing the love of his life, then he would make damn sure the billionaire bankrolled his oldest son's business venture. Sheriff Fuchs showed up—unannounced—at Greene Energy's Midland skyscraper with business plans in hand and murder on his mind.

"How the hell are ya, Sheriff?" huffed Sonny Greene, after his receptionist failed to block the lawman's entry.

"Been better."

"Sit down, Chuck," he said, folding up his *Midland Reporter-Telegram*. "If you're here about Weesatche Transport, I'm not buying your paper."

"I don't want a partner," answered the Sheriff. "We need trucks."

"Fine," he said, lighting a Winston. "But that's it! I can sell trucks for scrap after the cartel blows'em to hell."

"You let me worry about the cartels, Sonny," answered the Sheriff, finally taking a seat in front of the oil man's vast mahogany desk.

Sonny Greene puffed his cigarette, stared out the window into the Permian wilderness.

"Listen, Chuck, I had nothing to do with Sister . . . you know," he said, shifting uncomfortably in an oversized leather chair. "She was fine when she left the ranch. She was fine when she got home. Called me when she got there."

"No, you listen," he said, rising up from the chair to loom properly. "I'd just soon throw your ass out that window."

Sonny loosened his necktie, smiled up at the scowling lawman. "Aren't you supposed to *uphold* the law?"

"I am, and I do," said the Sheriff, putting both hands on the table. He pointed a meaty finger at Mr. Sonny Greene. "I'll make an exception for you."

"Bullshit. Sit down, Chuck," replied the old-timer, pulling up to the desk. "What the hell do you and Archie know about transportin' gas, anyway?"

"Plenty," replied the Sheriff, taking a seat. "We got solid partners; Waylon Bishop at SandTech took ten percent, and will probably take more; Miles Mathis, the biggest gas producer in the Eagle Ford, he's got fifteen percent."

"I know Bishop; lucky bastard," opined Mr. Greene. "Where's this Mathis fella from?"

"McMullen County," said the Sheriff. "Lives in Houston now, but Hilcorp and Chesapeake found enough gas on his land to supply the whole state."

"Who else?" demanded Greene.

"Fast Eddie Lau over in Snyder came in for five percent," said Chuck. "And security—I got *Federales*, DEA, *and* cartel on board."

"Yeah, and they're gonna steal you blind," said Mr. Green with a derisive laugh. "You mark my words."

"Like I said, Sonny, we're in this together, whether you like it or not," said the Sheriff. "Figure out how you're goin' to help."

"I've got no problem investing in a company that's got a chance to be successful," said Mr. Greene, stubbing out his cigarette. "Not sure your concept is sound. Transporting jet fuel and LNG through the Chihuahua Desert. Insurance has got to be high on that."

The sheriff didn't say a word, but Sonny Greene was right about that. The quote from Lloyd's of London was astronomical. The purloined $6.5 million was all the insurance Weesatche Transport had, at present. And that was far from the bank.

The Sheriff leafed through the business plan, then placed a list of required physical assets in front of the billionaire. After a cursory glance,

Sonny Green agreed to buy five propane trucks, five gasoline trucks, three jet fuel trucks, and two LNG tankers—a $10 million investment—minimum.

Sheriff Fuchs sat back, gratified that he'd bullied the bastard into action. "I appreciate you gettin' us on the road."

"On the road," repeated Mr. Greene. "I like that. Yeah, I'll get you on the road, if you'll get off my ass. I know you and Sister Ernestine were practically married. I'm sick as hell about what happened, Chuck. But this is business."

"Bullshit."

Chuck Fuchs squared his Stetson, looked Sonny Greene in the eye, and walked out.

As the Sheriff strode to the office tower elevator, he called Arturo on speed dial. He'd been in touch with his head of security almost daily.

The Sheriff reminded Arturo of the huge debt the Honduran owed him, and the DEA, who'd plucked him from certain death in a Zeta stash house, scrubbed his identity and turned him over to the Sinaloans. It took six months of intense lobbying, but somehow, *Lobo Loco* convinced the Culiacán bosses that he was the man to run the Ojinaga plaza.

With three rival cartels encroaching on their prized territory after years of undisciplined leadership under Pablo Acosta and Rudy Leos, the Sheriff and the DEA cut a deal with the Sinaloans to establish Arturo Villalobos, a stable presence, in the Big Bend Corridor.

"Is this going to work?" demanded the Sheriff. "*¿Si o no?*"

"*¡Si, Sherif! ¡Si!*" he said, still warming to his role as *Lobo Loco*, but grateful for a second chance. "The Sinaloans would rather do business with American law enforcement than fight the Zetas and this crazy CNJC. It's a new world, *jefe*."

The Sheriff wanted to believe Arturo but didn't trust him.

As a result, Sheriff Fuchs packed Wacey off to Marfa to keep an eye on him. Her Kozy Coach at *El Cosmico* was a semi-safe distance from the border, but close enough to keep tabs on the new plaza boss and his platoon of hand-picked Honduran mercenaries while they mapped out Mexican routes for Weesatche Transport's fuel deliveries.

By Christmas Eve, ten RSVPs had been received for the inaugural Weesatche Transport shareholders meeting and over 150 for Sister Ernestine's Celebration of Life scheduled for the Tuesday afternoon and evening between Christmas and New Year's. It was a perfect time and the perfect place. Nobody was working. Everybody wanted to party at the fabulously refurbished Hotel Settles.

Meanwhile, it was slow going at the Nice House.

Everybody involved agreed to a low-key Christmas. Wacey came back from Marfa in time to open presents with the Sheriff, Archie, Matt, and Tallulah around the last of Sister Ernestine's elaborate Christmas trees and a houseful of decorations.

It was Sister's habit to have all of her holiday finery on display by the Sunday after Thanksgiving. She'd put the finishing touches on the massive front porch manger scene the afternoon Sonny picked her up for the weekend.

Everybody tried to be jolly, but being surrounded by so much of their mother's Christmas spirit was too much. They all longed for Sister Ernestine.

Finally, after unwrapping a few joyless gifts, and having no appetite at all, Sister Ernestine's brood plopped down in the living room, drank themselves into an early stupor, tried to watch Charlie Brown, and went to bed with the setting sun.

KNOCK-DOWN DRAG-OUT KARAOKE DEATHMATCH

Weesatche Transport was, at last, a reality.

The principal investors were coming to order.

Archie stood at the head of the twelve-seat conference table in the Birdwell Room at Hotel Settles. Sonny Greene had backed out at the last minute and Waylon Bishop was dove hunting in Argentina. But Miles Mathis and Fast Eddie Lau had come in from Houston and Sweetwater, respectively.

Josefina and Ricardo Montemayor were also in attendance, although neither had indicated the size of the Montemayor family's investment in the new company. They were waiting for Archie to make good on his promise— the transfer of $650,000 for the release of $6.5 million.

"Ida, let the record show that the first meeting of Weesatche Transport has come to order," said Archie, nodding to his long-time KOT dispatcher turned Weesatche Transport Corporate Secretary. "The agenda is approved and we have a quorum."

The Weesatche Transport investors opened their presentation packets and settled in.

"I want to thank you again for coming to Big Spring during the holidays," Archie began, holding the top of his chair, trying to calm his nerves. "We've got a big party planned in the Grand Ballroom, in honor of our dearly departed mother, Sister Ernestine Ducornet. We hope you can stay to celebrate her remarkable life and enjoy some holiday cheer."

Noticeably late, Arturo Villalobos, nattily attired in full Plaza Boss regalia, and two soldiers in desert fatigues entered the conference room and sat in chairs lining the perimeter. Sheriff Fuchs got up, shook a man's hand, and ushered *Lobo Loco* to the table.

When everybody was settled, Archie continued.

"Ladies and Gentlemen, Weesatche Transport's business concept is simple: transport refined fuel: propane, gasoline, jet fuel—and most importantly— Liquefied Natural Gas, from Texas to key industrial destinations in Mexico. My friend and fellow investor Miles Mathis identified this emerging business opportunity with MexGas, a Pemex subsidiary. MexGas desperately needs refined fuels while they continue to build oil and gas pipelines in northern Mexico.

He nodded thanks to the gentleman rancher.

"Mexico has deregulated its oil and gas sector for the first time since 1917 and is woefully behind in drilling, exploration technology and downstream infrastructure. It's a known fact that Mexico is desperate for refined fuels to power its *maquiladora*s.

"As you well know, the shale boom in the Eagle Ford and Permian Basin has made the US a net energy exporter for the first time in over fifty years. Texas needs a market for its excess natural gas. Mexico needs the fuel. Bottom line: MexGas requires a partner to transport refined products until they can complete new pipelines. Weesatche Transport can fill that need. Any questions at this point?"

Everybody around the table shook their heads, except Josy.

"What if the next President of Mexico rescinds deregulation?" she asked, looking every inch the Master of Business Administration. "Will our contracts be honored?"

"I have to say, yes," Archie ventured. "We have iron-clad contracts in place that guarantee Weesatche Transport's right to move oil and gas into Mexico until 2025, or until the MexGas pipelines are operational."

"I've never encountered an iron-clad contract in Mexico," said Ricardo with a grin.

"That's why we're so pleased," said Archie. "To have the Montemayor family as Weesatche Transport's primary Mexican investor."

"We haven't committed a *peso*," said Ricardo. "Has my sister made arrangements to which I'm not privy?"

"No," answered Archie, ceding the floor to Josefina.

She joined Archie at the head of the table.

"The final percentage of the Montemayor family's commitment to Weesatche Transport won't be finalized until after the New Year," she said, looking directly at Ricardo. "My brother knows this."

She turned her attention to her fellow board members.

"The Montemayor family *is* committed to Weesatche Transport. I alone will make the final monetary determination, as my brother's focus is on our father, who is gravely ill, as well as the farm and cattle operations in Tamaulipas."

Miles Mathis and Fast Eddie Lau nodded, seemingly impressed with the sophistication and intelligence of their Mexican partner, not to mention her beautifully tailored suit of black crushed velvet accented with red and green floral appliqués.

"Thank you, Josy," said Archie, pulling his partner's chair. "It's essential that Weesatche Transport have the strongest possible partners in Mexico. We look forward to a prosperous relationship with the Montemayor Family for many years to come."

On his way back to the head of the table, Archie pat-patted Ricardo's shoulder, a gesture met with an audible grunt.

"So, the final piece of the business plan, and most crucial, is security. Specifically, protection for our trucks on the Mexican highways."

As Archie approached the head of the table, Arturo stood. Sheriff Fuchs stood with him.

"Everybody in this room knows Weesatche Transport fails if we can't safely transport MexGas's oil and gas from Texas to Mexico," he said, reaching to shake Arturo's hand. "This is Arturo Villalobos, head of transportation safety, representing our friends in Ojinaga and Culiacán."

The Sheriff stood. "Most of you know me, I'm Chuck Fuchs. I'm in charge of Weesatche Transport's security on the US side of the border. Arturo and his team will take over as soon as the trucks cross into Mexico."

Archie was relieved when Arturo stepped up and calmly explained, in plain, if halting English, his role as personal escort for all Weesatche Transport shipments. Each truck would be surrounded by his hand-picked squad of Honduran ex-military, men with no connection to any other Mexican cartel. Loyal to Arturo, and Arturo only.

The newly anointed *Lobo Loco* went on to explain that he was headquartered in Ojinaga, and was completely transparent about his employment with the Sinaloa Cartel. His Mexican bosses were keen to see their first foray into a major U.S.-Mexican oil and gas business go well. Arturo assured the investors that the Sinaloans were ready and able to guarantee every truck's safe passage. In addition to the Presidio-*Ojinaga* corridor, his team had also identified less frequently traveled crossings at Eagle Pass-*Piedras Negras* and Roma-*Ciudad Aleman*.

After the Sheriff and Arturo took their seats, Archie wrapped up the meeting.

"Thank you, Chuck and Arturo," he said, pausing to make eye contact with each.

"As investors, we all know the risks involved with transporting valuable commodities on Mexican highways," Archie continued. "Frankly, this risk-reward is what makes Weesatche Transport's Return On Investment so compelling. Mexican companies will pay handsomely for these products. The margins are significant, *if* we deliver.

"We have strong financial commitments from the men and women around this table. We have years of transportation and security experience. Finally, we have the Montemayor family and the Sinaloans working in tandem to ensure that a new day has arrived for Texas and Mexico on the wheels of Weesatche Transport.

"Thank you for your time, your commitment, and your confidence. Let's get a drink!"

SISTER ERNESTINE'S CELEBRATION OF LIFE WAS EXUBERANT.

To say the least.

The Hotel Settles was born again. Hosting a Staked Plains wake/rave for the ages.

It seemed, throughout the holiday evening turned dawn, that every carouser in the county helped their favorite French nurse educator, "put the big pot in the little." Around 3:00 a.m., the party got to rocking so hard that Tallulah pulled the huge, crystal chandelier down from its decorous ballroom alcove.

With an elegant leap and artful swing, Tallulah's trapeze act started swimmingly but came to a crashing halt upon the return—a shower of plaster and lead that covered the best athlete in the building in a cloud. Tallulah, nineteen and bullet-proof, picked herself off the floor, unscathed. Fortunate indeed that the bulk of the ancient luminaire remained suspended above her, inches from a gruesome impaling.

And with that, DJ Matt went to work.

He calmly put the mixer on Genius Shuffle, helped his giddy sister dust herself off, then located a ladder. With the Settles staff long gone, and the total extent of the damage unassessed by management, Tallulah, Matt, and Roger Tedesco (who'd arrived from Sterling City wanting to get a look at the girl who stole his girl), pushed the chandelier, wires and all, back into alcove and proceeded to re-plaster the entire mess with box after box of wet, white cocktail napkins. That, and a few strategically hammered nails.

Talk about Genius!

And the night did not wind down. The 4:00 a.m. *grand finale* was a knock-down drag-out karaoke deathmatch. Hours in the making, the sing-off started as soon as the last napkin was stuffed.

Josefina Montemayor and Ruth Bishop had been circling each other all night. Prideful, toothsome barracudas. Both resplendent in their respective Christmas finery. Both alpha females were also powerful singers with voices that required no amplification.

What the alcohol-soaked *Princesa* and the Hell Bitch from Rising Star didn't expect was Tallulah taking charge. As soon as she jumped down from the ladder, the lithesome volleyballer sprung into an impossibly long-legged cartwheel right in Josy's face.

"My girlfriend sings better than you," slurred Tallulah, taking the bottle of Cristal from Josy's manicured claw, and drank deeply, unfazed by her chandelier demolition.

Flinging her fitted jacket to the floor, Josy shouted for a Mexican tear-jerker.

Matt quickly queued up the request.

The crowd of super-inebriated Big Springers roared their approval as Josy, prowled the hardwood, singing a soulful rendition of Amanda Miguel's *El Me Mintio*. They howled even louder during the final chorus when Josy wiggled down to a bedazzled bra embedded with Savorski crystals. Josy scraped and bowed, enraptured by the wild applause. So much so that she invited the entire crowd of handsome young Texans up to her suite.

Not to outdone by her high-octane rival, Ruth Bishop requested Tanya Tucker's *It's a Little Too Late* and quickly took the burlesque to the next level. Exhibiting a fine, operatic voice, the Hell Bitch paraded around the room in her gangsta green Adidas tracksuit, bringing the drunken multitudes to their feet.

Young Roger Tedesco, thoroughly enthralled by both performances, finally couldn't take it. The Sterling City baller was so flummoxed by the buxom crooners that he got down on one knee and asked Ruth Bishop for her hand in marriage.

"I need you," declared the party's youngest, drunkest attendee, proffering the only jewelry he owned, a huge Josten's headlight he'd just received for being Texas 1A First-Team All-State Linebacker/Tailback.

Ruth appreciated the young stud's google-eyed gesture, but it didn't work.

"I don't like dick," declared the Sand Queen, throwing a rough arm around Tallulah. "But I bet you can make some time with Selena, over there."

Roger Tedesco did not tarry.

Following a precise pursuit angle, he met a breathless Josefina in the hole, swept her out of the ballroom and into the elevator. She took one look at Ramblin' Roger's bulging biceps and purred, "*Hola guapo.*"

As they elevated to the tenth floor, the farm boy took a deep breath, entranced by *La Princesa's* wild eyes and liquid curves.

"Damn girl."

Archie and Wacey, who'd escaped to their Gregg Street bungalows shortly before Tallulah's floor-length crash, rose at 5 a.m., already packed. They drove back to the Settles, curbed the Cougar Red Cadillac, then wandered into an eerily quiet lobby.

A fat, cooing pigeon kept watch at the front desk, nary a Settles staffer to be seen. In the lobby, sleeping women, in various stages of undress, elegantly draped across the Santa Fe furnishings. Snoring men, some bleeding, sprawled on spacious Oriental rugs.

As Wacey and Archie surveyed the party carnage, three stray dogs poured in through the wide-open back door, scaled the stairs, and quickly returned from the ballroom, chunks of tenderloin dangling from their drooling snouts.

Finally, a holiday itinerant, from the nearby Greyhound Station, peeked his head in from the outdoor patio.

"Mind if I take a bath in your hot tub?"

Archie and Wacey looked at each other and smiled.

"Absolutely!"

As the wraith disappeared into the gathering dawn, a roar of laughter drifted up from the basement. Ears pricked, the gambler and his bodyguard sauntered to the stairs.

Following the sounds of merry-making down and through a narrow hall, they happened upon Fast Eddie Lau at the head of a half-moon poker table dealing hands to a wide array of holdouts. To his left was Okinawa Watkins and his beautiful lady friend, Miss Pam Rogers. Lovely Melissa Mathis, held down mid-table in a devastating red halter dress along with Mr. Lau's raven-haired Relationship Manager from Texas Tech, who was, just now, raking a large pile of chips.

Lobo Loco, looking devilishly handsome in red Versace, threw his cards on the table in disgust. "*¡Mamon!*"

Miles Mathis and Tallulah snored on opposite ends of a crushed velvet couch, while Ruth Bishop and DJ Matt moved swiftly around a massive pool table, edging toward the end of a hotly contested game of nine-ball.

Archie and Wacey canvassed the room with utter glee, acknowledging the stalwarts as they walked about, slapping backs and hugging necks. As

Wacey canoodled with DJ Matt, and Okinawa introduced Archie to Pam, the Hell Bitch was setting up for an epic trick shot.

A little too tricky.

Ruth ripped the cue ball off the table and right into Pam Roger's lap.

"She the one been talkin' smack all night?"

The Midland College event planner flipped the errant cue ball from hand-to-hand.

"Just give it back," said Okinawa, not in the mood for late-night drama.

Ms. Rogers had other ideas. She'd endured a full night of Ruth acting like a spoiled brat billionaire's daughter.

"Why you tryin' to steal people's shine, girl?"

"What?" said Ruth, her mischievous grin turned churlish. "Hell you say."

"Call me a gangbanger, bitch," continued Ms. Rogers, rolling the ball across the poker table as Fast Eddie cleared the table of cards and chips. "I'll crack your cracker head."

The Hell Bitch was caught flat. No doubt about it.

But not two seconds later, Ruth Bishop was crowding the rail, poking her fuchsia fingernail in Pam Roger's flawless face.

"I'll call you whatever the fuck I want, BITCH!"

Okinawa restrained Pam, but just barely. The rest of the room froze.

"Go on, Karen," said Pam. "Make your move."

Ruth Bishop read the room.

Nodded good game to Matt as he sank the nine ball with a beautiful bank shot.

The Hell Bitch took a deep, dramatic breath—raised the pool cue like a samurai—then broke into a full-on kung-fu routine, whirling and twirling the stick around the pool table, straight up the stairs, and out of sight. Nary a racist peep out of her foul mouth.

As the room heaved a collective sigh of relief, Pam Rogers took her seat.

"Deal me some cards, Fast Eddie," she said, giving Okinawa a sweet kiss on the cheek.

"The game's Texas Hold'em," said Mr. Lau, grinning at the sassy educator. He dealt five cards, face down. "Pot's right. Bet's to the big man from C-City."

All-out war averted; Archie pried a full bottle of Veuve from Tallulah's sleepy grip.

"Raise your glasses, friends! Raise 'em high!"

Everybody crowded around the poker table, grateful for the miraculous change of mood. Archie raised the bottle and cried, "Long live Sister Ernestine!"

After Archie's long pull, Wacey grabbed the bottle with tears in her eyes. "Love you, Sister! Love you! Love you! Love you!"

As the adoration and praise continued, and new drinks were poured, Sheriff Fuchs ambled in from his twelfth-floor room, amazed that so many celebrants were still at it. He raised a steaming mug of coffee, among the champagne held high, as his oldest orphan continued to toast:

"To *Sister Ernestine!*" Archie exclaimed. "*¡A mi madre!*"

"Hip hip hooray!"

"Hip hip hooray!"

"Hip hip hooray!"

Lobo Loco raised a bottle of bubbly and enthusiastically cheered. "*¡Que viva! ¡Que viva!*"

At the last hurrah, an eye-piercing ray of sunlight penetrated a basement casement.

And that was that. The party was over.

As Sister Ernestine's rowdy acolytes headed for the door, Sheriff Fuchs gathered his children—Archie, Matt, and Tallulah—in a great group hug.

"Let's live," he said, to his circle of orphans. "Let's move on. Make your mother proud."

The orphans knew their father was right. But their assurances wouldn't come. Their most fervent wishes could not be spoken. Not yet . . . maybe never.

SUNSET ON THE VEGAS STRIP

LAS VEGAS, NEVADA
DECEMBER 30, 2015

Somehow, Wacey and Archie made their flight to Las Vegas.

Nursing two-day hangovers, the tuckered out West Texans slept like the dead in the city that never sleeps. Thankfully, they were booked in a swanky suite at a hip new hotel on The Strip, The Cosmopolitan.

Lots of lounging. Lots of room service. And no gambling. Not even a little blackjack.

In no time, the fated December 31 arrived. Early. Really early.

The Peach Bowl, live from Atlanta: 10 a.m. Mountain Time.

After a monumental breakfast at the transcendent time warp also known as The Peppermill, Archie wasn't even sure he wanted to, or could, watch the game. On the ensuing stroll to destiny, he and Wacey filled their lungs with fresh air, striding football field-size blocks from the restaurant to the Westgate Hotel at the corner of Las Vegas and Elvis Presley Boulevard.

It was Show Time.

"I'd like to place a two-way parlay on the Houston Cougars."

"And how much are we betting today?" asked the Westgate sports book, temporarily blinded by Wacey's new Arctic-white hair, her only concession to Vegas extravagance.

"Two hundred fifty thousand dollars," said Archie, not quite believing his own words.

"Yessir!' said the young chip slinger. "Are you staying at the Westgate?"

"No, we've over on The Strip," said Archie, checking to see if his angry girlfriend had a pistol pointed at his ribs. "Everybody knows the Westgate has the best sportsbook."

"We like to think so," he said, raising a hand to hail the manager.

A large, well-dressed man strode over to surveille the prospects and their attire. At Archie's insistence, both were handsomely turned out—coat, loosened rep tie and khakis for the gentlemen; a flawlessly-fitted Missoni frock and cork heels for the lady.

"Mr. Weesatche, we have you down for a two-bet parlay on the Peach Bowl: University of Houston plus seven over Florida State and over fifty-five. Two hundred fifty thousand dollars to win six hundred fifty thousand dollars. Is that correct?"

"That is correct," said Archie, holding pious hands.

"That's quite a bet," acknowledged the manager. "You understand the risks?"

"Yessir."

The manager smiled, settled a huge hand atop the cashier's shoulder. "Good luck, Mr. Weesatche. Would you like us to arrange a private viewing room?"

Perfect, thought Archie, preferring such decisions to be made for him.

He nodded at Wacey. "Little Coog watch party?"

"Whatever," said the somber bodyguard, who hadn't touched a drink during their stay.

"Let's do it!" said Archie, ignoring Wacey's frown, clapping with excitement.

"Excellent," said the manager, as the cashier processed the wager. "Would you prefer a private room in the sports lounge, or a suite. We have a room with an outstanding view of The Strip available."

Archie checked with Wacey, who shrugged.

"Let's watch it in the sports lounge," said Archie. "Thank you so much."

"I'll set it right up," said the manager, watching as the cashier handed Archie his ticket to ride—a small, innocuous slip of paper.

"Good luck," said the cashier, beaming, as he flashed his class ring and three-finger UH hand sign. "Go Coogs!"

Archie stood, blinking at the Cashier, then the ticket. He looked up at the beaming young man and flashed his own, mangled, three-finger salute. "Go Coogs!"

"Come on, goofy!" said Wacey, pulling her clueless client by the coat sleeve.

IT WAS THE SLOWEST THREE AND A HALF HOURS OF ARCHIE WEESATCHE'S LIFE.

He shouted at the TV. Pleaded with the players. Implored Coach Herman.

The Coogs came out hot and raced to a 21–3 halftime lead on the strength of two Greg Ward touchdown runs and a flea-flicker pass executed to perfection.

After the first UH score, Wacey asked their private waitress not to pick up the empties, so she could keep count. Archie drank three Budweisers before the end of the first quarter but slowed down as UH's lead grew.

The stress began to amp during an almost scoreless third quarter. Suddenly, Dalvin Cook, FSU's All-American running back, took one to the house.

24-10 to start the fourth quarter. UH was still looking good, but over fifty-five was shaky.

Archie started pounding Buds. The bottle count began to soar when the Seminoles scored again to make it a one-score game, 24–17. "Sweetie, sweetie! Calm down," Wacey cried, trying to coax Archie back to the couch in their super high-tech viewing room.

Archie stared up at the thirty-foot projection screen, his beloved Coogs moving like giant ghosts across the wall. "I still need two touchdowns," he said, head in hands during yet another TV timeout. "We gotta hold'em *and* score. Madness!"

Wacey rolled her eyes.

But as if on cue, FSU's quarterback, feeling cocky after a sixty-five-yard touchdown, threw an ill-advised sideline pass. A Coog cornerback jumped the route and returned the interception deep inside Seminole territory.

On the next play, Greg Ward threw a seventeen-yard touchdown pass: UH 31 FSU 17.

With 4:54 left in the game, FSU scored again: UH 31 FSU 24.

"I CANNOT TAKE THIS!" shouted Archie.

He was so close.

The over/under was stuck at exactly fifty-five. Archie's be-all, end-all bet—was a push.

"You did this to yourself," she soothed, calmly guiding Archie back to the couch. "Just relax and enjoy it."

"That's what Claytie Williams said."

"Who?"

"Nothin'," he muttered. "Just shoot me. Where's your nine?"

"Nope," she said, gently pulling him back into the couch. "Three more minutes."

And then that moment.

Every degenerate gambler's dream:

The UH defense comes up with its fourth interception. And with 1:59 left in the game, Ryan Jackson crashes over the goal line and the University of Houston Cougars are the 2015 Peach Bowl champions.

Final score: UH 38 FSU 24. Coogs win straight up and way over fifty-five.

Two hundred fifty thousand to win six hundred fifty thousand.

Archie Weesatche was—officially—the luckiest sumbitch on the planet. And didn't waste a second, although Wacey practically tackled him on the way to the cashier.

Archie stepped up with his winning ticket. Requested the accommodating manager to wire transfer his winnings to an account registered at the State Bank of Happy, Texas.

"Please don't do this," Wacey pleaded. "Please!"

Despite the loudest of protestations, the Automated Clearing House did its thing.

The transaction was complete.

"I can't believe you just did that," she said, staring, as Archie accepted the receipt verifying the ACH.

"What?" he asked, tucking the tiny ticket into his billfold.

"What about us?" she screamed. "All that, 'we're gonna spend the rest of our lives at the Settles bullshit!' What about that?"

"I'm keeping my promise, Wacey," said Archie, shaking his head, but not surprised. "Now, Josy keeps her promise. It's called business."

"It's called bullshit!" cried Wacey, so loudly that even the barflies looked up from their tonics and gin. "You believe for one second that, that . . . that whore is going to do anything but spend every dollar that's rightfully ours. You and me, Archie! What about you and me?"

Archie took in his bodyguard's query. "I'm keeping my promise."

"To who?"

"You'll be the first to know."

Wacey slapped Archie hard across the face.

Done.

Headed for the exits.

"Fine! Whatever!" Archie yelled at her backside. "Come on, Wacey! What the hell?"

Hella nothing, said Wacey's middle finger, bobbing away at a high rate of speed.

Archie watched his tough girl crash into the blinding Sin City sun.

Marching as to war.

VAYA CON DIOS

Don Jose Montemayor was gone.

After months of declining respiratory capacity and non-existent mobility, *El Leon de Victoria* kissed his hovering children's tear-streaked cheeks, closed his eyes, and drifted into a netherworld of morphine slumber.

As soon as Archie returned from Vegas, still ecstatic from his epic win, Josy called to report her father's passing. She was sending the G5 to bring him to Ciudad Victoria as an honored guest of the family.

Wacey was already there.

"We need to meet," said Josefina "After the funeral. Ricardo wants to finalize the family's commitment to you, Archie. To Weesatche Transport. We're grateful."

DON MONTEMAYOR'S FUNERAL SERVICE, PLANNED FOR OVER A DECADE, WAS A two-day, tradition-laden festival of mourning and celebration. First, a Latin funeral mass was held at *Catedral del Sagrado Corazón de Jesús*, in a sanctuary banked wall-to-wall with spectacular floral arrangements and pews packed with black *rebozos* and dark suits.

After the burial, Josefina and Ricardo hosted an endless, bacchanalian wake at *Hacienda Montemayor*. A grateful city, state, and country—thousands at the funeral, hundreds at the wake—acknowledged the passing of a colonial giant, the thirteenth generation of Montemayors in *Nuevo Santander*, the current-day State of Tamaulipas.

The entire affair was an exhilarating, exhausting whirlwind. At the end of the second night, Archie and Wacey bid a final goodbye to a legion of old friends and new acquaintances, retired to their separate rooms, and slept for ten full hours.

They woke at the break of a beautiful winter dawn. The season was brief in Ciudad Victoria but wonderfully cool and dry; more reminiscent of southern California than the swelter that dominated the weather nine months out of the year. Both were showered and dressed well before the 10 a.m. breakfast meeting.

As Archie and Wacey trundled across the patio, Josefina, Ricardo—and surprisingly, Arturo Villalobos—waited inside a poolside gazebo, seated at a round concrete table inset with artful mosaic. The table was formal with placemats, chargers, all manner of plates and silverware and glasses, all surrounding a riotous bouquet of fresh roses.

A trellis of dark cedar covered with flowering bougainvillea shaded them from the tropical sun. The Olympic-size pool shimmered. In the land of Mexican milk and honey, in the bucolic foothills of the Sierra Madre Oriental, it seemed to Archie, that all was well—sad, for certain, but peaceful.

Granted, he had not received dollar one of his promised $100,000 bonus or the $650,000 principle. That said, Archie the Optimist, assured Wacey, as they approached the gazebo, that today was the day.

"It's going to happen," assured the gambling man.

Wacey rolled her eyes.

Elaborate greetings and salutations eventually gave way to a seated table of five.

"*Archito*, you've been busy since last we met," said Ricardo, directing a hulking manservant to pour chilled champagne with a dash of orange juice. "Rumor has it, you've been quite lucky."

Archie looked at Josy, seated to his left, who immediately dropped her eyes.

"I've been waiting a long time for you to recognize your debt," continued Ricardo. "It's what honorable men do."

"*Ricardo, porfavor. No seas ridiculo,*" sighed Josefina. "Can we please stick to business?"

Ricardo unfurled his napkin with a flick of the wrist.

Archie paused for a moment; considering his response, while Wacey shifted in her seat.

Arturo, dressed business casual in a cream *guayabera* and knife-creased linen slacks, chuckled ever so slightly with sunglasses firmly planted above his handsome Honduran nose.

"Ricardo, with all due respect," said Archie, taking a long sip of *mimosa*. "I don't owe your family *un peso.* Your sister and I are good. And I sure as hell didn't kill your ancestors in Victoria."

"Fascinating," replied Ricardo, adding an audible belch. "Do you realize you're named after the scourge of my existence?"

"Yeah, *huizache* is a real nuisance," replied Archie, wishing for an immediate escape from this point of diminishing returns. "How do you keep your pastures so clean?"

"Slash and burn," said Ricardo, grinning "Slash and burn."

As Archie laughed off the comment, he noticed a subtle signal from Josy to Arturo.

Lobo Loco stood, folded his napkin, and walked away, stopping to smell the rose blooms lining the side of the pool.

It went largely unnoticed when Arturo re-appeared.

It was quite noticeable when *Lobo Loco* plunged a long, terrible needle into Ricardo's neck, delivering a quick dose of lethal liquid into the brother who would not be *Don.*

When Ricardo's body began to twitch and gurgle, Arturo jutted his chin. Two thugs rushed in from the shadows of a pool-side pergola. Words were exchanged. The men took charge of the near-corpse. Minutes later, Arturo's men silently rejoined the shadows having properly disposed of Brother Ricardo.

Arturo reached for his champagne to raise his flute.

"*¡Saludos!*" he said, nodding to Archie. "To promises kept and futures created!"

When Archie stood, Josy—even Wacey—stood as well, glasses raised.

"To promises kept!" cried Josy.

As they drained their glasses, Wacey spoke up.

"Where's our money?"

Josy lowered her fabulous sunglasses.

"Really?" she said. "*Our* money?"

"Here's the receipt," said Archie, pulling a folded Westgate Casino ticket from his wallet. "Six hundred fifty thousand dollars wire transferred to the Happy State Bank."

"And there it will stay," answered Arturo. "The money was always Don Pablo's. Now it's mine, *el jefe de Ojinaga.*"

"Dammit to hell," said Wacey, glaring at Josy, then at Archie. "I told you."

"Unless you can prove yourself worthy."

"Who?" asked Wacey, Archie, and Josy, simultaneously.

"All of you," replied Arturo, the sun glinting off a mass of gold chains beneath his open collar. "*El Tejano Afortunado.* Did you know that's what they call you, Archie? Let's trade your games of chance, for a game of skill."

"Arturo?" pleaded Josy. "*¿Que esta pasando?*"

He answered by removing a pistol from the small of his back.

"You want to be my partner?" he asked, handing the gun to Wacey. "You want to make *my* money, *your* money? Then earn it."

"What'd *she* do to earn it?" said Wacey, lifting an eyebrow. "Archie did all the work."

"Maybe she'll tell you someday," said Arturo, blowing Josy a kiss.

The newly-crowned Doña Montemayor flipped a lustrous wave of jet-black hair. Cast covetous eyes on Archie. Said nothing.

At that, Wacey broke and ran.

She was quickly manhandled by the two sun-glassed thugs and returned to the table.

Arturo directed the two men to march Archie—guns to his head and heart—around the pool and up against the sandstone pergola.

Arturo quickly followed. He stood Archie straight against the wall. "Hands! Spread your fingers."

"*¡No Arturo!*" cried Josefina. "*Porfavor.*"

"*¡Callate perra!*" roared *Lobo Loco*. "We are the ghosts of *Don Pablo.*"

"What the fuck does that mean?" Wacey asked.

"It means: you can't steal *my* money."

He paced in front of *El Tejano Afortunado*, "Are you feeling lucky?"

"Could be," said Archie, oddly free of nerves. "Why do you ask?"

"Why do you ask?" parroted the Plaza Boss. "You sound like a *Tejano Pendejo.*"

Archie shrugged, suddenly very nervous.

"Time to prove your skill, *bruja.*"

"I'm not shooting anybody," said Wacey, her Arctic-white hair reflecting the sun.

"*Si bruja*, you are," he said, pointing to Archie's bandaged digit. "Remove the finger. Or we remove the head."

To underscore his instructions, Arturo curled all but Archie's ring finger into a fist. "Get it up there. Give her a good target."

"This is stupid," said Wacey.

Arturo tisked. "No *bruja*, this is real."

When Wacey walked closer, Arturo barked. "No, no, . . . *across* the pool, *bruja.*"

Wacey racked a bullet into the chamber. "This is so fucking stupid."

"*Si, yo s*é," agreed Josefina, taking a seat for the morning matinee.

As Wacey prepared to shoot the luckiest man on the planet, Archie simply went away.

Back to his Technicolor Dreamscape.

Back to Big Arch and Bunny . . . he would join them soon.

As his bodyguard sited down the barrel, Archie bowed his head.

Time stopped as Wacey took a deep breath, exhaled slowly, and . . . squeezed.

With a deafening report, the supersonic slug cleanly removed flesh, bone and bandage. The top of Archie's mangled finger simply vaporized.

"*¡Ca-bron!*" stammered *Lobo Loco*, in mouth-gaped amazement, running to more closely examine the cleanly severed stump and its attendant red/yellow ooze.

Archie opened his eyes. He wanted to yell, but was so surprised to be alive, he laughed.

"*¡Bravo bruja!" shouted Lobo Loco.* "*¡Bravo! ¡Bravo!*"

Wacey dropped her arms. Raised her face to the sun. Breathed in the sumptuous tropical air tinged with gun powder and hyacinth.

Archie finally looked at his missing finger—considered passing out—then didn't. He wobbled around the pool reaching out for his avenging angel.

"Love you," he said, hands in Wacey's hair—blood red on arctic white.

"*Archito*," she whispered, watching Josy as her sweet boy swooned. "Love you."

Josefina scowled—defiant, sneering. In the slanted shade, she lit a long, elegant Davidoff. Floated a quavering smoke ring toward *Lobo Loco's* approaching face.

He waved away the smoke, stepped behind his prize, smiling. Snaked a manicured hand into the vent of Josy's starched white blouse, and stood, Napoleonic.

"Have you ever seen such a handsome Plaza Boss?" crowed *Lobo Loco.* "*¡Dale muchachas!* It's good to be King!"

And indeed, it was.

Before Doña Montemayor batted a single, extravagant eyelash.

Before Wacey introduced a full metal jacket just below the part in the accountant's freshly-cut fade.

"*Pinche pendejo*," spat Josy, slapping away *Lobo Loco's* sinister hand.

The fifth Plaza Boss of Ojinaga staggered—dead on his feet—then dropped like a sack.

Archie stood witness, shaking. Catatonic. Wishing it would end. Now.

He looked at Wacey.

He looked at Josy.

"Ladies," he said, rivulets of ruby red flowing down his hand. "I'm gonna go bleed out in the *biblioteca*."

Archie took one more step, then sank to his knees, curled on the terrazzo. Done.

Josy and Wacey smiled across the courtyard. Came together. Sauntered alongside.

The girls hovered over *their* prize. Thrilling at the fruition of a painstaking plan.

The most unlikely of Mexican power couples grabbed Archie by the wrists and dragged him under the gazebo shade.

El Tejano Afortunado looked up at his *conquistadoras*—smiled—and closed his eyes.

Dissolved into the sound of his mother's warm, soothing words.

Sister Ernestine's sweet song:

Holy Mary, Mother of God,
Pray for us sinners,
Now, and at the hour of our death,
Amen.

ACKNOWLEDGMENTS

Writing, editing, and revising *Beneath the Sands of Monahans* has been the most exhilarating collaborative experience of my life. An amazing, indispensable process.

First and foremost, I'd like to thank Macarena Hernández for her constant encouragement and support. Thank you for providing the perfect space, time, and team to whip this novel into shape. Also, *mil gracias, Maca,* for your uncanny command of Spanish/Spanglish and its masterful deployment throughout.

Muchas gracias to Doña Elva for feeding me like a soldier and treating me like a son. Thank you to Jorge and Nancy for grilling the finest *carne asadas* in *El Valle.* Thank you to Elva and Hector, Veronica and Santiago, Amador and Gracie, Gumaro and Imelda, Abel and Catalina, Jose Luis and Olivia, and all the *primos y primas,* for making me feel like family. *¡Puro 956!*

Thank you to poet John Olivares-Espinosa for his spot-on line editing and intuitive command of image on the page; teacher/author/scholars Natalia Trevino and Yvette DeChavez for their thoughtful reading, feedback, and suggestions; editors Eric Miles Williamson, Bill Crawford and Erasmo Guerra for making me think hard about plot. About how best to tell this story. And for gently pushing me across the finish line. To all, I am forever grateful.

Thank you to publisher Will Evans and Deep Vellum Publishing for believing in the story and having the confidence to make *BTSOM* the first offering of the La Reunion imprint. It's an honor. From editing, production, cover art, marketing and publicity, I have immense gratitude for everyone at Deep Vellum including Sara Balabanlilar, Walker Rutter-Bowman, Linda Stack-Nelson, and Serena Reiser. Kudos to Team BTSOM!

Huge thanks to the University of Houston, my teaching/fundraising/literary/athletics haven for the past twenty-two years. It's been an honor to witness and contribute to UH's phenomenal growth over the past two decades. Big Love to Cliff, Eloise, and the amazing Chancellor Khator. Go Coogs!

To David Felts, for singlehandedly putting me on the literary map. Long overdue thanks for your pitch-perfect editing and design efforts on *Argument Against the Good-Looking Corpse*.

To John O'Brien, founding publisher of the iconic Dalkey Archive. I am forever grateful for your friendship, mentorship, and exceptional ability to actualize long-held dreams.

Rest in Peace, Sir John. *Slainte!*

Charles Alcorn has lived in and written about Texas his entire life. A former all-state linebacker, Alcorn founded Splendid Seed Tobacco Company, was a sportswriter, and worked as a packaged goods copywriter before receiving his PhD in English Literature/Creative Writing (Fiction) from the University of Houston. Alcorn is the author of the short story collection *Argument Against the Good-Looking Corpse* (2011, Texas Review Press). *Beneath the Sands of Monahans* is his debut novel. Alcorn currently lives in Edinburg on the US-Mexico border.

La Reunion

La Reunion Publishing is an imprint of Deep Vellum established in 2019 to share the stories of the people and places of Texas. La Reunion is named after the utopian socialist colony founded by Frenchman Victor Considerant on the west bank of the Trinity River across from the then-fledgling town of Dallas in 1855. Considerant considered Texas as the promised land: a land of unbridled and unparalleled opportunity, with its story yet to be written, and the La Reunion settlers added an international mindset and pioneering spirit that is still reflected in Dallas, and across Texas, today. La Reunion publishes books that explore the story of Texas from all sides, critically engaging with the myths, histories, and the untold stories that make Texas the land of literature come to life.